FIRE
IN THE
OCEAN

K.D. KEENAN

DIVERSIONBOOKS

ALSO BY K.D. KEENAN

The Obsidian Mirror

Diversion Books
A Division of Diversion Publishing Corp.
443 Park Avenue South, Suite 1008
New York, New York 10016
www.DiversionBooks.com

For more information, email info@diversionbooks.com

First Diversion Books edition February 2018.
Paperback ISBN: 978-1-63576-186-3
eBook ISBN: 978-1-63576-185-6

LSIDB/1801

This book is dedicated
in loving memory of my mother,
Barbara M. Doyle.

In beauty it is finished.

ACKNOWLEDGMENTS

Without the good people of Moloka'i and their aloha spirit, this book would not have been possible.

My deepest gratitude is owed to the following people. Everything I got right is because of them, and the errors are all mine.

- Louella Albino (Auntie Opu'ulani), who consulted with me on usage of the Hawai'ian language and ancient traditions. I will always be grateful to Auntie for her kindness and aloha.
- My long-suffering husband, Tom Keenan, who accompanied me on my travels and took pictures of anything I asked him to.
- Ken Love, agricultural consultant, who helped me with contacts on the Big Island.
- Bob Matsuyama, barber extraordinaire of Shear Magic, Keleakakua, the Big Island, who regaled me with stories of the Night Marchers, ghosts, and spirits while trimming my hair.
- Joan and Casey McCarty, owners of beautiful Camp Aloha, our helpful hosts on the Big Island.
- Jim Miller, docent at the Bishop Museum Ethnobotanical Garden in Captain Cook, who patiently answered all my questions and gave me a tour of the gardens.
- Ray Naki, also known as Leimana, who spent hours talking with me about the ancient fishponds on Moloka'i, hula, the Hawai'ian language, and many other topics.

- Anakalo Pilipo, who told me stories about the moʻo of Halawa Valley and how the people lived there long ago. If you want to hike to Moʻoula Falls and learn more about ancient Molokaʻi, contact him through halawa-valleymolokai.com.
- Apelila (April) and Josh Qina, of Mo's Kava Bar in Keleakakua, who educated me about ʻawa, and introduced me to Apelila's uncle Leimana in Molokaʻi.
- Jeanine Rosso, who generously provided me with invaluable contacts in Molokaʻi and tutored me on island etiquette.
- Wayne Sentman, of the Oceanic Society, who gave me information about the Midway volunteer program.
- Peter van Dyke, of the Bishop Museum Ethnobotanical Gardens in Captain Cook, who gave me full access to ask questions about the ancient Hawaiʻians' use of native plants.
- My alpha readers, Cynthia Bournellis, Linda Duyanovich, Sean Keenan, Tom Keenan, Cindy Knoebel, Susan Monroe, David Pease, Abbe Seitzman, and Cara Alexandra Sundell, for providing me with invaluable feedback.

HAWAI'IAN LANGUAGE PRONUNCIATION

The Hawai'ian language has two punctuation marks not used in English: the 'okina (') and the kahakō (a bar, or macron, across the top of a vowel). The 'okina indicates a glottal stop, as in "uh-oh." The kahakō indicates a drawn-out sound, or emphasis, as in "kahak-OHH." (I would like to note for the record that using these pronunciation marks in Microsoft Word is a true test of the author's dedication. It wasn't easy figuring out how to do it, and using the symbols involved several keystrokes each and every time.)

Other than the syllables marked for emphasis by a kahakō, all syllables are pronounced with the same emphasis (or lack of emphasis). All syllables are pronounced, and there are no silent letters.

Hawai'ian uses the same vowels as English (but there is no Y). A and E are given their short pronunciations, as in "far" and "set." I is pronounced EE, as in "green." O is long, as in "mole." U is pronounced OO, as in "moon."

Hawai'ian words never end with a consonant. There are seven consonants, H, K, L, M, N, P, and W. All except W are pronounced as in English.

The pronunciation of W is a bit confusing (at least to me):

- After E or I, W is pronounced as V. "Lewa," meaning the sky, is pronounced "leh-vah."
- After U or O, W is pronounced as W. "'ōwili," meaning a roll of paper or cloth, is pronounced "OH-wee-lee."
- At the start of a word or after A, W is pronounced

as either W or V. (I don't know if this is decided by individual choice or by custom.) So Hawai'i is correctly pronounced as either "Havai'i" or "Hawai'i."

There's more, of course, but this should suffice for pronouncing the Hawai'ian words used in *Fire in the Ocean*. I have provided pronunciations below for the Hawai'ian words used here. I can only add that listening to a competent speaker of Hawai'ian is like listening to water running over smooth pebbles, sibilant and beautiful.

Ali'i: [ah-lee-ee] The hereditary ruling class of ancient Hawai'i.

Aloha: [ah-low-ha] "Hello," "goodbye," and "love."

'Aumakua: [aw-mah-koo-ah] A family or personal spirit. It may take the form of a plant or animal, or it may be an unmodified stone. It serves roughly the same role as a guardian angel in Western culture.

Auwē: [ow-WAY] An expression of dismay, similar to "How awful!" or "Alas!"

'Awa: [ah-vah] Known as kava throughout most of Polynesia. The roots of the *Piper methysticum* plant are pounded and mixed with water to produce a thin, whitish drink that is used to relax and soothe sore muscles and produce an elevated mood. 'Awa does not cause intoxication like alcohol, and the author assures you from personal experience that no one drinks 'awa for the flavor.

Hale: [hah-leh] House.

Haole: [how-leh] Caucasians. It is sometimes used as a derogative, but not always.

Heiau: [hay-ee-ow] Ancient Hawai'ian temple.

Houngán: [hoon-GAHN] A priest of Voudún.

Huaka'ipo: [hwah-kah-ee-po] Night Marchers, ancient Hawai'ian warriors who march inland from the sea. If they come upon you and recognize you as one of their bloodline, you are safe. If you are not of their bloodline, you will never return to your home and family. While on the big island, the author met two people—neither of them native Hawai'ians—who had heard or seen the Night Marchers personally. One said the Marchers pass straight through her house, so she leaves the front and back doors open on those nights.

Huixtocihuatl: [weest-OH-KEE-WAH-tl] Mayan/Aztec goddess of salt water. Her name means "She of the Jade Skirt."

'I'iwi: [ee-EE-wee] *Drepanis coccinea*. The Hawai'ian honeycreeper. A threatened native Hawai'ian species.

'Ili'ili: [eely-eely] An instrument used in the ancient hula (hula kahiko), practiced before Europeans came to the Hawai'ian Islands. Each dancer finds her own 'ili'ili, oiling them and keeping them carefully wrapped between performances. The stones are used in fours, two in each hand, and clicked together to create a rhythm.

Imu: [ee-moo] Underground oven.

Kaho'olawe: [kah-ho-oh-la-vee] An uninhabited island off the coast of Maui. The US Navy used it as a bombing range for many years. It is currently being cleared of munitions and non-native species like goats and rats to become a nature refuge. Sadly, many ancient Hawai'ian sacred cultural sites were destroyed by the bombing.

Kahuna: [kah-hoo-nah] In ancient Hawai'i, a priest, most of whom were credited with supernatural powers. In today's parlance, a kahuna is a wise person, a teacher, or a healer.

Kāne: [KAH-neh] Man. Kāne is also the name of one of the four greatest gods in the Hawai'ian pantheon, the creator god and the god of those things necessary to life.

Kapu: [kah-poo] The same as taboo—forbidden.

Kapualei: [kah-poo-ah-lay-ee] This is the name of Moloka'i's most famous mo'o, which is supposed to make her home at Mo'a-ula (or (Mo'o-ula) Falls in Halawa Valley. She is out of place in Kama's refuge, but I needed her help here, so perhaps she will forgive me.

Keiki: [keh-ee-kee] Child.

Kukui: [koo-koo-ee] *Aleurites moluccanu.* Also known as candle-nut. Kukui nuts are rich in oil that allows them to be used as candles in the manner described here. The ancient Hawai'ians had a myriad of uses for the nuts and oil.

Loa: [lwa] The gods of Voudún.

Lomi-lomi: [low-me-low-me] Lomi means "rub." In Hawai'ian, doubling a word is the equivalent of adding the adjectives "very" or "much." So lomi-lomi means "well-rubbed." In this case, it refers to the preparation of the fish, which is rubbed with salt before cooking.

Luau: [loo-ow] Traditional Hawai'ian feast.

Mahalo: [mah-hah-low] "Thank you."

Ma'i: [mah-ee] Genitals.

Maile: [my-lee] *Alyxia oliviformis.* A member of the periwinkle family. Maile leis are reserved for special occasions. They are sometimes formed into a circle, as most leis are, but more commonly worn as a long garland.

Malo: [mah-low] Loincloth. There are different styles of malos, but they often do not cover the buttocks.

Menehune: [meh-neh-hoo-nee] A legendary race of "little people." Many ancient temples and fishponds throughout the islands are said to be the work of Menuhune, who formed long lines and passed the rocks from hand to hand. In this way, the Menehune were said to have built many of these structures overnight.

Mo'olelo: [moh-oh-leh-low] Traditional story, or chant.

Mo'o: [moh-oh] Giant black lizards or dragons. They are usually female and often found protecting freshwater springs and pools. Some are hostile to humans, others friendly or neutral. Though no such creature has ever lived in the Hawai'ian Islands, mo'o are important elements of Hawai'ian culture and mythology.

Necocyaotl: [Neh-koh-kyah-OH-tl] Brother to Quetzalcoatl, the plumed serpent god of the Aztecs, and his opposite number, being the god of night, sorcery, storms, etc. See *The Obsidian Mirror* for the whole story.

'Opihi: [oh-pee-hee] Limpets.

Pali: [pah-lee] Sheer sea cliffs.

Pele: [peh-leh] The goddess of fire, volcanoes, lightning and wind. She is the creator of the Hawai'ian Islands. Many Hawai'ians—and many non-native-people living in Hawai'i—continue to believe in Madame Pele.

Poi: [poy] *Colocasia esculenta*. A starchy staple food made from the cooked, mashed corms of the taro plant.

Tī: [tee] A multi-use plant found across Polynesia. Its broad, flat leaves are used to wrap foods for cooking, but tī has many other culinary, medicinal, and practical uses.

Voudún: [voh-DOON] The proper name for a religion birthed in Haiti as an amalgamation of African slaves' religious beliefs and Roman Catholicism. It is a religion based on healing and a charismatic relationship with the gods. Much of what we hear about Voudún is incorrect.

CHAPTER 1

Sierra glanced up from her in-flight magazine and stared at her companion with concern. Chaco's face, normally a warm, glowing brown, was a sickly gray with green undertones. She scrabbled hastily in her seat pocket for the barf bag and handed it to him.

"If you feel like you're going to be sick, use this," she said. "I didn't know you get motion sickness." They had just taken off from San Jose International Airport—how could he be sick already?

Chaco waved away the bag with a weary gesture. "I don't have motion sickness."

"What's the matter, then?" she asked. She hoped he would recover soon—and that he wasn't contagious. But then she remembered: Chaco was an Avatar. He was thousands of years old, and had literally never been sick a day in his long life. If he was sick, something was seriously awry.

"I dunno," Chaco replied, closing his eyes. "Do you…do you suppose you could just leave me alone for a while?"

Sierra returned to her magazine, glancing at his tense, gray face every so often. When the stewards came by with trays of lunch, Chaco shook his head without opening his eyes.

When the screaming began, Sierra nearly jumped out of her skin, and she wasn't the only one. A female flight attendant was shrieking incoherently in the rear of the plane, where the galley and restrooms were located for economy class passengers. Other attendants crowded around her, and her shrieks stopped abruptly. But not before Sierra heard, "Green! Monster! I saw it…!"

"Oh no," Sierra moaned. "Oh no, no, that's just what we need!"

People were still craning in their seats, trying to see what was going on. The curtain had been drawn across the galley space, concealing whatever was happening.

Roused by the commotion, Chaco asked, "What was that all that about?"

"It's Fred," Sierra whispered grimly. "It has to be Fred. The flight attendant was screaming about a green monster. Sound familiar?"

Chaco closed his eyes again. "Figures." Sierra waited for more, but he remained silent.

"What are we going to do? Fred will be a disaster on this trip, which is why I told him—firmly!—that he couldn't come with us," Sierra asked.

"I don't know."

"We have to do *something*."

Chaco shifted his long body slightly to face her and opened his eyes. "Look, Sierra. I have no more idea than you do. In fact, I think I'm in real trouble here."

Sierra looked at his pale face and anguished eyes. "Are you sick?"

"It's worse than that," he responded miserably. "I'm mortal."

"Mortal? Mortally ill, you mean?"

"No. Mortal. As in, I'm just like you, now. I'm not an Avatar anymore. I can get sick. I can die."

All thoughts of Fred forgotten, Sierra said, "How do you know? How is that even possible?"

Chaco shook his head. "Wouldn't you know if all your blood left your body? I mean, just for an instant before you died? I've been severed from the numinous, the sphere in which we Avatars exist. The power source has been unplugged, if that makes more sense."

Sierra absorbed this in silence. Finally, she said, "But you're still alive. So cutting you off from the, um, numinous doesn't kill you?"

Chaco rolled his eyes. "Apparently not."

"Okay. Why don't you try to turn into a coyote? If you can do that, it proves you're okay." In addition to being an outwardly young and indisputably handsome young man, Chaco was Coyotl the Trickster, demigod and culture hero of many Native American traditions. Sierra was so rattled that she didn't consider what her fellow passengers' response might be to a coyote lounging in a nearby window seat.

Chaco looked at her, his golden-amber eyes now dulled to hazel. Dark circles beneath his eyes made them appear sunken. "What do you think I've been trying to do for the past hour?"

"Oh." Sierra sat quietly for a long time, thinking. Eventually, she asked, "How did you get separated from the, um, numinous, anyway? How could something like that happen?"

Chaco roused himself from his lethargy. "I don't know. It's never happened before. I could make an educated guess, though. I think it's because I'm no longer connected to my land, the land that created me. I think my land is the source of my power. I've never been on an airplane before, so I didn't know this would happen."

"We're thousands of feet in the air. When we get to Hawai'i, we'll be on land again—maybe you'll get it back. Hawai'i is part of the United States, after all," Sierra said, trying to comfort her friend.

Chaco brightened a little at this, but his enthusiasm flickered and died. "I don't know as much as I should about things like history and geography, but wasn't Hawai'i built by volcanoes in the middle of the ocean?"

Sierra nodded.

"And when did Hawai'i become part of the United States?"

Sierra's dark brows knit together as she tried to remember. She gave up. "I'm not sure, but it was probably about 60 years ago."

Chaco groaned, almost inaudibly. "So Hawai'i isn't part of my land at all. It's something different. The people there are probably not even Native Americans."

This Sierra did know. "They're Polynesians. They came from Tahiti, I think. Once you get your feet on the ground, maybe you'll feel better."

"Maybe," he said, directing a morose gaze out of the little window at the clouds.

• • •

The trip was originally supposed to be a fun vacation with Sierra's fiancé, Clancy. At least, Sierra thought it would be fun, but as Clancy pointed out, his idea of an island vacation had more to do with drinking fruity tropical drinks on the beach than with counting albatross chicks. Nonetheless, he had gone along with her plans for a one-month stint on Midway Island. It was an ecotourism gig that allowed some twenty volunteers at a time onto Midway to help biologists monitor the bird life. The island was a national wildlife refuge that provided breeding grounds for millions of sea birds, including several endangered species. The volunteers lived on Midway for a month, counting chicks and cleaning up plastic from the Great Pacific Garbage Patch so that adult birds wouldn't mistake the colorful bits of plastic for food and feed it to their nestlings—thereby killing them.

But Clancy's boss had asked (demanded) that he cancel his scheduled vacation. Sierra was upset by this, but she understood. Clancy was head of security at a high-tech Silicon Valley firm. The president of the United States had scheduled a visit to the plant to highlight her support of American technology—and Clancy's vacation was sacrificed amid promises of more vacation time later.

"I'm going anyway," she had told Clancy. At his look of surprise, she added, "Remember? My job is paying for it. I have to go so I can report on the wildlife conservation work on Midway." Sierra worked for Clear Days Foundation as a communications executive.

"Oh. Well, sure. I just thought…"

"I'd like to ask Chaco to go with me," Sierra had said. "That okay with you?"

There was a long silence. "Chaco? Isn't he with Kaylee? Wouldn't that be kind of awkward?"

"I thought you knew. Kaylee is dating someone named Guy now. She moved on. Kaylee always moves on."

"Oh. Well, what about taking Kaylee with you? Or Rose? Or Mama Labadie?" Clancy listed off Sierra's closest female friends.

"All three of them are going to some animal spirit guide workshop in Sedona, so they're not available. Look, please don't worry about this. Chaco and I are just friends. We've never been anything else. And I'm going to be on a remote island in the middle of nowhere for a month with a bunch of people I don't know. I'd like to have a friend with me."

"I'm not worried. Well, maybe I am, a little. Just tell me you're sorry that it won't be me."

"I'm really, really sorry that it won't be you!"

He would have to be content with that.

• • •

Discovering that Fred had decided to stow away on the airplane was unwelcome news to Sierra. But there could be no other explanation for the ruckus among the flight attendants and that telling shriek of "Green! Monster!"

Fred was a mannegishi. When visible, Fred looked like a green melon with pipe-cleaner arms and legs, six flexible digits on each paw, and swiveling orange eyes that resembled traffic reflectors. He had the ability to disappear at will, which had been handy in Sierra's earlier adventures, but he was a mischievous creature with little or no impulse control and an enormous appetite. Fred was not Sierra's first choice of companion for a visit to a delicate ecosystem populated by endangered birds.

Now she had to deal with an errant mannegishi as well as a mortal and extremely miserable Chaco. As they walked through the loading tunnel to the gate, Sierra whispered, "How are we going to find Fred?"

Chaco shrugged. "My guess is that Fred will find us. Don't worry about him—he's been around the block a few times in the past few thousand years." He was still drawn and tired-looking, with none of his usual sexy saunter. Sierra guessed that returning to the earth had not restored his supernatural powers or immortality.

They made their way to baggage pickup. When Chaco hefted his suitcase, he nearly dropped it, then frowned.

"I think Fred found us," he reported.

Sierra looked at him, puzzled.

"My suitcase." He hefted it again. "It's a lot heavier than it was when I dropped it off in San Jose. It's either Fred or someone stuffed a bowling ball in here."

Sierra was horrified. "Well, let him out! He must be smothered in there."

"Not likely," scoffed Chaco. He gave the suitcase a good shake. "Serves him right."

"What if he's lost his powers like you have?" she hissed, not wanting to be overheard.

"I don't think so. He disappeared on the plane fast enough when the flight attendant started screaming. Otherwise, there would have been a lot more commotion."

Acknowledging that Chaco was probably right, Sierra turned her attention to finding transportation to their hotel. It was located right on Waikiki Beach and wasn't far from the airport.

On the bus ride to the hotel, Sierra took in the tropical plants, caught glimpses of turquoise ocean, and, cracking the window a trifle, breathed in the scent of many flowers—and the usual smells of any big city. The people walking on the streets all looked like tourists to her. Many were wearing shorts, flip-flops, and Hawai'ian print shirts. *Surely not everyone in the city is a tourist,* she thought. At one point, Chaco's suitcase began to squirm, but he kicked it sharply, and the suitcase subsided.

Their hotel was an enormous complex of tall buildings, and they had a room on the seventeenth floor, overlooking the ocean. Sliding glass doors on a balcony opened to let in breezes, and the afternoon air smelled soft and sweet with an underlying sharper tang of salt. They dumped their suitcases on the floor—in Chaco's case, none too gently. Chaco unzipped the bag and Fred rolled out onto the carpet.

"Ow ow ow ow," he complained, rubbing his fat bottom and glaring at them reproachfully.

"It's your own fault," Chaco said coldly. "I'm going to bed." He commandeered one of the two queen-size beds and pulled the covers over his head.

"What's his problem?" the little mannegishi asked. "He didn't spend hours balled up in a suitcase."

"He's lost his powers," Sierra explained. "He's a mortal now, and it disagrees with him. Anyway, why'd you do it, Fred? I asked you not to come. Now I don't know *what* to do."

She felt nearly as weary as Chaco. The trip had started with Clancy dropping out. Now Chaco had lost his powers and become mortal—and who knew what that would mean? She supposed it would be like a human losing the ability to see, or walk. And she had to deal with Fred, too. As fond as she was of him, Fred was a nuisance at the best of times.

"Lost his powers? How does *that* happen?" asked Fred, looking worried. He disappeared briefly then reappeared. He looked relieved but puzzled. "I haven't lost my abilities. Why did Chaco lose his?"

"He thinks it's because he's no longer in contact with his birth land. He says he's cut off from the numinous, whatever that is."

"I dunno about numinous, but I'm still okay."

"How nice for you!" came an irritated growl from under the humped covers on Chaco's bed.

"Look, Fred, I could really use a drink right now. Disappear yourself, and we can talk. There's got to be a bar in this hotel somewhere."

As it turned out, the hotel had many bars. Sierra picked one with an outdoor seating area on the beach and ordered something unfamiliar with rum in it. The drink arrived, bedecked with chunks of fresh fruit, small umbrellas, and plastic hula girls and accompanied by a bowl of peanuts. She cleared away the ornamentation, ate the fruit, and began working slowly on the remaining fluid. It was cold, tart, and sweet. She still felt grubby from the trip, but at least she was near a beach—she could see surfers from where she was sitting—with a fruity tropical drink. And an invisible mannegishi. She could see the imprint of Fred's bottom on the chair cushion next to hers, and the peanuts were disappearing at a rapid pace. She picked up her phone and pretended to tap in a number, then said, "Hi, Fred. We can talk now." Anyone observing would see a trim woman with tanned skin and long, dark hair, sitting alone and talking on the phone.

"So what happened to Chaco?" Fred asked.

"As soon as the plane took off, he started to look kind of green around the gills. Then he slumped down and acted like he was sick. He says he's mortal now. He can die."

"That's not good," Fred observed.

"Tell me about it," said Sierra. "I've been mortal my whole life."

"Oh, sorry. I didn't mean to be insensitive."

"It's all right. I'm used to it. Chaco isn't. Do you know if he can ever regain his connection to the numinous? Whatever that is?"

"Dunno."

"And why didn't *you* lose *your* powers?" Sierra demanded. The mannegishi was quiet for a few minutes.

"Chaco and I aren't exactly the same sort of thing, you know."

"How do you mean?"

"Chaco is—was—an Avatar. Much more powerful than a mannegishi. I'm just a, ah, kind of an…well, I don't know exactly. I have certain powers, but what I can do is born inside me. Like bees can make honey? I can do what I do. That's all I know." Sierra could tell by the sounds next to her that the mannegishi was sucking his digits—a nervous habit.

"Stop that!" The sucking sounds ceased, and the peanuts began to disappear again. Sierra flagged a passing waiter and asked for more peanuts and another round of whatever she was drinking.

"What about your powers?" Fred asked abruptly. Sierra sat for a moment, considering. She had discovered during her earlier struggles against the Aztec god Necocyaotl that she possessed certain disturbing powers of her own. Rose had helped her to strengthen her control over these powers, but Sierra still didn't understand how they worked. Given a choice, she preferred not thinking about them. But Fred's question was a good one, so she closed her eyes and searched for the glowing ribbons she visualized when her powers were at work. After a moment, she opened her eyes again.

"I still have my powers, such as they are. No difference." Why were she and Fred untouched, while Chaco had been drastically changed? The illogic of magic, as always, annoyed her, but she couldn't do anything about the situation today. Right now, she was sitting in the Hawai'ian sun on a Hawai'ian beach, drinking a Hawai'ian drink, and watching the Hawai'ian waves. Almost against her will, she began to relax. The waiter brought her a fresh drink and another bowl of peanuts. She thanked him, took a long swallow, and closed her eyes. She began to think about Chaco and Fred and their attendant problems. Not relaxing. She opened her eyes again, only to find the rest of her drink gone, as well as all of the fruit.

"Fred!!!"

CHAPTER 2

Sierra knew from experience that Fred with alcohol onboard was infinitely more trouble than Fred without alcohol, so she wasted no time getting the mannegishi back to the hotel room. Chaco was still under the covers, silent and unresponsive.

Fred wanted to sing, but he had forgotten the words to "Let It Go" and was blearily attempting another favorite, "100 Bottles of Beer on the Wall." Sierra persuaded him to curl up in a drawer with a pillow and take a nap.

Listening to small, drunken snores from the bureau and the heavy silence from the lump under the covers on Chaco's bed, she decided to take a walk.

Her hotel was right on the beach, so within a few minutes Sierra was walking barefoot on the white coral sands of Waikiki. The beach was smaller than she had imagined. It was a long stretch of sand, but not very wide. Diamond Head, the towering corpse of a long-dead volcano, made a dramatic statement at the end of the sweep of beach. Hotels lined the shore as far as she could see.

It was May and a warm day. Sierra waded into the lukewarm water up to her knees. What to do now? She had a drunken mannegishi on her hands and an Avatar who was now just an ordinary depressed guy. She thought about going home. Maybe if she took Chaco back, he would regain his powers. *That would certainly cheer him up,* she thought—*if it worked.* If it didn't work—Sierra shuddered. It *had* to work. And taking Fred home was the only way to solve the Fred problem.

All right, then. She'd get tickets for home tomorrow. So much for her first trip to Hawai'i. So much for her eco-adventure to

Midway. But that's the way it had to be, she decided glumly. She walked for a long time, watching the happy tourists sunning on the beach and splashing in the clear, bright water. She wasn't much for sunbathing, but now she wasn't going to get the chance to do it in Hawai'i. Nor would she have the chance to count albatross chicks on Midway, which apparently wasn't everyone's idea of a vacation, but she had been looking forward to it for months all the same.

When she returned to the hotel, she could practically see the little black raincloud hanging over her head. She ate an early dinner alone in one of the hotel's restaurants and turned in early.

Chaco surprised her the next morning. When she woke, he was sitting, fully dressed, on the side of his bed.

"I'm hungry," he announced. He wasn't smiling, but he wasn't hiding under the covers, either.

"Me too!" piped Fred, apparently none the worse for his escapade.

"Good morning to you too," returned Sierra tartly. She climbed out of bed, slightly self-conscious about appearing in front of Chaco in her nightgown. The room had been intended for her and Clancy, of course.

She ordered up a large breakfast for three. Chaco and Fred always had hearty appetites. Fred disappeared when room service arrived, but as soon as the waiter left, he reappeared and flung himself on his breakfast like a starving hyena. Sierra tucked in at a more measured pace, and Chaco—even though she knew he hadn't eaten, Chaco was picking moodily at his food.

"I think we ought to go home today," Sierra said, sipping a second cup of excellent coffee.

"Oh noooooooo!" wailed Fred, pausing in the middle of his macadamia nut French toast. "We just got here. I don't want to go home yet." He gazed at her imploringly, maple syrup dripping down his—well, what passed for a chin.

To her astonishment, Chaco shook his head. "No. Let's do

what we came here for. I don't want to be the second one to completely wreck your trip."

"But maybe if we get you home, you'll regain your powers."

"And maybe not. In any case, I guess I can put up with this for a month. And it's probably good practice," he said glumly, stirring his scrambled eggs with his fork.

"Practice for what?" asked Sierra.

"Being mortal. I may need to get accustomed to it. I think it takes practice, because you mortals walk around acting like nothing is wrong."

"That's because we avoid thinking about it. Most people do, anyway—how else could we enjoy life? Anyway, nothing *is* wrong. For us, it's just the way things are."

Chaco shuddered delicately and drank some coffee. "So, let's just go ahead and do what you would have done in the first place."

"What about Fred? He's already gotten into trouble." She told him about Fred drinking half of her rather strong rum drink.

"Idiot." Chaco glowered at Fred. *He really is in a bad mood,* thought Sierra.

"Hey! I didn't break any rules. Except for the one about not coming. You always told me I couldn't have wine or beer. You never said anything about fruity drinks." Sierra kept wine and beer at home and had instituted the no-wine-or-beer-for-mannegishis rule after Fred drank a glass of Zinfandel and broke several dishes in a tipsy attempt to wash up.

"Okay. Fair enough, Fred. From now on: no wine, no beer, and no drinks with alcohol in them, fruit or no fruit," Sierra said.

"Okay." Fred started on scrambled eggs and bacon, having polished off the French toast.

"So Sierra, what did you plan to do while we're in Honolulu?" Chaco didn't sound enormously interested.

"If you're sure you don't want to go home today…?" Chaco nodded without enthusiasm. "Then I thought we could go whale watching. The waters here are a national marine sanctuary for humpback whales. It's not too late in the season to see them."

Chaco nodded, but Fred bounced up and down. "Whales? I'd love to see whales!"

Sierra and Chaco looked at each other. Chaco shrugged. "Why not? I'll take him in my duffle bag. I can unzip it so he can see. But!" Here he glared at Fred. "Stay disappeared! No surprise appearances like on the plane. Got that?"

Fred stopped bouncing and attempted to look serious, but his eyes gave him away. They were rolling wildly in different directions. "Yes. I promise!"

"Hmph," was all that Chaco said.

The whale-watching boat was moored at a dock in front of the hotel, and Sierra was able to get two reservations for the afternoon excursion. They walked across the coarse coral sand, Chaco with his duffle bag sagging under Fred's weight. He looked hot and sweaty, thought Sierra, realizing she'd never seen Chaco break a sweat before.

"Chaco, how about some sunscreen? The sun's going to reflect off the water, and you might get a burn."

"A burn? From the sun? Can that really happen?"

"Trust me, mortals get sunburned here." She handed him a tube of sunscreen when they boarded the little boat. Chaco looked puzzled at first, but she explained that all exposed skin had to be covered with the cream in the tube.

"And this really works?"

Sierra assured him that it did. "I brought along a super-large tube of the stuff, so we can share," she said. "But we might need more when we get to Midway, so I'll stock up before we leave Honolulu." The prop plane that would fly them to Midway left in three days. Plenty of time to do a little shopping.

The little whale-watching boat chugged away from its dock. The water swirled around it in the most amazing variety of colors. Turquoise shone where there was a sandy bottom, then a succession of deeper blues and blue-greens—even purples—appeared as they passed over the corals. As they reached deeper water, it became hard to see past the surface, where the light danced off the waves.

The water was fairly calm until they were a fair distance from land, and then the swells and chop made standing a challenge. They saw the island of O'ahu in the distance, the softly blue-gray land rising to the central mountains.

"Whale! Ten o'clock," came the captain's voice over the PA system. Having been briefed on using the clock face as a directional reference, everyone on the boat rushed to the forward port side to look. First they saw the spout, like a seagoing geyser. Then a huge, black body rose up out of the water, mountainous head first. They were close enough to see details—barnacles crusting the whale's body and the grooved folds of skin along the animal's throat. Sierra snapped photos as fast as she could. She had decided to take her little digital camera, leaving her cell phone in the hotel room, because the camera had a zoom function. She wanted to get the best pictures possible.

Chaco unzipped his duffle, whispering fiercely to the occupant to stay disappeared—or else. Sierra was so awestruck by the whale's appearance close to the boat that she didn't even check to see if Fred was invisible, unwilling to take her eyes or her camera lens off the mammoth creature.

Again, the whale rose majestically out of the sea. It seemed impossible that a creature so huge could propel itself so far out of the water. Then it disappeared again below the waves with a gasping sigh, leaving only spume behind. Soon, there were more and more sightings, and the passengers went from port to starboard, from fore to aft to catch a glimpse of the massive animals.

"It's like being visited by gods," breathed Sierra.

"You should know," Chaco responded. He wasn't exactly lively, but he was definitely interested and engaged. Sierra smiled to herself. As she'd hoped, the whale-watching excursion was bringing Chaco out of his slump.

After about half an hour of multiple sightings, Sierra noticed an odd, white disc forming on the starboard side, a few hundred yards from the boat. She nudged Chaco and pointed. "What's that?"

Chaco peered at the water. "I don't know. Let's ask someone who works here."

He zipped the duffle, the sound of the waves and the chatter from the other tourists drowning out the squeaks of protest from within. They went forward and found a crewmember, a young Hawai'ian man wearing (no surprise) shorts and a Hawai'ian print shirt, distinguished from the tourists only by his official-looking badge.

"What's that thing over there?" Sierra asked inelegantly, pointing at the white disc, now spinning along the water. The crewman looked, stared, and turned without a word to climb the ladder to the cockpit.

Sierra and Chaco looked at each other, puzzled.

"That didn't seem like the right response," Chaco said.

Sierra started to reply, but then the captain's voice came over the PA system, loud enough to drown out all other sounds.

"Folks, at about four o'clock you'll see a waterspout forming. It's a fair-weather spout, which means it's not likely to last very long, so you'd better have a look."

Everyone rushed aft and starboard. By this time, a spout was clearly forming, rising up to meet a cumulus cloud overhead. Everyone had smartphones or cameras out to take pictures. As they watched, the spout, trailing a wake, began moving toward the boat.

"We're moving away, now, folks," said the captain. "Fair-weather waterspouts aren't usually very strong, but we're not taking any chances."

The boat's motors roared, and they began to move away from the spout. There were no whales visible in the surrounding waters, so Sierra took as many pictures of the spout as she could, and then she and Chaco sat down on benches attached to the deck. The ride was rough now that they were traveling faster. The waves were hitting the boat head-on, creating a bounce and slap motion that made it hard to stand up.

Oddly, the spout continued to follow the boat, twisting and

writing across the water. It reminded Sierra uneasily of a tornado, though much smaller. Despite the boat's speed, it drew closer.

Sierra stood up. "I don't like this. I'm moving to the other side of the boat." She walked unsteadily to the port side, clutching the railings as the boat heaved over the swells. Chaco followed with his duffle.

"What's happening?" wailed Fred inside the duffle bag. The noise of the boat's engine and the slap of the waves made it impossible for anyone else to hear him.

"Um, just a waterspout. I'm sure everything's okay," Chaco said to the bag.

"Lemme see!"

Chaco unzipped the duffle. There wasn't much to see from Fred's viewpoint.

"Where is it?" Then the mannegishi caught sight of the upper reaches of the spout, now visible above the cockpit. "Oh!"

The tourists and two crewmen were gathered in a knot on the starboard side, leaving Chaco, Sierra, and Fred by themselves. They couldn't take their eyes off the towering spout, which now seemed ominously close. They never saw the long, white tentacle that rose from the sea and swept Sierra, Chaco, and the duffle bag containing Fred overboard.

The waterspout quickly diminished and died. The tourists breathed a sigh of relief, chattering excitedly among themselves. The captain never noticed he was missing two tourists until he reached the dock on Waikiki and counted the departing guests. But of course, by that time it was too late.

CHAPTER 3

Clancy sat at his desk, reviewing security reports. This was not his favorite activity, but it was a critical element of his job. So far, the reports had all been incredibly humdrum, and he was beginning to feel sleepy.

He had just decided to get a cup of coffee to wake himself up when his cell phone rang.

"Clancy Forrester."

"Hello. This is Tammy White at Clear Days Foundation? Uh, Sierra Carter's manager?" The high, feminine voice had a habit of lifting into the interrogatory at the end of a sentence. "Is this Clancy Forrester?" Clancy, who had a great deal of experience judging voices, detected significant strain in this one.

"Yep."

"I'm sorry to disturb you, Mr. Forrester. I, ah, I'm not catching you at a bad time, I hope?"

"Nope." What the hell was this all about, he wondered, wishing she'd get on with it.

"Um, I take it you are Sierra's fiancé?"

He grunted affirmatively.

"I, ah, I have some bad news, Mr. Forrester. About Sierra?"

Clancy felt his fight-or-flight response ratchet into high gear. "What?"

"Um, she went on a whale-watching tour out of Honolulu, and apparently she went overboard? They think one other person went overboard with her. They've been searching the water, but so far, they haven't found her? Or the other person."

Clancy felt an icy spear of horror lance down his spine.

"How long has it been?"

"It happened yesterday afternoon."

It was now eleven a.m. She would have been in the water for hours. All night. Was the other person Chaco? It seemed likely.

"Who can I talk to in Honolulu?"

Tammy White gave him the name of the police officer in charge of the case.

Clancy felt himself begin to quiver with tension and anxiety. He thanked the woman from Clear Days and ended the call.

His first step was to call Sierra's closest friends to tell them what had happened. He had never been entirely comfortable with the Three Weird Sisters, as he privately called them. Kaylee was a marketing executive for a semiconductor company by day—and a Voudún practitioner by night. Mama Labadie, tall, willowy, and acerbic, was a Voudún mambo, a priestess. She was also a network technology engineer, considered nothing short of brilliant. Gentle Rose Ramirez was a Native American shaman, a healer. Each of them was intelligent and interesting in her own way, but Clancy was just not at ease with them.

He first called Kaylee's house phone. No answer. He tried Rose, then Mama Labadie. Then he remembered that all three women were away at a conference together—something New Age-y, he recalled. Clancy did not want to leave a voicemail about what had happened. He decided to call them later—maybe when he had more information—and turned to his computer to buy a ticket to Honolulu.

Clancy locked up the house and left. Twenty minutes later, he pulled into a long-term parking spot at San Jose International Airport.

• • •

Clancy met with the police in Honolulu and discovered the Coast Guard was searching for Sierra and her companion. Based on prevailing currents, the Coast Guard was focused on the island of Moloka'i. He promptly purchased a ticket for Moloka'i and returned to the airport.

In contrast to the jumbo jetliner that brought him to O'ahu, the plane to Moloka'i was tiny. He walked across the tarmac and up a mobile staircase onto the plane. The little prop plane took to the air and headed across the channel. The view from his window seat was not reassuring. The water was visibly choppy, even from this height. And it seemed like a long way to Moloka'i. It was painful to envision Sierra and Chaco, lost in that endless sea of blue, but Clancy could not tear his eyes from the water. After all, what if he saw them, miraculously floating on the white-capped surface of the sea? He strained his eyes the whole way, knowing that it was futile.

After twenty minutes, the plane began to descend and prepare for landing. The land that appeared below was rusty red and flat with bright green patches. He began to see fields and houses, and then they landed.

There was one building at the airport, a bit larger than a large suburban house. The luggage was quickly deposited on a steel bench to one side of the gate. Clancy had only a carry-on, so he went directly to the car rental window. Paperwork completed, he stepped outside to collect his car. A young Hawai'ian man drove up in a black Range Rover, parking directly in front of the terminal building. No one challenged him, as they would have at a large international airport. The man stepped out of his car and introduced himself.

"Aloha. Kevin Kapule. Coast Guard liaison. You're Mr. Forrester?"

Clancy nodded affirmatively. "Any news?"

Kevin shook his head. "Sorry, sir." Then he went on gently, "There aren't a lot of places to stay here, and I know you didn't have time to make arrangements. Some of the local people have heard why you're here and have offered their homes to you. Is that all right?"

Clancy said, "Yes. It's more than all right. It's amazingly generous. Thank you."

"You'll find that's pretty typical of Moloka'ians," said Kevin. "They're friendly and generous to a fault." He walked Clancy to his rental car. "Just don't cross them, is all. They're tough folks who fight for what they believe in."

"You're not from Moloka'i?"

"Not me," said Kevin. "I'm from O'ahu. Honolulu. I'm just here temporarily. Because, ah…" he paused.

"Because of the search," Clancy put in. Kevin nodded.

"Before we go into town," said Kevin, "let me give you a few tips on etiquette here." He saw Clancy's bemused face and grinned.

"Moloka'i is kind of old-fashioned. They believe in the old courtesies. So when you meet someone, you take their hand and lean forward to kiss a cheek. Just one." Kevin demonstrated this technique in pantomime.

"Right. Now, when you meet someone older than you, or at least someone wiser than you," he grinned again, "address them as Auntie or Uncle. That's respectful. Also, if someone helps you out, especially if you ask them to, don't be shy about offering money. You won't insult anyone."

Clancy gazed at him, waiting for further instruction.

"That's about it. Follow me into town," said Kevin, getting into the Range Rover.

Following Kevin turned out to be extremely easy. There seemed to be one main highway. Even when they reached the town of Kaunakakai, there were no traffic lights and very little traffic. They pulled up to a little green-painted house. Kevin parked in front and exited his car as Clancy parked behind him.

"This is Auntie Keikilani's house," he said as a Hawai'ian woman came through the front door, wiping her hands on a dishtowel. She was a short, broad woman with a round, good-natured face. Her hair was long and curly, black streaked with silver. She walked up to Clancy and held out a hand. As instructed, Clancy took the proffered hand and leaned forward to kiss Auntie Keikilani's cheek. The woman reciprocated, then stepped back and smiled.

"Aloha. Please come in." She picked up Clancy's bag over his protests and turned to go back into the house.

Her house was a small, green clapboard structure with a peaked roof. It was built on stilts that were hidden by latticework, with an open verandah in front. It was clearly old but well kept. The yard boasted several different kinds of hibiscus. There were a few banana trees hung with hands of bananas, the small, fat fruits pointing incongruously toward the sky.

Auntie Keikilani ushered them into her living room. She showed Clancy his room and deposited his suitcase on the bed, then returned and offered both men some refreshment. They sat on elderly bamboo furniture, with its bright tropical fabric-covered cushions, and sipped lemonade.

"There's a Coast Guard cutter leaving tomorrow morning around six a.m.," Kevin told Clancy. "It's just down at the Kaunakakai Wharf—you could walk from here. Auntie will tell you how to get there." Kevin took another swallow of lemonade, which seemed to stick in his throat. He looked at his feet, then up again at Clancy. His dark eyes clouded. "I have to be honest with you, sir. We aren't going to continue the search after tomorrow, assuming today's run comes up empty." He held up a hand as Clancy began to protest.

"I know that it seems hard-hearted. But I have to be blunt. There just isn't a lot of hope that they could have made it. They went overboard in deep water, a long way from shore. Even if they were good swimmers, it just isn't likely they could have survived. I'm sorry. I'm so sorry, but I can't lie to you."

Clancy heard this in silence. The gloom in the little living room was as thick as cold oatmeal. Kevin got up from the couch and checked his watch.

"I should be getting along. Thanks again, Auntie. Aloha." He went to the door, waved, and left.

Clancy sat on the bright floral couch, lemonade forgotten. Auntie patted his hand.

"You've had a long, hard day. Tomorrow will likely be pretty long, too. Why don't you lie down and have a nap? Dinner's at six-thirty."

"You don't have to do that, Auntie," Clancy said, feeling awkward about calling an unrelated person "Auntie." But Auntie Keikilani seemed completely comfortable with it.

"No, I don't have to, but I want to do it." Auntie smiled an incandescent smile, revealing a gold tooth and a gap. "Get a taste of good, local Moloka'i food."

Clancy felt tired, yes. Also hollowed-out like a rotten log. He had known the chances for Sierra and Chaco were slight, but no one had been willing to say so. Kevin had broken the spell and opened the door to doubt and grief.

"Kevin's right," he said. "By tomorrow morning, they would've been in the water for three days. How likely is it that they could survive that?"

"What makes you think they're in the water?"

Clancy stared at the woman. "Where else would they be?"

Keikilani shrugged. "I once heard of a man who went overboard in a sailboat and washed ashore on Kaho'olawe. A shark got his girlfriend, but he made it to shore and managed to live for a week on 'opihi—limpets—until they finally found him."

Clancy's eyes widened. Shark! Why had he never even thought about sharks? That seemed like the final blow to hope. He felt tears sting his eyes and closed them. His throat ached with the effort of suppressing his fear and anguish for Sierra and her friends. He felt Auntie Keikilani sit beside him on the couch. She put a comforting hand on his shoulder.

"You can't do anything about it now," she told him gently. "Go get some rest."

CHAPTER 4

"Before you leave," Houghton Roberts said to his administrative assistant, "please bring me the most recent report on the West Wind Project. Thank you." As Shelby softly closed the heavy koa wood door to his office, he leaned back in his leather chair. He had a magnificent view of the water from his Honolulu office and could see miles out to sea. He could also see, far below, sailboats clustered together in the marina.

Shelby opened the door silently and stepped back into his office. She was a tall young woman, elegantly dressed, with a blonde coil of hair at the nape of her neck. She was efficient, intelligent, and fulfilled his expectations for a CEO's administrative assistant. Though she was undoubtedly lovely, he wouldn't have touched her with a ten-foot pole. Romping with employees did not fit his self-image, and he was well aware that doing so would result in a loss of respect within the company—something he was unwilling to risk for any reason. Shelby laid the bound report on his blotter. Blotters were, of course, as outmoded as buggy whips, but he liked the way they looked. His was framed in gold-stamped red leather. The report was also bound in red with the company name stamped in gold on the cover: "Ahi Moana Energy Corporation."

"Will that be all, sir?" Shelby asked in her melodious voice.

"Yes, Shelby, thanks," he replied. He opened the report and began to read. He could have easily accessed it from his computer, but he enjoyed leafing through real paper, printed on the fine rag letterhead his firm used (another somewhat outmoded notion in this digital age).

Fifteen minutes later, he laid the report aside with a faint smile.

Everything seemed to be going well at the WestWind installation. Good. Time for his next meeting.

Roberts sat down carefully at the head of the long, gleaming conference table. Shelby was there, sitting to one side with her notebook. The others were heads of various departments within Ahi Moana, with the exception of one young man. Roberts recognized him as a new hire on the WestWind project, Gary Chisholm. Chisholm was chatting easily with Coral Tsukino, vice president of Exploration Services, seated to his right. The others were quiet, and kept their eyes on Roberts.

Roberts removed his gold watch slowly and deliberately, placing it in front of him. All eyes followed his movements, even Chisholm's. The young man looked mildly puzzled.

Roberts began, "You all have the agenda for this meeting. We'll begin with—"

Chisholm leaned forward, his arm outstretched. "Houghton? I'd like to introduce a new topic, if I may."

Roberts, whose employees never called him "Houghton," was too surprised to respond. Chisholm went on, as the other attendees glanced uneasily at one another.

"I've noticed that there are some budgetary discrepancies regarding the deep-water equipment being delivered to WestWind. Now, I'm sure there's a reasonable explanation, but..."

Roberts, recovered, cut him off. "Mr. Chisholm, you're new to Ahi Moana. You're still learning how we do things around here. And one of the things we don't do is add new business to an established agenda. If you wish to add a topic, please see Shelby at the end of this meeting and ask her to add it to the next meeting's agenda. Thank you." And he returned to the business at hand. Chisholm subsided into his seat with raised eyebrows. The others listened to Roberts discuss labor issues on a project in Norway.

All was as it should be. But that new man needed watching. Maybe it was time to go to Moloka'i to inspect the WestWind installation. As he pondered this idea, Houghton had no inkling that his routine visit would galvanize a chain reaction, changing everything.

• • •

At six a.m., the Kaunakakai Wharf was brilliantly lit. Several small boats were moored to the sides of the dock. The largest was the Coast Guard cutter, so Clancy headed straight to it. Kevin, dressed in crisp navy trousers and light blue shirt with a peaked cap, welcomed him on board. He gave Clancy a cup of coffee and a bearclaw and asked if he ever got seasick as the engines roared to life and the cutter began to pull away from the dock.

"Nope."

Kevin nodded. He handed Clancy a bright orange life jacket and showed him how to use it. He then introduced him to the crew and told him what the day's agenda would be.

"We're going to go around to the east and north of the island," he explained. "We expect to be on the water for about five or six hours. If we find nothing by noon, we come back. You can come up to the observation deck or stay out here. I suggest the observation deck—you can see farther."

Clancy followed Kevin up to the observation deck. As they chugged out of the small Kaunakakai harbor, Moloka'i's shore slid slowly by to port. Before long, Clancy began to see what appeared to be large oval stone walls built out into the water. Only the tops of the walls protruded, making them look like gigantic necklaces floating on the sea. Each wall enclosed large pools. Some of the walls had gaping holes in them, and vegetation grew on top of the stones. After the boat passed the fourth one, Clancy asked Kevin what they were.

"Ancient fishponds. I've heard the fishponds here are the oldest in the islands," Kevin replied. "These are hundreds and hundreds of years old, but they're still here. They were beautifully engineered to last so long. Some have legends surrounding them."

As Clancy knew all too well, legends were sometimes reality. "What kinds of legends?"

"One of the fishponds was supposed to have been built overnight by the Menehune. They formed long chains and passed the rocks hand to hand until the pond was completed."

"Menehune?"

"Uh, little green men," said Kevin, looking distinctly out of his depth. "They're supposed to be small, incredibly strong, and mischievous."

Sounds familiar, Clancy thought. He wondered where Fred was. Had he come along with Sierra and Chaco—or was he comfortably at home, eating chocolate? Clancy hoped for the latter.

The shore showed scattered houses and other evidence of habitation for many miles, but then the land began to rise, forming steep-sided cliffs, and the houses disappeared. They followed black lava cliffs for many miles. At one point, Kevin pointed out Halawa Bay, a double-lobed sandy bay fronting a valley choked with tropical growth. As they progressed, the high cliffs (pali, as Kevin called them) became still higher and more precipitous. The surf crashed wildly against these stony palisades, sending gouts of seawater high up the rocks, only to cascade in sheets to the ocean again.

"These pali are the highest sea cliffs in the world," Kevin informed him. "Almost four thousand feet high in some places. From sea floor to top, I mean."

The north coast seemed a forbidding place. The waves were fierce, hurling themselves against the pali and sending white spray several yards into the air. Wild-looking valleys occasionally broke the continuity of the high cliffs. When they reached the Kaluapapa Peninsula, it was a relief to see flat land and eventually, a tiny town—the site of the infamous leper colony. Then, it was more unbroken pali, towering into the sky in their robes of green, until they rounded the western end of the island. At this point, the engines kicked into high gear, and they began moving more quickly.

Clancy asked Kevin, "Are we heading back to Kaunakakai?"

Kevin nodded and looked somber. "Yes, Mr. Forrester. I'm sorry. This is it."

Clancy sat down heavily. He ran his hands through his dark hair, making it stick up in unruly peaks.

They're giving up, he thought. He really had hoped they might find Sierra and Chaco—or at least one of them. He felt emptied out and exhausted. He wished with all his heart he had gone on the Midway trip, and then none of this would have happened. He would gladly, cheerfully count all the albatross chicks in the world if it would bring Sierra back safely.

Then it struck him. The Coast Guard might be giving up, but he didn't have to. He could hire a boat locally—with a captain, of course—and continue the search on his own.

By the time they disembarked at Kaunakakai, Clancy had picked Kevin's brain and was in possession of the names of three or four dive boat owners who might be willing to charter their boats. Within an hour of reaching dry land, he had booked a charter for the next morning.

"The boat's called *Polupolu*," he reported to Auntie Keikilani that evening as he sat opposite her at the kitchen table. Keikilani broke into giggles. Clancy looked at her quizzically.

"It means…it means sort of like 'Fatso,'" she explained. "That's Sam Skinner's boat. It is kind of tubby, but Sam's a good captain. If anyone can find your friends, Sam can."

CHAPTER 5

Sierra flew backward over the railing and into the water without the slightest idea of what was happening. One minute she was standing high and dry, staring at the waterspout, the next she was plunging into the ocean.

She hit the water hard, nearly forcing the breath from her lungs. Something soft and heavy was wrapped around her waist, like a wet kidskin bag filled with lead. She held her breath, kicking and thrashing against whatever was dragging her down into the deep water. Black panic obscured her vision. When she began to think instead of merely react, she saw a thick, white *thing* looped around her midsection. She pushed against it hard, but while the thing was soft, its grip was unyielding. It inexorably propelled her farther and farther down. As she descended, she could see nothing through the roiling, bubbling waters—not the boat, not Chaco, not whatever it was that gripped her. Her thoughts were incoherent with terror as she began to see flashes of light and black spots and knew she was running out of air.

The downward plunge ceased and the bubbles began to dissipate. In front of her, a vast creature hovered motionlessly in the clear water. It was an enormous white octopus with iridescent blue eyes the size of beach balls. Its mammoth bag of a head floated behind it as it held her up to inspect her, its pupils horizontal and eerily like the eyes of a goat.

Sierra continued to struggle, desperate for air, vision beginning to darken. She felt compelled to open her mouth and suck in seawater; it promised relief from the terrible yearning to breathe even as she knew it would be her death. But then the pain stopped. The desperate compulsion to breathe ceased. She drooped, exhausted, in the loop of muscle supporting her.

When Sierra stopped fighting, she was able to take stock of her surroundings. Another massive tentacle held Chaco in its grasp like a baby gripping a tiny doll. His eyes were wide, showing the whites all around, and his dark hair whipped around his face as he struggled, impelled as she had been to reach the life-giving air above. Finally, he too realized that breathing was unnecessary and ceased to writhe in the monster's grasp.

Obviously, this was not a natural creature. Sierra desperately ransacked her memory for what Rose had taught her about combating supernatural beings. Sierra envisioned her magic powers—a talent she had not discovered until she had become involved with Chaco and company—as twining, glowing ribbons. Now she gathered these tendrils into a glowing mass, praying that she possessed enough power to resist the creature. As hard as she could, she hurled her accumulated power against the massive white octopus.

This volley of energy would have dissipated an illusion, as she had learned in the Nevada desert when defending herself against a phantasmagoric serpent. But this creature merely turned from contemplating Chaco to observing her with increased interest. It held her firmly, but without causing pain or uncomfortable pressure. The great, gleaming eyes examined her without haste as Sierra scrabbled desperately and unsuccessfully to regroup her powers. Then words formed in her mind. They weren't English words. The language sounded more like the rolling cadence of what little Hawai'ian she had heard so far, but she understood it.

"What are you?" The words emerged clearly in her mind. There was no voice, but if there had been a voice, it would have been as deep as the ocean.

There was no way to verbally respond, so Sierra pictured herself, her friends. Images of her past adventures whipped by, almost unbidden.

"Not an Avatar. Not a kahuna. A mortal. Merely a mortal?" Sierra offered mental agreement.

K.D. KEENAN

"But you have powers of a sort." It wasn't a question, yet Sierra sent an affirmative.

"And the other?"

Sierra knew the huge creature meant Chaco. She pictured Chaco in her mind. As a man. As a coyote. Chaco's friendship, his bravery, his kindness. She skipped over Chaco's more lecherous nature, as that was none of the creature's business, even if a cephalopod could understand such things.

"So. An Avatar? But he has no powers."

Sierra shrugged mentally, sending as best she could an explanation of Chaco's sudden disempowerment.

There was a long pause. The octopus turned Sierra and Chaco gently back and forth in the current. This time, Sierra asked, "What are *you*?"

The pale, opalescent eyes stared at her. The absence of lids made the eyes seem fixed and expressionless, but there was never any doubt when the creature was looking directly at her.

"Kanaloa," came the answer. Sierra's brain began to fill with images, most of which she did not understand. A Hawai'ian man, tall, straight, and handsome, finding a spring of sweet water and showing it to thirsty people. Images of things under the sea, some beautiful, some hideous. Another Hawai'ian man, as beautiful as the first, walking with the first man and talking. Volcano fire and slow-oozing lava, burning its way to the sea.

"Are you an Avatar?" The unblinking eyes never changed expression, but Sierra knew the answer was yes.

"Why did you take us from the boat?"

"I sensed you. And the other one. I was curious. But there was a third? I sensed a third thing, not like you. But it reminded me of something. Something…"

Sierra's heart nearly leaped from her chest. Fred! In the confusion of being yanked from the boat and submerged in water, then the terror of the creature confronting her, she had forgotten all about Fred. She began to writhe and twist in the tentacle's grasp, turning to see if she could spot the mannegishi, or at least the

42

duffle bag he had occupied when she last saw him. There was no one else but Chaco. Chaco was staring at her wide-eyed and open-mouthed. He appeared to be shouting, but of course, she could hear nothing.

"Where's Fred?" she sent, heart pounding. "Did you see Fred?" She transmitted a mental picture of her blobby green friend.

"No. I don't know what a Fred is. You are the only ones I saw."

Sierra hung limply in Kanaloa's grasp for a moment, letting the water rock her. Poor Fred. Did he even know how to swim? She didn't know. Had the duffle bag been zipped? She couldn't remember. If Fred went overboard with them, he was likely drowned—if mannegishis could drown. She also wasn't sure if Fred qualified as mortal or not. He was thousands of years old, but that didn't necessarily mean immortal—or did it? She wondered if it were possible to cry underwater. How would she know if she did? Finally, she returned her gaze to the twin blue galaxies of Kanaloa's eyes.

"Can you take us back to land?" Even as she asked the question, her terror returned. Having a pleasant chat with this gigantic octopus was no assurance that she and Chaco weren't on the menu.

As if in answer, the thing turned in the water and propelled itself forward, dragging her and Chaco along like hapless underwater skiers in its wake. As it turned, it exposed an immense, cruel, black beak, like a parrot's beak magnified a thousand times, centered in the radiating star of eight tentacles. Its vast siphon, a tube in the crook formed between the eye and the head, pulsed as it expelled seawater in a powerful jet.

This underwater version of a Nantucket sleigh ride went on for perhaps a half an hour at a stunning speed. The bubbles from their passage roiled the water and made it impossible to see anything. It didn't matter; she had to shut her eyes and mouth against the force of the water for most of the journey, pinching her nose to prevent water being forced into her sinuses. Her hat, shoes, hair clip, dark glasses, and pocket change flew away into the deeps—and she almost lost her shorts as well.

Finally, Kanaloa slowed and stopped. He held Chaco and

Sierra before his eyes again and reached two other tentacles out, gently touching the tips to their throats. Sierra could feel the soft stickiness of the suckers against her skin. Her body bucked with a sudden influx of power. Her throat burned fiercely, making her think she couldn't possibly survive the contact. What could Kanaloa be doing to them? It felt like an attack, but the sensation quickly subsided to a warm glow. She saw Chaco jerk and squirm as well. As the tip of the tentacle receded, Chaco held a hand to his brown throat as though he had been burned there.

"My gift," said Kanaloa. The vast tentacles whipped up, and Sierra jetted above the surface, rising perhaps six feet into the air. Plunging down into the water, she realized that breathing had once again become a necessary chore, so she struggled to the surface with a gasp. She wiped her hair away from her eyes and looked around. There was Chaco, furiously dog-paddling toward her. And beyond him—land!

They were off the coast of an island. Precipitous cliffs (*They're called pali,* she thought in wonder. *Now how did I know that?)* rose in high, vertical folds above the sea; sheer, black lava rock furred with a thick coat of green vegetation. She couldn't see a beach, she realized, heart sinking. There were no boats in sight. Only the forbidding cliffs, rising straight from the turbulent sea.

Chaco dog-paddled up to her, panting.

"Are you okay?" he asked.

"Yeah. Sort of. Don't you know how to swim?"

"I *am* swimming."

"You're dog-paddling. I don't know if that's going to be good enough to get us into shore."

"I'm coyote-paddling," returned Chaco, spitting seawater. "That's got to be good enough, because it's all I've got."

"Well, let's get going. The sooner we get there, the better," she said. For the first time since hitting the water, Sierra thought of sharks. She cringed, hoping this didn't occur to Chaco, who had enough problems.

They began to swim, each in his or her fashion, toward the

black cliffs. The pali towered above the ocean like an uninterrupted ribbon of skyscrapers. Higher than skyscrapers, she thought. After ten minutes, Chaco's dogged rhythm began to slow and become ragged. The cliffs looked no closer.

"Take a rest, Chaco," said Sierra, whose slow crawl had not much tired her. Chaco paused in his efforts, but began to sink, so Sierra taught him how to tread water. After several minutes, Chaco's breathing slowed and evened, and they struck out for shore again.

They made slow progress in this way as the high cliffs gradually neared. She saw that her hands had turned white under her tan, and felt chilled to her bones. This didn't seem fair—Hawai'ian water was supposed to be bathtub-warm. But she was cold in a way she had never felt before, not even while snow camping, the chill creeping into the very center of her body. She called for another rest, and saw that Chaco was pale as well, his eyes taking on the desperation of someone at the end of his endurance. Then she heard it.

"Chaco, I hear waves! We must be close to land!"

Chaco's tired eyes brightened, but he was too exhausted to speak.

They swam onward. Chaco's labored strokes echoed her own. Her arms and legs felt like tree limbs, heavy, inert. It was all she could do to take one leaden stroke after another. She thought Chaco, with his inefficient paddling, must be in even greater distress. Stroke. Stroke. Stroke. She inadvertently sucked in a mouthful of salt water and began to cough, each spasm scraping her lungs and throat raw. This at least served to distract her from the grinding ache of her chilled and weary muscles.

Then she was lifted up on a wave. For a second as the wave hovered, she saw a wall of unbroken black stone before her. They were going to be dashed against the cliffs. There was nowhere to take refuge, no way to escape the angry waves crashing against the stones.

Then the wave broke, rolling Sierra in its grasp like a bread maker kneading dough, slamming her down on the lava rocks scattered throughout the shallow water. Shallow water. Sand. A beach, where a second previously, she had seen nothing but the end of her life as she was hurled against the unbroken rock of the cliffs.

Pain! Raw, branching pain sizzled across her abused body. She lay unable to move in the receding water. She thought muzzily that she must pull herself up and away from the dragging, sucking waves. She heard another wave roar up behind her, the inexorable power of the water forcing her back across the grating rocks and sand. She simply didn't have the strength to resist. The treacherous sand gave way beneath her body, allowing the greedy waves to grip her again. Sierra clawed her hands, desperately attempting to gain some purchase in the sand to prevent being dragged back into the ocean, but it was no use—she was fatigued and weak. As the waves scraped her over the rocks again, her fingers scrabbling uselessly, muscular brown arms seized her and began to pull her up the beach.

With the last of her strength, Sierra croaked, "Please—get Chaco too. Please save him. Please…"

CHAPTER 6

Roberts worked late the night after Gary Chisholm questioned the records for WestWind. He had Shelby bring in all reports, documents, and financials for the project. He dismissed her and pored over them for several hours.

Finally, he rubbed his eyes and relaxed into his leather chair. He felt enormous relief. There was nothing he could see that indicated any financial discrepancies or irregularities of any kind. What was Chisholm playing at? Or had the younger man merely made an innocent mistake?

The idea that any project under Roberts' command could be operating in any way other than perfectly aboveboard filled him with anger. He worked hard to assure his company was squeaky clean and resented any implication it was otherwise.

Chisholm. Roberts' annoyance centered on him. The man had dared—publicly—to impugn Ahi Moana's ethics. Chisholm was definitely a problem, but that kind of problem was easy to fix.

• • •

Sierra woke up. Her first take was confusion. She wasn't in her bed at home. She wasn't in the hotel in Honolulu. She shifted her position and winced. Her arms and legs were wrapped in large, wet leaves. She peered under a leaf wrapped around her forearm and winced again. There was a long scrape on her arm, raw, red and painful. It and multiple other scrapes around her body stung as she moved. She remembered being dragged across the lava rocks by the waves—the rocks might as well have been cheese graters.

She appeared to be lying on a mat of some sort that rustled as she moved. She was covered with a sheet of—was that paper? It was thick, like handmade paper, and soft. Geometric designs had been stamped into it to make a textured pattern, and there were other patterns composed of red and brown triangles and diamonds that looked as though they were printed with some kind of tool. Sierra sat up and took stock of her surroundings.

She was lying on the floor of a house, but it was a house made like a basket. Sturdy poles formed the framing, lashed together with thick, rough cord. The interior was one large room, with a peaked roof. The building was thickly thatched with dried grasses, from the peak of the roof to the ground. As Sierra clambered to her feet, the floor gave slightly beneath her, and she realized that there were many layers of mats beneath her. There were no windows, and the tall doorway in the center of one long wall had no actual door in it—Sierra could see the blue of the sky and the green of tangled growth outside. The papery stuff that covered her dropped to the sleeping mat, and she realized she was naked. Hastily, she retrieved the paper blanket and wrapped it firmly around her.

The large leaves covering Sierra's other wounds dropped to the matted floor as she moved. She hoped she wasn't interrupting some important treatment in process. Then she saw Chaco.

He was lying on another mat not far from hers. His eyes were closed and he appeared to be unconscious or sleeping. She forgot about the leaves and her injuries and went to his side. He didn't look good, she decided. He was pale, his dark lashes lying quietly against his high cheekbones. He was covered with another papery blanket, and he also had large, wet leaves plastered against his body and around his head. But his breathing was steady. She checked his pulse and it seemed regular and strong. At least, she thought so. Her last first aid course had been a long time ago.

Sierra placed a tentative hand on Chaco's bare shoulder and whispered his name. No response. She shook him gently and said his name louder. Still no response. So he was unconscious, not sleeping. This was worrying, but there was nothing she could do about it.

Sierra tucked her paper wrapping around her more firmly and went to the door. She could see what looked like a garden, and beyond it, the beach and the ocean, a few coconut palms fringing the sand. Behind the house was a thickly overgrown mass of trees and vines. The air was soft, almost syrupy with humidity, and smelled wonderfully of flowers and salt air.

Then she noticed there was someone in the garden. She hadn't seen him at first because he was wearing a hat woven of green palm fronds. Until he moved, he looked like another flourishing plant. Sierra cleared her throat, suddenly aware that she was extremely thirsty.

"Er, ahem," she croaked. Not her best effort, but the head turned, and the man began to make his way out of the garden toward her.

As he emerged from the garden plot, it was all she could do to stop herself from drawing in a sharp breath. The man was as tall as Chaco, but more heavily muscled. He had thighs like a weight lifter, broad shoulders slabbed with muscle, and arms that looked as though they could pick Sierra and Chaco up together and throw them a seriously long distance. His body, arms, and legs were covered with black tattoos inscribing geometrical patterns composed of triangles, diamonds, and spirals, but his face was unmarked. Under the swaying fronds of his hat, his face was definitively Polynesian—large eyes the color of uncreamed coffee; a broad, flattened nose; sensuous, sculpted lips; and smooth bronze skin. He was wearing nothing but the palm-frond hat and a loincloth. Long, curly black hair cascaded over his shoulders, carelessly tied back with a length of rough cord.

Sierra had trouble swallowing, which she put down to the fact that she was so thirsty. As the man approached, he began to speak. What issued from his lips sounded to Sierra like water running over smooth pebbles—and she understood every word.

"Aloha! How do you feel?" he was asking.

Sierra tried not to stare, but failed. "Are you, I mean, um, are you speaking Hawai'ian?" she asked.

The man grinned at her, teeth very white against his brown skin. "Yes, I am speaking Hawai'ian. And you are too!" he said cheerfully. "How do you feel?"

Sierra halted in confusion. "I…I am speaking Hawai'ian?" To her knowledge, she knew three words in Hawai'ian: aloha, mahalo, and mysteriously, pali. But the words she had just spoken were not English. Confused, she shook her head.

"Not feeling too well, then?" the man asked, concern wrinkling his forehead. "Why? Other than your scrapes and cuts, is there something else wrong?"

"Ah, no. The cuts hurt, but I feel okay. Do you have some water?" She felt she could not say another word until she had a drink.

"Over here." The man turned and walked behind the house where Sierra had awoken. He strode quickly down a narrow path between the trees, vines, and bushes. Sierra, unused to walking in bare feet, had more trouble. Her tender soles encountered sharp stones and thorny sticks, slowing her progress.

When she caught up with the man, she saw they had come to the foot of the cliff forming the walls of this little valley. From a cleft in the rock above jetted a stream of water, pouring down into a natural rock basin. The overflow from the basin gurgled down a small channel that diverted it toward the garden. The man handed her a coconut shell cut in half, forming a bowl. He plucked some long leaves from plants growing by the edge of the basin, twined them together and dropped them in the water. The leaves floated around in the current created by the water pouring into the basin. As Sierra watched impatiently, parched with thirst, the man watched the bobbing leaves and finally indicated she should help herself to the water. She drank deeply and looked up in surprise.

Given the humid heat of the day, the water was shockingly cold, as cold as though it had been refrigerated. It held a pure sweetness unlike anything she had ever encountered. Snowmelt from the peaks of the Sierra Nevada mountains had never tasted this wonderful or been so refreshing.

"It's sweet!" she exclaimed, and drank until she could drink no more. As she set down the coconut shell on the edge of the rocky basin, she realized she must have been dehydrated. She felt immeasurably better, if somewhat awash.

"What's your name?" she asked.

"I'm Kama," said the young man, accompanying this with a blinding smile that carved dimples into his cheeks and made Sierra a trifle breathless. "What's your name?"

"Sierra. Is Chaco going to be all right?"

"You're both going to be fine. We need to keep those cuts and scrapes clean, keep them from scabbing over. I've been bathing them in seawater and keeping them moist with tī leaf poultices. Your friend—Chaco?—got a pretty bad bump on the head, so he'll need to take it easy for a while."

Well, she was all right, and Chaco was alive and accounted for. But where was Fred? She couldn't ask this nice young man if he had seen a smallish, green, blobby creature washed up with them.

"Did you find anything else along with Chaco and me?" she asked. "Maybe a navy-blue duffel bag?"

Kama shook his head. Sierra's heart contracted with grief, but it wasn't something she could share with Kama. She felt her paper covering slip a bit and clutched it to her. "Where are my clothes?"

"I hung them up to dry, but I'm not sure they're going to be good for much. Lava rock has a way of tearing things up—skin, clothes, whatever. You can use the kapa cloth instead."

Sierra realized he was talking about the papery blanket she was using as a dress. She pointed to it. "This? This is kapa cloth? I thought it was paper."

Kama laughed a rolling, infectious laugh. "I suppose it is paper. It's made from beaten mulberry bark. Let's go back to the hale and get you some twine to help hold your dress up."

Clearly, Kama had undressed her and tended to her wounds while she was either passed out or lying in an exhausted sleep.

Sierra was relieved that he didn't make any knowing remarks. She followed him to the hale. Chaco was still deeply asleep or unconscious. Sierra remembered that people with concussions should not be allowed to fall asleep, at least not for a while.

She turned to Kama anxiously as he handed her a length of coarse twine. "Is he asleep? Or unconscious?" She wound the twine around the kapa cloth above her breasts and tied it securely, folding the kapa over the twine to keep it from slipping.

Kama glanced at Chaco's unmoving form. "He was unconscious when I found him. He must have banged his head on a rock. I hauled him up to the hale, and he woke up. He was mostly worried about you, but I told him you were just sleeping, there was nothing he could do in his state, and to let me take care of you. I got him cleaned up and poulticed his head. He passed out again after that."

"Thank you. Thank you for saving our lives. I'm sure we would have died if you hadn't been here. Mahalo!"

"You're welcome," said Kama. "Let's go outside so we can talk. I've got some questions, and I bet you do too."

They sat in the shade of an odd-looking tree with long, frond-like leaves and roots that sprang out from the trunk above ground before sinking into the earth around it. They could see the waves crashing on the rocks from their vantage point beneath the tree and Sierra shuddered at the memory of trying to swim through the rough waves and rocks to the safety of the beach. But this spot was gorgeous, she had to give it that. The water was brilliant turquoise, the sky was a soft blue with a few white clouds, and the repetitious roar and retreat of the waves was soothing. She could see how tiny this little valley really was, just a small pie wedge in the high pali, enough for a miniature jungle to grow up. Chickens clucked and pecked in the garden, jealously guarded by a magnificent rooster with a thick plume of blue-green tail feathers and a rainbow of orange, red, yellow, and green feathers embellishing its body. It looked more like the jungle fowl she had seen in zoos than a typical farm rooster.

"How did you come to be swimming up my beach?" Kama inquired. "I don't get a lot of visitors here, which is one reason I like it." He didn't sound annoyed by this; it was a statement of fact.

"Sorry about that," Sierra responded. She explained about the whale-watching expedition and getting swept overboard by a waterspout. This wasn't true, of course, but she was not willing to start babbling to this stranger about a gigantic white octopus.

Kama was quiet for while. Then he said, "That doesn't make any sense."

Uh-oh. He's not buying it. "Oh? Why not?"

"If you were on a whale-watching boat out of Honolulu, there's no way you could have made it all this way alive. It's too far. The water is extremely rough out there. And then there's the sharks."

"That's what happened," she said defensively. "I can't explain it. It just happened."

Kama nodded, but said nothing.

"And what are you doing here? Do you live here all alone?"

"Yes. I'm living in the old way, the way of the ancestors. I make everything I use here." He nodded around at the hale and the garden.

"May I ask why?"

Kama seemed a bit reluctant to answer. After a moment or two of thought, he raised his head and said, "I was in one of those toxic relationships. You know—fiery passion one moment and even more fiery rage the next?"

Sierra nodded. She had been in one or two relationships like that herself. Not Clancy, of course. He was almost too calm and cool most of the time.

"So I decided to get away from her. Trust me, when it comes to this lady, that isn't an easy thing to do."

Oh, a stalker? Poor man.

"I needed to find somewhere she wouldn't track me down. And I wanted to live the ancient lifestyle, like I always have. So I came here. Believe me, no one else ever comes here. Until you and your friend."

"So, how do Chaco and I get back to Honolulu?"

Kama shrugged, making his muscles ripple. He seemed utterly unaware of the effect this had on Sierra, who quickly, if reluctantly, glanced away. "I don't think there is a way. There's no way out of this valley by land—the pali here are two thousand feet and nearly straight up. You need a boat, but the only boat I have is my outrigger." He pointed to an elongated canoe with an outlying arm resting on the beach. "I'm sorry, but I can't give you that. I rely on it for fishing. Besides, as I said, the water between here and O'ahu is really rough. It's more than 50 miles to Honolulu from here. You need to know how to handle an outrigger—you and your friend look to be in good shape, but I don't think you can paddle an outrigger from here to Honolulu."

Sierra quickly realized Kama was right. She and Chaco didn't have the skills to handle a tiny boat in that vast expanse of turbulent water. Maybe if Chaco were himself again with the strength of an Avatar, but as it was…no. Did this mean they were going to live out their natural lives right here? Where was here, anyway?

"What island are we on?" she inquired.

"Moloka'i."

Sierra didn't know anything about Moloka'i, except for the leper colony.

"Could you take us in your outrigger to someplace on Moloka'i where there are more people? And electricity and telephones?" *And coffee?*

"No."

"Well, what would you do if you wanted to leave this place?"

Kama looked at her frankly. "I might take my outrigger, but I've been using it all my life, and I know what I'm doing. I have some other ways, but they aren't open to you."

"What do you mean, not open to us?" Sierra balanced on the edge of annoyance and alarm. *What could Kama possibly be talking about? What is this guy's deal? Who in this day and age doesn't have a freaking cell phone?*

But Kama rose to his feet. He held out a large hand to her. "It's time to treat your wounds. Sea water soak, three times a day." He drew Sierra to her feet. They went back to the hale for gourds, then to the beach. Kama showed her a small pool among the rocks, full of clear salt water and deep enough to immerse at least one adult body. Kama dipped his gourds full of water, explaining he would bathe Chaco's wounds with it, then told her, "Climb in there and soak for a while. No, don't worry, I won't peek." He grinned at her. "You haoles. Always so worried about your bodies." He turned and began to walk back to the hale with the gourds. True to his word, he never looked back. As Sierra eased out of her kapa covering and into the water, she watched his muscular rear, openly displayed by the loincloth, recede and disappear into the house.

CHAPTER 7

Polupolu was set to go out the following morning. Clancy wanted to spend more time searching the north shore of the island.

"I didn't think the Coast Guard went in close enough," he explained to Auntie Keikilani, forking a piece of tender mahi-mahi into his mouth. He had purchased the fresh fish from a boat earlier that day and brought it to Auntie Keikilani, along with vegetables from the farmer's market. Auntie had been more than generous, and he didn't want to be a freeloader. "I want to see if we can get closer in so that we can see better. The problem is, as far as I could see, the north side is pretty much pali, except for Halawa Valley and Kalaupapa."

Auntie Keikilani leaned forward with interest and said, "Not quite. There are a few little valleys up there that are accessible from the ocean. If you were far enough out on the water, you might have missed some of them."

"That seems promising," said Clancy, his heart lifting a little.

Auntie had invited a neighbor, Jack Kane, to share their dinner. Jack was a cheerful older man with two daughters living in Honolulu. As Jack explained, there had just been no jobs for the girls on Moloka'i. Now Jack said, "You can borrow my binoculars, if you want."

"Thanks, Jack," said Clancy. "That would be really helpful."

After a few more minutes of discussion about tomorrow's plans, the conversation drifted on to other topics.

"Anyone heard what's happening out at the WestWind project?" asked Keikilani, passing around a pitcher of iced tea.

Jack wrinkled up his broad nose and shook his head. "Nah.

They don't employ locals, you know, so we never hear anything. Sam says they've got at least two construction vessels working out there now." He pursed his lips as though tasting something sour.

"What's the WestWind Project?" Clancy inquired.

"It's a big wind farm that they're building out in the channel between western Moloka'i and O'ahu," said Jack. "There's an extinct underwater volcano called Penguin Bank. That makes the water shallower than you would expect, so it's easier to build there. And there's lots of wind. We're not too happy about it, though."

"Why is that? I would think wind power would be ideal here in Hawai'i—I mean, all the oil has to be shipped here, so electricity must be really expensive," commented Clancy.

Keikilani and Jack exchanged glances. They appeared to be on the same page when it came to WestWind.

Jack responded first. "It's not that simple. First, that area is a national marine sanctuary for humpback whales. The wind farm will disturb the whales and affect their ability to breed and calve. Whales are sacred to the Hawai'ian people, you know—we never hunted them. It's an important area for the monk seals, too. Both the whales and the seals are endangered."

"Isn't that sufficient reason to stop the project?" Clancy asked.

"Nope. You have to understand, the power is intended for O'ahu, and O'ahu is where most of the people and all of the money are in this state," Jack responded. "The political clout is all in Honolulu. But there's more. Each tower—and there are at least 100 towers planned—is supported on three legs. Those legs have to be sunk in the bedrock, which will create a huge disruption of sea life."

"Last—and maybe this is selfish, but it's important—we Moloka'ians won't benefit from it. They're bringing in workers from other places, so we won't get any benefit from the added employment, and none of the electricity generated from the wind farm will go to Moloka'i. So we won't even get a break on our electricity bills."

"Couldn't you stop it?" Clancy asked.

"We tried," Keikilani responded gloomily. "You have no idea how corrupt politics are in this state."

"Well, who's behind it?"

"Ahi Moana. They're located in Honolulu, but they have operations all over the world, or so I'm told," Jack said. The conversation drifted back to tomorrow's search. Auntie and Jack got into a mild argument about how many valleys on the north shore were accessible from the sea.

The next morning Clancy appeared at the wharf before the sun was up. *Polupolu* was waiting for him. She did seem like a tubby little boat, but her seaworthiness could be judged by the years of hard work she had put in, evidenced by the many scars and patches scoring her sides. Sam Skinner, along with a young crewman named Mike, greeted Clancy, gave him a brief safety talk, and handed him a life jacket.

"When I was out with the Coast Guard, I didn't think they came close enough to shore," said Clancy. "We wouldn't have been able to see my friends if they had reached land—we were too far out. I found out that there are some small valleys in the cliffs on the north side, places where someone might come ashore safely. Can you get us close enough to check them out?"

Sam nodded. "I'm sure I can get closer than the Coast Guard. But the water can get really rough, you know? And there are rocks and the reef to deal with. I'll do my best, but no guarantees, okay?"

That was as good as he was going to get, so Clancy nodded.

Sam went up the ladder to the cockpit. Soon, *Polupolu*'s engines grumbled and sputtered to life, and they began to move into the channel. For the first part of the journey, Clancy relaxed and watched the shore slipping by. This part of Moloka'i was well populated, and in the unlikely event that Sierra or Chaco washed up here, they would be discovered immediately. The sun lifted over the horizon, tinting the eastern sky with rose and gold; the fresh, salt breeze lifted his spirits and hopes. He saw dolphins and in the distance, the geyser-like spouts of whales. He didn't go on full alert until the sea cliffs began to rise out of the ocean and the signs of habitation disappeared. Clancy held Jack's binoculars to his eyes almost constantly after that point.

Sam did bring *Polupolu* in closer than the Coast Guard had done. As he explained, he had been fishing these waters since he was a kid. But there were places where he pulled out because of rocks or too-shallow water. As they chugged slowly past the pali, Clancy did indeed see a few small valleys that they had missed on his first tour around the island. At one point, he saw a house perched above the crashing waves, at the foot of a tiny stream. There was no sign of a dock or of a road leading away from the house's perilous perch above the sea. It was obvious from the neatly planted fields behind the house and the general state of tidiness and good repair that there were people living there. Clancy wondered how they managed to live in such an isolated place.

There was one great consolation in seeing this lonely house there were people here. If by some remote chance Sierra and Chaco made it this far, there were at least people who might be able to help them.

Finally, they reached the Kalaupapa Peninsula, where Sam took *Polupolu* a bit further out and ratcheted up the motors. Kalaupapa might be one of the most isolated communities in the world, but it was a community. If his friends washed up here, there would be help for them. Past Kalaupapa, the pali was bare black rock, with no little valleys, only wild waves pounding against the sheer face of the cliffs. *Polupolu's* motors revved, and the boat began to move briskly through the water. The day's search was over.

It was a subdued Clancy that disembarked at the wharf. He thanked Sam and Mike, confirming another search the following day. He trudged back to Auntie Keikilani's home. Auntie met him at the front door, eyebrows raised in silent inquiry.

"No luck."

She clucked sympathetically and stood aside to let him into the house. He went to his room and called Kaylee, figuring she had to be home from her conference by that time.

This time, Kaylee answered her phone immediately. "Clancy!

That you? Where you been keeping yourself?" He could picture her wide, happy smile, teeth gleaming white against her chocolaty-brown skin, and knew his next sentence would erase the happiness from her face like a wet rag over chalk marks.

Clancy explained where he was—and why. There was a long silence at the other end of the line. Finally, Kaylee spoke.

"I'm going to call Mama Labadie and Rose. Maybe we can help at this end. Mama could ask the loa what's happened to them. I simply do not believe that Sierra and Chaco are anything but okay. I mean, Chaco's an Avatar. He wouldn't let anything happen to Sierra."

"Uh, Kaylee, I…"

"I'll call you back, Clancy. Gotta go."

Kaylee ended the call, and Clancy sat disconsolately on the side of his bed. In the beginning, Clancy had viewed Voudún with suspicion and disgust. Once he had gained a better understanding of Voudún, he was more understanding, if not accepting. "Voodoo" as depicted by Hollywood movies was his only exposure to this religion—witch doctors, Voodoo dolls, and zombies. In talking with Kaylee and Mama, he realized his error. Voudún appeared to focus on healing, but that didn't make him comfortable with it, even when Mama Labadie's pronouncements from the loa paid off time and again.

Mama Labadie was a Voudún mambo, or priestess. This would have placed her beyond the pale as far as Clancy was concerned, except that Sierra was deeply attached to her. And Mama had admittedly been quite helpful in more than one crisis. She was a tall, willowy, black woman with fierce eyes who brooked no nonsense from anyone. She was also a loyal friend to Sierra, which Clancy viewed as her most redeeming characteristic.

Rose was an entirely different kettle of weirdness. She was a Native American shaman. More mumbo-jumbo, in Clancy's opinion, so it frustrated him that Rose's insights were almost always right. Rose had trained Sierra to use certain powers that Rose claimed were available to anyone, but required constant development. That might be so—Clancy had seen Sierra's powers in action—but he had been profoundly unsuccessful in detecting any such powers in himself.

Auntie Keikilani came to the door of his bedroom. "I'm sorry you didn't find your friends," she said quietly. "Let's go out to eat tonight. Maybe have a couple of cocktails. Listen to the music. You can't do anything more tonight."

They walked to the Paddler's Inn, a nearby restaurant that was a favorite with locals. It was a live music night, and the restaurant was crowded. Clancy did have a couple of drinks, although Keikilani declined. They listened to the music, and Clancy thought how soothing slack-key Hawai'ian guitar music was. Several times, he found himself beginning to relax, but then he would remember, and his mood would plummet again.

They returned to the house. As he switched on the light in his room, his cell rang.

"It's me. Mama Labadie," said a familiar, deep voice. "I talked to the loa tonight. They say Sierra and Chaco are alive."

Clancy wanted to believe, he really did. He was silent for a long moment, then asked, "Are you sure?"

"The loa know. No mumbo-jumbo, like you call it. They were clear as a bell. For once."

Clancy was glad that Mama was several thousand miles away and couldn't see his embarrassment. "Okay. It's just hard for me…"

"Yeah, I know it, but trust me on this. They say Sierra and Chaco are alive. By the way, I stopped by Sierra's place to water the plants. Fred wasn't there. You know where he's at?"

"Did the loa tell you anything about Fred?"

Now it was Mama Labadie's turn to be silent. Then she said, "No. Nuthin' about Fred."

"Maybe he was invisible when you went into her house."

Mama snorted. "Even if he was invisible, there'd still be chocolate wrappers all over the place."

CHAPTER 8

Roberts enjoyed being interviewed by the media. The young man now ensconced in his leather visitor's chair was from *Forbes Magazine*. Roberts' PR director, Alana Singh, deserved kudos for setting this one up.

After Shelby brought in a coffee tray, complete with porcelain cups and saucers, Alana spoke. "Mr. Jacobs is writing a story on alternative energy firms, their strategies, how they will compete with fossil fuel companies, and the future of renewable energies. Ahi Moana has been selected as the representative wind power company, so of course, we're very pleased to be included."

Roberts smiled and nodded. He'd been down this road before with the press, and it was familiar and comfortable territory.

"Mr. Roberts," Jacobs began, earning Roberts' immediate approval for not using his first name, "Could you tell me a bit about your background? I've read your bio, of course, but I'd like to get a little deeper. You grew up in Pennsylvania?"

"That's right. A little town called Nanticoke, near Wilkes-Barre."

"What did your parents do?"

"My father was a coal miner. My mother was a housewife, but she did laundry and ironing to bring in extra cash."

"So they were poor?"

"Poor as church mice." Roberts began to warm up, as he usually did when talking about his origins. "Of course, everyone thought when I graduated high school I would go into the mines, like everyone else. But I watched Dad come home night after night, covered in coal dust and exhausted. I saw a lot of folks die of black lung. Of course, they were also almost all smokers, and that didn't help. Every morning, you could hear the coughing all over Nanticoke. Like living in a TB ward some days."

"Did your father get black lung?"

"Died of it. But two good things came out of all this for me. First, I decided that there was no way in hell I was going into the mines. I wasn't afraid of hard work, but I hated the coal, the dirt, and the dust, and I was terrified of black lung. So I decided to get myself out of Nanticoke, go someplace where there were no coal mines.

"The other big thing was when I got interested in alternative energies. I decided that somehow I had to go to college. Nobody in my family had ever been to college before. They really didn't see why I had to go, and there wasn't the money for it in any case."

"Then how did you do it?"

"I worked from the time I was old enough to pick up a broom. I washed cars, swept floors, minded the cash registers in stores, ran errands—whatever I could pick up. And I studied like a fiend. Being good in school wasn't a huge priority for a lot of kids in Nanticoke, but I didn't care. I was too busy working to have a lot of friends anyhow…"

He could tell this story in his sleep. It was a good story—the poor boy bootstrapping his way to CEO of an international alternative energy corporation. But as always, there was a lot he didn't say. He didn't talk about his father staggering home blind drunk to beat him and his mother as they tried to shelter the younger kids. He didn't mention the bullying he suffered as the town's prize student, the dude who was always too busy studying or working to play sports or hang out. In particular, he did not mention the times he had been cornered in the school bathroom and beaten bloody because "the little shit acts like he's better than us." His chosen path was lonely, humiliating, and frequently painful, but each beating only set his resolve more firmly to get away and stay away.

After graduating and working in a lucrative engineering position for several years, he went back to Nanticoke only once, right before he moved to Honolulu to join Ahi Moana. He drove his Lamborghini, a low, panther-like machine that hugged the road, and he wore his best Italian silk business suit. He wanted to visit his mother and those siblings who had remained in town, but in his heart of hearts, he was hoping to impress some of the gorillas who had terrorized him in his youth. The morning after his arrival he emerged from his childhood home to find the Lamborghini covered in smashed raw eggs and flour. Farewell to Nanticoke.

As the interview progressed, Roberts assured that it all went just as he intended. It was a familiar process. Jacobs departed with respectful thanks. Later, Roberts praised Alana's achievement in setting up the interview and gave her a well-deserved raise.

● ● ●

That first day, Kama insisted that Sierra soak her wounds in seawater three times. While she did this, Kama bathed Chaco's wounds with salt water as well, filling gourds and taking them to the hale where Chaco lay unconscious the entire day. While she bathed in the saltwater pool, Sierra scanned the ocean for ships. Or boats. Or jet skis—anything that might take her and Chaco back to civilization. She also walked the small beach, obsessively searching the waves and rocks for a small green figure that never appeared.

Neither she nor Chaco showed any sign of infection, but she was nervous about having no recourse to antibiotics. She knew from personal experience that scrapes and cuts from beach rocks were quick to fester. And Chaco's continued state of unconsciousness worried her desperately. Kama seemed like a nice guy and all, but she had little faith in his doctoring skills.

In the early evening, Kama roasted fish and served it with a seaweed concoction that also contained some peculiar looking orange and black ovals. Sierra, sitting near the open fire in front of the hale, took her portion and prodded at it tentatively. Kama dug in with relish.

"Kama, do you mind telling me what these things are?"

"'Opihi," Kama said through a mouthful of the same. With her new and mysterious acquisition of the Hawai'ian language, Sierra had no difficulty understanding that these were limpets.

"Oh. Okay," she said, and took a gingerly bite. They were rubbery and salty, but Kama had evidently added additional ingredients, and the flavor was quite good. They ate in silence for a while.

When they had finished, Sierra asked, "So, do you ever get any visitors here? There must be boats from time to time."

"No."

"Oh. I just thought that some time or other, people must be fishing out there or exploring, and this is such a pretty little valley, you would think people would come in for a closer look."

"No."

"Never?"

"No."

Frustrated, Sierra got up. There were no dishes to wash; everything had been served on broad tī leaves. These were tossed into the fire. The sun was just beginning to set, and she wanted to check on Chaco while the light was still good.

She entered the hale. It was dim inside, but there was enough light from the doorway to see Chaco's still form on the sleeping mats. She knelt beside him and peered into his face. His head was still wrapped in tī leaves, as were his scrapes and cuts. Despite her concerns, Kama seemed to be taking good care of his patient. Chaco's face was still somewhat pale beneath his brown skin, but he had no fever, his breathing was easy, and his pulse—so far as Sierra's first aid training could tell—was good. To her amusement, he was snoring slightly.

Kama came in and stood over them. "He's doing okay. Should be up and around soon."

"How can you tell?"

Kama smiled at her, displaying large, even teeth that gleamed even in the dim light of the hale. "Excuse me for a few minutes. If you'd sit over there," he gestured toward Sierra's sleeping mat. "I have a few things I need to do for him."

Sierra moved over to her mat and sat down cross-legged to watch, tucking her thick kapa cloth around her more securely. Kama went to a basket and pulled out a length of pure white kapa. He took this to Chaco and wound the kapa around Chaco's head, binding it crosswise. He began to chant in Hawai'ian, but Sierra understood the chant as:

> *"Kapo is dwelling in the beautiful growth*
> *Standing at Ma'ohe-laia*
> *'Ohai trees standing on Mauna-loa*
> *Kauana-'ula celebrated gives aloha,*
> *Here is what is red, a sacrifice,*
> *A sacrifice, a gift by me to you."* [1]

Kama flipped the kapa cloth from around Chaco's head, then looked down at him and frowned. He remained in this pose so long that Sierra became alarmed.

"What's the matter?"

Kama shook his head. "There should be an 'aumakua sitting on his chest by now, giving me further instructions."

"A what?"

"'Aumakua. His personal god, or his family's personal god. But there's nothing there. I don't know what to do now."

Sierra considered this. Another woman might have run screaming out of the hale, but she had more personal experience with gods than most. "Chaco's not Hawai'ian, you know. Maybe that's why?"

Kama shook his head. "Everyone's got an 'aumakua. They might not know it, but they've got one. If his 'aumakua isn't here to help him, I fear for his life."

Sierra did not know how to respond to this. Up to this point, she had been completely unaware of 'aumakuas and their role in human life. And then she remembered. Chaco wasn't human.

"Um, Kama? I don't think you should worry about his 'aumakua."

"Why not?"

"It's just that I don't think he ever had one." She didn't mention that, if anything, Chaco *was* an 'aumakua of sorts.

Kama looked puzzled. "There's something strange about him, that's certain. He's almost...well, he's different."

Sierra nodded. More different than Kama could imagine, she thought, but she wasn't about to explain exactly how.

"Let's see how he's doing in the morning. If he isn't any better, can you please, *please*, take us someplace I can get him medical help?"

Kama stood over her, his massive body blocking the light. He shook his head. "No," he said. "I can't do that."

CHAPTER 9

Kama loomed over Sierra in a way she hoped was not intended to be threatening. "If he needs it, why wouldn't you take Chaco to get medical help?" she asked, staring up at him.

"I don't want anyone else coming here. I didn't want you and your friend here, either, but here you are, so let's make the best of it. Come outside, and let's talk." His tone wasn't hostile, merely matter-of-fact.

Sierra left Chaco's side reluctantly. He looked so vulnerable lying there—and she knew that he really *was* vulnerable, shorn of his powers. She followed Kama back to the fire, which he stirred, making orange sparks fly up.

"Why don't you want anyone else here? Aren't you lonely?"

"As I told you, I'm hiding out. If there are people around, someone I don't want to notice me might just notice me, if you see what I mean."

Sierra had a sudden suspicion. "Are you really just hiding out from a bad relationship, or are you hiding from the law?"

Kama stared at her in surprise, hunkered on his heels by the fire. "The law?"

"Yes. Did you, um, rob someone or something? Are the police looking for you?"

Kama sat down abruptly on his admirable posterior and, to Sierra's astonishment, began to laugh. He clutched his firm midriff with both arms and let loose with a series of deep, resonant guffaws. *If that doesn't wake Chaco up, maybe nothing will,* she thought, watching tears begin to roll down his brown cheeks. His laughter trailed off into giggles, and then he gulped a few times, quelled another fit, and regained his composure. Finally, he shook his head at her.

"No, Sierra, I am not hiding from the law. I promise you. Feel better?"

She nodded. She believed him.

"I'm going to drink some 'awa," he said. "Would you like some too? It'll make you forget about your cuts and scrapes."

Well, why not? Sierra nodded at him. Kama produced two coconut half-shells and poured a thin, pale liquid into them from a gourd. He handed a shell to Sierra, who sniffed at it. Not at all strong-smelling. She lifted it to her lips and took a swallow. And choked.

Kama glanced up from his own shell. "What's the matter?"

"It tastes like ground-up chalk in dirty water, Kama. How can you drink this stuff?"

"Oh, just gulp it down. You won't be sorry."

Three bowls later, Sierra's lips and tongue were completely numb—and her wounds didn't hurt at all. She felt pretty good, in fact. She raised her half-full bowl in a salute.

"Here's to you, Kama. Chaco and I—we owe you our lives. Thanks again."

Kama smiled at her and nodded. It was getting dark. The first stars of the tropical night began to shimmer overhead, where the sky was darkest. He rose easily from his cross-legged seat on the sand and went back to the hale. When he returned, he had several long, slender stakes threaded with what looked like chestnuts. He drove several of these into the sand and lit a small branch from the fire. He then applied the burning branch to the top "chestnut," which blossomed into flame.

"What are those things?" asked Sierra.

"Kukui nuts," Kama responded. Sierra watched one of the stakes as the top kukui nut burned away and ignited the nut just below, maintaining a steady light.

"So, Chaco—is he your husband?"

"No. Just a friend." *Okay, where is this going?*

"Boyfriend?"

"Uh-uh. Friend."

"Come over here, Sierra. Sit next to me." He smiled invitingly and patted the sand next to him. *Now we know where this is going.* She thought he looked like a beautiful statue, every firm muscle limned in the light from the kukui nut candles and the waning fire. Tempting.

Before he took up with Kaylee, Chaco had tried something similar, but she had the good sense to decline. She knew that if she offered, Chaco would accept her in an instant, but she felt odd about having a relationship with a non-human entity—even if he was a handsome and charming human male at least part of the time. But Kama was a man, and an enticing one at that. He was maybe a tad more on the beefcake side than she usually went for, but then, he wasn't wearing any pesky clothing to disguise his assets. Except for the loincloth, which hardly counted. Well, temptation was one thing, but acting on it was another. She had Clancy, and that was that.

And on the other hand, she had been drinking 'awa. She didn't feel even slightly intoxicated, despite the numbness of her lips. But might her judgment be…somewhat flawed?

"Actually, I think I'd better turn in now," she said, stretching and yawning for effect and hoping he wouldn't be offended by her evasion. She began to rise to her feet—and found she was just a trifle wobbly. Not wobbly with vertigo in the way one feels after too many margaritas, but loose-limbed and -jointed. Mustering what dignity remained, Sierra tottered back to the hale, checked on Chaco, who lay as quietly as ever, and dropped to her sleeping mat. If Kama re-entered the hale, she never noticed, slipping into a profound slumber, unbroken until the sun shone through the hale door the next morning.

When Sierra awoke, she turned on her mat to see how Chaco was doing. His sleeping mat was empty. Sierra rocketed up, barely remembering to clutch the kapa cloth in her flight. She ran outside, heart pounding wildly—to be met by the peaceful scene of Chaco and Kama sitting by the fire, eating roasted chicken. Sierra halted, panting slightly and hitching up the kapa. Kama smiled up at her and offered her a tī leaf with a piece of chicken on it. It smelled wonderful, and Sierra's mouth began to water. She accepted the food and sat down next to Chaco. Like her, his clothes had been shredded on the rocks, and he was wearing a loincloth similar to Kama's. *Between the two of them, you'd have to go a long way to find a more beautiful view,* she thought.

She sat down and took a bite of the chicken. The skin was crisp, all the fat rendered in the chicken's leisurely spin above the fire. Delicious, even if she was unaccustomed to chicken for breakfast. Which made her think of coffee, prompting a pang of profound longing that she sternly suppressed.

"So, how are you feeling?" she asked Chaco. He was still pale, in her opinion, but he grinned at her.

"Mortal. Feeling very mortal," he replied. "I still have a bit of a headache. But I have some 'awa here that Kama says will help that." He took a deep sip from a coconut shell, clearly repressing a shudder.

"Where's Fred?" he asked.

The gladness that Sierra had felt at seeing Chaco awake and healthy deserted her. "I haven't seen Fred since we were snatched off the boat. I don't know what happened to him."

Chaco took another cautious sip of 'awa. "What about the duffle? Any sign of that?"

Sierra silently shook her head.

"There's another one of you?" inquired Kama.

"If Fred hasn't shown up yet, there's probably not much hope for him," Sierra said tightly. Her throat felt as though she had a rock the size of a baby's fist stuck in it.

Chaco shook his head. "Don't give up, Sierra," he said, placing a comforting hand on her shoulder. "You know Fred—he's pretty tough for a little fellow. And he has a way of popping up unexpectedly."

Sierra smiled in spite of herself. Fred did indeed have a way of appearing—and disappearing—without warning. But this was different. Even if Fred could swim (an unknown factor), the open ocean where they had been swept off the boat was unbelievably dangerous. She felt tears prick at her eyes and wiped them away with the back of her hand.

"Truly, I'm sorry about your friend," Kama said. "But both of you need to keep up the seawater baths today." He pointed in the direction of the natural rock basin where Sierra had soaked the day before. "You don't want to get an infection."

Chaco looked over his many scrapes and bruises ruefully. "Right. Infection would be bad—I think."

Sierra knew a bit more about infected wounds than Chaco, who had never had an infection in his multi-thousands-of-years life. "What if we do get infections? Is there anything else you can do?"

"Oh, sure. I have many other plants I can use. It's just that it's better not to get infected in the first place." Kama stood up, tossing his tī leaf "plate" into the fire. "Got some gardening to do." He placed his green, woven hat on his head and strode off to the garden. Today, his long hair was tied back in a man-bun—but Sierra doubted that it was slavish adherence to current fashion.

Sierra watched his broad back recede. She put a hand on Chaco's shoulder. "I'm so glad you're okay," she said in a low voice to Chaco. "We really need to talk. Let's go down to the water and soak. Kama won't hear us there—it's too far away, and even if he came closer, the sound of the waves will cover us." Chaco gave her a questioning look, but rose without a word and followed her to the rocky basin at the shore.

Standing at the brink of the pool, Sierra realized that to bathe their wounds, they would have to remove what passed for clothing. She glanced at Chaco, who seemed to understand the issue.

"You go first. I'll sit over here with my back turned," he said, but then ruined his pose of masculine sensitivity by grinning evilly and saying, "Of course, I've seen it all before!" But true to his word, he sat on the dry rocks on the landward side of the pool, his back turned to the water.

Yes, he had seen it all before, Sierra thought with annoyance. That didn't mean he was going to get to see it again. In any case, it had been in a situation similar to this one where Sierra had been wounded and unconscious, and Chaco had been desperately trying to help her. She nervously removed the kapa and sank into the pool. The water was bathtub temperature, warmed by the sun on the rocks. She stretched out and inspected her wounds—those she could see. They all seemed to be healing normally, with no tenderness or swelling. They stung for a few seconds as the water enveloped them, then it actually felt wonderful.

"Chaco, when we went off the boat, did you see what I saw?"

"You mean the Avatar? The white octopus? It was kind of hard to miss." Chaco shivered a bit, though the sun was hot. "I thought we were dead at first. Of course, I've never been dead before, so I wasn't sure."

"I knew it was an Avatar when I realized I didn't need to breathe underwater. Could you hear us 'talking'?"

"Yes. What do you suppose he meant by 'my gift'?"

"I have a theory about that. What language are we speaking right now?" asked Sierra.

"Huh? What language? Why, we're speaking…" Chaco broke off. Sierra couldn't see his face, but she was willing to bet that he was looking puzzled. "Um, I don't know."

"We're speaking Hawai'ian. Kama speaks Hawai'ian, and we understand every word. I think that was Kanaloa's 'gift.' Also, I feel as though he—okay, this is hard to explain—you remember that Rose tutored me on how to use my powers? The powers I didn't know I had?"

"Yeah, I remember."

"I felt those powers ramping up after Kanaloa touched me. Like blowing on a flame. I don't know what that means yet, though."

"Well, if the Avatar hadn't dumped us off here, we'd be dead by now."

"Chaco, if Kanaloa hadn't snatched us off that boat, we'd be flying to Midway by now. He didn't do us any favors. Apparently, he was just curious." *Not unusual for an octopus,* she supposed. Then she switched topics.

"Chaco, what do you think about Kama?"

"I really just met him, Sierra, but he saved our lives, didn't he? There's something odd about him, though. I'm not sure what…" his voice trailed off on a puzzled note.

"He's odd all right. He says he's hiding out here, living the traditional lifestyle. He told me he was getting away from a bad relationship, but that doesn't explain why he has to be in the middle of nowhere, living all alone. But worse than that, he says he can't take us back to Honolulu. Or won't."

Chaco started and almost turned around. "He won't take us back? Why not?"

"He says he can't give us his outrigger, and we couldn't manage the trip anyway because we don't have the experience and the ocean is too rough. He also said something really strange; he has other methods of leaving the island, but we don't have access to them. He also says that other people never come here to this little valley, but he didn't explain that, either. There's just something not right about all this."

Chaco was silent for a few minutes. Then he said, "Where are we, anyway?"

"Moloka'i. There's fifty miles of open water between Moloka'i and O'ahu."

"I don't know anything about Moloka'i. Are there people living here?"

"Yes. Somewhere. But I don't see how we can get out of this valley. The pali goes straight up for two thousand feet." She had another thought. "Do you think maybe there's a secret path up the cliffs, and that's what Kama was talking about when he said he had 'other methods'?"

"Could be. Let's poke around and see if we can find one. Do you think Kama wants to prevent us from leaving?"

Sierra shrugged even though Chaco couldn't see her. "I don't know. Maybe."

"Then we should be cautious about looking for a path up the pali. We can look for it while he's off doing something else. But you know," Chaco continued, "that's not what bothers me about Kama. All that stuff about hiding out and a bad relationship, I mean. It's something else." He smacked his fist into his palm in frustration. "If I hadn't become mortal, I would *know*. I would just know what's off about him. As it is…" Sierra couldn't see his face, but Chaco's shoulders shrugged expressively.

"Stay where you are," said Sierra. "I'm going to get out and dry off in the sun. Then it's your turn. When Kama goes fishing, *we* will go exploring."

CHAPTER 10

Roberts leaned across his polished rosewood desk and tapped the intercom. "Shelby?"

"Yes, sir?"

"I'm flying to Moloka'i tomorrow. Please put me on a morning flight. I'll need a rental car, and I'll stay at the company condo. Also, please let Peter Chapman know that I'll be there tomorrow afternoon, and tell him I want to go out to the construction site. I'm taking a few vacation days on Moloka'i, and I want to be back here on Monday, so please arrange a return flight early Monday morning."

"Yes, sir. Anything else?"

"No. Thank you."

Roberts ended the connection and went back to his computer. It was time to check things out in person. It wasn't a question of not trusting his team. If he didn't trust someone, they weren't on his team very long—like Gary Chisholm, who was now looking for a new job. No, he trusted his team, but there was no substitute for his own eyes and ears and instincts. He wanted to be able to see for himself how the men were working and what the conditions were like. He would stretch out his mental antennae, looking for things another man might miss: small indicators of morale problems or issues that might lead to substandard work. No one could afford slipshod quality when it came to an expensive installation like WestWind. Because it was critical that WestWind be the finest installation of its kind.

Shepherding the project through the Hawai'ian State Legislature had taken years and a great deal of money. Endless environmental concerns had to be addressed, and there were many watchers hoping to catch Ahi Moana cutting corners on environmental protections in a sensitive marine reserve. The project had to work, work well, and ensure the investors their expected return. And it needed to pay for itself as quickly as possible—another challenge, given the cost of erecting an offshore wind farm.

Yes. It was definitely time to go to Moloka'i. Besides, he secretly enjoyed his time on the smaller island. It was quiet and informal. He could take a few days to rest and relax, and no one would bother him. Or so he thought.

• • •

Kama piled his fishing net into the outrigger later that afternoon. He pushed the heavy, hand-hewn vessel into the waves, launched himself into it with athletic grace, and paddled out to sea. Sierra and Chaco watched him from the beach.

Just after Kama disappeared into the distance, they saw a boat—not a huge boat, but one that would have dwarfed the outrigger many times over. It was travelling parallel to the shore, appearing from their right as it cleared the cliffs and moving slowly to their left. Sierra and Chaco leaped to their feet, shouting and waving their arms. They could see little detail from that distance, but a figure with binoculars was standing on the port side of the boat, nearest the pali, and he appeared to be scanning the shore.

"They're looking for us!" shouted Sierra, jumping as high as she could and waving desperately. She and Chaco leaped madly, flailing their arms and screaming. But the boat chugged on by, never slowing or speeding up. Soon, it passed the pali to the left of the little cove, and was lost to view.

Chaco and Sierra dropped to the sand, panting with exertion and frustration. "They had to have seen us!" exclaimed Sierra. "Maybe they couldn't hear us from out there, but they *had* to see us. That guy was using binoculars."

"I know," puffed Chaco, whose headache had not been

improved by the exercise. "I don't think they could've missed us. Unless…"

"Unless what?"

"Unless we're invisible."

Sierra stared at her friend. "Invisible? What do you mean?"

"As in, not visible. There's something funny about this place, about Kama, about everything. Maybe there's a spell that prevents people from seeing this place, and that's why they don't come here. It *could* happen," he finished.

Sierra sat silently for a few moments, considering. "That actually makes sense in a crazy kind of way," she said. "Do you remember swimming toward the pali? I couldn't see the beach or the valley—just cliffs. I thought we were going to be smashed against the rocks. I didn't see the beach until I was actually in the breaking waves. A spell, some kind of magic—that would explain why other people never come here. Do you think Kama is the one responsible for the, ah, invisibility spell?"

"If he isn't, I don't know who would be. I think we have to assume that Kama isn't what he appears to be. Actually, I'm *certain* he isn't what he appears to be, but I can't put my paw, um, finger on it." A discontented expression darkened Chaco's face, and Sierra thought he must miss being a coyote. After all, he might never be a coyote again, and it had been half his nature for thousands of years.

"I'm thirsty," she said. "There's a lovely pool of fresh water in the trees behind the hale. Let's go get some before we start poking around."

Sierra showed Chaco the basin of cold, sweet water and the little waterfall that fed it. Halved coconut shells and some gourds were stacked on the bank by the pool, and there were tall trees all around providing dappled shade. With the sound of falling waters and the cool breath from the waterfall, it was a wonderful relief from the afternoon heat. Sierra handed Chaco a coconut shell and took one for herself. They filled two gourds with water, then dipped more up for a satisfying drink from the shells. As Sierra had, Chaco commented on the cold sweetness of the water.

Without warning, a black, scaly head erupted from the basin, mouth gaping wide to display fangs that would put a crocodile to shame. Its maw stretched wide, and they could see teeth studding the inside of its red mouth, even protruding from the lining of the gaping throat. The thing hissed at them angrily and lunged. Coconut shells flying, Sierra and Chaco scrambled backward, away from the pool. Sierra heard the distinct sound of whimpering, and was surprised at Chaco until she realized she was the one making the noise.

As they hastily retreated from the pool, the huge creature did not follow. It poked its head above the water and glared at them with obsidian eyes.

"Okay, this isn't right," panted Sierra as they stumbled back down the path. "There aren't any big reptiles in Hawai'i. The biggest lizards they've got are those little geckos we've been seeing. That thing can't possibly be real."

"Oh, it's real enough. It's just not mortal," responded Chaco.

"Okay. You know what I mean. Anyway, there was no sign of it when Kama took me there. You'd think he'd have warned me!"

"That would've been nice," Chaco agreed. "Speaking of Kama, we'd better get busy if we want to make any progress before he gets back."

Exploring the walls of the little valley was much more difficult than they had anticipated. The trees grew thickly all around the perimeter and marched up the side of the cliffs, tightly interwoven with bushes and vines. In many places, this tangle was completely impenetrable unless they wanted to hack away at the thick undergrowth. This would only attract Kama's attention, which neither felt was a good idea, and they didn't have so much as a pocketknife to do the hacking. After an hour and a half of trying to pick their way through this jungle, they were hot, sweaty, and thirsty again. They had abandoned the water gourds back at the pool, so they gave up and went back to the hale, where there were more gourds full of water. Thirst quenched, they returned to the beach. The outrigger was still gone, so Kama had not yet returned.

They decided to do some more medicinal soaking in the salt water, and took turns as before. While Chaco was drying in the sun, Kama's outrigger appeared in the distance, heading home. Kama maneuvered the little craft masterfully through the waves and rocks, leaping out in the shallow water as he approached the beach. Sierra and Chaco helped him drag the boat well up beyond the reach of the waves, where it would be safe from the incoming tide.

"Mahalo. It was a good catch today," Kama said, pointing at a large parrotfish lying on the bottom of the boat. Its brilliant blues, greens, reds, and yellows were dimming with death.

"Kama," Sierra said, "we went to the freshwater spring today to get some water. There was something big and black in there, and we thought it was going to kill us."

"Oh, that," said Kama, carefully folding his net. "That's just Kapualei. You shouldn't have used the pool while she was in it."

"What is a Kapu-whatever?"

"She's the mo'o that guards the pool. I make sure she has what she needs, and she ensures strong 'awa, plentiful taro, and good fishing. She means well."

"You might have warned us!"

Kama continued arranging his net. "I showed you how to tell if Kapualei was using the pool. When she's in the pool, don't disturb her."

"No, you did *not* show me!"

"I did. I bundled up some tī leaves and put them in the pool. The tī leaves floated, so I knew the mo'o was not in the pool. If the tī leaves sink, Kapualei is using the pool, so I come back later."

"It would have helped a lot if you had explained that," grumbled Sierra. "As it was, we've pissed her off, and Chaco and I almost needed a change of clothing. And while we're talking, Chaco and I have some questions."

"Really? All right. But first I need to clean this parrotfish and get it roasting. Yum!" he concluded, smacking his lips. He reached into the outrigger and heaved the fish out.

Kama served the roasted fish with poi and coconut. Sierra hadn't cared for poi at first. It was a purplish substance with the consistency of library paste and a bland flavor, but she found that it complemented many of the foods that Kama prepared. Kama had avoided her questions while he was cooking, but he had no excuses left, she thought. However, Chaco jumped in before Sierra got started.

"Are you an Avatar?" *Okay. Straightforward, if a tad blunt.*

Kama smiled, square, white teeth gleaming against his dark skin. "I guess you could say so. It takes one to know one, as they say." He cocked an eyebrow at Chaco.

"I'm not an Avatar. Not anymore," said Chaco unhappily. "I lost my powers when I came to Hawai'i."

Kama nodded. "Mana. It's tied to the land. Auwē, man! What a disaster!"

Chaco looked at Kama with both hope and trepidation in his eyes. "If I go home, will I get my powers back?"

"I don't know. I've never left these islands. Why would I?"

Chaco drooped slightly. "Oh." He lapsed into silence, obviously revisiting the pain of his—*what would you call it?* Sierra wondered. *Mortalization?* In any case, the cards were on the table and they could start talking openly. She hoped.

"Kama," she said, "we saw something else while we were in the ocean. Chaco and I both thought it was an Avatar. It was a gigantic"—she stretched her arms as wide as she could for emphasis—"*enormous* white octopus. That's actually how we came to be in the water. It snatched us off the deck of a whale watching boat. It held us underwater for a long time, but we didn't need to breathe. And it gave us a gift, it said. I think the gift was being able to talk and understand Hawai'ian. It called itself Kanaloa. What the hell was it?"

"So the waterspout story wasn't true? Somehow, I didn't think it was."

"Um, sorry. I thought you were a human. I mean, a

mortal person who might be freaked out by my story," she said, blushing slightly.

"Kanaloa," he said reverently. "You saw the sea-god Kanaloa. And you are alive to tell me about it."

Chaco and Sierra exchanged glances. "Is seeing Kanaloa usually bad news?" asked Sierra.

"Well, he's the lord of the ocean. He's a lot like the ocean. One day, it's blue and calm and warm and welcomes you like your mother's arms. The next day, it's tempestuous and wild and can kill you in an instant."

"So he's an evil Avatar?" Sierra thought she already had a lifetime's quota of evil Avatars.

"No, not evil. Just…changeable. Unreliable. You obviously caught him in a generous mood."

"Generous? We almost died. Why did he snatch us off the boat?"

Kama shrugged. "Who knows? Maybe he was just curious. He was in his octopus body,[2] so he was curious like an octopus. Maybe, like me, he picked up on Chaco being an Avatar. Mortal or not, once an Avatar, always an Avatar. Either way, you are two very lucky mortals."

Kama did not notice Chaco's wince at this comment. But Sierra did.

CHAPTER 11

Just before dawn on the last day of the search, Clancy drove his rental car through the sleeping streets of Kaunakakai toward the brightly lit wharf. *Polupolu* was there, rocking gently against the dock. Sam and Mike greeted him with coffee and muffins, and *Polupolu* set off, again heading for the north side of Moloka'i.

This day's journey went precisely as the others had. Today, Clancy ignored the breaching of whales, the dancing of spinner dolphins, and the other delights of Hawai'ian sea travel as he focused Jack's binoculars on the shore. The green and black pali slid by, an occasional beach or cove claiming his most focused attention, but there was no sign of Sierra or Chaco and certainly no sign of Fred.

Clancy kept Jack's binoculars clamped to his eyes until his eyes watered so badly he couldn't see. Then he passed them to Mike, who took up the vigil. Sam idled along slowly, and he took *Polupolu* as close to shore as he dared.

After an hour's scanning, Mike handed the binoculars back to Clancy. Clancy held his position on the port side, lenses stubbornly fixed on the land. No one said anything as the miles of coastline slowly rolled by.

• • •

Roberts picked up his rental car at the tiny Moloka'i airport and called Peter Chapman, the engineer overseeing the construction of WestWind. Then he drove east to the heliport where Chapman would pick him up to take him out to the site.

The helicopter headed out to sea, soon clearing the west end beaches. Looking down, Roberts could see the development where the company condo was located, and then they were out over open water. Before long, he was able to see the jack ship towers poking up, then the jack ship itself. The helicopter landed on the mammoth ship's helipad, and Chapman and Roberts exited the cabin.

The jack ship was a marvel of engineering. It consisted of a 500-foot self-propelled barge with six towers constructed of steel girders, each around 150 feet high. When the barge maneuvered into the right position, these towers were lowered to the sea floor, becoming legs. The barge was jacked up along the legs with a rack-and-pinion system until it was well above the ocean surface, providing a stable platform for construction. The ship, dubbed *Jack of Diamonds*, was a small city with crew quarters, laundry, gymnasium, coffee shop, and other amenities for the workers and crew. The WestWind Project had two of these ships on the site, each busy installing the wind turbines through the use of massive cranes.

Roberts took his time inspecting the site. His sharp eyes missed nothing, but he came away satisfied. The jack ship was clean and organized with safety equipment and first aid stations clearly marked and well stocked. The crew was working hard, it seemed to Roberts, with a good deal of cheerfulness. He saw no evidence of slipshod work or bad attitudes.

He found the second ship, *Jack of Hearts*, to be likewise in excellent order. As he boarded the helicopter to return to Moloka'i, he praised Chapman for his management skills and good work. He also asked Chapman to convey his approbation to the crew. Then he boarded the helicopter and headed back to the island. Now he could disappear into life on the island, relax, and enjoy a little free time.

• • •

"You know, Kama, we've been eating really well since we got here," Sierra said, picking a fishbone out of the delectable portion in front of her. "Fish, all kinds of seafood, coconut, bananas, papayas, poi, sweet potato, chicken, eggs. But you haven't served pork even once, and I thought pork was one of the ancient Hawai'ians' favorite foods. I read somewhere that the first Polynesian settlers brought pigs with them."

Kama looked faintly nauseated. "No pork," he said emphatically.

"Why not?"

"That would be kapu for me."

Chaco cocked his head, eyebrows raised. "Why?"

Kama settled himself more comfortably away from the fire. The sun was gaining altitude, and the morning was beginning to heat up, despite a pleasant sea breeze. "I was born on O'ahu as a pig…"

"Huh?" The exclamation came simultaneously from Chaco and Sierra.

"You heard me. I was born a pig. My full name is Kama Pua'a. In your language, that sort of translates to 'Pig Child.' I guess I must have been a mischievous little keiki—stealing chickens and so forth—because a lot of folks got mad at me. I was always getting into trouble." Kama smiled reminiscently. Evidently, getting into trouble held a lot of nostalgic appeal for him.

"Anyway, I grew up and I assumed my man-form—as you see me now. I have many other forms as well, but I most enjoy being a man. I have been told,"—and here, Kama looked down modestly—"that I am the most beautiful of men."

A strangled snort was heard from Chaco.

Kama carried on serenely. "Pele, the goddess of fire, became aware of my manly charms and sent her smoke to tempt me." He shook his head. "I have never been one to resist temptation, you understand. Food, sport, women—I enjoy them all. I scented Pele's seductive smoke and followed it to the island of Hawai'i, where she and her family live. Her favorite house is Kilauwea, the southernmost volcano. And then it got complicated."

Sierra and Chaco waited for Kama to continue, but he

seemed lost in thought, his generous mouth skewed as though in regret. Finally, Sierra said, "Yes? Then what happened?" Kama shook himself.

"It was true love, you know. I wanted Pele more than I have ever wanted anything in my existence—and I have been here for longer than I can remember. You should see her—what a woman! Tall, with a spine like the pali—straight and strong. Her hair is a waterfall of obsidian, shining like a river. Breasts like full moons, and her eyes...!" Kama stopped talking again and sighed heavily.

"But when I approached her, she scorned me, again and again. She sent her sisters to seduce me. She was trying to show what a pig I was. I was happy to be seduced, of course—Pele's sisters are almost as beautiful as she is. Finally, she succumbed to me and we made love. And that was the problem." Kama shook his head and sighed again.

"Why was that the problem?" Chaco asked, clearly intrigued.

"Once a woman has me, she cannot stop," said Kama, raising tragic eyes to Chaco. "We made love for four days and nights without a break. Now, that is not a difficult thing for a man such as I..."

Eye rolling from Chaco.

"...but although Pele wouldn't stop, she was on the verge of death."

"Then why didn't *you* stop?" asked Sierra tartly.

Kama looked at her blankly. "Stop? She wanted me to go on!"

Eye rolling from Sierra.

"So one of her sisters came by to tempt me to leave Pele. And I did."

"How did she do that? Seems to me you had the one you wanted in hand, so to speak," Chaco commented.

"Actually, she didn't come by in person. She sent her detachable, flying maʻi to tempt me. I couldn't resist."

Both Sierra and Chaco were so startled by this image they remained silent.

"Her maʻi flew over the ocean to Oʻahu, and I followed.

Eventually I returned to the island of Hawai'i, but Pele and I always wound up fighting. Mainly, I stay on the rainy side of the island while Pele and her family live on the dry side, in Kilauwea."

"So how did you end up here?" Sierra inquired.

"Auwē! That last fight was a bad one. We had agreed to meet one more time, to see if we could work things out. We got to talking about her family, and I made the mistake of mentioning that her sister's ma'i was one of the sweetest, most delectable—"

"Oh, good lord," muttered Sierra.

"Well, anyway, Pele didn't like it much, even though that very same ma'i saved her life. She just erupted right then and there, and I barely escaped. I've been living here ever since." Kama stirred the fire. "Believe me, you don't want to be in the way when Pele's mad at you."

"I can see that," said Sierra. "Thanks for telling us all that, Kama. It answers a lot of questions." *And temptation flies out the window like Pele's sister's ma'i.*

Kama stood up. "We have important visitors tonight," he said. "We need to look our best. First, we should go to Kapualei's pool and apologize for your rudeness. Then maybe she will let us bathe there." He bundled up some food in a basket and strode off toward the path to the pool. Sierra and Chaco trotted behind.

"What important visitors?" Sierra asked. "I thought you were here all alone, that you didn't want anyone to know where you were because of Pele."

"They live here. They've always lived here, so I'm really their guest. They say they have some important news for me."

"That's odd," said Chaco, "We've never seen another person here. It's such a small valley I would think we'd have run into them. Unless they're invisible."

But that was all Kama would say about it. They soon reached the rocky basin. Kama tied a large bunch of tī leaves together and set them in the pool. They sank promptly. "Good. Kapualei is here." He arranged the food on the bank and began to sing. He had a beautiful baritone voice, and as he sang, he began to dance. His movements were emphatic and sharp, not the swaying, sylphlike grace of the dancers she had seen at the hotel in Oʻahu. It was far more masculine, with thrusting arms and stamping feet.

As they watched, the black, scaly head appeared above the water. Kapualei observed the dancing and singing calmly, her scarlet forked tongue flicking in and out of her mouth. Kama ended his chant and dance and told Sierra and Chaco to extend the food to the moʻo on the palms of their hands.

Sierra and Chaco looked at each other, each with the same image in mind of Kapualei's endless tunnel of teeth. But they picked up the food and approached her, hands outstretched. With the greatest delicacy, the giant lizard flicked the food into her mouth. Sierra never so much as felt the touch of her tongue. The moʻo swallowed the food in one gulp, then turned her black eyes on them. And burped.

"Apologies accepted," Kapualei said in a voice like a gravel grinder in action. "You may bathe in the pool in one hour's time." The black head sank beneath the water again.

"Let's go see what we can pull together for you two," said Kama as they headed back down the path. "I want you to look your best. Then we bathe, then we prepare food, then we get dressed up for the occasion." Kama seemed in high good humor, obviously anticipating the company.

At the hale, Kama pulled out a basket and removed a few lengths of red and white kapa cloth. He stripped off his everyday loincloth without hesitation, and Sierra looked away hastily. Kama noticed.

"You haoles and your body issues," he said cheerfully. "There—I'm all covered up again." When Sierra turned around, she saw he was wearing one of the lengths of red and white kapa as a malo. It was considerably brighter and less worn than Kama's everyday attire, but as for covering him up—no way. Kama added a necklace that consisted of many fine, braided cords from which hung a carved whale's tooth. Then he donned a helmet covered in red and yellow feathers with a curved crest that reminded Sierra of the horsehair crests on the helmets of Roman soldiers.

"Now, let's see what we can do for you," he said, eyeing Sierra. He picked out another length of kapa and handed it to her. "Traditionally, you wouldn't be wearing anything on top except for leis, which is how I prefer it," he said. "But you can hitch this up under your arms. You still get the leis."

While Kama rummaged in his basket looking for something for Chaco, Sierra took the red and white kapa outside the hale and made a hasty change. When she returned, Chaco was arrayed in another red and white malo. He looked wonderful in a loincloth, Sierra thought. His long legs and torso, as brown as Kama's, were muscular without the bulk of Kama's body. He looked like a statue by Praxiteles, sculpted out of some smooth, brown stone instead of white marble. She had no intention of telling him so.

Kama explained that Chaco would have to make do with leis for additional decoration, as he had no more whales' tooth necklaces.

"Strictly speaking, you shouldn't wear one in any case," said Kama. "They're reserved for Ali'i."

"No problem," Chaco replied. "Where are the leis?"

"I'll show you," said Kama, and led them outside for a lesson in lei making. At the end of a two-hour session of flower picking and stringing, all three were adorned in flowers and foliage. Sierra began to feel quite exotic as the fragrance of her flower leis wafted to her nostrils. She tried a hula move or two just to see what it felt like.

"Not bad!" Kama said. "But we don't have time for lessons, I'm afraid. We need to bathe and get food ready for our guests."

They left their finery behind as they trooped to the freshwater pool. As always, Kama tested the water with tī leaves, which this time floated and did not sink, so they knew it was Kapualei-free. The two men stripped down easily and entered the pool. Sierra watched them splashing happily for a few moments. Then she pulled off her kapa and slid into the cool water. To her relief, there were no wolf whistles or comments from the men, who responded by splashing her in the face instead. The water felt heavenly, rinsing off accumulated grime, sweat, and salt. Sierra splashed them back, and a water fight ensued—something Sierra hadn't indulged in since childhood.

Twenty minutes later, Kama called a halt. Time was getting on, he said, and they needed to move on to food preparation. There was, of course, no pork, but Kama did have several large fish roasting in an imu. Sierra and Chaco shelled 'opihi, roasted sweet potatoes, and pounded poi. Kama hovered over both of them, fussing over every detail. Sierra wondered again just who these important visitors could possibly be.

By evening, a feast sat waiting for the mysterious guests. Kama, Sierra, and Chaco were resplendent in red and white kapa and festooned with flower leis. Kama had arranged many woven mats for sitting, and indicated that he would sit in a particular place, Sierra to his right and Chaco to his left. He had gourds full of 'awa ready to go, with halved coconut shells stacked up at the ready. Then they sat and waited as darkness fell.

It was full dark before they heard their guests approaching. First there was the sound of drums and chanting. Then they saw torches wending their way from the back of the little valley through the jungle. Finally, the guests of honor stepped into the firelight, and Sierra gasped.

There were ten of them. Normally, this would have caused Sierra anxiety about how to feed so many with the amount of food they had prepared, but in this case, she never gave it a thought. They were small people, perhaps two feet high, with squat, strongly built bodies. It was difficult to tell in the light of the torches and kukui nuts, but Sierra thought their skin color was rather greenish.

Then all thought ceased as a small cannonball hit her amidships and knocked her sprawling in the sand. As she lay gasping from the impact, a familiar, squeaky voice said, "I knew I'd find you, Sierra! I just *knew* it!"

"Fred?"

CHAPTER 12

Fred perched on top of Sierra's stomach and dripped happy tears onto her chest. "I knew you'd be okay, Sierra! You too, Chaco," Fred added hastily. "How did you get here? What happened?" The small, stocky people, both men and women, crowded around and stared down at her. Chaco lifted Fred off Sierra's stomach and set him down.

"I'm glad to see you too," said Chaco gruffly. It was hard to tell in the wavering light of the torches, but Sierra thought his eyes were filled with unshed tears. Perhaps Chaco had developed allergies along with mortality.

Sierra sat up, shaking sand out of her hair. She reached her arms out to Fred, who flung himself into her lap. "Who are your friends, Fred?"

"Menehune. I'm forgetting my manners! This is Ailani, this is Aloha, this is Kaapo..." Fred introduced each of the little people in turn. Each approached Sierra and rubbed noses with her (sitting on the sand, Sierra was about the right height for this). They greeted Kama and Chaco likewise.

Kama took control of the gathering as smoothly as any corporate CEO. "If we could all sit down, I welcome you to our luau. We should eat and enjoy ourselves. Then we will discuss the business that brings our honored guests here today."

During the feasting that followed, Sierra and Chaco told Fred about their encounter with Kanaloa and how they came to be in this little valley. Then Sierra realized something.

"Fred! You're speaking Hawai'ian! How is that possible? Did you meet Kanaloa too?"

Fred shook his head. "Nope. I've always known this language—all mannegishis speak it."

"Really? How is that possible?" Chaco asked.

"The Menehune—they came from the Americas[3] long ago. They're kind of distant cousins to mannegishi. They brought the language with them. I was so happy to find them! They're like our mythical lost tribe, and I found them!"

"But how did you get here? You were in the duffle bag I was carrying when I got snatched off the boat. We were afraid you sank in the duffle bag and drowned," Chaco said.

"I would have sunk if I'd stayed in the bag, but I got out as soon as I hit the water. Then I just went invisible. No one can eat you if you're invisible, you know. Mannegishis are pretty buoyant, so I just floated along until I arrived here. It was the middle of the night. By that time, I was starving, so I went looking for something to eat. There was some stuff to eat in the garden there," he pointed at Kama's garden enclosure, "and I just helped myself…"

"As per usual," muttered Chaco.

"…and then I went looking for water. When I found the waterfall, there was a nice mo'o there, and she told me I should be looking for my people, that they were hidden in the pali, living in caves. So I went looking, and they found me. What a celebration we had that night, whoooo-eee!" He looked up at Sierra with his cockeyed gaze. "You shoulda been there." Fred folded twelve spatulate digits comfortably over his tummy and smiled.

"Well, we can do some celebrating tonight," Sierra said, indicating Kama and the Menehune, who had already lowered the 'awa level in the gourds considerably.

The partying went on for another few hours. When everything edible had been consumed, Kama brought out more 'awa.

"Now, my brothers, why did you come to see me this night?" he asked.

The Menehune called Ailani rose and drew himself up to his full and dignified two feet. He had long, curly gray hair and was dressed much as Kama was, with a loincloth, red-feathered helmet, chief's necklace, and leis. Though he was small, he had strong arms and legs and a solid torso. He looked as though he could pick up a small boulder without breaking a sweat.

"We have come to tell you about a terrible thing that is happening here. Humans are building things in the ocean, where there should be no building. We learned of it from the songs of the whales. They call to one another about the noise, the vibrations, the filth arising from this building. We have come to implore Kama Pua'a for help to stop this building in the sea."

Kama looked puzzled. "I haven't seen this. Where is this happening?"

"West of Moloka'i. Out to sea. We haven't seen it either, because it is too far out, but we hear the whales talking about it."

"This does sound serious, my friend. I am not sure what I can do, but I promise I will find out more about it. And if I can help, I will." Kama placed his large, brown hand over his heart. "You have my sacred word."

Satisfied, Ailani resumed his seat. "That is all we can ask, Kama Pua'a. Thank you."

The 'awa drinking resumed, and soon all the Menehune and Kama were playing some sort of game that involved javelin throwing and betting. The penalty for missing was to drink a shell of 'awa. What with the 'awa and the flickering shadows cast by fire and kukui candles, this was more a test of luck than of skill. Sierra watched for a while, but found her eyelids drooping more than once. She jerked herself awake at one point to find Fred snoring in her lap and Chaco leaning on her shoulder, nearly asleep himself. She shook them both awake.

"Do you think they'd be insulted if we snuck out of the party and got some sleep?" she whispered. Chaco rubbed his eyes.

"I don't think they'd notice if we painted ourselves purple and started howling at the moon," he said. The three of them got up and quietly made their way back to the hale.

The next morning when Sierra emerged from the hale, the sun was already well overhead. Kama was sprawled in the sand near the smoldering fire, snoring. His feathered helmet lay some distance away, and his flower leis were wilted, giving him an air of rakish dissipation. The Menehune were gone with not a trace left behind. Sierra looked, but could find nothing, not even a small footprint.

Sierra rekindled the fire, wishing for the hundredth time that she could make a steaming cup of coffee. She could almost smell it. Instead, she peeled and ate a banana to still her internal rumbling. Kama was the usual provider of food, though Sierra was learning some of it on her own. She cracked open a coconut with a sharp stake and a rock, drank the milk, and shattered the rest into convex pieces so that the sweet meat could be picked out with fingers. Despite the noise this created, Kama slumbered on, merely twitching when a fly landed on his face.

Fred emerged next from the hale. "What's for breakfast?" was his predictable first greeting.

"Bananas and coconut, unless you want to go catch some fish," she replied. Fred dove into the food without another word.

It was at least noon by the time Kama and Chaco awoke. By that time, Sierra had had a saltwater soak and a nice bath in Kapualei's pool. The moʻo was sunbathing by the side of the pool and had no objection to Sierra's use of it. They had a pleasant conversation, in fact, with the moʻo asking how Sierra had happened on this isolated valley. Sierra told her story, and Kapualei was impressed.

"Not too many meet Kanaloa and live to talk about it," she hissed softly. "You must be powerful in your own right. A kahuna, perhaps?"

"I'm not a kahuna," Sierra returned. "But a wise woman named Rose trained me to use certain, um, powers I seem to have. Kanaloa sensed that, I think. He touched my throat, and I felt... something. Sort of a power surge. But I don't really seem to be able to use this power unless there's an emergency. I can't just sit here and blast a tree or something because I feel like it."

Kapualei's chuckle sounded like gravel under a car tire. "Just as well. The exercise of power for the sake of doing it usually ends badly."

Sierra was still mulling over this comment when she emerged from the path to the pool and saw that Chaco and Kama were awake. They were sitting by the fire, both looking the worse for wear. Fred was sitting with them, asking a barrage of questions such as, "So, when do we go home? I had a lot of fun with the relatives, but I'm kinda homesick, y'know? Say, Kama, what're you going to do about the stuff in the ocean that the whales don't like? I'm ready for lunch, how about you guys?" Both Avatars were ignoring him outright, but this did not deter Fred in the slightest.

Sierra was about to suggest an expedition into the trees for some breadfruit and other edibles, when a sound captured everyone's attention. Everyone—even Fred—fell silent to listen. And then they smelled it.

"Fire!" yelled Chaco, pointing toward the pali that formed the back end of their little valley. There was a huge coil of black smoke rising in the air. The sound was the crackling of flames, which they could now see through the trees.

Sierra, Chaco, and Fred all jumped up, eyes shaded against the midday glare. Sierra and Chaco began trading suggestions on what they should do—get to the ocean, bring water in gourds to protect the hale, then dig a firebreak between the hale and garden and the encroaching forest.

Kama stood, but he remained silent and tense, his eyes fixed on the head of the valley. The sound of the flames and the smoke rushed quickly toward them, as though impelled by the wind. And then they saw her.

She was a tower of flame burning though the trees. A woman clad in fire, eyes of flame, molten hair twisting like glowing snakes around her shoulders and writhing down her back. When she spoke, her voice was the roar of fire driven by unimaginable heat and pressure from deep within the earth.

"Kama Pua'a, I am here. You can't hide from Pele." As she spoke, lava flowed beneath her bare feet, black with red cracks splitting its surface to show the molten hell below. Sierra felt the heat sear her cheeks, and she closed her eyes in reflex.

Averting her face from the inferno, Sierra turned to look at Kama only to find a large, spotted hog running away toward the beach. *He even makes a handsome pig*, she thought, watching his nimble hooves swiftly negotiate the rocks at the water's edge. The instant Kama's hooves touched the salt water he leaped in the air, twisted, and...changed. By the time he hit the water again, he had taken the form of a little fish wearing a neat pattern of yellow, white, black, and blue, with touches of red.[4] The fish disappeared for an instant beneath the waves, then poked its snout above the water.

"Goodbye, my love! Come see me when that hot temper of yours has cooled!" said the fish in Kama's voice—and then it disappeared beneath the waves.

The vortex of flame that was Pele crackled and burned down to the water's edge then stopped as though looking out to sea. The fiery column stood flickering at the edge of the water, and they heard a scream, like a woman shrieking in anger. There was a hissing sigh like a campfire being extinguished—and then there was nothing. Sierra rubbed her eyes, smarting from the smoke that was no longer in the air. There was no Pele, no lava. Chaco pointed up the valley.

"Look. Nothing's burning!"

"Um, that's not quite right," said Fred. Their eyes followed the direction of Fred's stubby digit. The hale was burning. Made of wooden poles and dry palm thatch, it had ignited as though someone had poured gasoline on it. Nothing else was touched, even though they had seen the jungle burning in Pele's wake just seconds before. Sierra thought of the things in the hale that they needed: knives, gourds, kapa cloth, baskets, cooking vessels, rope, fish hooks, twine...the list was endless. Had Pele torched this one thing out of revenge? Or because it would make it difficult for Kama to stay here?

"What are we going to do?" she asked aloud. Chaco and Fred

turned to look at her, tearing their eyes away from the inferno of the hale. She saw in their expressions the dawning realization that without Kama and without his well-provisioned home, their existence here had just become precarious. At best, comfort was a thing of the past. They still had the garden, though, and the moʻoʻs pool of fresh water, and—the outrigger.

"We've got the outrigger!" Sierra exclaimed, running to the beach, Chaco and Fred following. "Help me get this thing into the water. If we can get around the island to someplace where people are living, we can go home!" *And get a nice, hot cup of coffee*, she added to herself. Chocolate ice cream also sounded good. Any kind of ice cream, actually.

They shoved the heavy craft down the beach into the water, where it bobbed crazily, evading their attempts to board it. Finally, Chaco clambered in, flopping clumsily to the bottom. Grasping a paddle, he was able to stabilize it long enough for Sierra to heave herself over the side as the outrigger washed back and forth among the waves and rocks. Sierra and Chaco tried to control it with their paddles, but it eventually wedged itself firmly between two rocks.

On the second try, Sierra boosted Fred over the side of the outrigger while she held it on one side and Chaco on the other, waves knocking against them and threatening their precarious toeholds in the sand and rocks. When the random slap of a wave made Sierra tumble into the water, the outrigger spun away, Fred shrieking at the top of his lungs as the boat headed for the open sea. Chaco had just hurled himself bravely into the waves, paddling madly, when the waves batted the boat back to them. Fred leaped into Sierra's arms, sobbing with relief.

After several more tries, Chaco nearly acquired a new concussion before they admitted they were exhausted and gave up. They dragged the heavy outrigger onto the sand and flopped next to it, panting and discouraged. After twenty minutes of damp and miserable silence, Fred sat up as though touched by a cattle prod. "Boat! There's a boat out there!" he squeaked. Sierra and Chaco leaped up to look.

It was the boat they had seen before and tried to attract. It was a small, rather tubby craft, and someone was on the port side, the person with binoculars scanning the shore, just as before.

Sierra began to leap up and down, waving her arms above her head. Perhaps now that Kama had departed, the searcher might be able to see them stranded on the shore. Surely they would see the smoke from the remains of the smoldering hale. Chaco jumped and waved as well. Fred did what he usually did in uncertain circumstances: disappear.

To their surprise and delight, the boat slowed. Three people were pointing at the shore and talking to one another excitedly. They had been seen.

"Now what?" asked Chaco. "How do we get out there?"

"We swim," said Sierra. "That's how we got here."

"Yeah. And nearly got killed on the rocks," he pointed out. "We have to try the outrigger again."

"The outrigger? Didn't we just prove that we don't have a prayer in hell of getting that thing going?"

"What do you suggest, O Wise One?" snapped Chaco.

"Maybe we could put Fred in the outrigger, and you and I could swim next to it. We can hold onto the outrigger and guide it."

"That won't work, and I'll tell you why…"

As they argued, the boat ventured closer to shore, but stopped while it was still a fair distance out. The three people on board appeared to be arguing with one another just like Sierra and Chaco.

"Ahem. I think I have a solution," said Fred. They turned to look at him. He had taken advantage of their distraction to run to the mo'o's pool. Kapualei had followed him back to the beach and now lay like an enormous black crocodile on the white sand.

"Fred says you need help," she said in her grating voice. "Everyone climb in Kama's outrigger. I will push you out to the boat."

"How can we ever thank you enough?" Sierra exclaimed, wondering if mo'o liked to be kissed and deciding not to find out.

"The peace and quiet will be worth it," returned the mo'o.

They climbed in the outrigger, and she began to bulldoze it into the water. Once in, she lashed her strong tail, and the outrigger shot through the waves, Sierra and Chaco using the paddles to steer. They approached the idling *Polupolu* so quickly that a white wake trailed behind them.

Soon, they were climbing aboard, greeting Clancy with hugs and tears. Fred had remained discretely invisible. Chaco lifted him to Clancy with a quiet word, and Clancy tucked Fred surreptitiously into a canvas bag—his greetings would have to wait until later. Trying to explain Fred to the uninitiated such as Sam and Mike was unthinkable. With this in mind, Sierra glanced over the side of *Polupolu* to see if Kapualei were visible to the boat crew. She thought she saw a long, dark shadow undulating toward shore, but it was hard to tell against the shifting shades of the water and the glitter of sunlight on the waves. She turned and fell into Clancy's arms. He enfolded her and they kissed. Clancy murmured incoherently into her ear. She could hear, "...lost you forever," and "...God I can't believe it," and the word "love" over and over. She melted wordlessly into him, breaking the embrace only when Sam and Mike came to congratulate the castaways. The couple parted, but kept their arms around one another as if afraid that the other would disappear unless anchored by touch.

"I never really thought we'd find you," Sam admitted. "We went by this area several times and never saw a thing."

"Well, I'm really glad you saw us this time," said Sierra. "Do you, by any chance, have some coffee?"

CHAPTER 13

Roberts drove to the company condo on the west side of Moloka'i after the helicopter dropped him near Kaunakakai. The condo was located in a quiet, shady complex on the beach. It was well-equipped but hardly luxurious—more like a standard tourist condo, with bamboo furniture and bright, floral prints. Unlike a tourist condo, there was a complete dinner waiting for him in the kitchen, and the bar was provisioned with a wide variety of alcoholic beverages and mixers. He preferred California wines, and there was a selection of his favorites. He chose a cabernet franc to drink with his locally raised steak dinner.

After dinner, he sat on the screened lanai and watched the breakers crest and foam onto the rocky beach as the sun began to set. He was startled when the doorbell rang. It wasn't as though he had any friends on the island that might want to visit. He knew people here, but they were all employees of Ahi Moana. He put his drink aside and answered the door.

Standing outside in the twilight was a small group of Moloka'ians, men and women. They didn't speak, but bore hand-painted signs that read, "No Wind Farm," "Save Penguin Bank!" "Leave the Whales Alone!" and similar sentiments. They stood silently, every expectant eye upon him.

Roberts gently closed the door and locked it. He went back to the lanai. There were no more visitors.

• • •

Rose ended the phone call from Clancy, tears running down her brown cheeks. She turned to her friends with a smile.

"Clancy found them! All of them—Sierra, Chaco, and Fred. They're alive and well!"

Even Mama Labadie seemed a little choked up, but she firmed her generous lips and her eyes remained dry as Rose and Kaylee hugged each other and wiped away tears of joy. "They really okay after all that? What happened to them?" Mama asked.

"I don't have the whole story—Clancy didn't have much time or privacy to talk—but they were swept off the whale watching boat by, um, something I didn't really understand. Something like an Avatar. The something delivered them to Moloka'i, where they were rescued by someone named Kama. He was living off the grid away from civilization. And apparently he is an Avatar or something, too—I never knew Hawai'i was full of Avatars. Anyway, they're just fine. Except for Chaco."

"What's wrong with Chaco?" asked Kaylee, furrowing her brows. "Was he hurt?"

"No, but he lost his mana. He's mortal now. Clancy said it had something to do with being separated from his native land."

"He must be on the way home right quick," Mama Labadie commented. "Can't think that old coyote would waste a moment gettin' back here."

"I don't know. Clancy didn't say. Anyway, that's pretty much all I know," Rose said.

"This is the first time in a week that I've felt hungry. Let's go celebrate!" suggested Kaylee.

• • •

Sierra and Chaco were still wearing the kapa cloth garments that Kama had given them, now sodden from their exertions with the outrigger and much the worse for wear. Sam and Mike had no extra clothes on board, but they did have wetsuits for tourists who wanted to dive or snorkel, so Sierra and Chaco donned two shorty wetsuits on loan. "Bring those suits back when you can," said Sam. "I got plenty."

Chaco discretely dropped the now-shredding kapa cloth over the side of the boat. The garments raised questions that he and Sierra might find awkward to answer.

Sam wanted to take Chaco and Sierra to the Moloka'i General Hospital in Kaunakakai, but Sierra declined for both of them.

"I don't know how or why you're in such good shape, but it looks like you just got a few scrapes and bruises," Sam said. "I've seen one or two people who've gone overboard and been recovered later. You guys are really lucky to be alive." Sierra agreed with Sam, but couldn't very well tell him what really happened. The journey back to Kaunakakai was oddly quiet. Clancy, eyes streaming with unaccustomed tears, sat with his arm around Sierra's shoulders as they traveled. She leaned into him, feeling safe for the first time since she went over the railing of the whale watching boat. They spoke little, and what they did say was inaudible to the others as they whispered into each other's ears.

Sam had radioed ahead with the news of finding the castaways, so they could not avoid having a chat with the Coast Guard or the police. Kevin Kapule, the Coast Guard liaison, was waiting at the wharf for their arrival with a police officer. The interviews took place aboard *Polupolu* while Clancy looked on and waited. Sierra and Chaco just claimed accident, confusion, and luck for their misadventures. Again, they were urged to go to the hospital, but continued to refuse.

"Your hotel in Honolulu is sending your bags," said Kevin. "They're pretty happy that you turned up."

"That's a relief," Sierra said. Everything they needed was in those bags, including their photo IDs and Sierra's cell phone.

A photographer and reporter from the *Moloka'i Dispatch* turned up to get the story on the castaways who survived the brutal ocean channel between O'ahu and Moloka'i, and they were told there were more reporters on the way from Honolulu.

"No," said Sierra, standing up. "No reporters. No photographs." Sierra's long experience in public relations led her to avoid the press in this instance. It would turn into a weeklong media circus if she let it. Although it might be quickly forgotten, there were too many holes in their story, and Sierra wanted to avoid the questions that would inevitably follow.

Clancy, carrying a canvas duffle bag that apparently had a bowling ball inside it, thanked Sam profusely, paid him, and climbed into his car with Chaco and Sierra. The reporter and photographer walked with them to the car asking questions, but did not try to follow them. Sierra reflected that they were lucky they were on Moloka'i. If this had been the Mainland—or even Honolulu—the reporters would likely have been more aggressive.

Clancy parked in front of Auntie Keikilani's house and led the way to the front door, where he stopped and faced Sierra and Chaco.

"I don't think Auntie has enough room for everyone, but we can figure something out. I don't know what we're going to do about Fred, though," he said.

"You found them!" Auntie's voice came from behind him. The screen door opened and Auntie emerged onto her front porch, arms wide.

"Aloha! I am so glad to see you safe and sound. You have no idea how miserable this man has been, looking for you every day and not finding you. Come in, come in!"

Clancy glanced down at his weighty duffel bag, shrugged, and went in as Auntie greeted Sierra and Chaco with handshakes and kisses. He went straight to his room and deposited the bag on his bed.

"Stay there!" he hissed at the bag sternly. "Stay there and don't make a sound!"

"But I'm thirsty," the bag complained.

"I'll get you a drink. Just don't move and don't make a sound."

Clancy got a glass of water, opened the bag and handed it to Fred. Slurping sounds ensued, causing Clancy to shush the little mannegishi again. Then he went back to the living room, where Sierra and Chaco were standing awkwardly in their wetsuits, unwilling to sit down in them and growing increasingly uncomfortable in the heat of the day.

"Don't worry about the furniture," Auntie Keikilani was saying. "The wetsuits are dry. I haven't got anything that would fit you, Sierra, but my friend May is about your size. I'm calling her now. And I have some old clothes of my husband's for Chaco. They aren't exactly stylish, young man—poor James passed twenty years ago—but they'll cover you up. That ought to take care of you until your suitcases come."

May arrived a few minutes later with a selection of clothes. Sierra picked out shorts, a T-shirt, and some flip-flops. Keikilani retrieved shorts, a Hawai'ian shirt and sandals for Chaco. Sierra and Chaco took turns using Auntie's shower and changed into their fresh clothes.

"I'm starting to feel human again," Sierra said, sipping coffee and munching a sandwich Auntie had prepared for them while they were bathing. She sighed with pure joy.

"I'm feeling more human all the time," said Chaco, without any noticeable pleasure.

"That's odd," said Keikilani, giving Chaco a shrewd glance.

Three pairs of eyes turned to the Hawai'ian woman. "What d'you mean?" asked Chaco, who had stopped chewing in the middle of a bite.

"I mean that it's odd that you feel human. Not being human in the first place, I mean," Auntie said placidly.

"How the heck did you know that?" asked Sierra. "And if you know it, why aren't you freaking out?"

"I'm a kahuna," returned the older woman. "That's a Hawai'ian healer. Shaman. Priestess in the old days. I know an Avatar when I see one—though I haven't seen many. I have seen plenty of spirits, maybe a ghost or two. And Menehune, of course."

A long silence followed Auntie's revelation. It would be a relief to avoid making up a story about how they survived. And it solved another problem, too.

"Fred," called Clancy. "I think you can come out now."

Fred appeared in the door of the living room, glass in paw.

"Oh my goodness, aren't you the cutest thing!" exclaimed Auntie. "What are you?"

"I," said Fred with as much dignity as a creature the general size and shape of a watermelon could muster, "am a mannegishi."

"Of course you are," Auntie crooned. "You remind me of something—now, what is it?"

"Menehune?" suggested Sierra. "Fred says mannegishi and Menehune are sort of cousins. Fred speaks Hawai'ian. He says it's his native tongue."

Fred blushed a pretty shade of spring green and said, "Loa'a kekahi kokoleka?"[5]

"I do indeed," said Auntie and went to the kitchen. When she returned a moment later, she had a chocolate bar in her hand, which she presented to Fred.

"Mahalo, 'anakē,"[6] said Fred, beaming. He plopped down on the floor and began stripping the wrapping away from his treat.

"Now," said Keikilani, seating herself. "Why don't you start from the beginning?"

It was a long, long story, and they took turns telling it. Auntie sucked in her breath sharply when they came to the part about Kama Pua'a, and again at the point where Pele appeared. She muttered a few phrases in Hawai'ian as they told about Kapualei. Finally, they came to the topic of the construction in the sea that worried the Menehune. Auntie nodded her head.

"That's the WestWind Project," she said. "We Moloka'ians are very much opposed to it." She proceeded to list the objections.

"Why is there even a debate?" asked Sierra. "It sounds like a really bad idea."

"Energy is at a premium out here," responded Auntie, "and wind power is something we have plenty of. The problem is that Penguin Bank is perfect for a wind farm—but it's also perfect for the humpback whales. And I don't know how much damage the construction will do to the ocean floor out there."

Sierra asked, "Isn't there something that can be done to stop it?"

"Not so far. They just started construction recently. We tried talking to the State Legislature, all the environmental agencies— everything we could think of. But it's going forward whether we like it or not."

Chaco felt that it was time to turn the conversation to something more immediate. "Are we staying with you?" he looked hopefully at Auntie Keikilani.

"I don't have the room," she said regretfully. "I need to get on the phone and find you someplace. I'd suggest the hotel, but it's not exactly within walking distance."

"I have a car," said Clancy quietly. He had not said much, but he had kept his gaze on Sierra the entire time. "I'll call the hotel to see if Sierra and I can get a room." His glance at Sierra left her a bit breathless. He called the hotel, but there were no vacancies.

Auntie Keikilani spoke up. "You're all welcome here at my house, but all I have is the one single bed, and that might be a bit crowded." She twinkled at them. "I'll call Jack Kane. He has two spare bedrooms since his girls moved to O'ahu. Chaco can stay here with me."

This was quickly arranged. Jack agreed to host both Sierra and Clancy. Before Clancy packed his bag for the move to Jack's house, he asked Sierra to come outside with him for a few minutes. The others took the hint and did not follow them into Keikilani's little garden. Sierra, a mug of coffee clutched firmly in her hand, sat on a garden bench next to a hibiscus bush studded with bright gold flowers. Clancy sat next to her, slid his arm around her shoulders, and tucked her into his side as closely as possible. Neither said anything for several minutes. Sierra—blissfully happy to be clean, safe, cuddled up to Clancy, and full of coffee—spoke first.

"Clancy, I'm so grateful that you came to find me. I almost can't believe it. Under normal circumstances, Chaco and I would've died out there. No doubt about it." Kissing and cuddling ensued.

Eventually, she emerged, breathless, from Clancy's embrace. "What happened to the presidential visit to your plant, by the way?"

"I told my boss I was coming here and why, and there was no problem. But if there had been a problem, I would've come anyway, you know." He bent to kiss her, and she leaned into him, enjoying the closeness.

"I'm more grateful and touched than I can say that you're here. Sometimes I think maybe I'm too much of a tree-hugger for you, and then you go and do something like this." She kissed him deeply.

"You spend too much time worrying about things. But it's part of what makes you *you*, so I guess I'll just have to put up with it." He stood up, smiled down into her upturned face, and held out a hand to her. "Here we are on a beautiful island in Hawai'i. We didn't plan it this way, but let's make the most of it. Let's see what there is to see and enjoy ourselves. Maybe we can just hang out for a few days and let the dust settle. No one's expecting me at work, and no one expects you, either. We can go play. How's that sound?"

Sierra took Clancy's hand, stood up and smiled at him. "That sounds like a plan. I missed the chartered flight to Midway, so I guess we're going to have a laid-back Hawai'ian vacation after all," she said. "Could you just kiss me another time or two before we leave?"

"You bet," said Clancy. "But first, I think you ought to call your boss. She's the one who told me you were missing."

"Oh, poor Tammy!" Sierra took his phone and began to dial. After reassuring Tammy, Sierra told her, "So I'm staying on here for a few days, just to recuperate. I'm not sure when I'm coming back..."

"We aren't expecting you for another three weeks," Tammy said. "Take as much time as you need?" It sounded like a question, but Sierra knew better.

"I don't know how long our hosts will be willing to put up with us," Sierra replied. "I'll let you know when to expect me. Wow, I'm looking forward to sleeping in a bed again!"

"And all the coffee you can drink?" said Tammy, who knew her employee well.

Sierra returned Clancy's cell phone and looked at him under her lashes, smiling. He needed no further invitation and bent to kiss her. At the touch of his lips and the closeness of his body, Sierra felt a slow fire building inside and melted into his arms. Clancy's breathing grew quicker, and Sierra felt his arms tighten around her. She had missed this. She had missed Clancy. She had missed...

"Say!" said a squeaky voice somewhere near their trembling knees. "Where am *I* going to sleep?"

• • •

Sierra asked Auntie about sleeping arrangements for Fred. Auntie produced a laundry basket filled with soft towels, which Fred found highly satisfactory. She left Auntie clucking over Fred and helped Clancy get his things together. Jack's house was only a few houses away, so they walked.

Jack Kane effusively welcomed them to his home. "I can't believe you made it," Jack said to Sierra. "You look great—not like I would expect after nearly a week in the wilderness."

"We found food and water," she explained. "If we hadn't landed where we did, it would've been a different story."

"What did you eat?" Jack asked.

"'Opihi." That was true, even if it wasn't the whole truth.

Jack looked at her, one eyebrow raised. "How did you know the Hawai'ian name for limpets?"

Sierra looked blank for a moment and said, "Sam—the boat owner—he told me."

"We'll have to teach you some more Hawai'ian while you're here!" Jack said enthusiastically.

"I'd like that."

Jack had two small bedrooms, each with a single bed, which he explained had been his daughters' rooms until both girls had moved to O'ahu. They came home occasionally, but he wasn't expecting them anytime soon. Sierra noted the two little beds with some dismay, but said nothing.

"Stay as long as you like," he said. He glanced from Sierra to Clancy. They were holding hands and could hardly look away from one another.

"If you wanted," Jack said, peering out the window as he spoke, "you could move one of the beds into the other room. If you felt like it." His suggestion was promptly accepted.

Although it was only mid-afternoon, Sierra felt weariness settle into her bones. The last several days had taken their toll on her body and mind, and now that she was safe—and Chaco and Fred were safe—the fright and tension and physical exertion stole over her like dark fog. She yawned cavernously.

"If you don't mind, I'm going to take a nap," she said. "A real nap." She glanced at Clancy, who understood perfectly.

Sierra went to their room and flopped onto one of the single beds, now positioned side by side. Covered with a worn cotton quilt, the bed was firm and comfortable. Lying down, she looked around at the little room. It had obviously once been the room of a teenaged girl. It was painted a cheery yellow, with white blinds. The walls were covered with posters of boy bands, mostly shirtless, and snapshots of teenagers, presumably the daughters' friends. The trees outside shaded the window, making a dappled pattern of light and shade against the quilt, and a slight breeze made the patterns waver and shift. Sierra closed her eyes, and with visions of bright white sand and turquoise sea, of Kama paddling his outrigger through the waves, of Kapualei's great, black body churning the water, of the Menehune marching by torchlight, of Chaco's bruised face as he lay unconscious, she fell away from the world into a deep sleep.

• • •

The news that Sierra, Fred, and Chaco were safe had been a huge relief to their friends at home in California. Chaco's abrupt transition from demigod to mortal had shocked them. The Three Weird Sisters (who knew perfectly well that Clancy referred to them as such behind their backs) had discussed Chaco's plight and developed a possible solution. They knew it was a long shot, but worth attempting if there were a chance of restoring Chaco to his old and powerful self.

"Where are you headed with that shovel?" asked Guy, watching Kaylee head out the door after dinner one night. Guy had been looking forward to some cuddle time in front of the TV.

Kaylee turned and regarded her current lover with a mischievous smile. Her coffee-dark eyes sparkled. She gestured with a small folding shovel, the kind Boy Scouts take along on camping trips. "I plan to dig up some dirt."

He flashed her a sunny smile. "Maybe you're going to do away with me and hide the evidence?"

"Not today," she returned, heading out the front door of her apartment. "I just have a little gardening project."

"At this time of night? You don't have a garden. Shouldn't you be cuddling up to me right now?"

She grinned at him. "First things first." Then she was gone.

CHAPTER 14

When Sierra awoke, it was early evening, and she felt refreshed. She went to the small bathroom next to her room and stared at her reflection with dismay. She had kept her long, dark hair braided, but bits of it splayed out at odd angles and the braid was coming undone. She went to ask Jack if he had a hairbrush she could borrow.

"There might be a brush left in one of the girls' bedrooms," said Jack. "But your suitcase arrived while you were napping."

Sierra grabbed her suitcase with cries of joy and retreated to the bathroom. When she emerged fifteen minutes later, her hair was wet and shining, newly re-braided, and she was wearing shorts and a T-shirt from her baggage. Her skin was a darker shade than usual from her sunscreen-free sojourn in Kama's little valley, and a delicate spray of freckles had come out across her nose and cheeks.

Clancy kissed the tip of her freckled nose and said, "Auntie's invited us over for dinner tonight. We'll see you later, Jack," he called.

"If I'm in bed, the door will be unlocked." Jack replied. "I never lock my door anyway."

Sierra and Clancy found Auntie in the kitchen and immediately volunteered to help make dinner. They were turned down because Chaco and Fred were already at work and the kitchen was crowded.

When dinner was served, the conversation naturally centered on Sierra's and Chaco's recent adventures.

"Because of Kanaloa, Chaco and I can speak Hawai'ian," said Sierra. "It came in handy talking with Kama."

Over a dessert of macadamia nut ice cream, Auntie and Clancy asked many questions about the adventure in Kama's valley.

"Now that's it's all over," Sierra said, enjoying her ice cream as if it were the first time she had ever encountered such a substance, "Clancy and I plan to stick around for a few days to relax before we go home." Chaco said nothing and ate his ice cream quietly.

After dinner, everyone drifted outside into Auntie's pretty garden. Shadows had begun to lengthen but the light was still golden as the sun edged toward the horizon. In a large breadfruit tree nearby, a flock of mynah birds settled in for the night with a cacophony of squabbling and loud calls for order.

Sierra broke a long and comfortable silence by saying, "If WestWind is bad for Moloka'i, bad for the whales, and bad for the environment, maybe we should be doing something to help stop it." Clancy turned his green eyes on Sierra and shrugged.

"What, exactly?" he asked.

"Maybe you *can* do something to help, Sierra," said Auntie. All eyes turned to her. "You have mana. You said Kanaloa gifted you with even more power. I have some mana and my family's 'aumakua are powerful. If we combine our efforts, maybe we can stop it."

"If I can help, I will," Sierra said. "But I'm not sure what I can do."

"Let's talk it over tomorrow," Auntie said comfortably. "There's no rush, and you need to recuperate and have a little fun. Let's leave it for now." She levered herself out of her plastic chair. "I'm going in. I need to pick three numbers for a big competition coming up in a few months. My hula school will be participating." She went inside, and soon the soft strains of hula music wafted through the screen door.

The conversation turned to what they would do the next day. Sierra wanted to go snorkeling—an activity she had planned to do in Honolulu while she was waiting for the plane to Midway. Fred was all for it, but his participation was immediately and firmly vetoed on the basis of logistics. Keeping Fred a secret onboard a boat—that had been done before. Finding a snorkel mask to fit his small, distinctly non-human face was another issue. Trying to explain an apparently unoccupied snorkel and mask zipping around in the water was simply unthinkable. Chaco declined, saying he had enough of ocean swimming to last him the rest of…whatever. He and Fred would hang out at Auntie's place and play cards or something. They both cheated, so it would be an equal contest.

"I'll call Sam right now," said Clancy. "Maybe he has room on *Polupolu* tomorrow." It turned out that Sam had a party going out first thing in the morning and had room for two more.

"We need to be on the boat by six a.m.," Clancy reported. "Sam provides the equipment."

After a bit, Sierra went in to see Auntie Keikilani in the living room. "What can I do for you?" asked Auntie, switching off the music.

Sierra looked at the other woman's lined face and kind eyes. "We're all so grateful for the help, and you have been very generous to a bunch of strangers invading your private space."

Keikilani waved this away. "It's been fascinating for me. I have known of these things my entire life—and experienced much that can't be explained by science—but I've never encountered anything like this before." She stood up and hugged Sierra warmly. "I'm glad you're alive and well, my dear." Then she cocked her head toward the kitchen. "Fred! You had your dinner already. You stay out of my pantry!"

There was a scrambling sound, and then Fred appeared in the doorway. "Sorry, Auntie," he said, waving one thin arm. "Goodnight!" He wandered off to his laundry basket, but not before Sierra had extracted a candy bar from behind his back and returned it to the pantry.

Sierra thanked Auntie for the delicious meal and walked back outside to say goodnight to the others. It was now full dusk, and immense black moths were flying about, indistinguishable from bats. Clancy bent to kiss her. "I'm exhausted," he said to her. "Let's go back to Jack's place."

Sierra looked at Chaco, a dark figure drooping in one of Auntie's white plastic lawn chairs. "I'll be along in a minute," she said. "I want to talk to Chaco."

"Okay. Don't be too long," Clancy said, kissing her again. He walked away in the direction of Jack's house.

The yellow light from the windows limned Chaco's handsome face with its high cheekbones and long planes. His shoulders slumped and his wide, sensual mouth drew down, as though he were in a small field of increased gravity that affected only him. Sierra put a hand on his shoulder.

"You know you can fly home tomorrow, if that's what you want," she said. Chaco shrugged, and she could feel the lean muscles tense and roll beneath her hand.

"It might not do any good," he said dully. "I don't know that getting home will help me."

"Well, wouldn't it be better to find out than to mope around here all depressed?"

That seemed to sting. "I'm not moping. I'm mortal. There's a difference."

"You don't see any of us other mortals getting all depressed about it, do you? If I were in your situation, I'd want to get home as fast as possible to try to get my powers back. My mana, as they say in Hawai'ian."

"You have your powers," said Chaco bitterly. "After meeting Kanaloa, you have even more mana than you did before. You aren't tied to the land the way I am."

Sierra thought for a moment. "Yes, I guess you're right. But I still don't control those powers. Only in emergencies, it seems, and even then I don't actually know what I'm doing. It's scary."

"But you have them."

"Maybe you'll get your powers back, along with your immortality. Why not find out?"

Chaco remained in his seat, his face twisted, hands working against each other, mouth turned even further down. His hazel, no-longer-golden eyes turned up to hers, then closed, and a tear escaped under his long lashes and trickled down his cheek. He put his hands to his face, shoulders shaking. Sierra had never seen her usually cheerful friend so distressed.

"Chaco! What...?"

Chaco sobbed, then managed to gasp, "I'm afraid. I'm afraid to go home. It might not work! Then I won't have any hope at all. I'll be stranded here, in this time, in this age, a mortal. I will die. I'm afraid to die! I'm afraid to do anything now because I might die."

Sierra pulled him out of his chair and put her arms around him. She let him sob against her shoulder for a while. When his sobs subsided, she said gently, "You know, we're all afraid to die. Humans are, anyway, because we all know there's only one way out of here. It's just part of being mortal."

"How can you stand it?" he muttered.

"I think it's just something you get used to," she said. "When you're a kid and you realize for the first time that you, yourself, will die someday—it's kind of a shock. But you get used to the idea, and to be honest, most of us try not to think about it. You haven't had time to get accustomed to it. It's a new idea, and not a pleasant one. Give yourself some time. Or better yet—go home and see if you get your mana back."

"I'm not going back yet. I need to be here."

"Why?"

"I don't know yet," Chaco said, shrugging. "It's just something I know. I'll go back with you after this is all over."

"After what is all over?" she asked. "A few days of swimming and sunning and drinking tropical drinks? They must serve tropical drinks somewhere on Moloka'i."

"I don't know yet," was all Chaco had to say, and Sierra didn't think he was referring to tropical drinks.

CHAPTER 15

The next morning, Clancy and Sierra brought the two borrowed wetsuits to return to *Polupolu*. Clancy drove to the Kaunakakai Wharf, driving all the way to the end where there was parking. *Polupolu* rocked at her moorings under the bright lights of the wharf in the pre-dawn quiet. Sam greeted them cheerfully, handed them aboard, and gave Sierra a cup of coffee without asking.

"Nice weather today," he said. "Should have good visibility."

There were a few others aboard the boat already—a couple of older women who looked fit despite their white hair, and a young man and woman who had the look of honeymooners, gazing soulfully into each other's eyes, oblivious to everyone else. There was also a man on his own who seemed to have his own equipment, which he had stowed in a duffel bag by his side. He was good-looking in a lean and hungry way, Sierra thought, with silvering dark hair cut short, a rather long-nosed face, and sharp blue eyes. He greeted the newcomers with a restrained smile and nod.

As *Polupolu* chugged away from the wharf, heading north, the scenery was as unfamiliar to Sierra as it was all-too-familiar to Clancy. He showed her where the ancient fishponds lay, like rocky nets cast from the shore. Sierra took it all in avidly, enjoying the fresh breeze and the colors of dawn as the sun rose. Spinner dolphins played around the boat for a while, and she saw several large sea turtles swimming near the surface.

Sam stopped the boat and anchored after a half an hour. He gave his passengers a brief lecture about do's and don'ts and said they would be here for about an hour. Then he and Mike helped the passengers find and don wetsuits and clean their masks to prepare them for snorkeling. The one single man brought his own equipment and donned it with a practiced air. He was first off the boat, falling backward into the water from a platform lowered from the boat's stern. He immediately began swimming toward the shore, which was a bit less than a mile away, going slowly and pausing from time to time, head down to watch whatever was beneath the surface. Sierra and Clancy followed.

The water was delicious, only briefly cool as Sierra fell backward and away from the boat. She and Clancy moved along together. Sierra saw schools of yellow and white fish floating lazily through the coral beneath her, then several large, rainbow-colored fish snacking on the corals. She recognized these as parrotfish from her sojourn with Kama. Then there were so many fish, of so many brilliant hues that the sight overwhelmed her. She wanted to know what they were all called. From time to time, Clancy would tap her shoulder and point to something unusual.

After several minutes of no one drawing her attention, she realized she had drifted away from Clancy and the others. She poked her head out of the water and stared around. There was *Polupolu*, looking disturbingly distant. She could see snorkelers in the middle distance, between her and the boat, but they were too far away to make out who they were. She began swimming in their direction, not liking to be so far from the boat and other people.

As she swam, she kept her head down, breathing through her snorkel. She saw an eel's head poking out of its coral cave, and a school of fish swarmed around her. She thought they were black at first, but closer inspection showed bright white lines like racing stripes outlining the back halves of their bodies, and the "black" resembled psychedelic neon blue and orange pixels in the right light.

Then the corals dropped suddenly away, and Sierra found herself in a deep blue "hole." She couldn't see the bottom, and there were no corals visible. She lifted her head out of the water to get a bearing on *Polupolu* and her fellow snorkelers. She was a bit closer than the last time she had checked, but not much. She put her face into the water again—and froze. Below her hovered the enormous white octopus, Kanaloa, watching her with its staring blue eyes, eight massive tentacles writhing slowly around his bulbous body.

Sierra remained suspended in the water, breathing too quickly through the snorkel. She began to feel dizzy. The creature reached out one coiling limb, studded with suckers, and grasped her. She instantly lost the dizzy feeling, and along with it the impulse and need to breathe, just as before.

The tentacle grasped her gently, but she could feel the soft, sticky sensation of suckers against her skin. The Avatar held her, turning her this way and that, then the voice in her head said, "I know you. You're the kahuna from the boat. You lived, then."

"I'm not a kahuna, Kanaloa." *Should I have said something more formal, like "O great Kanaloa" or "Your Mightiness"?*

The huge eyes stared at her. "You are. You are only ignorant of your powers."

Sierra stared back, her brain alight with a new idea. "Kanaloa. Have you heard the whales crying about the building in the ocean?"

"Yes."

"Can you help them? Can you do something about it—stop the builders? Maybe take down the towers?"

The coil of tentacle around Sierra's waist relaxed and whipped away as Kanaloa released her. Simultaneously, a cloud of swirling black enveloped her, blinding her. The need to breathe returned with a vengeance, but her snorkel was filled with water. Sierra swam to the surface and thrust her head out of the water, gasping as she checked the position of *Polupolu* and the other snorkelers, then cleared her snorkel and mask and put her head underwater again as the ink cleared. And froze again in shock and fear.

Below her was an immense white shark, as long as *Polupolu*. It wasn't a great white shark, which is mostly black, but truly a white shark, white as chalk all over. As white as Kanaloa. The shark swam lazily beneath her, and she felt the tip of its dorsal fin touch her leg. It felt like wet sandpaper. Then it turned and swam back, studying her, its lidless black eyes flashing electric blue as they caught the light, like a wolf's eyes in the dark. Its slash of a mouth gaped slightly open, showing rows of jagged teeth.

Sierra's heart was pumping so hard she felt she couldn't breathe through the snorkel, but she could not take her eyes off the great shark for a second, not even to grab a lungful of air. She hung suspended above the giant predator, not daring to move. The shark circled again, then glided under her upside down, its belly as white as its back, serrated teeth clearly visible in its upside-down smile. It looped back sinuously, stared at her for a long moment—then dipped its head once before it flashed away like pale lightning and was lost in the blue depths of the sea.

Later, Sierra did not remember her swim back to the boat. Sam described it as "water walking." She arrived at the stern platform, hauled herself aboard in one swift move and stood dripping and panting as she screamed, "Shark! Huge shark!" Sam wasted no time in ringing the bell that would alert swimmers to return to the boat as quickly as possible, and kept an anxious lookout until all his passengers were safely aboard.

"How big was it?" Sam asked Sierra.

"As big as this boat. Huge."

A shadow of disbelief crossed Sam's face, but all he said was, "What did it look like? Gray? Brown? Did it have stripes or other markings?"

Sierra shook her head, water flying from her hair. "No markings. It was white. Pure white all over, like an albino."

Sam stared at her wordlessly, his round, brown face expressionless where there was usually a cheery smile. Finally he said, "In all my years taking boats out here, I have never seen a white shark. I mean, a shark that is white everywhere. Are you sure?"

Sierra realized that Sam either didn't believe her or thought she was exaggerating. Or maybe he thought her memory was affected by fear and shock.

Whatever Sam might have been thinking, he calmly said to the anxious group, "There's another place we can go. Never seen any sizeable sharks there, but there are lots of fish and turtles. It'll just be fifteen or twenty minutes." He climbed up the short ladder to the cockpit. Soon, *Polupolu's* engines revved and they were off again.

Sierra sat huddled in her towel. She was dripping wet. The warm air did nothing to counteract the bone-deep chill she felt. Clancy sat beside her and put his arm around her.

"That must've been scary," he said.

"Terrifying," was all Sierra could manage between her chattering teeth. Mike offered her a cup of coffee. She took it gratefully and let the hot mug warm her cold hands.

The solo man removed his fins. He rinsed them and his mask before sitting on the bench next to Sierra and Clancy.

"Name's Houghton," he said, pronouncing his name "Huffton." He extended his hand, which she and Clancy shook. "Sounds like a scary experience, but I've been snorkeling here for years," he said in a quiet, friendly voice. "I've seen lots of sharks, but they've never bothered me. Of course, I keep an eye on them if they're anywhere near me. The tiger sharks are really the most dangerous, and they tend to keep to deeper water."

"Yeah," Sierra said, not wanting to get into a discussion of her particular shark. She didn't think it was just an albino shark. However, the fewer people who thought her insane, the better.

"You shouldn't let it scare you out of the water," said the man, standing and stretching. "That would be a pity. There's really very little danger as long as you follow Sam's rules."

"I suppose so," she said noncommittally. "Thanks." *This guy didn't see what I saw.*

After a few minutes, she took her coffee forward, where there was plenty of room to sit in the hot sun. Clancy followed. Bit by bit, the ice melted from her bones and she began to feel human again.

"Clancy. There was something else," she said quietly. He looked at her attentively, one eyebrow raised like a dark wing. "I saw Kanaloa again. Before the shark appeared, I mean. I asked him about the wind turbine project—WestWind—and he knew about it. I asked him if he could do something about it, and that's when he disappeared. Well, he didn't exactly disappear. He squirted ink everywhere and when it cleared—there was the shark."

"Do you think they were the same thing? The shark and Kanaloa?"

"I don't know," said Sierra, "but I'm not going back in the water."

CHAPTER 16

True to her word, Sierra did not do any more snorkeling that day. She and Clancy stayed aboard *Polupolu* and watched as the others snorkeled. They saw nothing but sea turtles and an occasional dolphin from the boat. When the others returned, they chatted happily about the gorgeous fish they had seen. One person had seen an octopus, but it was obviously a garden-variety octopus and not a huge and terrifying Avatar. No one had seen any kind of shark.

After returning to Kaunakakai, Sierra and Clancy met up with Chaco and Fred at Auntie Keikilani's house. Sierra told her story, which still sent armies of goosebumps marching along her spine and arms.

When she finished, Fred piped up, "It must've been Kauhuhu that you saw. The shark, I mean."

"Cow-who-who? What's that?"

"Kauhuhu is our shark god here in Molokaʻi," put in Auntie Keikilani. "I don't know anyone else who has ever seen him, but what else could it have been? There are no natural sharks that look like that."

"The Menehune told me Kauhuhu is terribly dangerous," said Fred. "But he can also be compassionate."

"A compassionate shark?" asked Sierra skeptically. "How does that work?"

Fred looked at Auntie Keikilani. "Tell us the story, Auntie," he begged. "It's a good one." He settled his fat bottom on a hassock in her living room, eyes rolling expectantly in several directions.

Auntie poured some iced tea for herself and sat on a couch, her

tropical floral dress almost disappearing against the floral uphol-
stery. "It's a long story," she began, "but I'll try to make it short.

"Once, long ago, there lived a priest on Moloka'i whose name
was Kamalo, who maintained a temple. Kamalo had two sons who
were very adventurous, and they were the light of his eyes. Not far
away was another temple where a priest named Kupa lived. Kupa
was one of the island's high chiefs and very powerful. Kupa had
two sacred drums in his temple, and only he was allowed to beat
on them. He was such a skilled player that he could communicate
with drumbeats alone, using no words.

"One day, Kupa sailed far out to sea to fish. Kamalo's sons
knew they weren't supposed to touch the sacred objects in a temple,
but they snuck into Kupa's temple and beat on the drums until
they were tired. Of course, they were observed by the people in the
village, who told Kupa about it when he returned home. Furious
that kapu had been violated, Kupa ordered his temple sacrifice
seekers to find and kill Kamalo's boys.

"Kamalo was deeply grieved when he discovered the deaths of
his sons, and he swore revenge. Being of lower status, he could do
nothing against the high priest Kupa, so he sought the help of other
powerful people. One after the other, they all refused because they
were afraid of Kupa and his power. With no other choice, Kamalo
decided to seek the assistance of the great shark god, Kauhuhu,
protector of Moloka'i.

"The shark god's temple was at the foot of the towering pali
of Kalaupapa. He braved the climb down the cliff to consult with
the priest there. The priest refused to help him, but told Kamalo he
could approach Kauhuhu directly, if he dared. Kauhuhu lived in a
cave in the cliffs south of Kalawao.

"Kamalo caught a black pig and carried it all the way to the
cave of Kauhuhu. The entrance to the cave was guarded by two
fierce mo'o. The mo'o warned him away, saying Kauhuhu would
devour him, but Kamalo told them his story, and the mo'o were
moved by his tragedy. They told him to hide himself and the pig

in a pile of discarded taro leaves, and not to move or make a sound until they told him to come out.

"Kauhuhu arrived and assumed his man-form. As he came into his house, he said that he smelled a man in the cave, but the two moʻo denied it. He sniffed around, but didn't find Kamalo. Just as he was turning his attention elsewhere, the black pig squealed and gave away the hiding place. Kauhuhu pounced on the man, swallowing nearly half of him, but before his great, sharp teeth came down, Kamalo asked him to hear his prayer before eating him. The shark god agreed.

"Kamalo told the sad story of his two boys, explaining that no one would aid him in taking revenge against Kupa. He offered Kauhuhu the black pig as a sacrifice. Kauhuhu's heart was moved. He accepted the offering and told Kamalo he was the only man to ever escape him alive. He pledged his help, telling Kamalo to return to the temple of the shark priest, carry him back to Kamalo's own heiau, and live with him there. Kauhuhu also told Kamalo to put up sacred staffs and collect specific types and numbers of fish, pigs, and chickens. When they saw a great rainbow spanning the valley where Kamalo lived, Kauhuhu would take revenge on the priest Kupa.

"Kamalo followed all of Kauhuhu's instructions. One day, the great rainbow appeared, followed by torrents of rain that destroyed Kupa's temple. Kupa and all his people were washed down into the harbor below. Kauhuhu had gathered his own people—the sharks—in the harbor, and they devoured Kupa and all his people, staining the water red with blood. This is how Kamalo avenged the deaths of his beloved sons."

Auntie took a long swig of iced tea in the silence that followed this tale. Finally, Chaco spoke.

"Kauhuhu sounds like a dangerous friend."

Auntie Keikilani nodded. "As he said to Kamalo, Kamalo is the only man to escape him alive." She turned her gaze to Sierra. "Until now, apparently."

Sierra recalled more than one fairy tale that might have a bearing on this. "I'm not a man."

Auntie beamed at her. "You have a point! But I don't know why he appeared to you, or what it means that he left you alone. Did he communicate with you at all?"

Sierra thought for a moment. "Not in words. He did give me a sort of odd head nod. He dipped his snout down and up, then swam away."

"Hmmm," said Auntie, looking thoughtful. "And this was right after your conversation with Kanaloa?"

Sierra nodded.

"A white shark—a true white shark, not a great white shark—is one of the body forms of Kanaloa," she said slowly. "Kanaloa is the lord of the ocean, so all ocean creatures, including the shark gods, are ruled by Kanaloa and are also part of Kanaloa at the same time."

Sierra stared at Auntie Keikilani. "I don't think I understand," she said.

Before Auntie could respond, Chaco said, "It shouldn't be difficult for you, Sierra. You grew up going to church, right?" Sierra nodded.

"You worshipped the Father, Son, and Holy Ghost, but you were also told that they were all one God. The same holds true in this instance. Kanaloa is a creator and sharks are his creation, but they are still a part of the creator."

"Yes, but," began Sierra, but Chaco cut her off.

"You can't rationalize it or try to understand it through the lens of science," he said gruffly. "It just is. Trust me on this."

"Okay, but I don't know where this leaves me," said Sierra. "Am I supposed to do something, or am I supposed to get a tan and go home?"

"Why don't we call Mama Labadie and see what the loa have to say?" asked Chaco. "After all, the loa told Mama that we were both alive. Maybe they can tell us the right thing to do here."

"Lwa?" asked Auntie.

"L-O-A—the gods of Voudún," replied Sierra, as Clancy shifted uncomfortably. "Mama Labadie is a houngán, a priest-ess of Voudún. A bit like a kahuna. Sometimes the gods speak through her."

"Which gods?" asked Auntie. "Are they the same as the Hawai'ian gods, or different?"

Sierra looked puzzled. "I don't know," she responded. "I never thought about it that way. I suppose they're not the same. They don't have the same names, but I'm not exactly an expert."

Everyone turned and looked at Chaco, as the only represen-tative of the supernatural present—other than Fred, who never seemed to know the answer to questions like this, being more concerned with the dinner menu than anything else.

Chaco looked uncomfortable. "How would I know? I know how things work back home. I don't know how they work here or anywhere else. In any case, I can't exactly go ask some other Avatar, because I don't know any in this part of the world—except Kama—even if I could find one, not having any powers left to me." Now he looked more sullen than uncomfortable. It was such a foreign expression on his clever, lean face that Sierra almost didn't recognize him. Where was her cheerful, devil-may-care friend? Who was this surly stranger? She wondered if mood-elevating medications worked on Avatars.

"I vote that we ask Mama Labadie to ask the loa," Sierra said firmly. "They don't always come through, but it's worth a try."

Clancy had looked increasingly uncomfortable throughout this conversation. *Well, that was normal,* Sierra mused. Clancy didn't like anything that his rational mind couldn't parse as being logical or scientific. She looked at him fondly. *Nonetheless, he's gone along on these adventures. He tolerates—even loves—my weird friends. Not many men would stick around this insanity for the love of a woman.*

Sierra got out her cell phone and dialed Mama Labadie. "Hi," she said, "It's me. Sierra. Yes, everything's fine, but let me tell you what happened today!" And she launched in on the tale of her latest encounter. "So we aren't sure what that means, or what we should do. Maybe we shouldn't do anything, but then again, maybe there was a message in all that. Could you ask the loa for advice? Yes. Sure. We'll be on pins and needles waiting to hear. Thanks! Goodbye."

"She'll do a ceremony tonight and call us tomorrow," Sierra said, putting her phone away.

Pins and needles aside, they all went out to dinner at the Paddler's Inn. Between the fruity tropical drinks and fresh seafood, they managed to forget about Kanaloa and Kauhuhu and WestWind for the evening. *There's something about Hawai'ian guitar music that insists that you relax and enjoy life,* Sierra thought, savoring her third mai tai of the evening. She slipped another buttered roll under the table for Fred, who had promised to stay disappeared but still insisted on being fed.

They all walked back to Auntie's house, Chaco trailing forlornly behind. Sierra and Clancy paused at the front door as Auntie went in. As Chaco came up the front walk he gave them an expressionless glance and said goodnight. He went through the screen door and disappeared from view.

"What's with him?" Clancy asked, taking Sierra in his arms and kissing her warmly. She returned the kiss with enthusiasm.

"He's down in the dumps because he's mortal," she explained when she came up for air. "And I think he's a bit jealous."

"Being mortal isn't so bad," Clancy said, kissing her again. "Not when it involves kissing you." Then he stepped back a pace, holding Sierra's shoulders and looking into her eyes. "I thought you said Chaco was just your friend. Why would he be jealous?"

"Chaco *is* just my friend, but you have to understand. He always got to kiss girls when he was immortal, plus he had all the other benefits. Now he's mortal, and he's not kissing anybody." Sierra didn't really mean "kissing," but she thought it was sufficient to communicate her meaning.

"What about Kaylee?"

"What about her? She's with Guy now. As fickle as Kaylee might be, she doesn't cheat. She breaks up and moves on."

Silence followed this observation, as Clancy demonstrated how uninterested he was in the affairs of others. Finally, Sierra pulled away, regarding him with more sobriety than her three mai tais should have permitted. He held her close, and she could smell him, clean sweat and something spicy. She loved the feel of his arms holding her close. His urgency was firing hers. Her face was getting hot and her mouth dry. She swallowed hard.

"Let's get back to Jack's place," she suggested.

They walked back to Jack's house through the heavy, flower-laden night air, arms twined around each other's waist. The huge moths—Sierra knew by now they were called black witch moths—floated by overhead, silent as the stars.

Jack had gone to bed, but the front porch light was on and the door unlocked. They left their sandals at the door, according to Hawai'ian tradition, and padded quietly to the bedroom they shared. They fell onto one of the small beds, trying not to make any noise that would wake their host. Something about this heroic restraint seemed to fuel their urgency rather than dampen it, and Sierra felt as if she were melting into him, body and soul. Time suspended, all thought erased from her consciousness as they moved together. When Sierra reached her climax, she screamed but made no sound, the pressure of holding back that scream driving her into wave after wave of pure pleasure.

The next morning Mama Labadie called. "Girl, I have some news for you."

"What is it?"

"Yep. I can't make head nor tail of it. Maybe you can."

"What?" Sierra almost yelled.

"All Madame Ézilee say to me was 'Heaven's child.' That's it. Frustrating, huh?"

"Actually," Sierra said slowly, "I think I understand."

CHAPTER 17

Sierra thanked Mama Labadie, shoved her phone into her pocket, and told Clancy she was going to see Auntie. She found Chaco outside on the porch of Auntie's little house, sipping a cup of coffee. He looked broody, as he often did these days. Sierra told him that Mama Labadie had called.

"I need to talk to Auntie," she said.

"Oh." Chaco stared at his coffee as though he expected it to say something.

"Do you want to come with me?"

"Why? You don't need to talk to me," he said, still staring down the coffee.

"Don't be a jerk. Of course I need to talk to you."

"What about Clancy?"

"Clancy is a great guy, but he isn't comfortable discussing these things. He's more of a problem-solver-action-guy. Come or not. Suit yourself."

Sierra turned and walked away. She heard Chaco shift in his lawn chair, but he didn't follow. *Fine. If he's going to mope around feeling sorry for himself, I'll just carry on without him.* But Sierra missed her bright, energetic, and somewhat lecherous companion. Chaco as a mortal was getting to be something of a drag, and she wished he'd flown home as she suggested. Maybe he'd have regained his powers and with them, his sunny outlook.

Dismissing Chaco and his problems, she went back inside and found Auntie Keikilani reading in the living room. "Auntie, would I be correct in saying that your name means 'child of heaven' in Hawai'ian?"

Keikilani nodded.

Sierra told her about the loa's message. "They never give very specific messages," she said. "They never say anything like 'Your accountant is ripping you off.' It's always 'The snake is eating the fruit' or something, and you have to figure it out. But this time they said "heaven's child,' which wouldn't mean anything to me except that I now understand Hawai'ian."

Sierra thought for a moment. "I bet if they knew I spoke Hawai'ian, they would've said something much more obscure."

Auntie turned off the low music and turned her kind eyes on Sierra. "I think I know why the loa wanted you to talk to me. I've been thinking since our last conversation, and I'm convinced we need to be working together on this. You have a lot of mana. I know about the gods and spirits of Hawai'i, and I have mana of my own." Sierra nodded.

"But I don't think you're going to like what I have to suggest." Auntie Keikilani fixed her with a sharp gaze. "I think you should go back in the ocean and confront Kanaloa and Kauhuhu again. Maybe we can appeal to them as protectors of Moloka'i to do something about WestWind."

"I. Am. Terrified. To go back into the water. Absolutely freaked out, spooked, petrified, aghast."

Sierra was pale beneath her tanned skin. Her body was rigid, and she worked her slender fingers nervously. It was warm, but not hot enough to warrant the sweat trickling down her cheeks. Her eyes looked haunted.

"I have some…mana," she continued. "But Kanaloa is a great power. You can sense it. I've got nothing compared with him. And Kauhuhu…! He's beyond terrifying."

Keikilani reached out and patted Sierra's shoulder. "When you first told the story of being taken by Kanaloa, you said he gave you a gift. Part of that gift was speaking Hawai'ian. But you also said you felt your powers flare, as though he had charged you with additional mana. We should take a look, examine your mana. If you will let me."

Sierra consented to this, as it didn't involve immersing herself in the ocean. Keikilani drew all the blinds and curtains in her living room, reducing the available light to a soft twilight. With the curtains and blinds closed, the room rapidly became even warmer. Sierra lay on the couch, trying to relax her stressed mind and body as the other woman sat beside her, chanting. Sierra's mind gradually surrendered to the sound, and her body followed, every muscle softening as she relaxed. Waves of peace washed over her as the chanting continued, and she was nearly asleep when the chanting gently came to a halt. Then there was a restful silence.

This sleepy calm ended abruptly as Sierra began to see visions behind her closed eyelids. She saw ribbons of light—every color of the rainbow and some she was sure were not even in the rainbow. The ribbons pulsed and twisted, glowing as though super-heated. She reached out mentally and began to play with the ribbons, making them move just so or twine in a different direction. She even braided some of them and let them untwine again. When she twisted them together, they seemed to grow stronger and brighter, dimming a bit as they unraveled. She manipulated the tendrils of light, playing with them, experimenting to see what happened if she did this…or that. She noticed after a while that the light in the room had become brighter, and she opened her eyes blearily, squinting against the light. Auntie Keikilani had opened the curtains and blinds, letting in the midday sun.

"That answers that question," Auntie said with satisfaction.

"Huh?"

"You've been on that couch for four hours."

"Really?"

"Yes, really. And your mana is strong. Can't you feel that?"

"Well, no. I mean, not until now. I've never played with the powers before. I usually only remember them when there's an emergency."

"Oh, no. You need to keep using them. Grow your powers, exercise them. Then you'll be strong when you need that mana."

Sierra sat up, a bit disoriented. Four hours had disappeared while she wasn't paying attention. Auntie Keikilani sat down next to her.

"I think you have more than sufficient mana to face Kanaloa or Kauhuhu. I don't think they intend to harm you. Quite the opposite. They have both taken an interest in you," Keikilani said.

"But you're Moloka'ian. And a kahuna. Wouldn't they be more likely to listen to you?"

Auntie Keikilani sat silently for a bit, looking thoughtful. "As a Moloka'ian, maybe it's my responsibility. But the fact is that Kanaloa has never appeared to me, despite all my years swimming and fishing in the ocean. It seems he plucked you off that boat merely out of curiosity, but now you have encountered him twice. And Kauhuhu knows you are under his protection."

"Really? I am?" Sierra said, looking more cheerful.

"I think so, because neither of them has harmed you. However, as you pointed out, I am Moloka'ian. My home is threatened, not yours. I think I should be the one to ask him."

"How can I help?" asked Sierra.

"Come with me. I have a little putt-putt boat we can take out on the reef. I'll go in the water and call to Kanaloa. You stay in the boat and help me out if I need it."

"Okay," said Sierra slowly. "I think I can handle that."

"I can say the appropriate prayers and make an offering," Auntie said. "Does that make you feel any better?"

It did not.

"Are you sure it's safe, Auntie?"

Auntie Keikilani looked directly at Sierra when she answered. "Safe? No. I don't think it's safe at all. We're dealing with powerful beings, beings we don't really understand. The real question is: do you think the risk is worth it? You don't have any stakes in this game. Moloka'i is not your home. If the WestWind project goes forward, it won't change your life at all."

Auntie might have been reading Sierra's mind, expressing Sierra's half-guilty thoughts out loud. "Think about it for a while,

Sierra. I am willing to call the shark-god. I'd like your help, but as I said, you have no personal stake here. Think it over."

Sierra went to her bedroom, mind churning furiously every step of the way. It was mid-afternoon now, and hot, although there was always a cooling sea breeze. She didn't want to see Chaco. She didn't want to talk to anyone. She needed to get out of Kaunakakai, but she didn't want to ask Clancy to drive her. She realized with a start that she now had her wallet, a driver's license, and credit cards. She could rent her own car if she could get to the little airport.

A short taxi ride later, Sierra pulled out of the Kaunakakai airport in a compact white rental car and headed west. She had no destination in mind, determined to wander wherever the road took her. She saw a sign to Palaau State Park and turned off to the north. She drove through scattered residential areas as the road rose gradually higher. Eventually, the houses dropped behind, the vegetation changed with the altitude, and she found herself driving through a forest. By the time she reached the parking lot at the end of the road, tall trees blotted out the sky. Their foot-long, soft needles made them look, Sierra thought, like towering green haystacks.

She got out of the car and stretched. Though the day had been quite hot in Kaunakakai, it was cool under the trees—almost too cool for her shorts and T-shirt. There were two signs, one pointing to the Kalaupapa Overlook, and the other sign reading, "To the Phallic Rock." Sierra opted for the overlook, following a clearly marked path. She arrived at a low stone wall and saw she was standing at the very top of the towering pali. Below—far, far below—was the Kalaupapa Peninsula, which she knew could be reached only by boat or plane—or by a precipitous trail down the pali by mule.

No one else was around. The wind blew in from the sea, making the trees' long needles whisper and hiss. It was the only sound. She stood and stared for a long time. She might as well have been in an airplane, she was so high above the peninsula and the tiny settlement below. She could see miniscule buildings down there, but they were so far away that she couldn't distinguish whether they were houses, stores, or something else. The wind seemed to blow right through her, sending her fears spiraling up and away, at least for the moment, into the blue vastness of the sky and the sea.

Sierra made the short hike to the Phallic Rock before she left, and decided that it was very phallic indeed. A basin had been carved in the upper surface of the stone, and a lei rested in the hollow. She contemplated the delicate flowers for a moment, then stretched out a ribbon of mana and "felt" the stone. She immediately encountered a Presence. It wasn't a spirit or a ghost or an Avatar. It was something else, an awareness. Something knew she was there. Silently she asked for guidance in this latest challenge, the directive to confront the terrifying Kanaloa and Kauhuhu yet again. The Presence stirred in response to her question, but she received no answer. Disappointed, she returned to her car and descended again into the flat, red lands of western Moloka'i.

Somehow, she missed the turn to Kaunakakai. There weren't many roads on Moloka'i, so she was annoyed with herself for getting lost. But she seemed to be heading for a beach, and beaches were some of her favorite places, so she continued. She drove past several condominium developments, and then saw a sign for Papohaku Beach Park. She turned in and parked, noticing several other cars in the lot. She guessed that Papohaku was probably a good swimming and/or surfing beach.

Sierra followed the path to the beach, winding through a fairy-forest of delicate acacia trees. A steady stream of people was arriving and leaving. Was an event happening in the park? She emerged from the acacia forest onto a long, white sand beach. The waves were fierce, racing toward the land in multiple tiers and pounding angrily on the sand as they arrived. Not a good swimming beach after all, Sierra decided, noting the many jagged black rocks in the water. Everyone seemed to be heading downwind, and there was a gathering about a half a mile away of perhaps thirty people. She began to make her way in toward the crowd, curious about what was drawing people to this spot.

The stench was her first indication. She had almost reached the crowd when a sudden shift of the breeze filled her nostrils with a deathly reek. It was as though someone had distilled the essence of all rotting things, a putrescence that clutched at her throat. Sierra nearly gagged and stopped short. People were in motion, walking, taking pictures, talking, and pointing. A gap in the throng revealed the focus of the crowd's attention: a dead whale.

She could see that it wasn't a large whale. It was a baby, but still bigger than a minivan. It was collapsed like a pile of old, black rubber tires. She could see the long grooves of its throat. In California, it would have attracted hundreds of scavenging sea gulls. Hawai'i had no seagulls, but black clouds of flies were doing their puny best to contribute to the dissolution of the corpse.

Sierra went no closer but stared at the pathetic cadaver. She saw the baby whale alive and swimming in the sea, next to its mother, singing with her. That was where this baby should be now, not stinking up a beach and being stared at and prodded. She thought about the mother whale, swimming alone, surely with a gaping wound in her heart where her baby had been.

Sierra turned and sprinted back down the beach toward her car.

CHAPTER 18

"I'm nearly finished with this part," muttered Kaylee, pins held between her lips. "Could someone hand me the scissors?"

Mama Labadie handed her a pair of shears. Kaylee used them and held up her handiwork. "I think it will work, size-wise," she said critically.

"Looks perfect to me," Rose said. "But I think I need to do my part before we use this." She gestured at a filthy shoebox lying on the floor.

"That's right," Mama Labadie said. "First you do your bit, then we can finish it. You ready?" she asked Rose. Rose felt for the medicine bag at her throat, its weight familiar and comforting. As her hand clasped the leather bag, she said a silent prayer for the success of their endeavor.

"Yep, I'm ready," said Rose.

"How long will it take, d'you think?"

Rose examined the object lying in her lap. "I won't get too fancy. But it will take me the tomorrow and the next day. Maybe longer."

The women worked long into the night.

• • •

Roberts decided to spend a few more days on Moloka'i. It never hurt for the top guy to be seen on site for a while. It let people know that management had eyes on the project. It also gave him opportunities to find ways of encouraging good work and discouraging sloppy practices.

He'd spent a couple of days deliberately relaxing, as though he were just one more tourist. Nobody bothered him on Moloka'i and he'd swum, snorkeled, and fished. He'd spent time alone at the condo, reading, cooking, and watching sunsets from the lanai.

He'd also taken his on-site managers out to dinner at Paddler's. It had been a curiously stilted evening. The men and women who worked for him consumed cautious amounts of alcohol and kept the conversation on business. There was a certain camaraderie between the managers, but only respectful deference toward Roberts himself, which left him feeling like a specimen in a jar sitting at the head of the table.

Well, wasn't that what he wanted? Roberts firmly believed that familiarity bred contempt, and had sidestepped any attempts at intimacy or even friendship from those who worked for him.

But still, it all felt a bit…empty.

• • •

"No!" yelled Clancy, slamming his hands down on Keikilani's kitchen table, making the dishes—and Keikilani—jump. "You can't be serious, Sierra. It would just be fucking nuts to take that kind of risk!"

Clancy almost never swore. Hearing "fuck" come out of his mouth was like hearing your old granny say it, and Sierra was slightly shocked. She also realized just how upset he was. Auntie murmured something polite and left the room.

"I have to try, Clancy. No one seems to be able to stop WestWind. And now I think it really must be stopped."

"It's too dangerous. I thought I'd lost you before, Sierra. I *do not* want to go through that again."

Sierra couldn't help but be touched, but she was determined. "Auntie Keikilani says that I can handle it, and anyway Auntie is the one going in the water to call Kanaloa. I'm staying in the boat to help, so I think I'll be okay."

Clancy rolled his eyes. "I hate this. I hate all of it. Why do you have to get involved, Sierra? This isn't your fight."

"Are we doing this again? If it affects my world adversely, how is it not my fight?"

"How do you know it will affect your world adversely? The whale might have died of some…some whale disease."

"Yeah, I suppose so. On the other hand, the whales are unhappy about WestWind for some reason. The Menehune are unhappy about it. The Moloka'ians are unhappy. If I can help, I need to do something."

Clancy covered his eyes with his hands and groaned. "I see that I'm not going to talk you out of this. Okay. Let's think out of the box for a sec. How about finding out who's running this project and talking to them directly? That's got to be less dangerous than swimming around with giant sharks and squid."

"Octopus." Sierra looked at him, this new idea glimmering in her eyes. "That's not a half-bad idea, Clancy. Thanks!" She pulled out her cell phone and began to type in "Ahi Moana + WestWind Project." The search results included images. Clancy looked over her shoulder at the photographs, intrigued by the jack ships Ahi Moana used for offshore wind farm construction.

Sierra muttered to herself, "Stop! No, go back one…there! That's him!"

"That's who?"

Sierra was pointing to the photograph of a slender, dark-haired man in a suit, standing at a podium, evidently speaking at some event. "That's the CEO of Ahi Moana. We met him the day we went out snorkeling!"

"We did?" Clancy peered at the photo doubtfully. "Really?"

"Yeah. Remember the guy on the boat who had all his own equipment with him? We said maybe five words to each other? That's Houghton Roberts, CEO of Ahi Moana."

"Are you sure?"

"Yes! He even told us his name was Houghton. I'm absolutely positive. Actually, he seemed like kind of a nice guy," Sierra said.

Somehow, "nice guy" wasn't consistent with her mental image of a corporate CEO, but who could tell from the few words they had exchanged? "So he's here on Moloka'i! Maybe we can find a way to talk to him."

"The only way to do that is to ask around," said Clancy, now back on solid ground. "Let's start asking."

Sierra and Clancy asked Auntie if she knew whether Roberts was currently on Moloka'i, but Auntie had no idea. They walked to Jack's house and showed the photo on Sierra's phone.

"So you're looking for Roberts, huh?" Jack asked.

"Yes. We met him when we were snorkeling. Do you know if he's still here on Moloka'i?" asked Clancy.

"He isn't here a lot, but he is right now. We got up a little protest group and went out to the company condo to let him know we weren't happy. He opened the door but didn't say anything. Just went back inside."

"So what did you do?" Clancy inquired.

Jack shrugged. "Nothing," he said. "We made our point, so we went home. We aren't interested in making a stink and getting the police involved. We just wanted to deliver the message."

"Can you tell me where he's staying?" asked Sierra eagerly. She was energized by this new direction—a direction that didn't involve chatting with Avatars in the ocean.

"Sure," said Jack.

That evening found Sierra approaching the Ahi Moana company condo. Clancy had wanted to accompany her, but she asked him to stay behind. She felt she could deal better with Roberts one-on-one. She rang the doorbell and waited. Before long, the door opened cautiously and she saw the man she recognized as Houghton Roberts.

Roberts held the door half closed, as though he were prepared to slam it shut. "Can I help you?" he asked, politely enough.

"Mr. Roberts, my name is Sierra Carter. We were out snorkeling together the other day, remember? Can I talk to you for a couple of minutes?"

Roberts hesitated for a moment, and the tension in his face loosened somewhat. But he did not open the door any wider. "Oh, right. I remember you. What did you want to talk about?"

"It's complicated, but it has to do with the WestWind Project. I promise not to be a nuisance."

He hesitated again, his blue eyes searching hers. *Probably wondering just how much of a nutcase I am.* Then he opened the door and stepped aside to let her in.

Sierra had been expecting a luxurious dwelling, but the Ahi Moana company condo was fairly modest. The front of the condo was all lanai, providing a beautiful view of breakers rolling up the beach. Sea spray bejeweled the lanai's screened-in sides. The furniture was the usual rattan-and-tropical-print stuff. One major difference from a tourist condo was the presence of a large desk in the living room, equipped with phone, computer, printer, fax, and several piles of papers. There was a half-full wine glass on the desk, and the desk lamp was lit. She had evidently interrupted Houghton as he was working.

"Can I get you a glass of wine?" he offered, picking up the bottle. She saw it was a California zinfandel from Amador County—a particular favorite.

"Yes, please."

He poured out a glass and handed it to her. "Let's sit in the lanai," he said, leading the way to the screened-in porch. Sierra followed him and sat down. He sat in a chair facing her and sipped his wine.

"So what did you want to say about WestWind?" he asked, staring at her over his wine glass as he turned it around and around in his hands.

She found she didn't know what to say. Driving to the condo, she had rehearsed a number of different openers, all of which now seemed lame. On the other hand, obviously she couldn't start babbling about Menehune, whales, and Avatars.

"Mr. Roberts, it's a mistake," she said, finally. "It's going to be terrible for the humpback whales, and it's damaging to the environment. It's not a good deal for the Moloka'ians. As a matter of fact, it's a terrible deal for them, because they aren't getting any benefit from it at all."

Roberts was silent for several minutes. He set his glass down on a side table and gave her a penetrating blue stare that made her extremely uncomfortable.

"May I ask," he said finally, "what your interest is in this project? I don't think you're from Moloka'i."

"No. I'm not from Moloka'i. I'm from Northern California. I'm just visiting, but I've been talking to people who live here"—*and some not-people,* she thought—"and they're pretty unhappy about WestWind. They think it will damage the whales' breeding and nursery grounds and perhaps damage other organisms as well. But the Moloka'ians also say that they won't benefit from the electricity the project will generate. That it will all go to Honolulu. And I've been told there are no Moloka'ians working on the project, so they won't even get a boost in employment during the construction."

He heard her out, his blue eyes never leaving her face. He paused courteously to make certain she had finished. "You know, I've heard all this before. What they aren't saying is that wind power is good for Hawai'i. The state needs renewable, non-polluting sources of power, and WestWind will provide some of that. The cost of electricity throughout the Islands should begin to drop because of projects like WestWind.

"As for the ecological impact, we did a full assessment, as the law demands, and we got a green light from the environmental agency and the state legislature. It's all legal and aboveboard, and we jumped through every hoop to get this project approved. We are doing this work for the Public Utilities Commission of the State of Hawai'i, and we were never asked to divert any of the electricity to Moloka'i. In fact, the subject never came up.

"Finally, we don't employ any Moloka'ians on the construction because everyone out there is a trained professional. Working onboard a jack ship is highly technical and can be very dangerous.

If there is anyone on Moloka'i with those qualifications, they didn't send us a résumé."

Sierra felt like a beach ball after an encounter with a broken bottle. She had been so full of purpose and intent, but this man had quietly deflated it all. She still had the knowledge of what the Menehune had told Kama Pua'a and the image of the dead baby whale, but she could hardly offer these as a substitute for rational argument with this calm and self-possessed man. He'd dismiss her as a hysterical crazy lady. *And maybe he's right about that,* she thought glumly.

"I see," she said aloud, in lieu of anything more intelligent.

"So what are you doing here on Moloka'i?" he asked to her surprise.

"I'm here on vacation, Mr. Roberts. Sort of. With some friends."

"Please. Call me Huff," he said with a quick, wide smile. Then he looked at her with sudden spark of interest. "You're not one of the tourists who got swept off the sightseeing boat and got stranded, are you?"

"Yes. But if you don't mind, I'd rather not talk about it." *Way too risky.*

"I understand. It must have been a terrible experience," he said sympathetically. *Brother, you have no idea,* said her cynical mind, but her more vulnerable self warmed to his sympathy.

"Yes. It was. This is a delicious zinfandel. Mind if I look at the label? I'd like to pick some up when I get home."

"Help yourself. So how long are you here?"

Sierra pretended to study the wine label. "Um, maybe another week? I didn't intend to come to Moloka'i at all, of course. We had other plans."

"Oh? Who's 'we'?"

"Chaco and I. Uh, Chaco's an old friend. Originally, we were going to Midway Island..." Sierra launched into an explanation of her original plans. Huff listened, clearly focused on what she was saying. He did not appear anxious to get back to the stack of papers on the desk.

"...and since we're here, we decided to spend some time relaxing and having a little fun before we go home," she concluded.

"I didn't know about the program on Midway. That's interesting. I wonder if they would accept corporate sponsorship," Huff asked to her astonishment.

"I suppose they'd jump at it," she replied. "I think the whole program is run on a shoestring—after all, I had to *pay* to go there and work, and they're suspending the program due to lack of funds."

"How much do you know about plastic cleanup in the Pacific Gyre?" he asked, prompting Sierra—who knew quite a bit—into an explanation of the various experiments being conducted on cleaning up plastic particulates in the water.

Two hours and the rest of the bottle of zinfandel later, Sierra roused herself from what had been an engrossing conversation about ocean conservancy to realize the afternoon had fled and evening was closing in. The sun neared the ocean's horizon and the palms outside the condo cast long, purple shadows. She jumped up.

"Wow! I didn't mean to take up so much of your time," she said. "I'm sorry..."

"I'm not," said Huff, rising from his chair. "I enjoyed it." He smiled warmly at her. Sierra realized with a start that he really was a most attractive man. He had short, dark hair, silvering at the sides—just the way a good CEO's hair should look. His face was lean—his nose perhaps a bit too sharp—but enlivened by warm, blue eyes and a charming smile that made the corners of his eyes crinkle. His teeth were white and even. *He looks like a CEO from Central Casting,* Sierra thought, then chastised herself mentally for stereotyping him. Huff had been genuinely interested in the ocean cleanup efforts, and had offered to get Ahi Moana's nonprofit donations manager to look into providing some funding to one or more of the programs that were trying to develop viable cleanup technologies.

"So, you're going ahead with the WestWind Project, I suppose," she asked, looking up into his bright blue eyes. "I don't think I've changed your mind, have I, Huff?"

Roberts shook his head. "I couldn't back out now if I tried. I'd be sued by everyone from our stockholders to the Hawai'i State Legislature. It would take legislation, a Federal court order, and/or an act of god to stop it now. I'm sorry. I mean, I'm not sorry, but I'm sorry that you're so upset about it."

He hesitated then. "Maybe if you came out with me to the jack ships one of these days you'd get a different perspective on it. It's pretty interesting. What do you say?"

"Oh, I, uh," Sierra trailed off. *That was articulate.* "I'd like that. Sure. When?"

"How about day after tomorrow? I'm flying out there in the morning. Meet me at the Kaunakakai helipad at nine a.m." He showed her on Google Maps where the helipad was, then walked her to the door.

"Goodbye, Sierra. See you soon."

Sierra waved and walked away. She didn't notice that Roberts stood in the doorway until long after she had passed out of sight, staring after her.

CHAPTER 19

"So he told me it would take legislation, a court order, or an act of god to stop it," Sierra told her friends over dinner that night. "So I guess it has to be an act of god. Gods."

"What's that mean?" Chaco looked up from Auntie's excellent lomi-lomi salmon.

"I'm going to try to speak with Kauhuhu," said Sierra firmly, taking a bite of fried plantain.

Clancy groaned. "Please don't do it, Sierra. You don't know what you're getting into."

Sierra cocked her head at him. "And you do?"

There wasn't much Clancy could say to that, so he replied, "Then I'm coming too."

Keikilani spoke for the first time since Sierra had begun relating her meeting with Roberts. "No, you can't. That really would be dangerous. You have no powers like Sierra. Kauhuhu and Kanaloa won't recognize you. Besides, it's just a little putt-putt boat. No room."

"I'm small," Fred put in. "Couldn't I go?" The chorus of "Nos" silenced him. Fred resumed his attack on a dish of coconut pudding, which he liked almost—but not quite—as much as chocolate.

"And then the next day," Sierra continued, "I'm going out to the construction site on Huff's helicopter."

There was a small uproar.

"Oh, it's 'Huff' now, is it?" This from Chaco, accompanied by a scowl.

"Why are you doing that?" from Keikilani and Fred in chorus.

"That *does* sound interesting," Clancy said. Sierra cast an appreciative glance his way.

"Maybe he'll take you, too, Clancy. Come with me to the helipad. The worst he can do is say no."

After dinner, Auntie Keikilani insisted that she and Sierra spend some time to prepare. "There's no guarantee that Kauhuhu will show up," she explained. "But with the proper chants and gifts, perhaps he will manifest. I'd like you to help me with the chants."

"What sort of gifts?" Sierra asked uneasily. She had an image of a dead goat being tossed over the side to attract the huge shark. It struck her that supernatural sharks might not be the only ones attracted.

"A lei. Some 'awa."

Sierra breathed a silent sigh of relief.

As Sierra had lost none of her knowledge of Hawai'ian, learning the chants was easy. Then Keikilani helped her run through a series of mental exercises with those twining ribbons of mana. They seemed brighter and stronger than before, and Auntie was satisfied.

"I hope—that is, I don't think that you'll need to call on your powers if you're not being attacked. But you need to keep practicing, keep your mana strong to protect yourself," she said. "From what you told us, the Avatars sense your powers and are drawn to them."

"Yeah," Sierra said. She was reassured by the apparent strength of her mana, but she still felt insecure about her powers when confronted by these ancient gods. She dreaded the next day's adventure, but said nothing to the others about her fears. They could do nothing, and she knew that sharing her fears would make Clancy even more insistent on being there, despite the fact he could contribute nothing beyond his own worry and desire to protect her. Besides, Keikilani would be the one in the water, not Sierra, and she felt a bit ashamed of her anxiety.

• • •

They drove in Auntie's battered Ford to one of the fishponds on the eastern shore of the island. This one was in good repair, unlike the ones Sierra had glimpsed from *Polupolu* as they chugged past. There was only one gap in the seawall, allowing water to flow in and out. The surface of the pond wall rising above the calm eastern waters was flat and frosted with white coral. It was broad enough to walk on.

"Cousin of mine lives here," said Keikilani, bending over a small, red boat that was hauled up and anchored on the sandy beach to one side of the pond. "He keeps up the pond, fishes in it. Grows taro. He likes living the simple life, I guess."

Sierra helped Auntie drag the little boat to the water's edge, where both women stepped in. Auntie deposited her duffel bag with snorkeling equipment and other supplies on the floor of the boat and revved the little outboard motor. Soon they were putt-putting gently over the swells, heading away from the shore. Peering into the glassy water and shading her eyes against the morning sun, Sierra could see corals and fish below. They passed a turtle sunning himself at the surface and saw some small manta rays "flying" along through the clear depths.

They were about a mile out from the shore when Auntie stopped the boat and moored to a floating buoy. Sierra peered over the side, seeing corals quite close to the surface.

"It's pretty shallow for being so far out from shore," she remarked.

"It's a fringe reef," returned Keikilani. "The most extensive reef in the Islands. It's pretty shallow for about a mile out in some places. Now, you say Kauhuhu appeared to you in deep water?"

"Yes. I'd been swimming along over the corals and before I knew it, I found myself in deep water."

"There's a deep hole just a few yards directly ahead. I'll swim out there—but not just yet," Auntie said. "We still have our chants and offerings to make."

As the little boat rocked on the swells, Keikilani dug into her bag and produced a long, leafy lei. There were no flowers in it, just long, slender leaves. It wasn't fashioned in a circle, but as a kind of long garland. Auntie draped this around her shoulders.

"Maile leaf," she said by way of explanation. Sierra could smell a delicate, almost vanilla scent from the leaves, discernible even above the briny smell of the ocean.

Auntie Keikilani began to chant, and Sierra joined in with enthusiasm as they asked for Kauhuhu's protection and good will. Auntie sprinkled 'awa and flowers over the water. Then she removed the maile lei from her shoulders and dropped it onto the surface of the water, where it floated, twining like seaweed.

Auntie Keikilani sat back, looking at Sierra. "Here I go," she said. "May my 'aumakua and all the gods protect me."

Auntie fitted the mask over her face and rolled over the side of the boat, where she expertly slipped on her swim fins. She waved at Sierra and began swimming slowly away from the boat. Sierra watched her closely, not wanting to take her eyes from Auntie for a second. The older woman swam gracefully to a point at least twenty yards distant, where she stopped and floated. Sierra assumed this must be the deep hole Auntie had mentioned.

Sierra sat in the hot sun and watched. Sweat drenched her even as the sea breeze cooled her skin. The boat rocked with a gentle, soothing motion. A pod of dolphins swam past, noted the boat and began tumbling around her, occasionally poking their heads out of the water and gazing at Sierra with bright black eyes. When the pod finally moved off, Sierra realized she had been so fascinated by the dolphins' antics she had lost track of Auntie.

Panicked, she scanned the patch of ocean where she thought Auntie should be, but there was no sign of her. Sunlight glanced off the ripples and speared Sierra's eyes, making them water. She rubbed her eyes fiercely and looked again. There she was! Auntie was no longer floating in one spot. She was swimming back to the little red boat.

Auntie handed up her flippers to Sierra. Getting her back into the boat was a bit precarious, but they finally managed it. She sat panting and dripping on the center thwart as she removed her mask and snorkel. Her long, curly hair snaked down her back like seaweed.

"Did you see Kanaloa?" Sierra asked eagerly, but Auntie shook her head.

"No. I called and called, but no luck. I started to get tired and came back." Auntie Keikilani sounded disappointed. Sierra reflected that disappointment wouldn't be her own response.

"So I guess it's your turn," said Auntie, handing Sierra the snorkel and mask. Sierra took them with a sinking in the pit of her stomach.

"What if he doesn't appear to me, either?"

Auntie shrugged. "Then we go home and have some lunch."

Sierra donned mask and snorkel, setting them on the top of her head like an awkward and ugly hat, and clambered over the side, setting the little boat to rocking violently. Once Sierra was in the water, Auntie handed down the fins and Sierra, floating on her back, slipped them onto her feet. Then she pulled her mask down, rolled over and as Auntie pointed the way, swam away from the fragile shelter of the little red boat. She snorkeled as she went, not looking for colorful fish this time, but seeking the deeper water. And keeping a sharp eye out for sharks.

Sailing over the colorful corals, she abruptly found herself suspended over nothingness—a deep, blue hole. She could still see the corals behind her, but directly below and ahead of her she could see nothing but blue. She hung suspended in the warm water, floating and—if she were to be honest—praying. She had no reason to trust Kauhuhu. From her point of view, there was every reason to distrust a god that took the form of a white shark the size of a decent-sized fishing boat. She frequently raised her head to get her bearings on the little red boat and Auntie Keikilani—the closest thing to safety. And she didn't venture too far out over the deep water, staying near the shelf of corals at the edge. It would probably make no difference if things went bad, but it prevented her from panicking.

After hanging in the water for what seemed like hours, chanting soundlessly to call Kanaloa, she looked up to spot Keikilani and the red boat, waved to reassure the other woman, who waved back, then put her mask into the water again—to find herself face to face with the dead blue eyes and grisly teeth of the great shark Kauhuhu. The adrenaline rush almost made her black out and she inadvertently took in seawater through her snorkel with a sharply indrawn breath of panic. When the black spots in front of her eyes cleared and she had coughed up all the salt water, the enormous shark was still there, unmoving except for the passage of water through its fluttering gills. The gills looked like knife wounds in a corpse, black against its pallid flesh. The shark's "face" had no expression, of course, but its mouth was open a few inches, exposing only the serrated bottom teeth. For some reason, this gave it, if not a friendly air, at least a less-threatening appearance.

Sierra, as still as death in the water, tried reaching out with her powers. This was not an offensive hurling of her mana, as she had attempted against Kanaloa. She untwined the glowing ribbons and allowed them to gently expand beyond her body. They coiled though the water and twined around the shark's heavy torso in streamers of colored light.

The shark hung motionless within this basket of light, as though the touch of her mana were a pleasant sensation. She addressed it mentally. "Kauhuhu, thank you for coming to me. I wouldn't have asked if it weren't gravely important."

As the shark studied her, Sierra explained about the wind farm west of Moloka'i. She asked Kauhuhu if he had heard the whales singing about it but received no response. She told him about the dead baby whale. A deep voice began to resonate inside her head. The voice was toneless, smooth, and somehow dark. It chilled her to her core despite the warmth of the sun and water.

"Things die," said the voice. "Everything dies. There are the eaters and the eaten, but even the eaters die and are eaten in their turn."

There wasn't much she could say to that, but she tried again. "The whales aren't the only issue. The construction will kill many corals and other animals. And the people of Moloka'i don't like it either. I asked Kanaloa about it, but he, um, left without saying anything."

The huge white shark rested in the water, still allowing Sierra's mana to caress it. "Who are you?" it asked finally.

Sierra tried to explain who she was and why she wanted Kauhuhu's help. "So you're the protector of Moloka'i," she finished. "That's why I've come to you. I think you—and maybe Kanaloa—are the last hope for stopping this."

The shark made no immediate response, but when Sierra glanced down, she saw movement in the deep blue. It looked like an enormous nest of pale eels writhing up toward her, but before she had time to react, she realized it was Kanaloa, swimming up swiftly from the depths. Kanaloa reached out a long, long tentacle and gripped her thigh, not pulling her under—Sierra's adrenaline-fueled first take—but merely contacting her. She could feel the cold, sticky softness of the Avatar's dead-white skin. Then Kanaloa's voice spoke.

"We hear. We understand."

Abruptly, the tentacle released her and Sierra was enveloped in a roiling cloud of bubbles. When the water cleared, there was nothing to be seen. She immediately set out for the little red boat as fast as she could go and arrived panting with exertion and frayed nerves. Getting back in the boat was a bit iffy and they came close to capsizing once or twice, but Sierra finally heaved herself over the side with Auntie's help. She collapsed on one of the benches and pulled off her mask. Keikilani offered her a drink of water and peered into her face with concern.

"Are you okay?"

"Yes," Sierra gulped. "Yes, but can we get back to dry land right now, please?"

CHAPTER 20

"How do you know that Kanaloa and Kauhuhu will actually help?" asked Clancy. They were having another dinner at Auntie's house. Chaco had picked up supplies in town and was preparing a delicious meal of locally raised pork tenderloin with pineapple and fresh veggies from Kumu Farms. Mortality hadn't impaired his ability to cook, Sierra decided.

"I don't," Sierra said. "Avatars almost never tell you anything straightforward. They're always mysterious. Why is that, Chaco?"

Chaco looked up from his work, surprised. "I'm never mysterious," he protested. "I always say what I mean." He blushed slightly under Sierra's steady gaze. "Well, almost always," he admitted. "If I'm trying to impress someone I might get a little obscure. Just for effect."

"So you're still going out to the construction site tomorrow?" Chaco asked.

"Yes!" Clancy said with enthusiasm. "I hope Roberts lets me go, too. I'd *really* like to see the jack ships." Sierra just nodded her head and looked at Clancy fondly. Chaco noted this quietly. He picked up his plate and glass and took them into the kitchen. No one noticed his glum expression because it wasn't much different from the glum expression he had worn almost continually since becoming mortal. And no one noticed when he quietly slipped out of the kitchen and went to his room.

The next morning, Clancy drove Sierra to the helipad near Kaunakakai. When they arrived, a helicopter was waiting and so was Roberts. Sierra introduced Clancy. He and Roberts shook hands and Clancy said, "I know I'm butting in here, but I was wondering if I could come, too? I was reading up on jack ships, and they're fascinating. I'd love to see one."

Roberts looked a bit surprised but readily responded, "Sure. You'll have to sit in the back, though."

"Not a problem."

"Then let's get going." Roberts gave them ear protectors and showed them how to climb into the 'copter and strap in. Within minutes they had lifted straight up from the ground and were flying west over the island. Conversation was impossible in the racket from the rotors. From the rear seat, sitting next to Clancy, Sierra could see a panoramic view of bright red earth, deep black lava rock, and the vivid green of fields, orchards, and grassy meadows. To the north, she could see the land rising gently to the top of the forested pali; to the south, ocean; and in the hazy blue distance beyond she could see other islands as dim, gray-blue shadows across the sea.

Before long, they passed over white breakers dashing themselves against the western rocks. Then they left the island behind and flew over the open ocean. Not long after leaving the west shore of Molokaʻi, one of the jack ships became visible, looking like a toy boat on the surface of the sea. As they drew closer and began to land, Sierra was astonished at the size of the ship. Longer by a third than a football field, it resembled nothing so much as a factory suspended above the ocean on six massive legs constructed of latticed steel girders. The helicopter pilot brought them down expertly on the ship's helipad and they debarked, bending low under the craft's rotors even though the blades were well above their heads.

"Welcome to *Jack of Diamonds*," Roberts said.

Roberts was clearly proud of his operation. He gave them a thorough tour of the vessel and explained how it operated. The crew was in the process of lowering one of the wind turbine shafts onto a base that had already been installed on the seafloor. The base poked up from the water, a bright yellow pillar with a railed-in work platform near the top. Sierra tilted her head up to look at the two-hundred-foot-long white tower, now suspended from a gigantic crane mounted on the jack ship. The crane was gently, slowly manipulating this upright length over the side of the ship, positioning it to slide into the waiting base. It quickly became obvious why the ship was jacked up on its six legs; it would have been impossible to achieve this precision work from the deck of a ship bobbing about on the ocean swells. As it was, the jack ship's legs provided a stable platform from which to work.

Although Sierra, Clancy, and Roberts were well away from the active work site, the installation made Sierra nervous. The shaft was huge, suspended from an even larger crane, and it seemed to sway dangerously in the steady offshore wind.

Then she gasped, "There are people working down there! In the base. Won't they be crushed?"

"No. It's dangerous work, but the crane operators know what they're doing. Just watch," replied Roberts.

Sierra did watch, hardly able to breathe, as the immense tower, as tall as a smokestack, descended onto the base, the workers in the base making micro-adjustments as the tube descended, a centimeter at a time. Finally, the massive shaft rested gently and precisely on the base, hiding the workers within.

"How do they get out?" Clancy asked.

"There's a ladder inside," replied Roberts. "Right now, they're joining the two parts together. When they're finished, they'll climb down and come out on the work platform below." He pointed to the bright yellow platform. "There's also a one-person lift inside the shaft, but it's not operational yet." Roberts suddenly stiffened, and craned over the railing of the platform where they stood watching the operation. "What the hell is *that*?"

Sierra and Clancy looked down where Roberts was pointing. The water around the base of the tower had begun to roil and bubble as though boiling. Gradually the entire base began to rock. The newly placed shaft was not yet secured to the base, so as the base rocked one way, the unsecured tower began to tilt in the other. At first, it was hard to see what was happening; the movement was slight, nearly imperceptible. As the water became more and more turbulent, the rocking became more obvious. Alarmed shouts went up all over the jack ship as people realized what was happening. Evidently this had never happened before because the crew seemed uncertain what to do.

Roberts pulled out a two-way radio. "Control! Do you read me, Control?" The crackling affirmation was returned at once. "Don't release the shaft! Repeat, DO NOT release the shaft!" The crane was still attached to the top of the shaft. The reason for Roberts' order became apparent as shaft and base parted and the shaft swung free—still under the control of the crane, though swaying in long arcs that brought it dangerously close to the jack ship itself. Sierra could see the hard-hatted workers cowering on top of the base. Then they swarmed down the ladder inside the base, evidently aiming for the work platform below. The water around the base boiled green and white as it continued to rock. Sierra saw the first worker emerge from the base onto the yellow work platform just as it disappeared beneath the turbid water, workers and all.

Sierra watched in paralyzed horror as boats were launched to rescue the workers. She didn't feel Clancy's strong arms around her. She didn't hear Roberts shouting orders over his radio. She didn't hear the cries and confusion all over the jack ship as workers struggled to bring the tower back under control and stow it safely onboard before another disaster occurred. She could not take her eyes off the water, scanning it obsessively for surviving men.

Though both Clancy and Roberts urged her away from the deck where they had stood to watch the installation, Sierra would not budge. She watched the boats cautiously approach the boiling water, now beginning to calm. She saw crewmembers on board the rescue vessels scanning for survivors. Finally, a small, yellow object drifted up from the depths. It was a hardhat, identical to the ones worn by every crewmember.

The next few minutes seemed to take forever as the boats patrolled the area so recently occupied by the bright yellow base. After what seemed years, five people appeared on the surface of the ocean, flailing and waving, and boats sped to their rescue, men hauling their sodden co-workers over the sides to safety.

As Sierra drew a long breath of relief, it turned into a groan. "Clancy!" she whispered urgently. "Look down there. Where the people were. In the water."

Clancy looked down again and drew in his breath. The workers were all safely aboard the boats, which were pulling back to the ship. But where they had emerged from the water there were several long, gray-brown bodies swimming, sharp dorsal fins cutting the surface like knives.

"Sharks," he breathed.

CHAPTER 21

Many long hours passed before Sierra and Clancy returned to Kaunakakai. Roberts—when he finally remembered his guests—had them escorted to the jack ship's mess hall to wait. No one else was there. Everyone was out trying to assess the damage, secure the equipment, or take care of the survivors.

Sierra collapsed into one of the chairs and put her head down on the table. She did not weep. The icy certainty that she had nearly caused the deaths of several innocent people was too great a weight for tears. Clancy put his arm around her shoulders.

"That was a terrible thing to see," he said somberly.

Sierra whipped her head up. "It was because of me. Kauhuhu and Kanaloa destroyed the tower and almost killed those poor people. And there were sharks there. Just waiting. Kauhuhu and Kanaloa must have sent them. There was no other reason for a bunch of tiger sharks to show up en masse." She shuddered. "Horrible."

"How do you know that? It might have been some underwater phenomenon. Maybe an earthquake."

Sierra shook her head. "No. You could tell no one working here has ever seen or heard of anything like it. They were completely unprepared for this. This happened because of *me*." She felt as though there were a steel fist around her heart, squeezing. Her hands felt numb and her head throbbed. Her eyes, dry as they were, ached. If only she had just spent her time relaxing on the beach, this wouldn't have happened. And it could have been so much worse. *What gives me the right to stick my nose into other people's business? What gives me the right to use these powers? Why did I not know what the consequences could be?*

"Clancy, I've got to stop them," she said. "What if they keep on doing this? Someone will be killed—maybe a lot of people. What if they attack the jack ship?"

"The jack ship is huge," responded Clancy. "Do you really think they could affect it?"

Sierra looked at him. "These things are gods, Clancy. Avatars. Kanaloa is the god of the sea. Can you imagine something he could serve up that would take the jack ship down?"

Clancy was quiet for a moment. Then his eyes widened. "Yes. I can. You're right. We have to stop them."

Sierra was not so deeply perturbed that she missed the "we" in Clancy's statement, and it filled her with warmth. She and Clancy spent the next several hours fretting over the delay in returning to Kaunakakai. They both wanted to consult with Auntie Keikilani about their next steps.

Roberts turned up late in the day. His normally sleek hair was sticking up in tufts. There were dark circles under his blue eyes, and his jaw was blue with five o'clock shadow. His clothes were rumpled, damp, and stained.

"Everybody okay here?" he inquired. When they nodded, he continued. "Sorry about all this. None of us have ever seen anything like this before. We're still trying to figure out what happened. The base had been securely installed. Everything was pretty much ideal—until it wasn't." He sat heavily on one of the chairs.

"I can't leave yet, but the pilot will take you back to Kaunakakai now. Again, my apologies." He gave them a worn, warm smile, and Sierra again realized that Houghton Roberts was an attractive man. "Here's my business card." He handed a card to both Sierra and Clancy. "Maybe if I can get to the bottom of what's happening here, I can bring you back and you can have a better experience."

The flight back to Kaunakakai was as noisy as before and equally devoid of conversation. As they touched down at the helipad, the sun was beginning its slow descent to the west and Sierra realized she was hungry. She and Clancy had eaten many hours ago, but there had been no thought of eating aboard *Jack of Diamonds*.

They drove back to Auntie's house and found Chaco preparing dinner. He was working on chalupas poblanas, one of his favorite dishes. Fred (who had been trained by Chaco) made tortillas with the concentration of a television chef de cuisine. Standing on a kitchen stool, he kneaded the masa flour and patted out little rounds with his green, six-fingered paws before frying them. He wore a small, frilly apron that would have looked entirely appropriate on a 1950s ad depicting the perfect housewife.

"How'd it go?" asked Keikilani as Sierra and Clancy entered the kitchen.

"Disaster!" Sierra replied, and told the whole story.

When she finished, there was a stunned silence in Auntie's kitchen. Everyone stopped what they were doing, including Fred. As he gaped at Sierra, a small, uncooked tortilla slipped from his paws and landed with a small plop on the floor.

"Auntie, do you know of any way to stop Kauhuhu and Kanaloa?" asked Sierra.

Auntie shook her silver-threaded mop of curly hair. "No," she said flatly. "You can go out there and ask them again, but I don't know if it will work. We've set some very ancient powers in motion."

"Yes, but I didn't think they'd kill people. Or try to." Sierra remembered the hunting tiger sharks in the water so recently vacated by the workers that fell from the base and shuddered.

Auntie gazed at her in amazement. "You haven't read any of our mo'olelo, our old stories, have you?" Sierra shook her head. "Sacrifice and death were always the dark side of the old ways," Keikilani said. "We pay more attention now to aloha—love—and the path of light. But death and violence were more prevalent in ancient times. Kanaloa brings us fresh water, delicious fish, and waves for surfing, but he also brings sharks, hurricanes, floods, and tsunamis. Kauhuhu is a protector of this island, but he has always brought death to the enemies of Moloka'i."

"Yes, I understand. But will they stop if I ask them?"

"I don't know."

Sierra pulled at her long braid with nervous fingers. "I suppose I should go back in the water. I should plead with them to stop. Oh, jeez," she groaned. The idea of confronting the Avatars again was bone-chilling. *What if I ask for the wrong thing again?* she wondered.

"Don't do that," Fred said quietly. All eyes turned to the mannegishi. He was sitting on the kitchen stool, his frilly apron spilling over the sides like a wedding dress. Flour dusted his paws and face.

"Why not?' asked Sierra. She hoped desperately that Fred had a good reason.

"This has gotten too big and too serious. You haven't got the mana to actively *oppose* these Avatars. Am I right, Auntie?"

Auntie Keikilani gazed at the little green creature seriously, then turned her eyes to Sierra. After a moment, she nodded. "Fred's right, Sierra. Kauhuhu and Kanaloa are working together. If they oppose you, if they view you as an obstacle to the work they've started—well, dangerous doesn't begin to describe it."

"I can't just sit here and let them kill people!" Sierra cried. "I'm responsible!"

"Actually," Fred said, "It isn't *your* responsibility."

"How so? I asked them—asked them personally—to stop the WestWind Project."

"And I heard Kama Pua'a promise the Menehune that *he* would do something about it," said Fred. "You heard him, too. Kama is a powerful Avatar, and you're not. Let's ask Kama to keep his promise."

Chaco looked at Fred with respect. "Fred, once in a while you're a real genius!"

At this unexpected and extremely rare compliment, Fred blushed a deeper shade of viridian and modestly returned to patting out tortillas.

"Well done, Fred!" said Clancy, obviously relieved that Sierra might not be required to confront Kanaloa and Kauhuhu directly.

Sierra kissed Fred on the top of his smooth, green head, and the little creature flashed her a pleased orange glance.

"Now, how do we find Kama Puaʻa?" Clancy asked, turning to Auntie Keikilani.

"I don't know," she said, shaking her curls. "But I do know he makes his permanent home on Hawaiʻi—that is, the Big Island. He lives on the windward side, the side that gets the rain. It's very jungle-y. But I don't know exactly where he lives on that side of the island, and it's a lot of territory to cover."

"I'll make plane reservations for tomorrow," said Clancy, rising.

"I don't think it would be a good idea for you to go, Clancy," said Auntie.

"Why not?"

"Kama Puaʻa knows Chaco and Sierra, but he doesn't know you. They might be able to find him if he wants to be found, but if you're with them, he may not reveal himself."

Clancy said nothing, but his scowl told it all. Sierra put her hand on his shoulder.

"Auntie's probably right, Clancy. I know you want to help, but Chaco and I will be fine. Auntie, can you teach me a chant? To call Kama? That might help."

Auntie nodded. "Let's learn it tomorrow, when we're fresher. Also, we can plan how to search for him. I know the windward side of the Big Island fairly well—I worked there for a few years as a young woman, and I have relatives there."

Sierra's cell phone rang, making everyone jump. "Hello?" she said. "Really? Right now? Yes, we'll come get you."

Sierra turned to the little group in the kitchen. "You won't believe this! Rose is at the Kaunakakai Airport. She says she, Mama, and Kaylee have a surprise for Chaco. I wonder what it could be?"

CHAPTER 22

Clancy and an extremely curious Chaco drove to the airport in Clancy's rental car to pick up the new arrival. Rose was waiting on the sidewalk outside the tiny terminal building, wearing her usual outfit of T-shirt and jeans. Her thick, black hair was neatly braided, and she wore a heavy Navajo silver necklace with her casual garb. Clancy felt an unaccustomed surge of warmth and friendship as he greeted her and picked up her luggage.

"You have a surprise for me?" asked Chaco. He tried not to sound hopeful, but there was anticipation in his voice.

"All in good time," said Rose with a sly smile. "Where we are going?"

"We want you to meet a local lady, Auntie Keikilani," Clancy started, but Rose interrupted him.

"Is that her first name? Auntie?"

"No, 'Auntie' or 'Uncle' are terms of respect," Chaco explained. "You're gonna like her. She's a kahuna."

"What's a kahuna?" Rose inquired.

"Like you. A shaman. Someone who preserves the knowledge of the old ways. She knows all about me and Fred, and she knows a ton about Moloka'ian lore."

"I'm looking forward to meeting her!" Rose replied.

"Anyway, as I was saying," Clancy broke in, "I'm taking you to Auntie's house. Sierra and Fred are waiting for you there. By the way, where are you going to stay? Auntie's house is kind of small, and so is Jack's house, where we're staying."

"I reserved a hotel room."

Clancy stared at her in surprise. "I tried to get a room, but no deal. I guess you've got influence here."

"Just lucky. Timing is everything, you know," said Rose, smiling at him.

Soon, they pulled up outside Auntie's house. Rose picked a colorful bag from her luggage and emerged from the car. Keikilani burst from the front door, arms held wide.

"Aloha!" she cried, and kissed Rose on the cheek. "I don't have leis to welcome you, but we do have dinner ready. Come in, come in." She bustled back into the house, followed by her guests.

Sierra greeted Rose fondly and served her dinner. Fred and Chaco had made plenty of food, more than enough to feed an extra mouth. Rose tucked in eagerly, having experienced Chaco's cooking skills before.

As the last of the chalupas disappeared, Rose sat back and regarded Chaco with a serene smile. "Sierra told us—me, Kaylee, and Mama—that you have a bit of a problem," she said.

"Yeah, Rose. A big problem," Chaco replied. "Can you help me?"

"We'll see. Sierra said that as soon as you lost contact with your native earth, your Avatar powers completely disappeared. She also said you didn't want to come home because you were afraid that even if you did, you might not get your powers back."

"That's not the only reason," Chaco said defensively. "I also have a strong feeling that I'm supposed to stay here for now. I may not have my powers, but I still have intuition."

"Right. Anyway, I was thinking about this, and I thought, why couldn't we bring you some of your native earth? Maybe contact with it would restore your powers even though you're far away."

Chaco sat forward, quivering. He reminded Sierra of a dog that has just sighted a squirrel. *"Where is it?"*

"Me and Mama and Kaylee talked about it, and decided that just bringing a suitcase full of dirt probably wouldn't work. You can't live in a suitcase. So we put our heads together and came up with a way that you can be in contact with your land and still be able to walk around and do what you need to do."

Rose opened the bag she had carried into the house and reached inside. She held up a vest-like garment made of tan canvas. It was quilted like the kind of vest that people wear to work outside in cold climates, but appeared far heavier. It was embroidered with Native American symbols and designs around the neck and down the front.

"We all worked on it," Rose said proudly. "Mama designed the vest, Kaylee sewed and stuffed it, and I embroidered it." She held it out to Chaco. "Try it on."

Sierra turned her attention to Chaco. He had gone pale beneath his tanned skin. She noticed beads of sweat beginning to form on his forehead. He made no move to take the vest.

"What if it doesn't work?" he half whispered.

"Then you're no worse off, are you?" Sierra said briskly. "Put it on, Chaco."

Chaco took the vest from Rose. He laid it across his lap and looked at the lining. It was made of some sort of fine mesh.

"The idea is that the earth we sewed into the vest can escape a little at a time to be in contact with your skin," explained Rose. "If it works, it won't work forever. But it should last until you get home. You can't wear it over your clothes, obviously, and I guess you'll need to bathe a lot..."

Chaco shucked off his T-shirt, revealing a long, leanly muscled brown torso. He slid one arm into the vest, then another. He fastened the zipper in the front and sat back, tense and expectant.

Sierra watched Chaco's face. At first, there seemed to be no change. Then she looked at his eyes. They were no longer a dull hazel, but a bright, feral yellow-amber: the eyes of a coyote. His skin seemed to glow with an inner light. Then he began to change, melting and twisting like warm wax. His legs and arms shrank, twisted and re-formed in a way that always made Sierra's stomach lurch. His face lengthened and sprouted luxuriant fur. Soon, a coyote stood in front of them. Unlike most coyotes, however, this one was wearing a beautifully embroidered tan vest.

Auntie Keikilani knew intellectually what Chaco must be capable of as an Avatar, but she shrieked at this abrupt transformation, then apologized. Everyone else was used to seeing their handsome friend turn into an equally handsome coyote, and they were busy congratulating him on this happy turn of events.

Sierra was close to tears. She had never petted Chaco in coyote form because although he had deep, soft, and eminently pettable fur, he was also an ancient god, and petting an ancient god did not seem wise or respectful. But now she was on her knees beside him, face buried in his thick fur. "Oh, I'm *so* glad for you, Chaco! This is wonderful! Now you know you can go home, and you'll be fine."

Everyone else offered more verbal congratulations, including Auntie, who had recovered from her shock. Chaco morphed back into his delicious human form again. He was grinning from ear to ear—*like a coyote*, Sierra thought—and he hugged everyone. Even Clancy accepted Chaco's happy embrace, clapping him on the back—then sneezing as a small cloud of dust erupted from the fabric of the vest.

"It's not a perfect solution," admitted Rose. And you're going to have to be careful around water. If the earth is washed away, you'll go back to being mortal, of course."

"I'll be careful," promised Chaco, and kissed her cheek, his wild golden eyes dancing. "Thank you, thank you, thank you!"

A little research and a long talk with Auntie convinced Sierra and Chaco to spend a couple of days preparing for their journey to find Kama Pua'a. Auntie felt that their best chance of finding him was somewhere around the Kohala Peninsula.

"Kohala is the wettest area of the Big Island," she told them. "Kama and Pele have agreed that because fire and water will always quarrel, Kama Pua'a stays on the windward side—the rainy side—and Pele stays on the dry side. Kohala is the wettest part of the island and it's also about as far as Kama Pua'a can get from Kilauwea, where Pele lives, without leaving the island."

Auntie also told them they would be traveling in extremely rough country. "There's a big nature preserve. You won't find Kama by sticking to the maintained trails, but if the rangers catch you off-trail in the park, you're going to be ticketed and escorted out. You'll need to plan for every contingency and be able to survive for several days. You can't carry enough water to avoid using the streams as a source, so we'll need water treatments—for you. I assume now that Chaco has his mana back, he doesn't get sick. We have very few harmful animals—maybe a few poisonous spiders or centipedes—but the terrain is hazardous. For heaven's sake, don't fall down a lava tube! Better take rope, and a first aid kit, and…"

She continued to list the necessities. Sierra longed for her camping gear at home, and she knew Auntie was right—she would have to prepare well. It was a bit different for Chaco. He could wear his bulky vest and morph into a four-legged, agile creature that could handle the rough terrain without difficulty. As an Avatar, he was also impervious to infection, injury, and all the other ills to which human beings are heir.

She knew she would be gone from Moloka'i for a few days and felt guilty about the damage Kauhuhu and Kanaloa might be doing out at the WestWind Project during her absence. Sierra fished around in her jeans pocket and pulled out Roberts' business card.

Roberts answered his phone curtly, taking her aback slightly. "Um, hi, Huff," she said warily. "It's Sierra Carter."

"Oh. Hi, Sierra." His voice warmed perceptibly. "How are you?"

"I'm great, Huff. Thanks for taking us out to the ship the other day. Sorry about the accident."

"Yeah. We're still looking into it."

"Has it happened again?"

"No. We aren't doing any new work until we get to the bottom of it. I sent divers down there but they couldn't see anything but the wreckage of the base. Strange. They had to be really cautious—we've seen a lot more sharks in the area than usual." He broke off, heaving a deep sigh.

"Oh, sorry to hear that. So you're not doing any more installations?"

"Nope. Listen, it's great talking, but I gotta run. Are you still here in Moloka'i? Maybe we could meet for dinner some night?"

"I'm on Moloka'i right now, Huff, but I'm going to the Big Island for a few days. I'll call you when I get back, okay?"

"Sure. That would be great. Take care."

Her conscience soothed, Sierra went to work trying to find the necessities she and Chaco would need. Moloka'i's stores had limited selections, so she and Chaco took the ferry to Mau'i and found much of what they required.

"I have some chants I want you to learn," Auntie told them. "You will need to take a chicken, a fish, a banana, and 'awa as offerings to him. Otherwise, he's not likely to notice that you're looking for him." She went on to list all the things they needed to be aware of, and taught them a chant of offering and appeal to the Avatar. Sierra and Chaco listened dutifully and learned the chants by heart. Chaco thought he could appeal to Kama on an Avatar-to-Avatar basis, but Sierra wanted to make sure they also knew the traditional and respectful approach.

After three days of frenetic preparation, it was time to go. They said goodbye to Auntie, Fred, and Rose. Sierra said a private goodbye to Clancy, who kissed her warmly, but he was obviously still unhappy about not going on the expedition.

CHAPTER 23

The plane touched down at Hilo International Airport. Chaco and Sierra collected their baggage at the terminal building which, though not huge, was gigantic compared with the dollhouse-sized terminal in Kaunakakai. Then they rented a car and began driving to the Kohala Peninsula.

The windward side of Hawai'i was indeed jungle, lush with giant bamboo, tall-canopied trees, vines, ferns, and flowers. It was a beautiful drive, with the ocean often visible to their right, and an occasional distant waterfall to the left, draining water from the mountains of the interior.

Neither Chaco nor Sierra said much during the drive. Sierra fretted over how they would ever find Kama Pua'a on this huge island with its dense jungle and difficult terrain. She wondered why Chaco was so quiet, and turned to ask him.

And smiled. Chaco, eyes bright, was sitting in the passenger seat and staring eagerly out the window. A half-smile curved his wide mouth, and he radiated energy, happiness, and enthusiasm. This was *her* Chaco, not the mopey wet blanket she'd been hanging around lately. He wore his tan vest over his bare torso, leaving long, nicely muscled arms exposed. If the vest was uncomfortable in this hot, humid climate, he didn't seem to mind. He wasn't even sweating.

After nearly two hours of driving, they came to the area Auntie thought was the most likely possibility for Kama's residence.

"Waipio Valley and Pu'u O Umi Natural Area Reserve," read the sign, and Sierra turned off the main road and followed signs to the reserve. She knew she and Chaco would be breaking many of the Reserve's rules—if not all of them—and she apologized silently to—whom? The god of park systems?

She didn't want to leave the car where rangers or others might discover it, so she took her time finding a secluded place to park under a stand of thickly canopied trees. They spread branches and debris over the car to further assure it wouldn't be spotted. Then she hefted her pack—Chaco had no pack, as he planned to undertake the journey as a coyote—and stood, staring at the dense undergrowth in front of them.

Chaco morphed as soon as he left the car and plunged into the heavy vegetation without hesitation.

"Wait, Chaco!" she cried. "I can't get through this stuff as easily as you can."

Chaco returned, tongue lolling. "Sorry. I forgot how pitifully slow and awkward humans are."

"Really? How soon you've forgotten your brush with mortality," retorted Sierra. "Slow down."

The rest of the day was, to put it mildly, a slog. Following Auntie's instructions, they traveled well away from trails, buildings, or other signs of human presence. The untrammeled vegetation was dense. Sierra had to work hard to avoid leaving an obvious trail of destruction behind her, so it was slow going indeed. Despite the sweat and liquefied sunscreen stinging her eyes, she was able to note and appreciate unfamiliar birdcalls and admire the exotic flowers. Once, she saw a long-legged yellow spider with a colorful "happy face" pattern on its upper abdomen. She recalled her encounter with Kóhk'ang Wuhti—Spider Grandmother—during her earlier adventures and passed by carefully without disturbing its web. Chaco, in the meantime, slipped through the undergrowth on four legs with incredible ease, never cracking a twig or making the branches slap in his wake. Panting and crashing behind him, Sierra tried to keep him in sight, but often she couldn't see so much as the black tip of his tail among the bushes, ferns, and vines.

The terrain was every bit as rugged as predicted. When the lush growth wasn't the issue, with vines and roots entrapping

Sierra's feet, she had to work around soft bogs for fear of literally bogging down in the deep mire. Jagged lava rocks threatened to trip her—and because the rocks were frequently covered with mosses or ferns, she sometimes didn't realize they were there until it was too late to avoid them. A map might have been helpful, except for the fact there was no map to wherever Kama Pua'a was living, and there were no maps documenting this off-trail and entirely illegal expedition.

The weather, which had been threatening, decided to carry through with its plans. It grew dark overhead, followed by grumbling thunder, flashes of lightning, and the torrential downpour of a tropical storm. Within seconds, Sierra was soaked to the skin. The footing, treacherous to begin with, became even more difficult, encrusting her boots in mud. Surfaces that had been reasonably firm became slippery, slowing her progress still further.

Chaco reappeared by her side, looking worried. "I can't let the rain wash the earth out of the vest," he panted. "I've got to find shelter!"

Chaco morphed back into his human form and they looked for a sheltered space beneath the trees. The storm let up, and they were able to find a fairly dry campsite. Sierra pulled her small tent from her backpack, and they began setting it up.

"Only one tent?" he asked, looking at her slyly with one eyebrow raised and a wide smile. His face was alight with cheerful mischief, and Sierra was struck again by the change in her friend. Attractive didn't begin to describe him. He was glowing with good health and happiness, and she realized abruptly that she was beginning to feel rather warm and yearning in parts that had no business yearning after anyone but Clancy.

"Right. As you have frequently told me, you can sleep outdoors as a coyote without difficulty."

"Yes, but that was when I didn't need this vest," he returned. "I can't sleep in the rain in this vest. I'll lose my mana again."

Sierra had to concede this, but still, the tent was very small. And it would rain again tonight, she was sure. "All right," she said grudgingly. "You sleep in the tent. I'll sleep under the tarp. I can't get any wetter than I am already."

"Why can't we both sleep in the tent?" he asked with a mischievous grin, his eyes dancing. "I don't want you to get cold."

She was cold. They had agreed not to use a campfire because it might tip off rangers—or others—to their presence. Bringing a camp stove—even a packable one—wasn't an option either. Sierra had the only pack, and it was bulging with needed supplies. She carried basic food that did not require cooking, so they would have to live on cold rations the whole time. But she certainly longed for a campfire now, shivering in her wet clothes.

"Okay," she conceded. "We can both sleep in the tent. But!"— as Chaco's eyes lit up with a feral gleam—"We will sleep. Just sleep. And stay warm. Agreed?" Chaco agreed without further argument.

As they munched their peanut butter sandwiches, Sierra realized they had forgotten something.

"Chaco! We totally forgot to bring a fish and a chicken to offer to Kama. We were supposed to buy them in Hilo. Damn it! Oh dear, we can't go back now. I mean, I just can't face it. We've come too far."

Chaco appeared unperturbed. "I wouldn't worry about it. We have 'awa and the chants, and there's several bananas in your pack," he said.

"What if that's not enough?"

"I'm an Avatar. I can use my mana to call to his mana. We'll find him."

Sierra was not as certain, but she either had to accept his assessment or slog back through the jungle and deadfalls for many miles to get a chicken and a fish. So she accepted his word, and after applying yet another layer of insect repellent, went inside the little tent. Chaco squeezed in after her and fell asleep instantly. Exhausted, Sierra followed suit. She awoke once to the roar of heavy rain, but the canopy of trees overhead prevented it from swamping the tent.

The next morning, she awoke to the delicious smell of fresh-brewed coffee. Completely disoriented, she peered out of the tent, to be greeted by Chaco with a steaming mug of java.

"I thought we weren't going to build a campfire," she said groggily. "And I didn't pack any coffee for obvious reasons. How did you get this?"

"Just a little trick of mine," he answered with a smile.

Sierra reached for the mug and slurped at it. It was hot. Mugs were another item she hadn't packed. "Why didn't you use that trick when we were marooned in Kama's valley? I could really have used some coffee then."

Chaco looked at her, one eyebrow cocked. "Short memory," he said.

"Oh. Right. You still didn't have your powers back."

"No mana, no coffee."

"What else can you do? I still don't know exactly what you're capable of."

"I never know until I try," he said cheerfully.

The rain had stopped, but the forest was saturated. The trees dripped continuously, and the soft growth underfoot was sodden with water. The skies were still gray and pregnant with moisture. After a quick breakfast of gorp and apples, Sierra shouldered her pack with a grunt and Chaco morphed back into coyote form. "I have a feeling about this direction," he said, plunging into a tangle of vines among some tall hardwood trees, plumy tail waving behind. Sierra followed, muttering under her breath.

The going was even harder than the previous day. Chaco headed steadily uphill, leaping crevasses that Sierra had to negotiate with painstaking care, making their progress even slower. He sailed up rough pebble scree on four agile legs, while Sierra slid and scrambled behind. It was at the head of just such an ascent that Sierra paused for breath, wiping torrents of sweat from her face—and stopped. She listened, trying not to breathe hard or make any noise. The forest was quiet. No birdsong, no sound of Chaco's claws scrabbling at rock, or branches swaying in his wake. Even the wind had died.

"Chaco?" she called. There was no answer. She waited for a few minutes, then called again. Nothing. Panic began to grab at her throat, choking her, and she fought it down with as much strength as she could muster, even bringing her mana to bear on it, golden ribbons twining around her heart and lungs, calming her. Her heartbeat and breathing slowed.

She proceeded cautiously in the direction she had last seen Chaco take. Black lava was close to the surface here, extruding as jagged ridges from the green growth struggling to conquer the primeval rock. Though the ground was steep, there were trees and vines even here, making it hard to see. Chaco was nowhere in sight.

He's a big coyote, she thought. *Chaco can take care of himself.* But she still felt apprehension prickling along her spine. She knew that even an Avatar was not entirely invulnerable, given the right circumstances.

Sierra picked her way carefully across the rocks. She glimpsed a clearing where no trees stood, and headed for it. As she emerged into the clearing, a black hole abruptly gaped in front of her. The lush growth surrounding the opening had shielded it from her view. Sierra stopped and peered into the hole. It looked like a gigantic wormhole in the lava. It was a nearly perfect circular tube, at least ten feet across, slanting down into the earth and darkness. It was steep, but not too steep to be able to walk down it.

She called down into the tunnel, dreading that Chaco might have fallen into it. Or that he had gone into the tunnel to explore, only to tumble down a hidden crevasse. "Chaco," she called again, her voice quavering a little. Her voice echoed down the rocky tube.

Then she heard a scrabbling sound deep inside. Before Sierra could fling herself back and away from the opening, a creature charged up the hole toward her. As she screamed and tried to throw herself aside, the thing collided with her. She sprawled on the soft growth around the opening with the breath knocked out of her as the creature disentangled itself from her embrace.

"Sierra! This is it! This is the place!" cried Chaco, dancing on all four paws with excitement and stamping repeatedly on her legs as she struggled to regain her breath. "We found it!"

Sierra took a few moments to allow the adrenaline to clear her system before she spoke. When she did, there was still an edge of exasperation in her voice. "Get off me! Why the hell didn't you answer me, idiot? You scared me to death."

"Oh, sorry about that," he said. "I didn't hear you." Being in coyote form, he licked her sweaty cheek in a conciliatory manner. "Yum. Salt. Yeah, this is the opening. It's perfect!"

"Why is it perfect? How do you know this is the place?"

Chaco sat on his furry haunches and cocked his head, amber eyes alight. "This is a lava tube..."

"How do you know it's a lava tube? You've never been here before."

"It's a tube, and it's made out of lava." Sierra had to concede these points, so she nodded.

"Anyway, the portals between the worlds—I mean the world of Avatars and the human world—are usually in caves. Remember where you first met Quetzalcoatl?" Sierra nodded. That memorable meeting had been in a deep cave in the eastern Sierra Nevada range of California.

"That is, if the Avatar in question is an earth power. Kama is the pig-god, and that's about as earthy as it gets. Further down in the lava tube, I can sense the portal—the opening—into Kama's world. Bring your pack, and let's get going."

Without another word, the coyote jumped up and sped into the blackness of the tube. Sierra followed with a great deal less enthusiasm. She had on good hiking boots, but she still had to negotiate the steep sides of the tube with two legs, not four. Her pack was overloaded—the unfortunate effect of having two people but only one pack. Occasionally it would throw her off balance by banging against a protruding rock as she struggled to move forward and down. The floor of the tube was not only steep, it was filled with rubble that had an unnerving tendency to slip and slide under the thick soles of her hiking boots. As daylight faded behind her, she pulled a flashlight out of her pack and switched it on. The walls of the tube were gray-black volcanic stone that swallowed the beam of her flashlight, but now she could see where she was going.

Chaco ran ahead with ease, but circled back frequently to check on her progress. At one point, he found her hesitating at a large crack in the floor of the tube. It was just wide enough to make Sierra wonder if she really could jump across it, or if she were risking a broken bone. Despite the flashlight, she couldn't see how deep it was.

Chaco morphed back into a young man, his dark hair falling into his eyes. He stood on the far side of the crack and said, "Toss me the pack. I can help." She heaved the pack at him. He caught it and placed on the floor of the tube. Then he held his long arms out to her and said, "Jump. I'll take care of you."

Sierra teetered at the edge. Chaco's hand was just out of reach, so she couldn't grasp it for support. She felt panic rising again, and sternly quelled it with her mana. She took a deep breath, gathered her courage, and leaped.

It felt as though she were flying, not jumping. She sailed easily across the gap and Chaco folded her tenderly into his arms. She thought for an instant that he might attempt more, but he kissed the top of her head and released her, instantaneously morphing back into his coyote shape and racing back down the tunnel. After a moment to reorient herself, Sierra followed.

The sensation of flying stayed with her for several moments. "Did you use your mana to help me across just then?" she asked.

"Uh-huh," came the reply from ahead. *So there were many things her personal Avatar could do if he put his mind to it*, she thought. *What else can this guy do?*

The tube twisted and turned, finally opening out into a large space. Chaco was waiting for her there, tongue lolling, a coyote grin on his furry face. Sierra's flashlight showed the ceiling of this space was perhaps thirty feet above their heads, and the walls were several yards apart all around. The tube continued at the far end of this space.

"Are we going any further?" asked Sierra. She hoped not.

"Nope. This is the portal. Get out the 'awa and bananas. Let's do the chants now," he replied, morphing into a man again.

They arranged three bottles of pale 'awa on a mat Sierra had brought for the purpose, and laid the bananas beside it. They sat on either side of this offering and began to sing the chant Auntie Keikilani had taught them to bring their presence to the attention of Kama Pua'a. Sierra stilled her mind and allowed her mana to expand, sending the glowing, colored ribbons trailing about the lava tube as though they were fingers seeking an opening in the glassy rock. She closed her eyes, allowing her consciousness to expand, looking for Kama.

"Aloha, my friends. What are you doing here?" boomed a familiar voice. Sierra opened her eyes. She was no longer in a lava tube deep beneath the earth. She was sitting in a thatched lanai, cushioned by many woven palm frond mats. The jungle surrounded the lanai—but what a jungle! There were more flowers than Sierra had seen since coming to Hawai'i. There was no trace of the storm that had soaked her and Chaco the day before and threatened them again as they began their second day of hiking. There was a rainbow shining with brilliant colors in the blue sky overhead—Sierra later found that the rainbow lingered, unfading and immortal, shining night and day. Kama stood before her, grinning from handsome ear to handsome ear. He lifted the bottle of 'awa and drank deeply, then offered it to her. Knowing the polite thing to do, Sierra flinched inwardly, took the bottle, and drank before handing it off to Chaco, now in human form. Chaco did likewise.

"I recognize you now, Avatar." Kama inclined his head to Chaco and his embroidered vest. "You regained your powers, I see."

Chaco nodded and smiled, but didn't explain.

"Kama," Sierra began, but he interrupted her.

"I don't know why you came to see me, but we must celebrate!" he exclaimed. He turned, lifted a large conch shell to his lips and blew. A long, shuddering moan went out over the forest.

People began gathering. They were clad in kapa cloth, as was Kama, with geometric tattoos on face, arms, and legs. They shone, as did Kama (and Chaco, too, for that matter) with an inner glow that made their brown skins alight with energy and life. They were all beautiful. Not one of them showed signs of illness, injury, or age.

Then came the Menehune, at least a hundred of them, bearing platters of cooked and raw foods of all sorts—fish, ʻopihi, seaweed, coconut, octopus, plantains, fruit, and bowls of purple poi. Sierra noted that no pork was present at this feast, of course. Drummers began to beat rhythmically on small gourd drums and dancers began to sway, accenting their dance by clicking smooth stones held between their fingers like castanets. Chanting accompanied the dance, and Sierra understood it perfectly. They were singing a song of aloha—a loving greeting to welcome guests.

A few moʻo showed up and were respectfully greeted by all. They were obviously known here. The moʻo tucked into a gleaming pile of whole, fresh fish apparently provided just for them.

Ah well, thought Sierra. *If Kama wants to put on a luau, we just have to go along with it. I know we're not getting any real business done until this is over.* She accepted a coconut shell of ʻawa and placed a scoop of ʻopihi on tī leaves offered to her by a young Hawaiʻian man with melting brown eyes and the physique of an elite athlete. *We just need to wait until this is over. I think I could enjoy this.*

Sierra began to sing along with the chants.

CHAPTER 24

Houghton Roberts was having a bad day, but all of his days had been bad since the accident at *Jack of Diamonds*. Work at both sites had been suspended while they investigated the accident, but so far they had found nothing to account for what had happened. The delay in construction was costing Ahi Moana a great deal of money, and contractual deadlines were in peril.

Now he was trying to decide whether or not to proceed with the work. There was nothing to indicate that what happened that day was likely to happen again. On the other hand, they didn't know what had caused it, so there was no assurance that it *wouldn't* happen again. Well, he had wanted a top position, with all the responsibilities that came with it. Now he had to make the right choice. Whatever that was.

Despite his worries, his thoughts occasionally went back to Sierra. She was definitely a tree-hugger type, not that he objected. After all, he was devoting his own time to alternative energy, and he felt good about it. She was interesting, though. Smart and passionate. It didn't hurt that she was beautiful—although perhaps not in a conventional way. Her shiny, dark hair wasn't fashionably styled, and it looked like the only thing she did with it was plait it into a single, long braid down her back. She had worn no makeup the times he had seen her. She was fit and tanned from hiking. Her high cheekbones and large, almond eyes gave her an exotic look, but her manner was down-to-earth. She had never flirted with him, which in his experience was unusual. At the company parties or industry events he attended, lovely women always flirted with him. These women, he had noticed, put a great deal of effort into their clothes and makeup. Sierra didn't even bother to paint her nails, much less grow them long. He had noticed, though, that she usually wore jewelry. It looked handcrafted, with unusual stones and creative designs. He had been surprised to learn that she designed and fabricated the jewelry herself.

He felt comfortable around Sierra in a way he usually didn't around women. Women often seemed to have a hidden agenda. Sometimes they seemed to want to get close to him as quickly as possible. Sometimes they seemed to be playing hard to get. Sierra had an agenda, but she had told him immediately what it was—she wanted him to stop construction on WestWind. Other than that, she had seemed interested in many of the same things he was, and she had enjoyed her visit to the jack ship until the accident occurred.

This thought reminded him of Clancy, and he frowned. Was Clancy her boyfriend? He wasn't sure. Sierra and Clancy had seemed close but hadn't been particularly affectionate with each other on their tour of *Jack of Diamonds*. Of course, cooing on a tour of a construction site would be inappropriate, so that was no indication.

Roberts wrenched his thoughts away from Sierra and back to WestWind. He still had a decision to make.

• • •

Sierra woke up gradually the morning after Kama's luau. The evening had been warm and rain-free, so she had eschewed her tent in favor of sleeping under the lanai. Kama had his own hale, as did his many friends, scattered about the forest nearby. As she opened her eyes, she heard a clear, ascending whistle. A brilliant red-orange bird with black and white wings sat on a vine growing next to the lanai. It had a long, downward-curved beak. Sierra knew without thinking that the bird was an ʻiʻiwi. She hadn't seen one on Molokaʻi, but the knowledge was clear and present in her mind. Another aspect of Kanaloa's gift? She lay on her mat, staring dreamily at the bird until she smelled coffee and sat up. Bless him, Chaco was approaching with a mugful of caffeinated bliss.

"Thank you," she said, taking the mug. "You know, I really like this particular talent of yours."

"I have lots more," he said, smiling broadly.

The subject needed changing. "Where's Kama?"

"He's still asleep. But breakfast is ready."

Sierra saw a large bundle of kapa cloth under the lanai. It was snoring loudly, so she assumed it was Kama. She left the lanai and entered the clearing where the luau had taken place the night before. Based on her earlier experience in Kama's valley, she expected to see sleeping revelers, the remains of the feast, trampled leis, and other detritus you might find after an enthusiastic all-night luau. But the area was immaculate. There were new bowls of freshly prepared food waiting for them. There were no flies or other obnoxious creatures flocking to the food for their share. The benefits of magic, she supposed.

After a breakfast of fish, poi, and fruit, plus Chaco's excellent, bottomless mug of coffee, Sierra and Chaco sat waiting for Kama to appear. As the sun approached the zenith—without diminishing the glory of the permanent rainbow overhead—the bundle of kapa cloth under the lanai stirred, stretched, and unrolled, revealing Kama. He bounded up with enormous energy and came to join Sierra and Chaco.

"Good morning!" Kama said, tucking into a dish of fried plantains. "I hope you had fun last night. I did!" He ate with enthusiasm. After demolishing the plantains, he went on to devour the fish and poi, then cracked a coconut, drank its milk and scooped out the crisp, white flesh.

"That's better," he said finally, patting his flat, hard stomach. He peered at Sierra's steaming mug. "What's that?"

"Coffee. You should try it—they grow a lot of it over in Kona." She offered the mug to him.

Kama took a huge mouthful. He held it in his mouth for a

few beats, then turned and spewed it into a bush. "That's bitter! It's horrible!"

"Sorry." *Now you know how I feel about 'awa.*

"So, what brings you to see me, friends?"

"I'm sure you remember the luau on Moloka'i, where the Menehune were the guests of honor?" Sierra said. Kama nodded.

"Now there was a party!" he exclaimed, rubbing his big hands together with glee. "I won the javelin toss, did you know that?"

"No, I didn't. Congratulations. Do you also remember why the Menehune came to talk to you?"

Kama sat back, eyes cast upward in thought. "Hmm. They had some sort of request, didn't they? Oh, I remember now! They were worried about the whales, was that it?"

"Yes," Sierra confirmed. "Do you remember what they asked you to do?"

"Um, no. Not really. It was a pretty wild luau."

"They said there was construction going on in the ocean west of Moloka'i," said Sierra. "The whales are unhappy about it. You said you would look into it for them."

"I did? I don't remember saying that," said Kama, looking sheepish.

"You gave your sacred word," put in Chaco. "That's why we came. People are building a wind farm in the ocean on top of Penguin Bank—the extinct underwater volcano west of Moloka'i."

"Wind farm?" asked Kama, his brow furrowing like earth beneath a harrow. "What's that?"

It took quite a while to communicate everything they had learned, and it was late afternoon when Kama, still looking bemused, stood and blew his conch.

"Time for a break," he explained, as the beautiful men and women began bringing bowls and platters of food and gourds full of 'awa, coconut milk, and fresh water. "Let us eat and refresh ourselves, friends, and then we will talk some more."

Chaco and Sierra were more than ready to take a break. Sierra's growling stomach had more than once interrupted her serious explanations of the situation on Molokaʻi. As she ate, she looked around the clearing. Kama's hale and several others were tucked in among the sheltering trees. The sky was a clear, bright blue, set off by the rainbow overhead. Small, wispy clouds floated past. The sun was warm, but not too hot, and the winds carried the sweet perfume of flowers. The entire place had a sense of peace and perfection that had never been features of Sierra's world.

"Does it ever rain here?" she asked Kama. "It was raining, or about to, when we left…where we were. But it's not storming here."

"Sure it rains here," replied Kama, sitting cross-legged on a mat and enjoying some roasted coconut.

"When?"

"At night. As long as there's nothing else going on. We don't want it to rain if we're night fishing or having a luau, or something like that."

So I'm in Fairyland, thought Sierra. *Well, well.* And she drank some ʻawa without thinking about it, the bitter taste becoming sweet in her mouth.

When everyone had eaten and drunk all they wanted, Kama sat up, alert once more.

"So you asked Kanaloa and Kauhuhu for help," he said, "and they tried to kill the men building the, the…farm of wind. But you say that's not what you wanted. Did you tell Kanaloa and Kauhuhu not to harm the men?"

Sierra felt a pang of chagrin. "No. It didn't occur to me. I asked them to stop the building, not hurt the workers."

Kama shook his head. "What about you, Avatar? Did you not warn her?"

"I am not of your land or your ways, Kama," Chaco replied. "I didn't know the character of these gods, or how to deal with them. I regret this, but it's true."

"Kanaloa and Kauhuhu are dangerous. Unpredictable. Did no one warn you?"

"Yes," said Sierra. "Auntie Keikilani warned me, but she also said she thought they were interested in me and wouldn't harm me."

"She was right about that," said Kama, "but apparently, they had no qualms about hurting others. You *have* been stirring the hornets' nest, haven't you?"

Chaco gave Kama a stern look, his golden eyes darkened to amber. "Sierra wouldn't have resorted to asking Kanaloa and Kauhuhu for help if you had kept your promise to the Menehune of Moloka'i."

Kama straightened his spine and nodded his head, "You're right, friend. But I have no power over Kanaloa or Kauhuhu. If they have decided on a course of action, I can't stop them."

Chaco, seated cross-legged across from Kama, leaned forward with deadly intensity. "You may not have the power to combat those two, but you have a friend who can."

Kama stared blankly at Chaco. "What do you mean?"

"Pele. Pele has enormous mana. She shaped this land. She continues to shape this land and exert her will throughout these islands. Who can stand in her way? Kanaloa can quench her fires, but he can't stop her; Pele stops only when Pele wishes. Am I right?"

Kama paled a bit and shifted uneasily on his mat. He gestured to an attendant to bring him more 'awa. "I can't go to Pele," he said flatly. "She'll kill me."

"I thought Avatars can't be killed?' Sierra asked.

"He's speaking metaphorically," replied Chaco. "But I'm sure she could make things pretty unpleasant for him." Returning his attention to Kama, he said, "You're a handsome kane—as you've told us more than once—and Pele still yearns for you. We could tell that when we saw her in Moloka'i. Right now, she's angry with you, but perhaps if you were considerate of her, behaved like a lover, she might warm up, er, be more amenable to your enormous, ah, charms."

"And for heaven's sake, don't go telling her about her sister's ma'i! Or anyone else's ma'i, for that matter," Sierra added hastily.

Kama looked resolute for a moment, then drooped. "I can't do it," he said. "I know I promised the Menehune, and I'm sorry I forgot about that, but I can't face Pele. You saw her. She'd burn me to a crisp if she could."

"Well, then," Chaco said, rising easily from his cross-legged position and stretching elaborately. "I guess I'll just have to go have a talk with her myself."

Sierra and Kama gaped at him. "About what?" Kama asked suspiciously.

"I'm afraid I will have to tell her how to find you," said Chaco with a malicious gleam in his eyes. "I bet she'll be interested."

Kama seemed to swell, reminding Sierra of a puffer fish. Sierra didn't know what he was capable of, but she was sure Kama controlled more mana than he had ever shown them.

Kama's face had grown dark and he scowled fiercely at Chaco. "You threaten me?" he said in a low growl. "Remember, I am a god!" His powerful shoulders hunched like a bull's.

"Yes. As it happens, I'm by way of being a god myself," said Chaco, shifting rapidly to coyote form. His black lips were drawn back from white fangs, his legs were stiff with tension, and his thick fur bristled around the tan vest.

A black and white hog stood where Kama had been sitting. Its heavy yellow tusks dripped foam, and its little piggy eyes were furious. The boar squealed and pawed the ground with a cloven hoof. The coyote crouched low, prepared to spring forward.

"Stop it!" yelled Sierra. "Don't go crazy on me. No fighting! Please!"

Boar and coyote, startled, looked at her, then Kama and Chaco were back in their human forms. Both were still panting and casting nasty glances at each other, but the fight was over before it began.

"Thank you," Sierra said, drawing a long breath of relief. "Now, let's settle this like gentlem…like the good, kind Avatars I know you both to be, okay?"

Feathers began to unruffle. The Avatars sat down again. Kama brushed imaginary dust from his arms while Chaco ran long fingers through his dark hair. Neither looked at his erstwhile opponent.

"I think as Avatars you two are evenly matched. Neither of you will win a fight here. So, Kama, I am asking you again to speak with Pele, implore her to intervene. Chaco doesn't want to spill the beans to Pele. He'd much rather you go speak to her. Right, Chaco?" She glanced at her friend.

"Right."

"Please, Kama? Then you will have kept your promise to the Menehune, people's lives will be saved, and maybe you and Pele can come to some sort of mutual agreement."

Kama rose majestically. "I will think on it overnight," he said grandly. "If you desire food or drink, you have only to ask one of my people." He strode with conscious dignity to his hale and disappeared into the interior.

CHAPTER 25

Sierra and Chaco glanced at one another as Kama retreated. "What do you think?" Sierra asked.

"He'll do it. He's just miffed because we called him out for forgetting his promise to the Menehune. Also, Pele scares him spitless. But she's also his true love. Outside of himself, I mean," said Chaco.

Sierra reflected that it takes a thief to catch one, but she said, "Well, now what shall we do? While we're waiting, I mean."

Chaco looked up at the fading sunlight and the unfading rainbow. "I vote we walk around and see what we can see. I'd be willing to bet there's nothing here that will harm us. Have you noticed there are bugs, but none of them land on us or our food? And they don't bite? It's never too hot or too cold. It rains only when Kama says it can. We're in paradise, or something close enough."

They began to stroll about the little village. All the people were gorgeous, with liquid brown eyes, full lips, and smooth brown skin. The women wore their hair long, rippling down their slender backs in blue-black waves, festooned with flowers. They wore kapa skirts, but left their upper bodies uncovered. Sierra noticed that Chaco kept his eyes fixed firmly above shoulder level, and was proud of him for his restraint under such trying circumstances. The men, all of the same tall, solid, stocky build as Kama, wore malos. Their long hair was tied back in a variety of interesting ways, and they wore lavish flower leis. Some also had kapa cloaks, stamped with geometric patterns. Both men and women sometimes wore shell leis, ropes of yellow, red, white, brown, black, and pink shells, strung together to form patterns.

"One thing is odd," whispered Sierra to Chaco. His eyebrow rose like a dark wing as he cocked his head at her.

"Really? I mean apart from the rainbow that never fades, the perfect weather, the polite insects, and all?"

"Yes. There are no kids here."

Chaco looked around. Men and women were busy doing various tasks or chatting. They seemed happy and occupied. But Sierra was right. No children.

"That might be one reason this is paradise," Chaco whispered back. Sierra elbowed him. "No, seriously. These aren't humans living here. These are all immortals. If you don't die, there's no need to reproduce, is there?"

"If they aren't human, what are they?" asked Sierra, a little uneasily.

Chaco considered this. "I'm not sure you have a word for it. Fairies. Good Folk. Some of them might be ghosts."

"Ghosts?"

"Not in the sense of wearing white bed sheets and clanking chains and moaning, no. But many of these people were once mortal. Now they are immortal. Don't ask me why."

"Why?" asked Sierra.

"What did I just say? There could be a million reasons. Maybe some man in ancient Hawai'i was a brave warrior and saved his village and Kama made him immortal. Maybe a maiden fell in love with a shark god and he devoured her but made her spirit immortal. Could be anything."

"Oh." As usual, the more Sierra tried to figure out how the supernatural worked, the more it eluded her. *It would be so much more convenient and comfortable if they just had a user's manual,* she thought. *As it is, I never know what to expect.*

Their wanderings brought them to the foot of a waterfall. It fell hundreds of feet down the side of a cliff into a large pool. Sierra looked at it longingly. It looked cool and inviting, the rocks all around covered with bright green mosses and flowering plants. She looked for tī plants, found them, and bundled several leaves together, setting them to float on the surface of the pool. They bobbed around merrily, indicating there were no moʻo present. Without thinking twice, she shucked off her dirty clothes down to her underwear and dove into the pool. When she surfaced, pushing strands of hair from her face, Chaco was still standing by the side of the pool, looking discomfited.

"C'mon in!" she shouted to him. "The water's fine!"

But he shook his head. "Nope. I'd have to take off the vest. I'd lose all my powers in an instant. Horrible sensation. I'm not doing that again. I don't mind watching you, though."

Sierra lounged and swam in the deliciously cool water, listening to the sound of the waterfall and enjoying the scent of flowering vines that grew all around the pool. The basin was quite deep, so she took a long lungful of air and swam down as far as she could. Surfacing, she exhaled loudly and splashed about, feeling like an extra in some tropical extravaganza.

As evening began to close in, she decided she'd had enough and climbed out of the pool by the soft light of the rainbow. She grimaced at having to put on her dirty clothes, but there was no help for it.

"Hungry?" she asked Chaco. He nodded, and they wandered back to the clearing in the center of the village. As before, fresh food awaited them. The men and women who served it were friendly and smiling, but they answered no questions. *Typical immortals*, thought Sierra. *Can't give a person a straight answer.*

Then there was nothing left to do but go to bed. Kama hadn't appeared for dinner. The men and women were returning to their hales, and finally the only light remaining shone from the blazing net of stars overhead—and the ever-shining rainbow. Sierra and Chaco waited for a while, hoping Kama would reappear, but he did not. They rolled themselves up in kapa cloths under the lanai and fell asleep to the sound of a gentle rain pattering down on the sleeping village.

Kama woke them in the morning. He was dressed in what Sierra now recognized as high formal dress. He wore a red and white malo. Around his neck, he wore the carved whale's tooth pendant that marked him as an Ali'i and a chief. Over his shoulders he wore a red and yellow feather cape, and on his head he wore a crested helmet also covered with red and yellow feathers. He stood stiffly in front of them, head erect like a Roman statue.

"I go to seek Pele," Kama announced. "Whatever fate awaits me, do not forget me or my deeds." He looked off into the distance, his chin held high.

"Not so fast, Big Guy," said Chaco.

"Yes, we're coming with you," said Sierra, scrambling out of her kapa cocoon.

Kama lowered his gaze, frowning at his guests. "It's too dangerous. Stay here, where you're safe."

"We'll be fine. I'm an Avatar, and Sierra is…hmm. Sierra has her own powers," Chaco said.

"You'll slow me down," Kama complained. "I travel the ancient paths and you can't come with me. Even if I wanted you to," he added crossly.

"We can travel the ancient paths with you," said Chaco with confidence, though Sierra remained silent, her brow furrowed in consternation.

"We can?" she whispered.

"Shush!" Chaco hissed. Then to Kama, "Yep. We're along for the ride. We should get going. The sooner the better and all that."

Kama relaxed his heroic stance. "I'd like to get some breakfast first," he said.

"Me, too!" Sierra said. Then to Chaco, "Can you do your coffee trick?"

It was perhaps forty-five minutes later that Kama, Chaco, and Sierra stood in the center of the clearing while Kama chanted.

"Hold my hand—and don't let go!" Chaco said to Sierra in an undertone.

"Do you know what he's doing? Where he's going?" she whispered back.

"No. But hang on to—aaaaarrrggghhh!"

Sierra felt as though she had been jerked off her feet, but instead of landing immediately nearby, she experienced enormous acceleration. She felt Chaco's firm hand slipping from her grasp, and grabbed his wrist with her other hand. She seemed to be rushing through a tunnel at great speed, then she abruptly decelerated, making her lose her grip on Chaco. She and Chaco tumbled forward, finding themselves breathless and disoriented in an unearthly landscape.

If it were not for the full moon shining above, she would have thought it was the lunar surface. Although it had been morning in Kama's land, here it was night. A desolate landscape of sand and rock gleamed silver and black in the moonlight. An occasional overambitious shrub struggled up from the sand, but there were few growing things. Sierra smelled sulfur. Black sheets of ancient lava spread out in wrinkles and swirls under her feet like petrified water. Though the sun had long since set, the barren rock and sand still reflected heat into her face, and she could feel sweat running down her back.

"Where are we?" she asked Chaco, who seemed a bit disoriented himself.

"Best guess? Kilauwea."

"Pele's favorite home? Her mai'i? The volcano? The one that is erupting right now?" Standing on an erupting volcano did not seem like the wisest or safest place to be.

"That's the one. But we're not in danger—from the eruption, I mean. Jack told me that Kilauwea has been erupting continuously for decades. The lava flows underground to the ocean most of the time. But we could be in plenty of danger from Pele herself, I think."

Kama Pua'a stood on an outcropping of lava several yards from them. His arms were spread wide, and he was chanting. Sierra stilled her pounding heart and listened.

"O Beautiful One,
Flashing in the heavens

Hear me.
O she whose hair is a river of obsidian,
O she whose eyes are the lightning of the heavens,
O she who commands the fires beneath the earth,
Hear me.
I come before you humbled, O Pele.
I come as a supplicant.
I come as a beggar before you.
My life is as nothing when the Beautiful One
Is not with me.
My soul is dry and my bowl empty.
Can you find it in your heart to forgive me, O Beautiful One?
Grant me forgiveness that I might live,
Your adoring shadow, your slave.
This is my prayer, O Pele."

Knowing Kama as she did, Sierra wondered how much all this abasement cost him. She had to admit that he sounded sincere.

A sudden crackling hiss behind her tore her attention away from Kama. When she looked around, she saw a terrifying—if familiar—sight: a writhing column of flame. Pele, her face so bright and beautiful that Sierra could scarcely look at it, was approaching Kama. And Sierra and Chaco were right in between them. She grabbed Chaco, who was staring, transfixed, and hustled him away. There was a boulder as big as a house embedded in a nearby small hill of volcanic ash; she dragged Chaco behind its shelter. From this refuge, they could look out at the scene below. The mass of the boulder shielded them from the blast-furnace heat pouring from Pele as she approached her humbled lover, who was now on his knees.

Pele overwhelmed all of Sierra's senses. The column of fire stood perhaps twenty feet tall, and the roaring of the flame was deafening. Molten lava poured in a continuous flood down her body, spreading around her feet, black where the lava cooled, with bright cracks of golden-red flame between. Her hair was a waterfall of fiery snakes, writhing and hissing. Bright orange and golden sparks flew from her at every step, sprinkling the sky with ephemeral stars that glowed and died against the darkness. Though the heat of her presence must have been unbearable, Kama stayed resolutely on his knees before her, looking up to meet her blazing eyes.

"Let us not quarrel further, my only love," he said, his eyes reflecting her fire. "I will never hurt you again. I promise." Kama held his arms out to her.

The twenty-foot column halted in front of him as though hesitating. The roar of internal heat and pressure continued as sparks continued to fly up and molten lava oozed around the figure's feet. Abruptly, the roaring ceased and the hissing died. The sparks cooled and vanished as twenty feet became fifteen, then ten, then congealed into the figure of a woman nearly six feet tall.

She stood straight and regal, a queen conscious of her great power. Her hair rippled down her back to her ankles, no longer fiery snakes but now ribbons of midnight, shining under the moon. She was naked and perfect, flower leis garlanding her shoulders, ankles and wrists. She walked straight into Kama's arms. He enveloped her in an embrace, their mouths meeting hungrily—and they vanished.

Sierra and Chaco stared. The heat had abated, so they ventured out from behind the boulder. They walked to the spot where Kama had stood. There was nothing but ancient lava, just as before, though the ground still radiated warmth. They peered around. The desolate wilderness around them was empty, glowing eerily beneath the light of the moon.

"Shit!" yelled Sierra. "Our car is way the hell on the other side of this goddamn island!"

CHAPTER 26

Roberts made his decision, picked up the phone and dialed Peter Chapman. "Find anything yet, Peter?"

"No, sir," Chapman replied. They discussed the various exploratory dives and tests that had been undertaken in an effort to discover what had gone wrong at the jack ship. After reviewing all the data, they were still left with a huge question mark; apart from the toppled base, there was no evidence that anything untoward had ever happened at that site.

"Well, I'm going to call it a freak accident," Roberts said finally. "Maybe we were wrong about the footing in that particular site. Leave that one alone and let's move on to the others. Tell *Jack of Hearts* to start up again, too."

"Yes, sir."

As he put the phone down, Roberts hoped he was doing the right thing.

• • •

"What do you mean, you can't take us back along the ancient ways? You got us here, didn't you?" Sierra snapped. She and Chaco (in coyote form) were tramping through the volcanic wilderness somewhere on the slopes of Kilauwea. The moon was bright enough to avoid most walking hazards, but the terrain was rough. She was grateful that it was nighttime and therefore cooler, but she was thirsty, and they had no water with them—an amateur mistake that made Sierra privately blush. Chaco produced a nice, steaming mug of coffee, but for once in her life, Sierra didn't want coffee.

She drank it anyway, on the basis that it had water in it. It helped, but she'd need a pee break soon. Sierra had brought the backpack with her, so they at least they had food.

"I didn't take us along the ancient paths, Kama did. I was just hitching a ride."

"Now that you've been on the paths, can't you find them again?"

"No!" Chaco chopped that one off short. Perhaps he was becoming a bit annoyed as well. They walked in silence for a long time, Chaco trotting easily across the rocks with Sierra stumbling along behind. For the umpteenth time, Sierra wished she understood how magic worked. For instance, if Chaco could produce a mug of coffee, why couldn't he just as easily produce a cold glass of water? If he could float her across a gap in the lava tube floor, why couldn't he just levitate the both of them back to the Kohala Peninsula and the comfort of their rental car? His answers to questions of this sort were never satisfactory, but she tried again.

"Um, Chaco?"

"Umph?"

"This is great-tasting coffee. Thanks. Can you also get me some water? Maybe?"

"No."

"Okay. May I ask why not?"

"I just can't. There's no reason."

"I don't understand."

Chaco planted himself on his furry haunches and regarded her, his eyes bright with moonlight. "You and me both. Listen. Do you understand how the universe began?"

"Sure. The Big Bang. Then all that energy and matter spread out and began forming stars and planets and things."

"Okay. So where did that enormous amount of matter and energy come from?"

"Um..."

"And what was there before the Big Bang?"

"Ah..."

"Have you heard of dark matter? Dark energy?"

"Yes."

"What are they?"

"Um…kryptonite?"

"Okay. So you don't understand the basic laws and history of your scientific universe. Is that a fair statement?"

Sierra sipped the last of her coffee. As she drained the mug, it disappeared. *Oh, good. No littering.* "I guess so."

Chaco stood up and shook himself all over as though he were shaking rainwater off his fur. He had a good stretch fore and aft, sneezed vigorously, then set off again, Sierra following. "As I understand it, even astrophysicists and cosmologists don't understand all of it," he said. "There are contradictions in the theories, right?"

"Yeah. So I've heard."

"So why do you expect the supernatural to be explainable and consistent?"

Sierra supposed maybe this was a bit unreasonable after all. "How do you know all that about the Big Bang and dark matter?"

Chaco snorted and scratched behind his ear with a hind paw. "I can read."

"But if you don't know how magic works, how do you know what to do? I mean, day to day?"

"Same as you know how to live from day to day. I learn what works and what doesn't. Making you a cup of coffee works. Making you a glass of water doesn't. At least, I can't do it now, but it's possible I might be able to do it later. I think it has to do with love. Love is my connection to the numinous."

"Love?"

"Uh-huh. Have you noticed that mana, magic, whatever you want to call it, is pretty dualistic?"

"What do you mean?"

"Truly powerful magic is either good or evil," explained Chaco. "That part is simple. Good Avatars use love to create good mana. Evil Avatars use hatred to create evil mana. The mana itself isn't good or evil, though. Mana is neutral. The wielder determines whether the mana is good or evil."

Sierra pondered this for several minutes as they tramped in silence. "So all magical creatures are either good or evil?"

Chaco shook his head, making his ears flap. "No, that would be too simple, wouldn't it? Mana is neutral, and there are also magical creatures that are neutral. Fred would be a good example of that. Of course, Fred isn't an Avatar."

"But Fred is good!" Sierra protested, narrowly avoiding twisting her ankle on a loose stone.

"Yeah, well, maybe," Chaco replied sardonically. "Anyway, Fred's abilities aren't tied directly to the numinous. And they aren't bound to his native land either. He just is what he is. He can't manipulate mana or increase it, the way you can."

"What about you? Can you manipulate or increase it?"

"Yes. But I don't necessarily know what I can or can't do until I try. Sometimes it works, sometimes not. Sometimes if I work at it, I can figure it out. Sort of like learning a new computer program, I imagine. It's a pain, but if you keep at it, you can succeed."

Morning found them at a marked trail. They followed this to a small road, and from there hitched a ride into Hilo. (Chaco switched to his human form based on the theory that a coyote—with or without a vest—would be unlikely to win a ride from sympathetic motorists.) It seemed silly to have to go all the way back to Waipio Valley to get the car, only to drive all the way back to Hilo to return it. She couldn't very well tell the rental agency that it was parked under concealing underbrush somewhere in the Pu'u O Umi Natural Area Reserve, so there was no help for it.

In Hilo they were able to hitch another ride all the way to the turnoff for Waipio Valley. They hiked most of the rest of the way back to their car, though a couple of surfers gave them a lift for a few miles.

At last, Sierra slung her backpack into the backseat of the rental car and slid into the driver's seat. "I'm exhausted," she said, gratefully turning on the car's air conditioning. By this time, it was late afternoon, and hot. "So, now what do we do?"

Chaco looked at her quizzically. "What do you mean?"

"Kama and Pele just disappeared last night. We don't know what they're going to do."

"I think we know perfectly well what they were going to do," retorted Chaco. "I do, at any rate."

"Not that. I mean, what are they going to do about WestWind and Kauhuhu and Kanaloa?"

"I don't know."

"What if Kama forgets again? I mean, he has other things on his…mind," said Sierra.

"I don't know. I guess we go back to Moloka'i and see what's happening," Chaco suggested patiently.

Sierra backed the car out from underneath its concealing bushes and pulled onto the road, heading for Hilo and the airport.

• • •

Clancy was bored and worried, always a bad combination. He had wanted to go with Sierra to the Big Island, but had to concede that his presence might be more of a hindrance than a help. He knew Chaco wouldn't let anything happen to Sierra any more than he would. Now that Chaco had his mana back, he was quite capable of handling almost any situation—but what sort of situations might arise in their quest for the pig-god was beyond Clancy's ability to imagine.

Now he was sitting in Auntie's little garden, worrying. Rose joined him and sat quietly for a few minutes.

"Don't you just hate waiting?" Rose said. "Let's go do something. I've never been to Hawai'i before, and I'd like to go to the beach."

"If you ask Auntie Keikilani where to go, I'll drive you," he replied. Maybe some beach time would help take his mind off his worries over Sierra. And Chaco too, of course.

A discussion ensued. Auntie was consulted about the best beaches. Finally, they were in their bathing suits with towels and beach equipment was assembled.

Auntie had recommended Kapukahehu Beach on the west end of the island. It proved to be a small crescent cove, safe for swimming. There was nothing built near the beach, only two other people were there, the waves were fairly calm, and the water sparkled in the sun. The sand was a blaze of heat that they could feel though the soles of their flop-flops. They spread out mats and towels, lathered up with sunscreen, and sat in the sun. Clancy regarded the idyllic scene before him and heaved a sigh.

Rose eyed him shrewdly. "You're obsessing about Sierra, aren't you?" Clancy nodded. No point in denying it. Rose hesitated a moment, then took something from around her neck. "Here. I can't swim with it, and maybe it'll help you." She placed it in Clancy's hand. Clancy looked down at the object resting in his palm. It was a small, soft leather bag, gathered at the top with a thong that went around the wearer's neck.

"What is it?"

"Medicine bag," replied Rose. "Don't look inside, please. It's got a lot of power." She shivered in the hot sunshine as though chilled, and Clancy saw goosebumps rise on her bare arms. "I just have a feeling that it may be helpful to you. Anyway, Sierra's with Chaco. She'll be just fine. Stop worrying!" She reached down, took the bag back, and placed the thong over his head. He thought she muttered something as the bag came to rest against his chest.

"What?"

"Nothing. I'm going in for a swim!"

Rose went down to the water's edge, leaving her flip-flops on her beach towel. She skittered into the ocean like a drop of water on a hot griddle. Clancy watched for a while as she splashed around, looking relaxed and happy. He looked down at the little leather bag and sniffed at it. It smelled like leather, with maybe a ghost of something fragrant and herbal. He let the medicine bag fall back against his chest. Nothing seemed to shake his worry over Sierra. He felt a sense of foreboding, even dread, that was foreign to his pragmatic nature.

When Rose tired of swimming she returned and flopped onto

a mat to dry off. "Not going in the water? It's delicious! It felt cool for just a moment, but then it was just wonderful. I could see fish even though I don't have a mask or goggles. Aren't you going in?"

As Clancy shook his head, his cell phone rang. To his surprise, it was Houghton Roberts. "Clancy? Hi. Huff here. Say, I've been calling Sierra, but there's no answer. Everything okay?"

"Um, yeah, everything's fine." *I hope.* "You know, cellular reception can be kind of spotty here."

"Tell me about it. Anyway, we're starting to work on the jack ships again, and I was wondering if you and Sierra wanted to come out again. Maybe this time it won't be as dramatic."

Clancy thought fast. If construction on WestWind were starting up again, would Kanaloa and Kauhuhu play the same terrible game as before? Or had Sierra and Chaco been successful in recruiting Kama Pua'a to help? He hesitated.

"It's okay if that isn't convenient," Roberts said. He sounded a bit disappointed.

"No, it's not that," Clancy said. "It's just that Sierra's still on the Big Island to, um, visit a friend for a while." That was pretty close to the truth.

"Oh, that's right—I thought she'd be back by now. Well, how about you? Want to come out to the site again?"

What a dilemma. Should he warn Roberts not to start construction yet? On what pretext? He made a quick decision. Maybe there was some way he could be helpful if things did go wrong.

"Yeah, sure. I'd love to go. I thought the jack ship was beyond cool."

"I'm going out to the other one, *Jack of Hearts*. It's pretty much the same, but it's working a different area. We leave from the helipad at two o'clock. See you there." Roberts ended the call. Clancy stared at his phone. What would he do if all hell broke loose again?

. . .

Later that day, after Clancy left for the helipad, Rose called Mama Labadie to bring her up to date. She told Mama she had given Clancy her medicine bag.

"I never knew you to be parted from that bag before now," commented Mama.

Rose was quiet for a moment. "I just think he's going to need it."

"Why?"

"You ever look at someone and think, 'That guy may not know it, but he's in for big trouble'?"

"Yeah. I sure have."

"I looked at Clancy this afternoon, and all I could see was trouble."

CHAPTER 27

Sierra called Clancy from the Kaunakakai Airport, but got no answer. She then tried Rose's phone and had no luck there, either.

"I can't call Auntie Keikilani," she fumed. "Auntie's already done so much for us that I'd feel guilty asking her to drive out here to pick us up."

Chaco pointed out that it was a quick drive, but Sierra insisted getting a taxi for the ride back to Auntie's house. When the cab pulled up, she saw immediately that Clancy's car was not parked on the street in front, as she'd expected it would be.

"Auntie," she called as she entered the house. "Chaco and I are back! It worked. We think. Where's Clancy?"

Auntie was in the living room, practicing hula. She halted her graceful swaying and fingered the off switch on her DVD player. "Clancy went out to the WestWind Project again with the CEO fellow, Roberts or whatever his name is."

"Oh. Too bad. We'll just have to tell you all about it and tell him again later," Sierra said, feeling a bit deflated. *And I'm a bit worried about Clancy being out there. What if Kanaloa and Kauhuhu attack while he's at the jack ship?* But then she remembered that Kama had promised to help, and tried to shrug off her uneasiness.

"Where's Fred?" Chaco asked, peering around.

"Fred? He ate enough bacon at breakfast for a football team, then told me he had to go visit the Menehune," responded Auntie. "Well! Let's get you some lemonade and you can tell me all about it." She bustled into the kitchen. "The two of you must've had some adventures, by the looks of you."

Sierra looked down. It was true. She and Chaco were coated

with dust and grime. Her new boots, battered and scarred from walking through the volcanic wilderness around Kilauwea, now looked like her oldest pair. Various rips and tears in her clothes and the occasional raw scrape and scratch proclaimed that she had not been drinking Blue Hawai'ians at the Hilton. Chaco was just as dusty, but his precious vest filled with earth was perfectly intact. He had been ultra-cautious about not letting anything tear or rip the fabric that protected the source of his mana.

They sat at the kitchen table with their lemonade. Auntie also produced a plate of cookies. "Tell me everything!" she said eagerly.

The tale took a while in the telling, as Sierra and Chaco each related part of the story, interrupted, corrected each other, and generally complicated the story, but eventually Sierra said, "And that's it. We finally got back to Hilo, dropped off the car, and here we are."

Auntie just sat and stared at them with shining eyes. "If only I could've seen it! The meeting of Pele and Kama Pua'a. It must have been magnificent!"

"It was," Sierra said. "Also terrifying. To be honest, we have no idea what Kama plans to do vis à vis WestWind. We're hoping he hasn't forgotten in the heat of the moment."

Auntie considered this. "So he didn't say how he and Pele planned to stop Kanaloa and Kauhuhu?"

Chaco shook his head. "No. I don't think Kama knew what he was going to do until he actually reunited with Pele. And then things got kind of wild, so it's not as though he had the time or attention to discuss it with us."

"We'll have to wait and see," Auntie said.

As they talked, the sun dipped toward the west and mynah birds began settling down for the night, setting up a cacophony in the trees around the house.

"It's odd that Clancy isn't back yet," Sierra noted. "And we still haven't seen Fred." Sierra looked at Chaco. "I'm worried," she said.

• • •

The helicopter hovered over *Jack of Hearts*. The ship looked like a toy boat at first, but grew rapidly as the 'copter descended and finally set down with a touch as light as a butterfly landing on a fingertip. The ship was a clone of *Jack of Diamonds*; Clancy couldn't see any difference between the two. Roberts donned a hardhat, gave another to Clancy, and walked him around the ship, introducing him to the crew and asking questions about the work. Roberts always asked if everything was proceeding normally. Had anyone noticed anything not quite right? The crew was well aware of events at *Jack of Diamonds*, but they all shook their heads. Roberts began to look positively cheerful as each crewmember affirmed a complete lack of the unusual. Finally, he led the way to an observation platform at what would be the stern of the ship when it was not jacked up on its steel legs.

"We're going to install a tower on its base," Roberts explained. "It's exactly the same maneuver we were doing when we were on *Jack of Diamonds*. Let's just hope it goes better this time—but there's no reason it shouldn't."

Clancy had his doubts about that, but didn't say anything. He peered intently at the ocean around the base. It looked normal enough, dark water slapping at the bright yellow column. He saw that the five men waiting inside the base to position the tower were wearing life jackets. The men at *Jack of Diamonds* had not had life jackets, so Clancy knew they were taking extra precautions. A few small boats were already launched, waiting a respectful distance from the base. *Good. They were ready for problems.*

As before, the massive crane swung the 200-foot tower gently from its resting place on the ship and positioned it above the base. The tower began its cautious descent, moving only centimeters at a time. The men in the base were looking up at it, as was nearly everyone but Clancy, who kept his eyes firmly fixed on the water below.

The tower dropped lower, always at a snail's pace, until it hovered just above the waiting crewmembers. Five pairs of orange-clad arms lifted to make the micro-corrections in trajectory that would snug the tower into the base.

"Stop!" Clancy yelled, pointing down at the water. Just like the incident at *Jack of Diamonds*, the water was beginning to roil green-white around the base. Shouts of alarm went up around the ship. Roberts leaped into action, grabbing his two-way radio.

"Abort!" he yelled into the receiver. "Get those men out of there!"

Clearly, new emergency procedures were in place. Crew-members sprang into purposeful activity as the base began to rock slightly, but discernably. The crane began to lift the tower away from the base. The men in the base scrambled down the interior ladder and appeared on the work platform below, where a bridge-like structure extended from the jack ship out to the platform. The workers ran hastily across this to safety as Clancy spotted the first knife-like fin in the water surging below.

Though the workers were now safely onboard the jack ship, the base continued to rock. The movement became more and more pronounced, and Clancy wondered how long it could resist what-ever pressure was destabilizing it from beneath the waves.

Roberts had been talking over his radio, but he holstered it abruptly once the workers were safe. His face was pale and shocked. "I need to go talk to the men," he said. "Please stay here. It's safe." He set off down the metal steps leading to the main deck.

Clancy began to follow, but reconsidered. He had an excellent view from this vantage point, and he was unlikely to be helpful down on the main deck, dodging the many crew members moving purposefully below. As he watched, the yellow cylinder of the base rocked ever more wildly, finally tipping over. The water closed over it, and the yellow faded to a ghostly green that wavered and disappeared into the depths. The sharks patrolled for several more minutes, hunting fruitlessly for the men. The fins disappeared as the water calmed, and within minutes, there was no sign that anything at all had happened—except for the activity aboard the jack ship, which now resembled a beehive ripped open by a marauding bear.

When Roberts finally reappeared, his face was gray with worry. "Let's get back to Kaunakakai," he said tersely. "This is a disaster.

I've suspended all work until further notice. There's no way I can make the milestones now. No way." He ran his fingers through his hair, looking as though he would prefer to rip it out by the roots. "The thing is, I just don't get it. What could possibly be doing this?" He looked at Clancy pleadingly, as though Clancy might have an answer.

"The ships are miles apart," Roberts went on. "Even if there was something anomalous about the other site, it wouldn't be duplicated here—right here, by some coincidence, the next location we decided to erect a tower. It's just crazy. And whatever it is leaves no trace behind. The divers went down the last time and found the base lying on the bottom. It had been knocked over like a toy block—but there was no indication what had caused it. None. Shit, I think this just might ruin us."

The straight-from-Central-Casting CEO had vanished. In his place was a man staring abject failure in the face. Sweat ran down his cheeks in streams, and his eyes were wide. Clancy took the man's upper arm and felt the tension that hardened his muscles.

"Huff, take a deep breath." Roberts gave him a sharp glance, but did as he was told. "Take another. Another. And another. That's it. Okay." Clancy watched Roberts' face regain some color. His body didn't exactly relax, but lost its rigidity. "That's better. Now, have you done what you can here? Yes? I'm sure you've got a lot of crisis management stuff to take care of back at the office. You do? Yeah, we should go."

Talking calmly, Clancy walked Roberts back to the ship's helipad. The pilot, as grim-faced as every other worker on the ship, prepared for takeoff and they were soon buzzing over the ocean swells toward Moloka'i. Roberts' eyes had the inward look of a man who is contemplating the end of all his hopes and plans.

• • •

When Chaco returned to Jack's house, he found Sierra waiting up. Auntie Keikilani had gone to bed, but Sierra was waiting up.

She was increasingly worried about Clancy and Fred, who was still among those missing in action.

"He's a big mannegishi, you know," Chaco had said. "He's taken care of himself for—oh, I don't know—several hundred years. Maybe a couple of thousand? He'll be all right."

Sierra had to concede that no matter how annoying and buffle-headed Fred might be, he was pretty self-sufficient. So was Clancy (minus the buffle-headedness), but she worried about him, too. When she heard his car draw up outside, she flew out the door, meeting him halfway to the house. Surprised, Clancy folded his arms around her and kissed her.

It wasn't a casual kiss. Sierra melted into him like warm caramel. He could almost feel her trickling into every nook and cranny of his being. She held herself against him with such urgency, such passion, that he could only respond in kind. Without speaking a single word, they turned and went to the car, arms around each other.

CHAPTER 28

"What was that all about?" Clancy asked, propping his dark head on one palm. His other arm curled around Sierra's shoulders. She lay tucked against him, her long hair spilling loose across his bare chest and arms. She smelled of coconut oil and plumeria.

Sierra stirred against him sleepily, utterly relaxed. "I love you," she murmured.

"I love you too, but what was that all about?"

Sierra reluctantly returned to full consciousness. "I was afraid for you. I was worried sick, really. Auntie told me you had gone out to the jack ship, and I was afraid Kauhuhu and Kanaloa would attack again—and who knows what they might do this time? But I guess Kama kept his promise and everything was okay. Because here you are."

"Well, no. It wasn't okay." Clancy sat up, resting against the hotel cushions. "They attacked again while I was out there with Huff."

Sierra's eyes flew open and she sat up abruptly. "What? Why didn't you say something?"

"I didn't say anything because you, um, directed my attention elsewhere," Clancy said reasonably. "Once you shot out of the door and into my arms, I wasn't thinking about anything else."

"Tell me what happened."

It didn't take long. Sierra had witnessed the first tower coming down, and the second incident was much like the first. Her face grew grim.

"And there were sharks in the water? Like the last time?"

Clancy nodded, his face as grim as hers. "The bastards! And no sign of Kama or Pele, I suppose?" He shook his head.

Sierra raised her knees and wrapped her arms around her legs. "I would've sworn that Kama would keep his promise. This time, anyway. Now what do we do?"

"Right this minute?" Clancy replied. He kissed the top of her head. "I can think of something to do." Gently, he tipped her over onto her back and kissed her nose, then her lips. She reached for him, and there was no more talk of WestWind that night.

• • •

When Clancy and Sierra strolled into Auntie Keikilani's kitchen the next day, Fred was still conspicuous by his absence, and Sierra asked about him.

"I'm sorry. I haven't seen him," Auntie said. "He's usually the first one to turn up for breakfast."

Sierra's happy mood evaporated like dew on the beach. "Oh, no. I wonder what's happened to him?"

"How old is Fred?" asked Clancy.

"I don't know. Hundreds, maybe thousands of years," said Chaco.

"He must be pretty good at taking care of himself by now," Clancy said.

"Yes, I suppose. But I can't help worrying. You know—he's like a kid in a lot of ways."

"He's no child, Sierra. Relax. He'll show up. He always does."

"I think we'd better have a council of war," said Sierra at last. "About WestWind. And about Fred. Let's find Chaco, Rose—who are we missing?"

"Houghton Roberts," said Clancy, and Sierra shot him a look. "Yes, I know that's impossible, but I feel for the guy. He seems decent enough, and everything's crumbling around him. The project will fail because of this, and he doesn't even know why."

"Yes. You're right. But telling him what's *really* been going on won't help anything. He'll just write us off as lunatics, and who could blame him?"

Clancy shrugged. There wasn't much else to say about Roberts. He phoned Rose and offered to pick her up at the hotel.

Before long, Auntie's little living room was overflowing with Sierra and friends. Auntie passed out iced tea and cookies. Clancy caught everyone up on the latest events at the jack ship.

"So all we know is that Kama and Pele aren't involved—not yet, anyway—and Kauhuhu and Kanaloa are still attacking the installation, deliberately putting the workers at risk. The question is, what do we do about it?"

Silence prevailed. Then Chaco said, "What *can* we do about it? Sierra and I played the Kama card, and that's the only card we had."

"Then we have to do it ourselves," said Sierra firmly. "I need to go out to the WestWind installation and talk to Kauhuhu and Kanaloa directly. I need to ask them personally. After all, I'm the one that begged them to stop the installation."

Everyone turned to stare at her. "You can't do that!" exclaimed Clancy. "You'll be killed. You remember the sharks in the water. And when those towers get knocked down—it's too dangerous, Sierra!"

"I have to agree," put in Auntie. "I asked you for help, but I didn't expect you to risk your life, Sierra."

Everyone began to talk at once, but Sierra held up a hand. They all stopped.

"I realize this is a very poor plan—if you can even call it a plan," she said, "and I realize it's dangerous. But I feel responsible for what's happening. I set something in motion that had unintended consequences, and none of them are good. It's bad for the whales. It's bad for the Menehune. It's sure not good for Moloka'i. And it's terrible for Ahi Moana and Huff Roberts. I wanted to hate him, but he's actually a pretty good person, and this is causing him a world of trouble. I have to try to set this thing right. I just wish I had some assurance it might work."

Then the buzz of talk broke out again. A few minutes later, Rose said, "Why don't we ask the loa about this?" Silence reigned as everyone thought about this.

"I guess we'd better call Mama Labadie," Sierra said.

• • •

"You wanna do what?" asked Mama's querulous voice on the cell phone speaker.

"A long-distance ceremony. You and Rose do the ceremony, and we watch via cell phone. Clancy can tell you how to set up the call."

"I believe I am quite capable of setting it up on my own," came the sharp reply without a trace of an accent. Sierra remembered a little too late that Mama was an engineer by profession who could probably design a telephone network, much less set up a conference call. "I'll call back when we're ready."

An hour later, the phone call came from Kaylee. On Clancy's phone screen, they saw a small altar laid with ritual objects as well as a bowl of cornmeal, bananas, and a bottle of rum.

In California, Kaylee began to play drums, setting up a slow rhythm that gradually built in pace and intensity. Auntie followed along in Moloka'i with her 'ili'ili, four polished black stones that she clicked together in her fingers like castanets, producing a crisp clacking sound. Rose began to chant.

Mama Labadie busied herself with arranging bananas, cornmeal, rum, and other items on the altar. Those not playing an instrument or chanting watched in silence. Clancy squirmed uneasily. Sierra recognized Clancy's usual response to anything supernatural, and wondered for the umpteenth time why he put up with her when he was so obviously uncomfortable with the weirdness that was her life.

Finally, Mama was satisfied with her preparations. As the odd accompaniment continued, she sat on the floor, head bent. Then she began to chant, melding her voice with Rose's. She rose to her full height of six feet and began to sway gracefully from side to side, still chanting. Her expression, normally rather stern, softened, and she spun in place, flashing a luminous smile around the room like a beacon. In fact, thought Sierra, she looked nothing like her everyday self. In place of the rather intimidating Mama Labadie, there now danced a stranger, lithe, beautiful, sensuous—and rudely cheerful. This stranger swigged a quarter of the bottle of rum—Mama never drank—ate some fruit, and danced. She danced flirtatiously, though there were no men in the room at her end, grinding her hips suggestively. Sierra could not imagine any behavior less like that of her sedate, serious, and sometimes caustic friend.

After a half hour of dancing and drinking, the woman abruptly stopped and faced the cell phone screen, giving the watchers in Moloka'i a clear view. Her eyes rolled back into her head, leaving blank white orbs in her eye sockets. Sierra shivered at the sight.

"Fred is in danger. Go! Hurry!" cried the stranger with Mama Labadie's face. Then she collapsed gently onto the floor, eyes closed and face streaming with sweat. Kaylee immediately knelt by her friend's side.

"Is she all right?" Rose asked anxiously.

Mama's face was as shuttered and still as it had been wild and open only a moment before. Rose brought a bowl of water and bathed Mama's face with a soft cloth, sponging away the sweat. After a few long minutes, Mama's eyes slitted open a crack, creating white crescent moons in her dark face. She turned her head, frowned and opened her eyes all the way, looking up into Kaylee's worried face.

"Did I pass out again?" she said crossly. "What'd I say?"

Kaylee sat back, regarding her friend with serious eyes. "You said, 'Fred is in danger. Go! Hurry!' The loa seem remarkably straightforward today."

Mama sat up, rubbing her eyes. "Could I have some iced tea, please, Kaylee? I can still taste the rum. Lord, but I hate that stuff." She gratefully accepted a tall glass of tea, drinking half the glass in one go.

"If you hate rum so much, why do you drink it?" asked Auntie Keikilani with interest.

"That's not me," responded the houngán, still seated on the floor. "That's Madame Ézilee. She loves it." She hiccupped slightly, still looking annoyed.

"I still don't quite understand," the Hawai'ian woman persisted.

Mama Labadie picked up the phone, rose gracefully and seated herself, still talking to Auntie Keikilani. "The loa are the gods of Voudún. We invite them to visit us, for healing or spiritual purposes. When I invoke the loa, I offer myself as a horse for the god to ride. Madame Ézilee is the one most likely to ride me. She's the goddess of beauty, love, sex, dancing—that kind of thing. Sort of our black Aphrodite." Mama stopped speaking for a beat and shook her head, dreadlocks shivering down her back. "I don' know why Ézilee likes *me* so much. But she does. Anyway, while Ézilee rides me, I *am* the goddess. I speak with her voice."

"Ah," said Keikilani. "Now I understand. Thank you."

"I should go look for Fred," said Clancy, frowning. "And I'd like to point out that the loa didn't say anything about WestWind. We still don't know whether Kama and his girlfriend are going to help."

"Where would you look for Fred?" asked Sierra. "You don't know your way around the island. It would be dangerous to just go wandering off into the back country."

"If Fred is in danger, of course I'm going," Clancy stated flatly.

Chaco cleared his throat. "I think I should be the one to look for Fred. As a coyote, I can get around better than any of you permanent humans. I have powers that may be useful. And I can't be hurt or killed—at least, there's not much that can do me in. So I'm the logical choice."

Clancy looked annoyed. "You don't know your way around here any better than I do, Chaco."

"True," was Chaco's serene response. "But you can't turn yourself into a coyote. And you *can* die. I rest my case."

CHAPTER 29

Chaco spent a long time with Auntie, planning his expedition. "Clancy is right about me not knowing my way around," he explained. "But you can tell me where to find the Menehune. I can negotiate almost any terrain when I'm in coyote form." The two spent hours with their heads together over a map of the island.

"I think you should take the Wailu Trail," she said, tracing something on the map with her forefinger. "It goes right past the Iliʻiliopae Heiau, but if you give the heiau a wide berth, you should be okay. Then you continue…"

"What's the Iliʻiliopae Heiau? Why should I avoid it?"

"The heiau is a place of great mana—but it's a dark and evil power. Too many people—hundreds of people, maybe thousands—were sacrificed there."

"Really?" Chaco slitted his bright amber eyes.

"Yes, really," responded Auntie. "Molokaʻi was once known as the island of sorcery. There was even a school of sorcery here. All the other islands knew of Molokaʻi's mana, and they could see from our many fishponds that our mana made us wealthy. The other islanders were jealous and sent many war parties to raid and plunder, especially from Maui, which is one of the closest islands to Molokaʻi. The old Molokaʻians asked the Menehune for help, and the Menehune formed a chain along the Wailu Trail, passing stones from one hand to the next. The Menehune built this great heiau in a single night on the hillside facing Maui. Anyone in a war canoe could see it for miles. The sight reminded them of Molokaʻi's great power, and discouraged war parties from landing. The priests sacrificed many people in this temple to Kanaloa. I've been there a few times." She shuddered. "It was never a pleasant experience."

Chaco didn't take anything with him on his expedition except for his vest. He didn't need to carry food or water because he could easily forage for these, nor did he require shelter. He planned to hike upcountry where he would be unlikely to be observed, change into a coyote, and quickly negotiate the upland crags and forests until he came to the area where Auntie said he would find the Menehune, living far from human habitation.

Auntie drove Chaco to the trailhead. The trip took them through now-familiar territory. They followed King Kamehameha V Highway east, along the coast. Long before the road began to rise up to the pali, Auntie stopped her car by the side of the highway in the shade of the vine-twined trees. She pointed across the highway to a tiny sign that read simply "Heiau." "There's the path," she said. Chaco exited the car and walked around to the driver's side. He leaned in and kissed Keikilani on the cheek.

"Aloha. Thanks for all your help, Auntie," he said.

"May all the gods and your 'aumakua bless you and keep you safe," she replied. "I hope you find Fred. Aloha."

The path led under sheltering trees as the trail began to climb upward. The trail here was steep and rather rugged, but he didn't feel the need to shift into his coyote form yet. It was still light, and he was still too near civilization to risk being seen while transforming. Before long, Chaco left the trees and followed a dry streambed under the sun for a short distance. Finally, he emerged at a wide plain dominated by a mass of tumbled stones.

"It's the size of a football field!" he breathed, and he was right. The foundations of the temple remained as an enormous, broad platform of stones. Before vegetation grew up around the heiau, it must have dominated the hillside, visible far out to sea. Many of the rocks used in the structure were as large as compact cars, and no mortar had been used; the heiau was held together by its own sheer mass and the skill of the ancient drywall builders—the Menehune, by Auntie's account.

It was now seven in the evening. He and Auntie had spent most of the day planning, and he had gotten a late start. It hadn't bothered Chaco to start his expedition late in the day; he could see in the dark as well as in the daytime. As the sun lowered to the west, it touched the great stone platform with golden light. Chaco stood and stared for a while. He thought that in his native environment the heiau would be a prime residence for snakes. But he had heard there were no snakes in Hawai'i—not that snakes were any danger to him when he was in his full powers as an Avatar.

Many of the stones had come loose from their original positions and lay tumbled about on the ground around the platform. Chaco walked up to a large stone with a flat top that looked like a comfortable overstuffed ottoman inviting him to sit. The hike had not been difficult, and he never tired, but he wanted to take stock of his surroundings. Seating himself on the stone, he allowed his eyes to wander across the great raised plain of rocks before him. The rocks that had been sitting in the sun all day looked hot; he could see the shimmer of heat waves in the air above them. The ones on the sides were less exposed, and many were covered with a thick fur of bright-green mosses where they were shaded by the encroaching jungle. As he sat and took in the scene, he began to feel something reach up to him from the stone. He tensed. It was not a physical touch; the tickling probe of some unknown energy was taking a stroll around his psyche without bothering to ask for permission. He attempted to leap up from the stone, away from the repugnant intrusion, but found that he couldn't rise. The tickling intrusion now seemed like a great fist, clenched somewhere in the middle of his body, holding him in place.

Chaco wasn't prone to panic. Despite his youthful appearance, he was an ancient being, and there was little he hadn't seen or experienced. This was outside of his experience, however. He focused his mana on whatever it was that held him to the stone, working fingers of power around the foreign force inside his body. As he did this, he scanned his surroundings. If there was a trap here, there must also be a trapper—every coyote knew that.

At first, Chaco was aware only of the expected paranormal activity around him. Small spirits darted among the trees like birds. There were a few slow, dark minds wandering about beneath the earth. None of these were a threat. As his mana worked against the grip of the power constraining him, Chaco sent his senses farther afield. *Ah, there. Approaching.*

• • •

Earlier, while Chaco and Auntie Keikilani had hunched over maps, discussing Chaco's rescue mission, Clancy had paced around and around the small living room until Auntie lost her patience and shooed him out.

"Go to the beach. Or go out to lunch. Or take a hike. You're making us nervous," she had said, making shooing motions with her hands at Sierra and Clancy. They left, but with no destination in mind, walked downtown.

"How about some ice cream?" Sierra suggested. Clancy shrugged. They began looking for ice cream. Downtown Kaunakakai consisted of two main streets off the highway with a number of smaller residential streets branching off. Grocery stores, tourist traps, galleries, a liquor store, some fast food restaurants, a dry goods store—there it was: an ice cream shop. Initially, Sierra was fascinated by the brilliant purple sweet potato ice cream, but settled for Hawai'ian mud pie instead. Clancy had the same, and neither was sorry about their choice.

As they sat outside the store under the shade of the eaves, Clancy's phone rang. He handed his cone to Sierra, who licked at hers to keep the delicious treat from melting into her lap, and patiently allowed Clancy's ice cream to drip over her hand and onto the sidewalk as he talked.

"Okay. Thanks for calling," Clancy concluded, and ended the call. Rose's medicine bag had escaped from its hiding place under his shirt. He tucked the bag away impatiently and retrieved his dripping cone.

"Who was that?"

"Roberts."

"Really? I'm surprised. What did he want?"

"He promised to call me to let me know what, if anything, they've found out at *Jack of Hearts* that made the tower fall. As before, they found nothing."

"We *know* what made the tower fall. Why did you want him to call?"

"I just wanted to know if they found anything. Also, it seemed like a normal thing to ask."

"So what are they going to do about it?"

"I gathered from what he said that they're continuing with the installation."

Sierra dropped her cone. It splatted at her feet, spraying melted ice cream over her bare toes, but she barely noticed. "They can't! Clancy, they can't go ahead. You know what will happen!"

• • •

Sam shook his head at Sierra, Clancy, and Rose, who were crowded into his tiny charter office. If Auntie Keikilani hadn't opted out of this trip, there would have been too many people to fit.

"I can't help you there," Sam said. "I don't want to go out there and get in the way of the construction crew."

"Yes, but," began Clancy, but he caught a sharp look from Sierra, and cut himself off.

Now is the time to start using mana, Sierra said to herself, and reached inside for those glowing ribbons. She spoke in a low, gentle voice. "I think going out to the wind farm would be a wonderful idea. It will be beautiful. You'll see how they are building the turbines. You want to see that, don't you?"

To everyone's astonishment, Sam began nodding his head. "Yes, I see that now. You're right, of course. I'll be ready to go in one hour. Meet me at the wharf." He bustled out, presumably to prepare for the trip. Sierra, Clancy, and Rose trickled out into the hot sunshine, everyone looking puzzled except for Sierra.

"Did you do that?" whispered Clancy. "Did you do a 'Star Wars' number on him?"

"What do you mean?"

"You know, 'These are not the droids you are looking for.'" He made a cryptic gesture with one hand.

"Well yes, I put a little spin on things to move him along," Sierra admitted. She couldn't help grinning just a little at the success of her attempt to influence Sam.

"You have to teach me how to do that," Rose whispered to her friend. But Clancy looked uneasy.

They gathered at the Kaunakakai Wharf an hour later and found Sam and Mike on board *Polupolu*, ready for their passengers. They churned away from the dock and out of the harbor, turning to the west this time instead of east. Rose turned to Clancy.

"Do you still have my medicine bag?"

"Yes," said Clancy, pulling the thong over his head. "Here."

"No, Clancy. You keep it. Be sure to wear it," Rose said, replacing the thong around his neck. She tucked it carefully into his shirt and smiled, but her eyes were worried. She walked away to stand at the rail, and Clancy gazed after her, looking puzzled.

"We want to go to one of the jack ships out there," Sierra yelled to Sam over the sound of the engine. "*Jack of Diamonds*. It's the one closest to shore." Sam nodded. Apparently whatever she had done was lasting.

The journey took much longer than it had by helicopter. Kaunakakai was located almost midway along the island's southern coast. *Polupolu* followed the coast past the westernmost tip of land before heading out into the channel. As before, they saw spinner dolphins near the boat and many whale spouts in the distance. Sierra spotted several turtles swimming gracefully near the surface, but as they left the island behind she saw no more of them. A flock of what appeared to be silver birds began soaring all around the boat. She saw they were fish—called malolo, she knew—flying fish, launching out of the water a hundred or more at a time, gliding incredibly far across the surface of the sea. As she watched these sleek, silver creatures glittering in the sun, the installed towers of the WestWind project began appearing on the horizon, growing ever taller as they neared.

The wind farm presented a surreal vision out here in the deep sea, with land barely visible as a streak of blue-gray on the horizon. Sierra thought there was something weirdly beautiful about this monument to human ingenuity standing alone in a vast expanse of water. The ocean was calm, reflecting the wispy clouds and the sky amid the evenly spaced towers and the installed bases not yet topped with towers. None of the turbines had been activated yet, so the towers equipped with blades stood silent and still. It resembled a strange, watery cathedral, unfinished, its pillars reaching to the sky instead of a roof. The uncapped yellow bases looked like the broken stumps of columns in an ancient temple. Instead of a stone floor, the gleaming sea stretched between the towers and stumps, a lake of quicksilver. Gradually, *Jack of Diamonds* grew larger, sitting atop its six legs like an enormous water beetle.

Polupolu chugged its determined way amid the bases and the standing towers toward the jack ship. As they approached, a small boat launched from a dock at the base of one of the jack ship's steel legs and headed toward them. A man with a bullhorn stood in the prow. As it grew closer, he raised the bullhorn to his mouth.

"Ahoy! What's your business? We weren't expecting anyone."

Sam peered down from his perch at the helm of *Polupolu*. He was holding out a bullhorn to Sierra. "Maybe you should answer him," Sam said. "I have no idea why we're here."

Sierra took the bullhorn, located the "on" button and pressed it. "*Polupolu* out of Kaunakakai," the bullhorn roared as she spoke into it, startling her. "Um, looking for Houghton Roberts."

There was silence from the other boat as this was absorbed. *Polupolu*, idling at low speed, rocked as waves sloshed against her sides.

"Mr. Roberts isn't here," came the amplified answer. "I can't let you board without authorization."

"Okay," roared Sierra's bullhorn. "We're just going to stay here for a little bit. Okay?"

A longer silence ensued. "Why? I told you Mr. Roberts isn't here."

"Well, call him and tell him that we're here."

"You're nuts. You can't do this." The speaker seemed flabbergasted. Apparently they hadn't had a lot of day-trippers at the construction site.

Sierra handed the bullhorn back to Sam. "Let's stop here."

But Sam seemed to have recovered from Sierra's persuasion. "I'm getting us out of here." He turned to go back to the cockpit.

"It's all right, Sam," said Sierra, again in that soft, soothing tone. Now Sierra could see tendrils of rosy light reaching out from her to Sam. She was reasonably certain no one else could see them.

"Alright. Sure. It'll be fine," Sam said. He cut the motors. Sierra began to don fins, wetting them first with seawater so they would slip over her feet more easily. "Please drop the platform so I can get in the water."

Freshly alarmed, Sam said, "You can't do that. There are sharks out here. And really strong currents. You'll be killed!"

Clancy pulled Sierra aside. "What are you doing?" he hissed.

"It's all I can think of to do," she responded. "If Huff tries to install another tower, Kanaloa and Kauhuhu will do the same thing again. Kama and Pele are still out of the picture, so I guess our trip to the Big Island was a waste of time. Pig!" she said, nastily.

"Did you just call me a pig?"

"No, no, no. Not you. Kama. He promised us. *Promised* us—and the Menehune. And he's done nothing. Except presumably frolic with his red-hot girlfriend. Well, someone's got to stop Kanaloa and Kauhuhu, and I started this, so I guess it's up to me to stop it."

"Sierra, please don't do this," Clancy said. "I'm really afraid for you. You know for a fact there are a lot of sharks out here, and most of them aren't Avatars."

Sierra looked up at him from her seat on the deck. "You know," she said, "the ancient Hawai'ians thought of sharks as their ancestors. They worshipped them and looked on them as guardian spirits, 'aumakua. Who are we to say they were wrong?"

"In general," Clancy replied, gritting his teeth, "sharks are huge, hungry animals with big, sharp teeth."

Sierra reached rosy tendrils out to him. "Clancy, I know what I'm doing…" Her voice was velvety, almost hypnotic.

"Don't try that shit on me!" Clancy growled. "Sierra, please listen…"

But Sierra silently continued adjusting her gear. Making sure the mask was clean and unfogged, she rose and walked to the stern platform. The boat that had launched from *Jack of Diamonds* was still there, apparently waiting to see what they were up to. She sat on the platform, fins in the water, eyes searching the depths anxiously. She was so frightened she could hardly breathe. Her chest compressed with dread of whatever waited beneath the waves for her. She began a chant of protection, imploring Kanaloa and Kauhuhu for safe passage, as Auntie Keikilani had taught her. She motioned with her head toward the duffel bag she had brought with her. A fresh lei waited there as an offering to the gods. Clancy, moving like a man with lead weights on his feet, went to the duffel and opened it. He picked the lei up in two hands and turned back to Sierra.

At that moment, a deep rumble shook the air. Everyone started and looked around, including the crew of the other boat. There was a long silence broken by nothing but the slap of waves against *Polupolu*'s hull. Then another rumble was heard, a deep, resonating sound that seemed to shiver up from the depths of the ocean. But there was nothing to be seen. Gentle swells continued to rock *Polupolu*, and the sea appeared calm.

After several more minutes, a grinding roar shook the occupants of both boats, which swayed and dipped as the water grew agitated. But it was not the green-white agitation in the water that had brought down the towers; a sullen red glow now became visible, shining up through the leagues of water beneath. The water began to boil—literally, this time. After a few minutes, Sierra was horrified to see the cooked carcasses of fish, including a thirteen-foot tiger shark, bobbing to the turbulent surface where the corpses were flung about like noodles in a soup pot. She tore off her snorkel mask and hopped back onto the deck as the water at her feet grew painfully hot. Mike swung the platform back and secured it, wide-eyed with uncomprehending terror.

Then she saw the face beneath the waves. It was a face of fire, fire inexplicably raging beneath the ocean, and she would know that flaming, furious beauty anywhere. Pele's face stared up at her through the water with incandescent eyes, her generous mouth parted in unmistakable laughter.

"What's going on?" yelled Sam from the cockpit. "What's happening?"

"Get us out of here, Sam!" Sierra shrieked back.

"Wait!" cried Clancy, running aft. "We need to warn them!" He was apparently going to shout at the other boat, where the crew was staring at the boiling water in disbelief. But as he raced toward the stern, Polupolu's engines revved, propelling the boat abruptly forward. Clancy tripped as the surface beneath him accelerated, slammed against the railing—and was gone.

Sierra shrieked and lunged toward the railing where Clancy had disappeared, but Mike caught her in a grip made powerful by years of earning a living on boats.

"Let me go! Clancy!" she wailed, fighting against his immovable arms. But all Mike did was yell at Sam, "Go! Go! He's gone." He wrestled her into the cabin and forced her to sit, never relaxing his grip. Rose sat beside her, holding her like a warm blanket against the horror of what had just happened. As *Polupolu* raced away from the WestWind installation, Sierra struggled miserably for a few minutes and then began to weep as though she would never stop.

She did not stop weeping for a long time. Black guilt tore into her soul—*He would still be alive if not for me! Why didn't I mind my own business? It's all my fault!* Worst of all: *Why Clancy? Why wasn't it me?* She was unaware of her surroundings until *Polupolu* docked at Kaunakakai. When *Polupolu* was securely docked, Rose reluctantly moved back, giving her air and space, and she became once more aware of her surroundings.

Sam, looking grim, saw them off the boat, saying, "I'm going down to the police station to report all this. I suppose they'll want to talk to you. Auwē! I don't know how I'm gonna explain what I was doing out there. I must've been off my rocker."

Somehow, they all wound up back at Auntie's house, though Sierra never could remember how they got there. Auntie took one look at her, enveloped her in a long hug, and put her to bed with a mug of something hot she had concocted. Then Auntie joined Rose in her living room. Rose was weeping softly.

"What happened?" Auntie asked, settling into her favorite chair.

Rose described the scene of disaster and chaos at the West Wind installation. "Sierra said it was Pele, that she saw her face in the fire under the waves. Maybe a volcanic eruption? The water started boiling, and dead fish were coming up from the depths. Sam revved up *Polupolu* to get us out of there, but it caught Clancy off-guard. He went overboard." Rose gulped, and a single tear slipped down her nose. "He must've been dead as soon as he hit the boiling water. There was no point in trying to save him."

Auntie put her head in her hands. "Oh, poor Clancy, how *horrible*. Poor Sierra."

CHAPTER 30

Chaco waited patiently, sitting on the imprisoning stone. Something was coming. It would get here in its own time. In the meantime, he probed cautiously at the thing holding him there.

It was more like a ghost than a being or a spirit. Supernatural beings were complete; they had their own personalities, abilities and goals. Spirits likewise were whole, though insubstantial to human senses. But ghosts were the sad echoes of things that had once lived and left only a resonating vestige of energy behind.

The thing that had been set to trap him was just a fragment torn from a once-living human. Chaco reached out with his mana to see if there were more like it in the area and found a virtual sea of drifting, lost remains. A horrific repository of tragedy, violence, terror, and loss lay upon the vast platform like a toxic miasma. Each mournful remnant had been ripped away and forsaken by a human sacrifice up there on the flank of the mountain.

Chaco quickly withdrew the searching tendrils of his mana. Evil had been poured over these stones like poisoned syrup, he thought. But Kanaloa wasn't really evil. In Chaco's opinion, Kanaloa had his good side, though he was unreliable, unpredictable, and often untrustworthy. Auntie had said Kanaloa traveled around the islands with Kane, the creator god, creating freshwater springs for the thirsty people. He provided the ancient Hawai'ians with food and other necessities from the sea. Perhaps the evil derived from the humans who had murdered other humans in the name of Kanaloa? Had Kanaloa even wanted or needed these ruined lives?

As evening closed in, the black moths began to flit overhead. The stars blazed brilliantly all the way down to the horizon, unaffected by the puny lights of Kaunakakai. Finally, the moon began to rise. It was a crescent moon, still waning from its fullest. The horn of the moon peeked over the tops of the trees, fading the stars and casting a veil of silvery half-light across the vast darkness of the heiau.

As the moon rose, Chaco began to hear strange sounds. They were not the sounds of the insects or birds or the wind in the branches of the surrounding trees. It was more like the sound of the Menehune as they processed into Kama's valley. He could hear far-off chanting and the sound of conch shells being blown. With the senses of an Avatar—and a coyote—Chaco became aware of a foul odor on the usually sweet night breeze. The sounds grew louder, and now he could see a line of torches proceeding down the trail, though he couldn't yet see the torchbearers.

Gradually, the processional approached near enough that Chaco could see. It was a group of warriors, ancient Hawai'ians arrayed for battle with clubs and spears. Their faces were tattooed with black spirals and geometrical patterns that appeared to whirl and spin in the light of the torches. And the foul smell became the reek of a violated grave.

To his dismay, Chaco knew who and what these warriors were: huaka'ipo, the Night Marchers. Auntie had told him about these spirits and warned him to avoid them should he hear them coming. She described their chants, conch blowing, the foul reek, and the tramp of many bare feet. He'd heard them coming, but due to the ghostly power that held him to the stone, he had been unable to keep clear.

Now the marchers came to a halt and surrounded him where he sat. They were faceless. Their bodies were powerfully built, shining like statues in the torchlight, but their faces were indistinct, as though each countenance were shrouded by black mist—except for the eyes, glowing luminescent green in the dark like something out of a horror movie. While they were terrifying to behold, Chaco himself was an immortal and had seen far more frightening creatures.

"This one is none of my blood," said one grim warrior. "He looks right at us. This is kapu, and he should die."

Another warrior peered more closely at their bound captive. "He's no mortal. We have no power over him."

A muttered discussion ensued. As much as Chaco wanted to hear what they were talking about—after all, it concerned him—he was distracted by a new glow, tiny and far off, a spark that flared in the middle of the great platform of stones. It started as a light no bigger than a firefly and grew rapidly. At this stage, Chaco could see that it was a man—or at least something in the form of a man. The form began to stride toward him, covering the uneven footing of lava stone with easy grace. The figure was that of a Hawai'ian man, much like Kama in appearance. He was clad in the trappings of an Ali'i chieftain, with a kapa cloth malo, feathered cloak, and whale's tooth necklace. On his head was the same type of red-and-yellow-feathered helmet Chaco had seen Kama wear, and one blocky hand grasped a long spear.

As the glowing figure strode toward the stone and the Night Marchers, Chaco saw that in the hand not occupied by the spear, the new arrival held a small, struggling animal. No, not an animal—Fred. The figure held the little mannegishi upside down, his twiggy arms and legs bound with rope. Despite being trussed like a turkey, Fred was wriggling in violent protest and screeching at the top of his lungs.

The Night Marchers stood back and lowered their eyes.

"Lord Kanaloa," said one. "How may we serve you?"

"This one is mine," said Kanaloa, gesturing at Chaco. "He betrayed me and his life is forfeit."

The Night Marchers fell back to the accompaniment of more murmuring. Then one of the spirits stepped forward. "He is yours, Lord. He has great mana and we can't harm him." The spirit's eyes glared green. The marchers turned as one and sounded the conches as they resumed their endless march.

The glowing figure strode to the stone where Chaco sat ensnared and stopped, glowering down at him. Chaco saw that despite the classically carved Polynesian features, the eyes were blue. Not the blue of human eyes. These eyes were all blue with no whites. Like…like the eyes of the giant white octopus that had swept Chaco and Sierra into the sea.

"So we meet again," Chaco said, affecting a casualness he didn't feel.

"Why did you do it?" growled Kanaloa, not bothering to acknowledge the question.

"Do what?" Chaco was genuinely puzzled.

"You called on the wrath of Pele to oppose me!" roared the figure, seeming to swell, becoming even more menacing.

"I did?"

"You and that witch you were with! Why did she plead with me for help—then turn around and send Pele to destroy my work? I want to understand before I kill you. Then I'll kill the witch."

Obviously something's happened since I left. Chaco hadn't yet been able to escape the bonds of the ghost-energy that held him, but he had no doubt that given time, he would find a way out of its mindless grip. With his Avatar powers intact, he had no fear of dying. But he was immobilized, looking up at a visage so suffused with rage he thought it might explode, and he had no idea what Kanaloa was talking about.

"So Pele finally showed up?"

"You admit it!"

"Well, sort of. You and your shark friend were trying to make mincemeat out of the workers out there. Sierra didn't ask you to kill the people, just stop the building."

"What better way to stop what people are doing than to kill the people doing it?" grated Kanaloa through clenched teeth.

Chaco paused. Seen from Kanaloa's perspective, this was perfectly reasonable. Kanaloa was an old god, older than Hawai'i, Auntie had told him, and the old ways had been bloody and grim at times. But hopefully, times had changed.

"Kanaloa, we objected to the building in the ocean because the whales hated it," Chaco said. "The Menehune asked Kama for help. Kama agreed. We just, uh, reminded Kama of his promise to the Menehune. Really. That's the truth." Not one hundred percent of the truth, but Coyotl the Trickster was comfortable with half-truths. And lies, if absolutely necessary.

"Liar!"

So much for that.

"Well, let Fred go, anyway," Chaco said in a reasonable tone of voice. "Why do you have him tied up like a chicken? He's harmless."

Kanaloa lifted his muscle-corded arm to look at Fred as though he had forgotten he was toting a rope-bound mannegishi. "This is a Fred? I am going to sacrifice it. It intruded on my holy space at a sacred time. This is kapu, and the penalty is death."

"If you want good results, my advice is don't sacrifice a mannegishi. Where he comes from, it's supposed to be a thousand years bad luck. Now, sacrificing me is another thing altogether. I'm immortal, of course, but if you can manage it, I'm supposed to be an enormously powerful sacrifice. A thousand years *good* luck, I should think. Let Fred go and take me instead."

Kanaloa dropped Fred from shoulder height and crouched, spear at the ready. "Die like the dog you are!" Kanaloa roared, and swiftly jabbed his heavy spear at Chaco. Chaco didn't bother to flinch, but to his surprise, his earth-filled vest tore away with a horrible ripping sound, and he felt his mana drain away. At the same instant, the ghost-energy released him and Chaco sprang to his feet. Although he was weak and sick from losing his mana, he managed to sprint away from the heiau like Fred after a chocolate bar, taking refuge behind an enormous boulder. He knew he couldn't last long against Kanaloa without his powers, but he hoped to gain a moment or two for negotiation.

The angry Avatar leaped after him, brandishing his spear. "Why even bother, you mangy puppy? Your mana is gone. No one can stand against Kanaloa!"

"Except Pele," Chaco shouted, and leaped up the side of the boulder to avoid a spear thrust that fountained green fire as it struck the stone. He might be merely a mortal now, but he was a mortal with a young, strong body.

Chaco scrambled over the boulder and slid down the other side, using the undergrowth to shield himself from Kanaloa. He yelled, "Come and get me!" then slid away through the trees to another sheltering boulder as Kanaloa's spear sparked green fire where he had just been hiding.

Kanaloa paused, peering around for his quarry in the entangled dark of the trees and brush. Chaco crept silently into another stand of trees, ears and eyes straining anxiously to locate Kanaloa's current position. His mortal senses were far less acute than his Avatar-powered senses, and he was feeling handicapped on all fronts. As he ducked to avoid a tree limb, a massive brown arm swept around his throat and held him in a chokehold.

"Got you!"

Chaco struggled against the arm, which felt like carved granite. He couldn't breathe. The arm lessened its grip slightly, enough for Chaco to take a full lungful of air. He drew in the warm, humid air, smelling of flowers and sea air, and wondered how many more breaths he could count on, as Kanaloa swiftly bound his arms with heavy rope. The Avatar began dragging Chaco back to the heiau. It was like being dragged by a mountain; Chaco could no more pit his mortal strength against this force than he could fly to the moon.

They came swiftly to the immense platform of stones, and Kanaloa leaped on it with a single bound, carrying his victim. Chaco's legs dragged across the jagged surface of the lava rocks, shredding skin and clothes, but that was the least of his worries. Kanaloa stopped in the center of the heiau. He dumped Chaco roughly onto the stones, where he sprawled without moving, waiting for an opening if it came. Kanaloa discarded Chaco's vest several yards away, where Chaco would not be able to reach it, even if he managed to free himself.

Kanaloa stood straight and tall beneath the blazing stars. The moon had set, so there was no light to compete with the stars. The night sky was a vast pavilion of blue-black velvet, pricked with the light of a billion ancient suns. He unsheathed an obsidian knife from his waist. Holding the blade in his huge right hand where its translucent blade caught and held the starlight, Kanaloa stretched his arms wide and muttered an incantation. Immediately a hulking black shape appeared at the far corner of the old temple and approached with a grinding rumble. As it neared the center of the platform, it became visible as a black boulder roughly the size and shape of a desk. The boulder ground to a halt before Kanaloa, now appearing to be precisely in its accustomed place. It was an ancient altar, impregnated throughout its porous bulk with the blackened blood of many sacrifices. Kanaloa turned to his victim, stooping to pick him up—and froze in astonishment.

Chaco's bonds were neatly sheared through, lying limp and discarded on the rough stones of the heiau. There was no sign of Chaco, Fred—or Chaco's half-empty—but half-full—vest.

CHAPTER 31

Sierra swam up from a dream. It had been a dream about vacationing in Hawai'i. She and Clancy had been swimming among colorful corals and fishes. They lay in the sun on a white sand beach drinking mai tais. Then they found themselves in a beautiful room. There was water below them, as if the room were a boat sailing on a calm sea, and the hull was fashioned of glass. They could see fish of all sizes and colors swimming beneath them among the waving fronds of seaweed and the coral trees. Then they made slow, delicious love in that sun-filled room, the light spinning and wavering around them as it shimmered across the ripples. But now, something was tugging at her, pulling her away from that lovely vision. Something unpleasant awaited her, but she didn't know what.

Sierra opened her eyes—no small task, as they were gritty and stuck together. She was in the guest bedroom in Auntie Keikilani's house, and morning light streamed through the slats in the venetian blinds. Sierra blinked at the light, trying to throw off a deep grogginess to remember her beautiful dream. It was, she recalled, a dream about Clancy.

Clancy.

Clancy was dead.

Sierra's head began buzzing, and there were annoying white flickers at the edges of her vision. Her head began to ache, and she was having trouble hearing anything over the buzzing. She was afraid of moving; it might make the pain worse. She heard the door to her room open quietly, but lay still with her eyes closed. She didn't think she could bear interacting with another human being. Someone sat on the bed next to her and laid a gentle hand on her shoulder.

"Sierra, wake up," said Rose's quiet voice. "I need to talk to you."

Sierra tried to pretend that she was still asleep, but Rose was having none of it. "Come on, Sierra, open your eyes. I have something important to tell you. About Clancy."

Sierra rolled over and put a pillow over her head. She was entitled to some privacy under the circumstances, and this intrusion was too painful to bear.

"While you were asleep, I meditated on my spirit guide. I ran through a number of exercises that Mama, Kaylee, and I learned at the conference in Sedona."

Sierra removed the pillow and stared at her friend. She was so numbed with pain—if that was a thing—that she didn't question why Rose was telling her about her spirit guide meditations when all that mattered was that Clancy was dead.

"I had a vision from my spirit guide. It told me that Clancy didn't go into the water yesterday."

No, this really was too much. Sierra began channeling Clancy. "No. I'm sick and tired of the mumbo-jumbo. I saw him go over the side with my own eyes. Just do me a favor and get out of here. Please."

Rose again laid a hand on Sierra's shoulder, which she tried to shrug off. "Sierra, I'm as sure as I can be. Don't you trust me?"

Sierra sat bolt upright. "I hate all this stuff. I just want to be a normal person. If I'd never met Chaco, never got involved with all this weird shit, Clancy would still be alive. He's the one who had the right idea—and he's the one who's dead. It's just not fair!" Tears began trickling down her cheeks, but Rose refused to budge.

"All right. If you don't believe me that Clancy is still alive, will you believe the loa?"

Sierra stared at her friend resentfully, but nodded. "I trust you, Rose. Of course I trust you. I just don't trust the supernatural.

Look where it's gotten me. And Clancy. If Clancy is still alive, where is he?"

"Clancy was wearing my medicine bag. I gave it to him earlier yesterday, and he was wearing it when he went overboard. I think that might have saved him. That doesn't answer your question about where he is, though. I'm sorry. I don't know."

Finally, Sierra asked, "What was in your medicine bag? How was it able to protect him?"

"What a shaman keeps in his or her medicine bag is very private and personal. I need to think about whether or not to tell you. No offense, but it's not something I would normally do."

Sierra got out of bed. "I'll be out in a few minutes. I'm going to take a shower."

The news that Clancy, if not accounted for, might still be alive, compounded with a hot shower, restored Sierra to a near-functional condition. The raw wound of his death was replaced by a tightly wound ball of worry lodged in her solar plexus, but that was more bearable than the awful grief of certainty.

Sierra joined the others in Auntie's kitchen. Auntie had served up pancakes with fresh pineapple and bacon, and Rose was just finishing her portion. After a cup of coffee, Sierra tucked into her share of pancakes with a newly restored appetite. She sighed and sat back.

"That's better," she said. "Rose, maybe you could tell me what you think happened?"

"As best I can," replied Rose. "I'm as surprised and clueless as anyone, you know. Anyway, for the last few days, Clancy had something dark hanging around him. I've seen this before, usually right before someone dies violently. I don't know what causes this. Maybe an evil spirit. Maybe a curse. I didn't want to tell him, given how much Clancy dislikes supernatural stuff—he'd have pooh-poohed it. I wanted him to have some protection, and the best I could do was to give him my medicine bag. It has—it had— great power, and I hoped it would shield him from whatever was threatening him. So I just gave it to him and asked him to wear it. I guess he trusted me enough to do it."

Sierra addressed Rose again. "I know it's not good form to ask about your medicine bag." Rose began to reply, but Sierra held up a hand. "However, I think whatever was in the bag might give us a clue as to what happened to Clancy. What do you think, Rose?"

Rose looked troubled. "It might. I don't know."

"If you revealed the contents, would that in any way invalidate the power of the bag?"

"Oh, gosh. I don't think so. It's just that, well, it's not traditional to share the knowledge. If someone were ill-intentioned toward me, they might be able to use that knowledge against me." Auntie Keikilani nodded at this. Clearly, this was a principle that fit into her own traditions.

"Nobody here would ever harm you, Rose. Am I right?"

"Yes, of course you are."

"Then maybe you could tell us what was in the bag? Just on the chance that it might help us to get Clancy back?"

Rose thought hard, tradition warring with need. Then she nodded. "Okay. The bag had a tiny figure of Kukulkan in it. A very ancient amulet. Along with cornmeal and white sage, of course."

"Of course," Sierra said. "What's Kukulcan?"

"The plumed serpent god of the Maya…"

"Wait a minute. I thought Quetzalcoatl was the plumed serpent god?" Sierra was personally acquainted with Quetzalcoatl from her earlier adventures, but she had never heard of Kukulcan.

"Yes. Quetzalcoatl was the plumed serpent god of the *Aztecs*. Kukulcan was the plumed serpent god of the *Maya*."

"There's *two* of them?"

"Yes and no. In a sense, they are the same god. In another sense, they are not the same."

"Thanks for clarifying that. Could you elaborate?" Sierra unsuccessfully tried to keep the impatience from her voice. She felt as though every minute that passed placed Clancy's continued existence—potential continued existence—in greater jeopardy.

"The Maya occupied Mexico's Yucatan Peninsula and down into Central America. The Mayan culture began to erode around the end of the ninth century CE. We don't know what happened, exactly, but some of them probably wound up joining other tribes and influencing them. A few hundred years later, the Aztec tribe followed a vision quest and founded what is now Mexico City. One of their key gods was Quetzalcoatl, which I think is obviously Kukulcan under a new name. They are both powerful creator gods and both are represented as plumed serpents. To the early Mayans, Kulkulcan was also the 'spirit snake,' the bridge between man and the numinous. The amulet I had in the medicine bag was the spirit-snake version of Kulkulcan. It depicted a spirit ancestor emerging from the jaws of the snake—and it looks almost exactly like the Aztec depictions of Quetzalcoatl. When I first I received the amulet, I knew it was a powerful object, so I put it in my medicine bag and called on it for power during healing ceremonies."

A long and thoughtful silence followed Rose's explanation. "Let's call Mama Labadie," said Sierra. "I want to believe, but I saw Clancy go over the rail with my own eyes. I almost don't want to hear what the loa say, but I need to. By the way, did Chaco and Fred ever come back?"

"Here we are," said a familiar voice at the kitchen door. And another, squeakier voice said, "What's for breakfast?"

•••

In between wolfing down pancakes and bacon, Chaco told their story. When he got to the Night Marchers, Auntie drew her breath in horror.

"No one survives the Night Marchers unless they are of the same bloodline," she breathed. "Yet here you are!"

Chaco explained that he had been unable to flee the Marchers due to the pitiful ghost that held him fast to the stone. "But then Kanaloa came along with Fred. He was intending to sacrifice him. I don't think he knew anything about Fred's role in getting Kama and Pele involved. But he knows about you, Sierra, and he's not happy with you, either.

"Anyway, Kanaloa didn't know about Fred's, um, special abilities," Chaco continued. "So I told him Fred was harmless, not a good sacrificial victim at all, and he ought to sacrifice me, instead. Much better results than a mere mannegishi." Fred looked up from his breakfast, snorting loudly.

"And who was it that rescued *you* from being sacrificed?" the little creature demanded indignantly.

"I'm getting there. Be patient." Chaco smiled fondly at Fred—possibly a first, thought Sierra.

"Wait a minute, Chaco," said Rose. "What about your vest?" She stared pointedly at the ragged, dirty remains of Chaco's vest, now tied awkwardly around Chaco's slim waist and shedding California dirt on Auntie's clean floor.

"I guess he knew that my mana source was in the vest. He dropped poor Fred like a hot potato and tore the vest off with his spear. And he got me, too. Eventually."

"So what was Fred doing?" queried Rose.

"That was the beauty of it. Once Kanaloa dropped him, Fred used his teeth to shear through his bindings." Fred paused his chewing of syrupy pancake long enough to smile, revealing an arsenal of jagged teeth that would make a mako shark proud. Chaco looked at Fred with an expression of open admiration, sharply contrasting with his usual expression of rage or exasperation where Fred was involved.

"When Kanaloa dropped him, Fred disappeared and grabbed what was left of my vest. When Kanaloa paused to perform his sacrificial ceremony—me being the intended victim this time—Fred slashed my ropes and gave me the vest. With my Avatar powers restored, it was easy for us to slip away undetected."

Fred stared up, both saucerlike eyes trained on Chaco. Amber syrup dripped down his face onto his rounded, green tummy and he clutched a rasher of bacon in one six-fingered paw.

"Fred," said Chaco solemnly, "You are the best friend an Avatar could wish for. Thank you for saving my life—as a mortal, there's no question I would've died up there. I can't promise I'll always be patient with you, but you have my eternal gratitude, and that's not an exaggeration. Thanks."

Fred began to blush. A slow, forest-green stain darkened his face and he blinked rapidly. He stuttered slightly, subsided, puffed, and sighed. Abruptly, he launched his small, sticky self into Chaco's arms.

"Argh! No! Yuck! Oh, okay." Chaco gave the little creature a hug and gently set him back in his chair. "Don't get used to it."

Fred tried to brush away the California dirt that now stuck to his front, but only succeeded in smearing it around in the syrup. Auntie abruptly stood, picked up Fred and hauled him off to the bathroom.

"You're a fine mannegishi, Fred," they heard her say as she strode down the hall. "And a fine, brave mannegishi should also be a clean mannegishi." No protests were heard from Fred, so he must have agreed.

"Then what happened?" asked Sierra. "Did you come back here right away?"

"No, but I can tell you about that later. First, you need to know that Kanaloa is after you as well as me."

"Me? Why?"

"Because you asked Kanaloa for help and then betrayed him by getting Pele involved."

"But that's not how it was," Sierra protested, and Chaco gave her a look.

"That's the way *you* see it. Kanaloa sees it differently."

Rose sadly regarded the stained, slashed, dirt-leaking mess of cloth around Chaco's waist. "That vest is just…I don't know. Awful. Can you part with it for an hour or two so that I can tidy it up a bit? I can't fix it, but you can't go around with that thing leaking dirt everywhere."

Chaco frowned. "If I take it off, I lose all my mana. It's a horrible sensation—I imagine it's like bleeding to death if you're mortal. Only I don't bleed to death, I just feel weak and puny and miserable and powerless and…"

"…mortal," Sierra finished for him. "Like the rest of us. You can tough it out for an hour or two, O Defeater of the Great Lord of the Sea."

"That's the other thing," Chaco replied. "We need to get out of here. Kanaloa is after you. And me. And Fred. We aren't safe here."

"But we haven't yet figured out what happened to Clancy," protested Sierra. "Rose says that Clancy may not be dead."

Chaco's fork hit the floor, and he stared at her, his wild amber eyes wide. "What? Clancy dead? What on earth happened while I was gone?"

As Rose and Sierra tried to explain simultaneously what had happened aboard *Polupolu* the day before, Auntie returned with a clean Fred, smiling and smelling of soap. When Fred picked up the gist of the conversation, he emitted a siren-like screech as hot tears splashed from his eyes, each of which was spinning in a different direction.

"Nononononono!" Fred squalled. "Not Clancy! Oh, nononono, Clancy can't be dead, he can't…"

It took several minutes for the others to break through this cacophony to communicate to Fred that Clancy might not be actually dead.

"Whaddya mean, *might not be*?" gulped Fred, sniffling loudly.

"I'm not sure, Fred," Sierra responded. "I thought we should ask the loa. It's not that I don't trust Rose's spirit guide, but I *saw*…!"

"No offense taken," Rose said calmly. "I'd like to hear what the loa say, as well."

CHAPTER 32

Auntie agreed that time was of the essence if Kanaloa had mobilized against her guests.

"You aren't safe from him on land or sea," she pointed out. "You'd be better off going home to California. I'm afraid there's nowhere in Hawai'i that is safe for you now."

"I don't doubt you," Sierra replied. "But I don't want to leave until I've heard from the loa. Clancy disappeared here in Moloka'i. If I leave, I may never be able to come back. I need to be certain I'm not leaving him here. Unprotected."

"If he has my medicine bag he's not wholly unprotected, Sierra," Rose said.

"Yeah, but we don't really *know* anything, Rose. We don't know whether he's here or somewhere else. We don't know if he still has the bag. Or what kind of danger he might be in. Or even if he's even still alive." Sierra felt her throat begin to close again and stopped speaking.

Rose tried again to call Mama Labadie and Kaylee, but both women's phones went to voicemail. She left another round of messages.

Sierra began pacing up and down Auntie's little living room. She was less concerned with Kanaloa's wrath than with finding Clancy. Nervous energy suffused her, and she couldn't relax or settle. She wandered outside to where Chaco was waiting impatiently for Rose to finish mending his vest.

Rose sat on a lawn chair in the shade of a breadfruit tree. She held Chaco's ruined vest in her lap and was carefully sewing it back together by hand, taking tiny, precise stiches. Her jeans were covered in dirt leaking from the torn vest. The garment itself would never look like anything again but a crazy assemblage of filthy rags with once-bright embroidery still clinging to the tatters. Rose hunched over this mess with a frown, silver needle and thimble flashing as she worked.

"I don't think Chaco can wear that thing in public," Sierra commented. "It's pretty awful."

Rose paused, looking up. "I know. And it's not going to look much better, even after I finish. But he's going to wear it as soon as I tie the last thread. He doesn't want to spend a second longer than he has to as a mortal. I suppose he can wear something over it."

"So where is our brave vanquisher of gods?"

"Muttering to himself and pacing around. Kind of like you. Over there." Rose indicated the rear of the yard with a tilt of her dark head. As Sierra looked, Chaco came around the corner of the house, hands working nervously, eyes immediately seeking out his vest. Sierra recognized what she now thought of as Chaco's "mortal look": hazel eyes, a bit pale, fidgety, and uncomfortable.

"Is it fixed yet?" he asked.

"No," came the patient answer. "I'll let you know the second it's done. I promise."

Sierra asked, "Chaco, did Fred ever get to visit the Menehune, or did you two just come straight back after you ditched Kanaloa?"

Chaco wrenched his eyes away from Rose's stitchery. "Yeah. Once we were well away from the heiau, Fred insisted we keep going. He said he had to talk to Ailani. You know, the chief."

"You went all the way to the Menehunes' home in one night? And back?"

"It wasn't that hard for me and Fred. Negotiating rough terrain on four feet will always be easier than on two. But it was a long trip. The Menehune live in the back of beyond, you know."

• • •

The trail past the heiau had been rugged and poorly maintained.

There were loose rocks and scree, the trees and bushes had intruded upon the trail in places, and there were many drop-offs where the earth disappeared into inky and unknown depths. Fred and Chaco both had excellent night vision and were able to avoid the pitfalls, scrambling over the many obstacles in the path. Their only burden was Chaco's vest. Chaco could maintain his coyote form only so long as he was in contact with the earth from the vest, and the vest was so damaged by Kanaloa's spear that Fred was constantly obliged to readjust it for him.

"Why do you have to see the Menehune again so badly?" Chaco asked as they negotiated a relatively easy stretch. Fred spoke for a long time, and Chaco listened with interest, only interrupting to ask questions until, at last, they came to the valley Auntie had described as being the entrance to the Menehunes' home.

By this time, Chaco and Fred were near the top of the great pali in the north. The Menehunes' valley was a steep and narrow defile in the pali. Auntie told Chaco that the defile slanted down and debouched two thousand feet above the ocean. Chaco was immortal, but he couldn't fly, so he made his way cautiously on four agile and slender legs down the grade as Fred scrambled and sometimes rolled beside him. As they descended, the rocky walls of this defile reduced the available light to the faint radiance of the visible stars. They were searching for something that might be too difficult to see in this Stygian darkness: a cleft in the left hand side of the gorge. It was the entrance to the Menehunes' home, but everything looked the same—black—and Chaco had difficulty focusing on his search as rocks slid underneath his paws. He could imagine all too well the bobsled slide to the cliff edge, ending by pitching out into the air far above the ocean. Hardly fatal to an Avatar, but it would be an unwelcome and uncomfortable detour, and a plunge into the sea would surely destroy what was left of his precious vest.

But Fred had no such difficulty. "There it is," he grunted, pointing with one stubby digit to a patch of ultra-darkness against the black of the rock.

The patch of dark-on-darkness was located some twelve or fifteen feet up the side of the gorge. It was a tough scramble without many footholds, but the two of them managed it on four paws each. They found a cave entrance and left even the star shine behind as they entered. Chaco promptly summoned an orb of gentle light that hovered above them. Fred began a solemn chant of greeting to let the Menehune know they had visitors.

After the echoes of the chant died away down the dark tunnel into the rock, there was a lengthy silence. Then a light began to glow, at first just a faint stain of flickering color as though the source were a long way away. As Chaco and Fred waited, the light grew stronger and brighter, and they began to hear chanting. Soon, a procession of small, squat, powerfully built people marched up the cave toward them, bearing torches and singing. Ailani headed the parade.

After the nose-rubbing and polite greetings were done, Fred cleared his throat portentously.

"Ailani, we thank you for your hospitality and we are most pleased to see you and your people again. But this is not a casual visit. We have a request for you."

"Before we talk, please come and feast with us," Ailani said. "By the looks of you, you've come a long way and need refreshment."

Chaco, now in human form, wore the rags of his vest tied around his waist. He was filthy, not just from the California dirt sifting down his lower body, but also from the rough hike. Fred looked a little dusty, but was otherwise presentable. Fred and Chaco exchanged glances. If they refused the invitation, it would be an insult to Ailani and his people. If they joined in a luau, it could last all night and into the next day. Chaco, for one, was uncomfortably aware that Kanaloa was unlikely to stop looking for him and Fred. And for Sierra, who had no clue that Kanaloa might be looking for her with vengeance in his heart.

"Why, yes, Ailani," Fred was saying eagerly, but Chaco stepped on the little mannegishi's rear paw and interrupted as Fred screeched indignantly.

"Ailani, you are the most generous of chieftains," Chaco said. "But I think we must discuss it now. Kanaloa is hot on our trail, and he isn't pleased with us."

"You've angered Kanaloa?" the Menehune asked in alarm. "Is Lord Kanaloa coming here? Now?"

"Not here. Not now, anyway. I think we lost him. But he wants to kill Fred and me, and our friend Sierra, so we have to move quickly. Fred, please tell Ailani what you've been telling me."

• • •

Sierra listened to Chaco's tale first with alarm, then concern, then astonishment, and finally, delight. She threw her arms around him and kissed him enthusiastically. "You're a genius!" she exclaimed. "And Fred's another one!"

"Actually, it was all Fred's idea," admitted Chaco. "I didn't know he had it in him. I may have underestimated our little green friend. But," he added with feeling, "Fred can still be incredibly annoying at times."

CHAPTER 33

Roberts opened the door at her knock.

"Thanks for meeting me, Huff," Sierra said as she entered the Ahi Moana company condo. "How are things going?" The latter was a throwaway comment. She knew how things were going.

Huff no longer looked like the CEO from Central Casting. Already thin, he had lost weight over the past two weeks, and his lean cheeks now seemed sunken. His hair was rumpled and seemed grayer than before and his eyes were tired. Little wonder, given the events of the last few days.

"I hear Clancy was killed out at the site. I'm so very sorry," Huff said, looking genuinely sorrowful. Sierra acknowledged his sympathy with a nod. Her eyes stung and she held off the tears that tended to well up whenever Clancy's name was mentioned.

He continued, "Why did you go out there? I don't understand. My men said you wanted to see me, but that couldn't be right. I mean, you're not crazy. You could've called me."

"It's hard to explain. First, I have something I need you to see. Then you might understand better," she said as he handed her a handkerchief. *A man who actually carries a clean linen handkerchief,* she thought in wonder.

"I wasn't there," he said. "I think you knew that at the time. What actually happened from your point of view?"

Sierra described everything to him as clearly as she could, leaving nothing out except for Pele's fiery face glowing through the waves—and Clancy's presumed survival. "It looked like a volcano erupting under the water," she finished. "But Penguin Bank is supposed to be extinct. Isn't it?"

"Yes, it is. At least, they thought it was. We have some volcanologists out there now. They're still investigating, but their favorite theory right now is that some deep tremors opened up an isolated lava chamber, and it erupted right at the *Jack of Diamonds* site. The preceding tremors are what caused the toppling of the towers, according to that theory. But you told the boat crew from *Jack of Diamonds* that you were actually going in the water. Why, in the name of—in the name of *sanity* did you want to do that? It's the deep ocean—the currents are fierce, and so are the sharks."

"I have an explanation, and it does make sense in a weird sort of way, but I don't think it would make sense to you right this minute. Can you spare little time to go somewhere with me? Trust me—you won't be sorry. And we won't be going far."

He looked at her curiously, with growing uneasiness. "Are you working for someone else? A competitor maybe, or a regulatory agency? No—if you were working for an agency, you would've just arrived with the right paperwork and investigated openly. What were you doing out there?"

"I was not—and am not—working for someone else."

"So who do you work for? You told me when we first met— some conservation organization, right? Are they investigating Ahi Moana? 'Cause they won't find anything out of line, if that's the case." His tone was sharp.

"I work for Clear Days Foundation but as far as I know they don't do investigative stuff. They raise money and do outreach to raise awareness about sustainable energy and waste reduction. I promise you, I was out there on my own—well, me and Clancy and Rose. I don't have a hidden agenda, it's just that you wouldn't believe me. Yet. Please come with me. It won't take long."

Huff looked at her for a long, uncomfortable minute. "I really don't have the time," he said. "I've got regulatory agencies and shareholders snapping at my heels, and it's likely we'll have to shut the whole thing down and take our losses."

"Believe me," she said, "you'll want to see this."

• • •

Rose set down her cell phone with a smile. "Finally!" she said to Auntie Keikilani. "I got through to Mama and Kaylee."

Auntie looked up from her book. "Are they going to do a ceremony to ask about Clancy, then?"

"Yes," said Rose. "They wanted to do it right away when I told them Clancy might still be alive, but I said, no, Sierra has to be in on this. So when Sierra gets back, I'll call Mama, and we'll do it as a conference call, like before."

Auntie shook her curly head. "Technology," she said, smiling, and returned to her reading. Stealthy sounds came from the kitchen, and Auntie's head came up sharply.

"Fred!" she roared. "Leave those cookies alone!"

• • •

Sierra and Huff stood at the side of the road, overlooking a broad, grassy stretch of land. The wind blew hard from the western sea, sending Sierra's braid flapping. The long, soft grasses rolled like breakers under the wind. Large stone constructions dotted the field at regular intervals. They were shaped like pyramids with the tops sheared off, rather like ancient Hawai'ian boundary markers, with trapezoidal-shaped sides.

Huff stared out over the grassy field and its odd stone piles for a while, clearly trying to make sense of Sierra's insistence that he come here. "What is this? Are these ancient monuments or something? They look like it."

"Actually," she replied, "They are new and incredibly well-constructed bases for wind turbine towers. Go ahead. Take a look."

Huff did take a look. He inspected three of the stone elevations with extreme care. Finally, he returned to where she waited for him, perched on one of the bases.

"I don't understand. These look custom-made as tower bases,

but they're made of rock. Just rock, no cement, no mortar to hold it together. They seem solid, but how can they support our towers? The towers are maybe two hundred feet high, and they have to resist very high winds and turbulence. Besides, where did these things come from? Who built them? Why did they build them? Who owns this property?"

"Sit down, Huff," Sierra said, patting the rocks next to her. Huff sat. "This is gonna be tough, but hear me out. First of all, the bases weren't here yesterday." She pulled her phone out of her jeans pocket, retrieved a photo and handed the phone to Huff. He peered at it. It was a photo of an empty field. The field they were now sitting in. Huff looked at the photo and looked around, searching for landmarks. He found three small acacia trees in a clump to one side of the field. The trees were in the photo as well. He scanned the dip and swell of the land as it dropped gradually toward the sea. Every detail was the same, except there were no rock constructions in the photo.

"I took this photo yesterday." Sierra said. "And no, I didn't Photoshop it."

Huff handed her phone back. "That's not possible," he said. His tone was both wary and flat.

"Yes, it is possible. The Menehune built them overnight. Like they built the fishponds. And the heiau."

Huff looked at her with dawning concern. He stood up and held out his hand. "C'mon, Sierra. You've had a tough time here, honey. I think maybe I should get you some kind of help. Let's go."

Sierra ignored his outstretched hand. "Chaco. I need you now."

Chaco stepped around the corner of the base where Sierra sat. He wore a colorful Hawai'ian shirt over the remnants of his vest, which no longer dribbled dirt, thanks to Rose's ministrations.

"Who is this?" asked Huff, turning to Sierra with a puzzled frown. "What are you two up to? What's going on here?"

"Take it easy," Chaco said, grinning at Huff. "Sierra just wants me to persuade you that she isn't crazy." As he spoke, his features began to blur and shift. It was a bit like watching a candle melt, then reform like an icicle in fast motion. In an instant, a coyote wearing a strange collection of dirty rags stood in front of Huff, panting gently and waving its plumy tail.

Pale beneath his tan, Huff sat down again.

• • •

The original idea had been Fred's, but Auntie Keikilani was the one who suggested bringing Jack Kane in on the idea. "Jack is a believer, like me. He's had his own experiences with the Old Ones. And he owns a huge stretch of land on the west island. Grazes cattle on it and hunts deer. Once he finds out how much his electricity bill is going to go down, I bet he'd jump at it."

Jack had indeed been unfazed to find that Auntie's houseguest was an ancient Native American Avatar. "Thought he was a bit odd," Jack said. "But live and let live. My motto." He shook hands with Fred and had a long conversation with him in Hawai'ian. At the end of this discussion, Jack asked Sierra, "How do we know that Ahi Moana will agree to dedicate three percent of the electrical output just to Moloka'i?"

"It's either that or no deal," Sierra told him.

So Fred had stealthily returned to the Menehunes' remote home—keeping a wary eye out for Kanaloa the entire time—and confirmed with Ailani and his people that they needed the Menehunes' help with the tower bases. The Menehune were delighted. They adored stonework, and it had been centuries since anyone had asked them to build something.

• • •

"So it's either three percent to the Moloka'ians—at no charge to them—or the deal is off and the bases go away overnight," Sierra explained to Huff, who was now sitting in the soft grass of Jack Kane's field and leaning against the side of one of the bases.

Roberts, like Clancy, had to accept the evidence of his own eyes and experience. He was still reeling from the barrage of strangeness but trying to cope.

"Well, yeah. I mean, that's only fair," he replied. "But how do I explain all this to the authorities? I can't just say we're moving the installation overnight to a new location. And what about the Moloka'ians? Won't they notice that all the bases popped up in a single night? Won't they be asking a lot of questions?"

"Trust me," Sierra said, "they won't be asking questions. They've lived with the Menehune since forever, and they know a Menehune-built construction when they see one. Auntie and Jack will take care of the Moloka'ians. As far as the regulations and legislators go, you can take your time. If you agree to the terms, the bases aren't going anywhere."

Huff shook his head. "I can't believe this is happening," he said. Then he looked at Chaco. Still in coyote form, Chaco was lying in the long grass enjoying the sun, all four paws in the air in an undignified sprawl.

"Chaco, would mind giving me and Sierra a little privacy?"

Chaco rose, stretched fore and aft, and cocked a bright amber eye at Huff. "No problem," he said, showing just a flash of fang in a grin before he trotted off across the field. He was soon lost to sight among the tall grasses.

Huff turned to Sierra, sitting next to him. Her black hair shone in the sun like obsidian, and her hazel eyes gazed at him steadily. She had a sprinkle of freckles across her nose.

"When do you go home, Sierra?"

Sierra drew her knees up to her chest and wrapped her arms around them. "Soon as possible. I have one more thing I have to do, then Chaco and Fred and Rose and I—you haven't met Rose or Fred yet—have to leave. We kind of got some people, um—Entities? Gods?—really upset with us, and it's too dangerous to stay here."

He looked at her, frowning. "What do you mean?"

Sierra was quiet for a few moments. If she told him why

Kanaloa was angry—and Kauhuhu too, no doubt—she would have to confess her role in the disasters at WestWind. She looked into Huff's gray-blue eyes, now filled only with concern for her. She did some mental girding of loins, took a deep breath, and told Huff the entire story.

"So it was really my fault all along. I truly didn't mean for Kanaloa and Kauhuhu to go as far as they did, and I'm deeply sorry. I was hoping maybe this"—she gestured at the stone bases dotting the field—"would make up for it, at least a little." She peered into his eyes again and found thunderclouds.

CHAPTER 34

They propped Sierra's cell phone against a stack of books in Keikilani's living room so they could all see the screen. On that screen, a miniature Kaylee and Mama Labadie arranged cornmeal, bananas, rum, and flowers around Mama's living room in Silicon Valley. Again, drums, rattles, and 'ili'ili provided rhythm while Fred played the flute. Again, Mama Labadie began a sinuous rhythmic movement that blossomed into a joyous celebration, Mama flashing a brilliant smile around the room and dancing with abandon. After three or four tours of the room, eating fruit and bananas and drinking generous swigs of rum, she stopped, swaying, in front of Kaylee. She seemed to be inviting Kaylee to dance with her, but Kaylee spoke instead.

"Where is Clancy? Is he alive?"

Mama stood swaying for several long moments, as though considering the questions. Then she beamed another wide, gleaming grin at Kaylee. She whirled around, white robes flying around her. She spoke again, this time somberly, without a trace of a smile, "*Time is not your friend.*"

She whirled around again, picking up a bowl of cornmeal. Carefully, she pinched the coarse meal between her slender, dark fingers and began to draw on the dark red carpet with the pale meal. Sierra winced.

"Mama's gonna be so pissed when she finds out Madame Ézilee's smeared cornmeal all over her priceless Bokhara rug," she whispered into Chaco's ear.

Mama completed her drawing, studied it carefully, took a long, thoughtful swig of the rum bottle she held in her left hand—and

252

as her eyes rolled back in her head, she crumpled to the floor next to her creation. Kaylee bent over Mama and wiped her streaming face with a cloth.

"It's no good askin' me," Mama Labadie said crossly, a quarter of an hour later. "Madame Ézilee didn't tell me any more than she told you. So quit buggin' me! I need something to get this rum taste out of my mouth." Kaylee handed her a tall glass of water, which Mama gulped eagerly.

Rose made a request at the Moloka'i end. "Could you please position the phone so we could see the drawing Mama just made?" Kaylee picked up the phone at her end and the image on the screen swung dizzily for a few moments until it hovered over the design on the rug.

"How's that?"

"Good," said Chaco, and they all leaned forward to try to discern the minuscule image on the screen.

"I think I know what it is," said Rose after several minutes of squinting at the little picture. "It's Mexico. Look, there's a glyph right over the Yucatan Peninsula. It's hard to make out..."

Sierra peered over Rose's shoulder at Madame Ézilee's drawing on the small screen. It looked like nothing to her at first, but gradually an image emerged from the imprecise lines formed by the spilled cornmeal.

"What is it?" she asked Rose.

"I'm almost sure...hang on...yes! It's the glyph for Kukulcan! It's the spirit snake glyph, like the amulet I kept in my medicine bag. It's the symbol for Kukulcan, imposed on the map of the Yucatan Peninsula. That makes sense!"

"It does?" asked Fred dubiously.

"Yes. The amulet came from the Yucatan. When it saved Clancy, it must have returned to its native land." Rose looked up, smiling. "Clancy must be in Mexico. The Yucatan, more precisely."

Sierra stared at the awkward drawing on the screen. "You're sure about this? Madame Ézilee didn't actually say Clancy is still alive."

Rose nodded. "As sure as I can be. Given the circumstances. The loa aren't usually this clear, really."

The image on the screen lurched and disappeared, to be replaced by the faces of Kaylee and Mama.

"Well, that pinpoints it," snorted Mama Labadie. "I'm no expert, but that's only about 76,000 square miles we gotta search."

"But if Clancy were in the Yucatan, wouldn't he have gotten in touch by now? He'd have contacted local authorities and gone to the U.S. Consul or whoever it is that Americans are supposed to see when they get into problems in foreign countries," Sierra said.

"Um, yes, under normal conditions," said Rose.

"What do you mean?" asked Sierra, hairs on the back of her neck rising with apprehension.

"Clearly, the circumstances that took Clancy from Moloka'i to the Yucatan weren't normal," Rose explained. "He could've landed anywhere—maybe miles away from civilization. And there are other possibilities. I hate to mention it, but Madame told us that 'Time is not your friend.' We don't know if Clancy is even still in the twenty-first century. Given the age of the amulet, he could be back at the time the amulet was created, when its mana was first charged."

"Ladies and gentleman," said Chaco. "I think it's time to go home."

• • •

Parting from Auntie was an emotional experience for everyone. "You've been so kind and so generous, Auntie," said Sierra, hugging the older woman. "I don't know what we would have done without you." She turned to Jack and hugged him.

"Jack, you're a hero! Thanks for everything, and I hope it all goes smoothly from here on out. I'll miss you. I can never repay either one of you. It doesn't look like I'll ever be able to come back to Hawai'i," she said with deep regret, and thought briefly of

Midway Island and its albatross chicks. "But if you ever come to California, there will always be a place for you to stay with me."

Fred tucked himself into a carry-on bag before they left for the airport. Chaco carried the bag, and this time he was careful to avoid banging the bag against handy obstacles. The tiny airport in Kaunakakai was uncrowded and trade winds swept gently through the open building, carrying the scent of flowers. And jet fuel.

As they approached the security station, Sierra gasped. "What happens when they X-ray Fred? They'll see there's something, um, organic in the bag."

"No worries," Chaco said. "He'll disappear. X-ray machines are no match for a mannegishi."

Sierra, Rose, and Chaco checked in, then sat to wait for their flight to Honolulu and from Honolulu, home. They sat quietly on the plastic seats, each lost in his or her thoughts.

"Sierra?" said a familiar voice.

She looked up. Roberts stood in front of her. She flushed. Their parting after her revelations about her role in the WestWind disaster had been awkward and miserable on her part, angry on his. She could hardly blame him. She peered up at him silently.

"I didn't want to let you leave without saying goodbye," he said. He no longer looked angry, just tired. "I was a bit…upset when we last spoke."

Rose excused herself to go to the ladies' room. Chaco rose gracefully from his seat and wandered into the minuscule gift store nearby. He picked up a coconut painted with a tiki face and turned it over critically as though examining a miniature sculpture by Degas. Huff took his seat beside Sierra, who could hardly bear to look at him.

"Look, Huff, there's absolutely nothing I can say or do that would begin to express how sorry I am," she said.

"I know." He sat quietly, looking at her downcast face. "I was really angry at first. But I remembered how passionate you are about the environment. All the things you wanted to do to protect the albatross chicks at Midway. You're kind of a nut, you know?"

"Yeah, I know," she replied. "Clancy thought so, too. It was a problem for us, sometimes."

Huff was quiet for several minutes. Chaco was now appraising a bobble-head hula dancer. "I realize this is too soon, but I'm going to ask anyway. Can I come to see you in California sometimes? I visit on business frequently. I'd like to see you again."

Oh. I didn't realize. Oh, dear.

"I would love to see you again, Huff. But one thing I didn't mention during our last discussion"—Huff's eyebrows rose in alarm—"is that Clancy isn't dead. At least we think he's not dead."

"That's not possible. He fell in, I mean…"

"The Menehune building a wind farm site overnight wasn't possible either, Huff. You're going to have to trust me on this. I don't have a lot to go on right now, but I do think Clancy is alive, and I'm going to go look for him."

Huff sat silent for several more minutes. "Well, we can still be friends, as the saying goes, right?"

Sierra nodded.

"Where is Clancy, exactly?" Chaco was draping plastic flower leis around his neck and admiring the effect in a small mirror the shopkeeper held.

Sierra decided to skip over the implications of "Time is not your friend," and said, "We think he may be in the Yucatan Peninsula. I'm afraid that's as exact as we can get."

Huff exhaled sharply. "How do you plan to find him?"

"I have no idea," she confessed, struggling not to give way to despair at the thought.

He stood up. "If you need help—any kind of help—you know how to get in touch," he said, then bent down and kissed her gently on the cheek. "Best of luck, Sierra. And thanks. Thanks for Jack Kane's field. Thanks for the Menehunes' help. Thanks for the tower bases." He waved at Chaco, who was sniffing fragrance samplers, and strode out of the airport as Rose emerged from the restroom.

Chaco rejoined the women. After a brief silence, the carry-on bag remarked, "You smell like Auntie Keikilani's garden." Nobly, Chaco refrained from kicking the bag as Sierra shushed Fred.

"What'd he want?" Rose asked. She had heard from Sierra about her last meeting with Huff and its unhappy ending.

"I think he was extending the olive branch. Well, not exactly," Sierra considered what to say for a second. "Actually, I think he was asking me if I wanted a relationship with him."

Chaco cocked his dark head, golden eyes alert. "What do you mean? You already have a relationship with him."

"I do have a relationship with him, but I think he's interested in a romantic relationship."

"Oh. Wouldn't that be kind of awkward? With Clancy being alive? Sort of alive. Alive as far as we know. Besides, he's going to have to take a number," said Chaco. Rose stood up abruptly and walked into the little gift store.

"Huh? Oh, I see what you mean, but who's next in line?" Sierra asked, wondering what sort of trinket made in China could possibly have attracted Rose's attention.

"Me." Chaco's gaze never wavered. Sierra wrenched her gaze back to his.

"Oh, c'mon, Chaco! You keep saying that, but you also told me once that you were footloose, unreliable, and never settled down. You know that's not what I want. Why do you keep saying that about me?"

"Because it's true," muttered Chaco as they stood up to stand in the security line. Rose set down a tube of tanning lotion in the store and hurried to rejoin them. There were no more than ten people in line. Fred's bag went through without a hitch.

Once through security, there was another short wait, and then they boarded the small plane for Honolulu. During the time they had been in the airport, the wind had freshened, blowing strongly from the southwest, and clouds were gathering out to sea. As the little plane taxied down the runway, Sierra could feel it shudder with the force of the wind, but it took off without incident.

Once at cruising altitude, the captain's voice came on the PA system. "Folks, we're the last plane out of Moloka'i this morning. Tropical Storm Afa, a class four or five cyclone, is headed in this direction. Please stay calm; we're well ahead of the storm and we will land safely in Honolulu. However, there will be no more flights out of Honolulu until this situation is over. Those of you who have connecting flights must shelter in place at the airport to wait out the storm. Emergency personnel will be waiting to assist you at the airport..."

"That's weird," Sierra said, after the captain finished speaking. "Isn't this the wrong season for hurricanes?"

"Is it?" Chaco responded. "I don't really know. But I have been wondering if Kanaloa had something more in store for us."

Sierra felt dread creep up her spine, raising goose bumps along her arms. "You think Kanaloa has something to do with this?"

"Kanaloa said he was coming for us, but it's been pretty quiet the past couple of days. We've been careful, of course, and stayed as far as possible from the ocean or the heiau or any other place we might encounter him. But he is god of the ocean. And aren't hurricanes caused by, um, oceanic water temperatures, or something? Anyway, he would be able to raise a storm without thinking twice, I bet."

They passed the rest of the short flight in silence, glumly watching the turbulent ocean below through the thickening clouds.

By the time they reached Honolulu, there was no doubt that a massive storm was on the way. It hadn't begun to rain, but the winds were high enough to send the tall palms bending like so many blades of grass. The sky to the south was purple-black, and as they descended, they could see that the waves breaking on the beaches below were not the gentle summer combers of before, but towering gray-black cliffs, slashed with foam, dashing against the sands and running far up the beach and over seawalls in many places.

The airport itself was primarily open-air, funneling the wind through its corridors. Emergency workers met the passengers and urged them to take shelter on the ground floor of the airport.

But Sierra didn't follow their suggestion. Instead, she ran in the opposite direction, toward an exit. Chaco shoved Fred's duffle bag into Rose's arms and ran in Sierra's wake yelling, "Wait! Sierra! Where are you going?"

Sierra threw herself at an emergency exit door. An alarm sounded and lights flashed, but between the train-whistle shriek of the wind, the sirens wailing all over the city, and the frantic rushing of passengers within the airport, no one paid the slightest attention.

"Sierra, stop! If you go out in that you'll be killed!" Chaco screamed over the wind, and she paused, looking at him as the rain began, driven horizontally by the storm.

"Stay inside with Fred and Rose, Chaco. Take care of them for me," she said, and continued to run. Chaco hesitated by the blaring emergency door, torn between his impulse to protect her and her directive to stay with their friends. In the instant of his hesitation, Sierra disappeared into the darkness, wind, and rain.

• • •

She headed straight for the ocean. She knew from taking off and landing at Honolulu International that its runways directly bordered the bay. Running against the wind proved to be more difficult than she thought, and as the storm gathered its fury, she feared she might actually be blown away. She could dimly see objects flying in the wind, but she couldn't see what they were—branches, perhaps roofing tiles torn away from their buildings.

And, of course, ran straight into a chain link fence that blocked her from approaching the ocean any closer, although the monstrous, white-toothed waves breaking over the seawall sent gouts of water flooding across the level tarmac. Water swirled around her legs, threatening to topple her. Sierra found a steel utility pole and planted her feet in the streaming water, leaning into the wind, arms wrapped tightly around the pole. Then she screamed at the top of her voice.

"Kanaloa! Please hear me! I'm waiting for you. Everything that happened was because of me, so take your anger out on me. Don't use your great mana to hurt others, Kanaloa!"

She then began an ancient chant that Auntie had taught her, imploring Kanaloa for mercy. In ancient Hawai'ian she begged him to lift his hand from his people and bring back the days of sun and good fishing. She gathered all her mana together, envisioning it as brightly glowing ribbons of green, purple, gold, fuchsia, silver—all the hues of the richly colored world she lived in—and offered it all, every bit of it, to Kanaloa in return for his mercy.

Sierra chanted with her eyes tightly shut against the stinging rain. She chanted with an intensity of feeling she had never experienced before. The horror of what this storm could do to thousands, maybe millions of innocent lives pared her down to just one intent: take me, not them.

She chanted with such utter concentration that she never noticed when the wind began to abate. The rain, too, grew softer, and the howling of the storm mellowed, but she chanted on, hoarse now with the effort of keeping her voice raised against the wind.

So when he touched her, she screamed and opened her eyes. She was face-to-face with a tall and muscular Hawai'ian man dressed as an Ali'i chieftain. He looked incongruous standing there on the runway, the storm surge flowing around his powerful legs, but Sierra didn't need to see his all-blue eyes to know who it was. She bowed her head in supplication.

"Kanaloa. You may do what you wish with me. But leave the others alone. Please."

He contemplated her in silence as the great storm gradually ebbed.

"You have great mana and great courage," he said. "But neither can save you from me."

She merely nodded and waited.

"Your Avatar friend tried to explain to me why you did what you did. I didn't care. You thwarted me—worse, you involved Pele. Fire and water don't mix. That was not well done."

Sierra nodded again. The wind had slackened, but she retained her grip on the steel post. "I'm sorry. I probably shouldn't have asked for your help in the first place. But I thought Kama had broken his promise—Kama did break his promise. But I shouldn't have meddled.

"Kanaloa, I don't expect you to forgive me. I haven't had these powers for very long. I don't know what the rules are. I...I don't really know how it works. I've made a lot of mistakes. I'll take whatever I'm owed for what I've done."

Kanaloa looked up into the black and gray sky, his strange eyes following the flight of an entire rooftop on the wind.

"I may have been a little bit hasty," he said, bringing his gaze back to Sierra. "After all, the whales are happy now that the construction has stopped. The Menehune are happy because the whales are. Pele has returned to Kilauwea. She enjoyed spoiling my game, but she won't be back—she only did it because that muscle-bound pretty-boy asked her to get involved."

Sierra thought that was an accurate description, but a little harsh. "Kama Pua'a is okay. He saved my life. And Chaco's life. He's a bit full of himself, but I think his heart's in the right place."

"And I think your heart is in the right place," said Kanaloa unexpectedly. "Go in peace. Aloha." Without any warning, he was gone. Sierra stood in the water, now beginning to recede. She was drenched, and she had small bleeding cuts where random objects driven by the wind had encountered her skin. Her shoes were gone, who knew where. The wind's piercing scream declined to a steady roar as the surf thundered against the rocks of the seawall bordering the runway.

She blinked the rain out of her eyes and limped back to the terminal building, carefully negotiating the debris left by the storm.

CHAPTER 35

Sierra sat on the lawyer's overstuffed brown leather chair, wondering why she had been summoned to this meeting. Clancy's lawyer, Robert Jamison, had called her shortly after her return from Moloka'i and asked her to come by. She assumed Clancy had left some kind of bequest for her in his will, but it was hard for her to be interested; there were so many urgent problems to solve. How would she find the time and the money to search for Clancy? How would she ever find him in the vast expanse of territory and time indicated by the loa?

Sierra visited Jamison's unassuming offices near downtown Sunnyvale about three weeks after returning from Hawai'i. He didn't keep her waiting long, bustling in with a sheaf of papers and a briefcase that he set on his credenza before turning to her. He adjusted black-framed glasses and cleared his throat.

"Ms. Carter? How do you do?" He held out a large, soft hand and shook hers. "First, please accept my condolences on Mr. Forrester's death. He was my client for several years. I am so terribly sorry."

Sierra nodded wordlessly. She'd had to endure a lot of what she hoped was misplaced sympathy in the past several days as she encountered friends and co-workers who knew about Clancy. It never got easier. She felt vaguely guilty for accepting their sympathy. And people sometimes asked when the memorial service would be held. She might accept their condolences under false pretenses, but she was damned if she was going to organize a fake memorial service.

"So, when is the memorial service?" Jamison asked. "I would like to attend. If that's all right with you."

"Of course it would be fine, Mr. Jamison, but I'm not holding a memorial service. It's just too…difficult. At this time. I hope you understand."

Jamison obviously didn't understand, but he nodded and adjusted the glasses, which had slid down his nose. "Indeed, indeed," he said and picked up a formal-looking legal document. "As you know, Mr. Forrester made you the sole beneficiary of his will—"

"WHAT?"

Jamison looked up in surprise. "Didn't he tell you? I assumed you must know. Dear me, let me get you some tea or something."

He hurried out of the room as Sierra, literally unable to speak, sat gasping in his brown leather chair. By the time he returned, closely followed by a young man with a laden tray, she had recovered somewhat. Jamison fussed over her, offering water, tea and coffee—how about some cookies?—until Sierra accepted a cup of coffee and a ginger snap. She despised ginger snaps but couldn't think of any other way to make him sit down again.

"Yes, well. Now. Feeling better? Ah, good. Now, back to Mr. Forrester's will…"

The upshot was that Sierra inherited Clancy's house, savings, investments, and all worldly goods.

To her astonishment, he turned out to have quite a lot of money. Apparently he had been squirreling everything away for decades, probably since he was quite young, and had made some excellent investments in Silicon Valley technology companies. In addition to her own modest holdings, Sierra was now the owner of a three-bedroom home in Sunnyvale—a million-dollar-plus ranch-style bungalow built in the 1950s and lately remodeled—a pleasantly plump bank account, and a stock portfolio that was currently close to three million dollars. Added to that, she was the beneficiary of his 401k and life insurance policy. Sierra Carter was now, if not fabulously wealthy, quite comfortably well off.

With care, she would never have to work again if she didn't want to.

But of course, Clancy wasn't dead, and this flood of worldly wealth didn't really belong to her.

Which was not something she could tell Clancy's lawyer.

But she couldn't just take Clancy's hard-earned money. He would need it someday. Hopefully.

Then it occurred to her that she could quit her job and devote all her time and Clancy's substantial resources to finding him and bringing him home.

The seesaw between conscience and guilt abruptly stilled. There was no problem. Clancy was the priority. Although he hadn't planned to use his resources in this way, Sierra was sure he would be the first to approve. After all, what good was a 401k if you never retired and claimed the money?

Her brain spun. One moment, she was wondering how she would ever be able to find the time and money that would be required to search for Clancy. The next moment, she was free to do as she pleased. Sierra listened politely to the rest of Robert Jamison's painstaking explanation, probably missing most of it, then rushed home to make some phone calls.

• • •

"But that's wonderful news," enthused Kaylee, sitting with Mama Labadie, Chaco, and Fred in Sierra's living room. "Now you can really concentrate on looking for Clancy full-time."

"I still have one little problem," Sierra said. "Namely, he may or may not be in 76,000 square miles of mostly jungle. And, if you recall, 'Time is not on our side.' It's kind of hard to know where—or when—to start." She looked hopefully at Mama. "Do you suppose the loa…?"

Mama shook her head regretfully. "Sorry. The loa don' wanna answer more a your questions. They say, 'Look to yourself.'"

Sierra stared at Mama in horror. "How am I ever going to find Clancy if the loa won't help me?"

Rose cleared her throat and leaned forward. "Sierra, this is as good a time as any to bring this up. You don't know your own strength."

Chaco, Fred, Mama, and Kaylee all nodded solemnly at this. Sierra stared at them, confused and worried.

"Tha's right," said Mama. "You the strongest of all of us. 'Cept Chaco."

"What do you mean?" Sierra asked.

"They mean that your powers make you magically stronger than anyone else here, except for me," Chaco said, watching Sierra closely. "I am still the stronger, but I hope we never fight." He smiled, but Sierra didn't.

"I don't feel powerful or full of mana or whatever," Sierra replied. "I feel like when it works, it's usually because there's an emergency. It's like I can't stop the mana from being used when there's trouble. But on an everyday basis? I don't have any special powers."

"That's where you're wrong," Mama said. "The loa say you close to an Avatar your ownself."

Sierra rounded on Mama. "Where did you say you're from? Just curious."

Mama eyed her. "Tha's nunna your beeswax, girl. Don' change the subject."

"Beeswax?" Really?

Rose cleared her throat again. "Sierra, I think what we're trying to tell you is that you are a hair's breadth away from becoming a powerful sorceress. You have the raw power. What you lack is the training and discipline to use it."

"Me? A sorceress?" Sierra snorted.

"Yes. And I hope I don't hurt your feelings here, but it needs to be said." Rose looked around at the others and received silent confirmation. "From the beginning, you've resisted your power. You didn't want to be involved in fighting Necocyaotl. You didn't believe in your own strength in Moloka'i. Think about it; why did you call on Kanaloa and Kauhuhu? Why didn't you look to your own powers to solve the problem?"

Sierra looked around at each face in disbelief. This was an intervention. Only she wasn't an alcoholic or a drug addict. Apparently, she was a delinquent sorceress who didn't want to use magic.

"You know," she said slowly, "I don't want to be a sorceress. I want to be normal. I'd like to settle down, marry, have kids, live in a rose-covered cottage, and keep chickens. I don't see anything wrong with that."

She looked around the room again. She did not like what she saw.

CHAPTER 36

Sierra drove across the mountains to the coast the next day. It was a lovely summer day, but it was a Wednesday so she didn't have to fight the beach-goers fleeing Silicon Valley. She reached her destination in under an hour. She wanted to walk on the beach, to take solitary time to think.

The purpose of the "intervention" had been to convince Sierra that she needed to train and develop her powers.

"Rose has been teaching me," Sierra had said. "She's done a great job."

Rose shook her head. "I can't take you any further, Sierra. Your powers are far greater than mine, and I have no idea how to guide you."

Mama Labadie agreed, saying, "Can't help you, girl. You need to find a teacher."

"Can't I just choose you?"

Mama shook her head. "No point a-tall in that. Find someone stronger than you."

"What if I don't want to be a sorceress?"

"That would be like giving a baby a loaded pistol," said Chaco. "A lot of firepower, but no idea how dangerous it is or how to use it."

Sierra had shaken her head and asked for privacy and time to think. The three women had departed, Kaylee giving her a hug and a kiss and a whispered, "Cheer up, honey. It could be worse. You could have ended up doing public relations your entire life."

So when Sierra arrived at her favorite beach, she was feeling annoyed. She was annoyed with her friends for insisting that she take on magical training. She was annoyed with the situation—she had never asked to be gifted with amazing magical powers. She was annoyed with herself for not understanding the powers better, not comprehending how magic worked. The only person she was not annoyed with was Clancy, who had landed in his current predicament for only one reason: he was a good man who was trying to help.

She walked south on the beach, heading for an empty stretch. The sandstone cliffs made the area unsuitable for building, so there was a miles-long stretch of largely deserted sand and waves. It couldn't have been more different from Hawai'i. The water was cold even in summer, and the waves heavy with sand and kelp. Swimmers without wetsuits braving the waves ended up chilled, wearing swimsuits now weighed down by several pounds of accumulated sandy grit. The sand wasn't ground-up coral, bleached white under a tropical sun. It was beige where dry and brown where wet, composed of minerals and shells.

Sierra walked along the water's edge, out of habit searching for shells and sea glass. She had found several perfect sand dollars and a lovely bit of cobalt glass, frosted from its years in the waves, when she nearly bumped into a small woman wearing a green skirt. Sierra's head had been lowered, searching the sand for treasures, and she hadn't seen the woman until she was almost on top of her.

"Oh! Excuse me," Sierra exclaimed. The woman wore a colorful green, red, and yellow squarish top over her skirt. Her straight black hair was arranged in an elaborate hairstyle bound with tasseled cotton bands. She wore a necklace of chunky jade beads and possessed the rich, deep brown skin and high-bridged, arched nose of an Aztec or a Maya Indian. The woman wouldn't have raised an eyebrow in downtown Santa Cruz, but she looked out of place on this beach.

Sierra's adventures had given her the ability to recognize an Avatar when she encountered one. "Who are you?" asked Sierra.

"Huixtocihuatl," replied the woman, smiling.

"I see. And if I may ask, who is Huixtocihuatl when she's at home?"

"The goddess of the sea," said the small woman, still smiling.

"I thought Kanaloa was the *god* of the sea?"

"It takes a village, you know."

Sierra did not know, but she decided to move on. "So why are you here?"

"A mutual friend sent me along with a message," said Huixtocihuatl.

"Mutual friend?"

"You know him as Quetzalcoatl."

"Ah, yes. What does the Big Q have to say to me?"

Huixtocihuatl gave her a quizzical look at this, but went on. "Lord Quetzalcoatl says he can help you to find your man."

Sierra's world suddenly became brighter. "Really? He'll help me?"

"Yes," replied the Avatar. "But he says first help yourself. Find a teacher. Become what you were meant to be."

"But what about Clancy?" Sierra almost wailed. "He might be in terrible danger, and I can't help him!"

But the woman just shook her dark head. "I can only tell you what Lord Queztalcoatl instructed me to say. I have no more to tell."

Sierra nearly imploded on the spot. More mystery! More obfuscation. More magical doings that she didn't understand. She pushed her palms against her eyes in frustration, and when she looked again, Huixtocihuatl had vanished and she was alone on the beach. At her feet lay a single large feather, blue-green and sparkling. Sierra knew the feather was from Quetzalcoatl, as she knew that when she touched it, it would chime like a distant crystal bell. She regarded the feather for several moments as it lay gleaming on the sand. The feather trembled as the sea breeze threatened to lift it into the air. Sierra picked it up. The faint chimes sounded clearly over the constant low mutter of the waves.

Aloud, Sierra said, "I'm coming, Clancy." She turned and set her feet on a new path.

AFTERWORD

WIND FARMS AND MOLOKAʻI

Fire in the Ocean is a work of fantasy fiction that bears little relationship to what we like to think of as reality. Needless to say, there are no Menehune-built wind farms on the west side of Molokaʻi. Penguin Bank is still an extinct volcano, as it has been for millions of years. However, I came up with the idea of a company trying to build a wind farm on Penguin Bank before I knew that such an attempt had actually been made. *Disappeared News* had articles about a company called Grays Harbor out of Seattle that wanted to build a wind farm on Penguin Bank.[7] Suits were filed in an effort to protect the area, which is a humpback whale breeding ground and nursery. The installation was prevented from going forward by the discovery that the permit for the site had been issued by a government agency that had no authority to do so.

An attempt to build a land-based wind farm on the western end of the island was thwarted by the Molokaʻians themselves. The installation would have transported the electricity via undersea cable to Oʻahu. All of it. None of the electricity generated on Molokaʻi would have gone to the residents of the island. There was a referendum and the Molokaʻians voted it down. This and a number of other stories convinced me that the Molokaʻians are not people to be trifled with. They will stand up and act if they feel their rights are being threatened, and they aren't quiet about it. People after my own heart.

MOLOKAʻI AND THE MOLOKAʻIANS

This book would not have been possible without the generosity and aloha spirit of the people of Molokaʻi.

Molokaʻi is perhaps best known as the leper colony island, but that doesn't begin to describe this island and its residents. The leper colony is still there, isolated on the Kalaupapa Peninsula at the base of 2,000-foot pali. Although what we now call Hansen's Disease is entirely curable, many of the colony's older residents chose to stay where they had lived most of their lives. You can visit Kalaupapa by mule, winding down the steep trail from Palaau State Park, or you can hike down. I did not visit, being disinclined to burden an innocent mule who had never done me any harm. I was even less inclined to descend—and then ascend—a steep, narrow trail on foot with gut-clenching drop-offs.

Molokaʻi is called the "Aloha Island." Aloha, you may remember, means "love," "hello," and "goodbye." In this context, aloha means a spirit of welcome and hospitality. I have rarely visited a place with such friendly people. A woman I met within sixty seconds of disembarking at the airport gave me the names of everyone I needed to meet to fulfill my research goals, briefed me on island etiquette, and gave me a lot of other useful information as well. I didn't know this person; she just asked me what I was doing on Molokaʻi, and when she found out I was there researching a book based on ancient Molokaʻian traditions, she generously gave me all the information I needed to get going. As I went about contacting the people she recommended, they welcomed me with warmth and did their best to help me out.

As the Molokaʻians say, "Don't try to change Molokaʻi. Let Molokaʻi change you." Molokaʻi is not the island to visit if you are into plush resort hotels, nightlife, fine dining, or touristy luaus. I didn't stay in a hotel, but there is at least one. And there is one resort I know of for certain. Most accommodations are in condos and cottages.

Molokaʻi is the island to visit if you want a relaxed, unpretentious place where you can get to know the people who live there, explore local cuisine (warning: this includes a lot of Spam and saimin noodles), or cook your own with fresh, local ingredients. In addition to fresh-caught fish, Moloka'i produces beef, pork, chicken, vegetables, fruit, honey, macadamia nuts, and coffee.

Moloka'i may be the island of longest human occupation in the Hawai'ian archipelago. Archeologists have dated some of the ancient fishponds back to 650 CE. When you consider that the substantial remains of those fishponds are still there, withstanding tides, currents and hurricanes for more than a thousand years, you can understand why many Moloka'ians believe their construction to be supernatural.

Snorkeling and diving are wonderful because Moloka'i is surrounded by the largest fringe reef in the islands. The fishing is also excellent. There are some boat charters in Kaunakakai, but you won't find parasailing or other tourist-type activities.

ANCIENT HAWAI'IAN SOCIETY AND RELIGION

Ancient Hawai'ian society was divided between the Ali'i, the nobility, and the maka'ainana, the common people. There were also the kahuna, the priestly class, but these were probably drawn from the ranks of the Ali'i. The Ali'i were physically distinct from the maka'ainana, being taller, heavily built, and lighter-skinned. The maka'ainana were significantly shorter and darker, leading some anthropologists to speculate that the maka'ainana were the original inhabitants of the islands, migrating from the Marquesas, while the Ali'i were conquerors hailing from Tahiti who subjugated the original people.

Hawai'i may be a paradise on earth, but ancient Hawai'ian culture was far from idyllic, especially if you were not an Ali'i. The higher in rank an Ali'i, the more kapu. For instance, in some cases, to touch the shadow of an Ali'i or to set your foot upon his footprint, was punishable by death. At any time, the temple mu, or sacrificers, could capture a random person (usually male) and sacrifice him. Human sacrifice was an integral part of the ancient religion. If you were maka'ainana, your life would have been infinitely less hazardous if you lived in a remote fishing village unfrequented by Ali'i.

Most religions have internal conflicts, fuzzy areas, and confusing bits, but the ancient Hawai'ian religion is more confusing than most. The religion is said to have 40,000 gods. This is because, in addition to the Big Four—Kane, Ku, Kanaloa, and Lono (each of whom had *many* different Avatars, earthly forms, and human descendants)—and a panoply of lesser gods and demigods like Pele and Kama Pua'a—any individual could adopt a personal or family 'aumakua. This might be a particular shark or owl or tree believed to embody the spirit of an ancestor, or it could be an unworked stone that someone decided was his god. It's not as clear-cut as, say, the Greek pantheon, where there's an accepted genealogy, gods and goddesses have specific responsibilities, and the stories are more or less consistent.

This lavish proliferation of gods is complicated by the fact that traditions vary somewhat from island to island. I have tried to stay true to the Moloka'ian take on the gods as much as possible, but perhaps I may be forgiven for any inconsistencies.

KAMA PUA'A

Kama Pua'a is a beloved cultural hero in Hawai'i, the equivalent to Coyotl the Trickster in Native American stories. Kama Pua'a is mischievous and prone to getting into trouble like Coyotl, and like Coyotl, he has a good heart. Everything related here about Kama is within the Hawai'ian tradition, except that he never went to Moloka'i.

MENEHUNE

In *Fire in the Ocean*, I have the Menehune originating in the Americas, an idea that was sparked by a Moloka'ian woman,

Louella Albino (known by everyone as Auntie Opuʻulani), who told me in no uncertain terms that the Aliʻi came from North America, not Tahiti. I will let others argue about this; Auntie Opuʻulani's version is fine by me.

Some think the Menehune were actually the original inhabitants of the Hawaiʻian Islands who were oppressed by invading conquerors and dispersed into the backcountry to live furtive, seldom-seen lives. On the *Wikipedia* page for Menehune, I read that a group of 65 people describing themselves by the term "Menehune" were listed in an 1820 census of Kauaʻi. The Wikipedia page for Necker Island, one of the more remote islands in the Hawaiʻian archipelago, notes clear evidence of former habitation (heiaus and other buildings), and the tradition in Kauaʻi is that Necker Island was the last refuge of the little people.

Various other theories abound, but many Hawaiʻians believe absolutely in the Menehune and will tell you of their experiences with them.

MIDWAY ISLAND, ALBATROSS CHICKS, AND THE PACIFIC GYRE

Sierra never made it to Midway Island—which is one of the most remote islands in the world, and part of the extensive Hawaiʻian archipelago. Midway and other uninhabited islands in the archipelago are important nesting and breeding habitats for a number of sea birds, including three species of albatross: the black-footed, the Laysan, and the short-tailed mōli. Many of these birds are threatened or vulnerable to extinction. Volunteers use their own time and money to go to Midway, staying there for weeks and sometimes months at a time, cleaning plastic off the beaches, counting albatross chicks and adults, and assisting naturalists with other duties. As of this writing, the volunteer program has been suspended indefinitely due to lack of funds.

The seabird chicks on Midway and the other islands are dying in large numbers because of plastic ingestion. Hawai'i is at the center of the Pacific Gyre, a gigantic whirlpool of currents. The gyre—also known as the Great Pacific Garbage Patch—is full of particularized plastic, swirling around and around like so much indestructible confetti. The plastic harms ocean life in a few ways. First, the plastic leaches chemicals into the water that affect the health of ocean life. Second, the colorful bits of plastic attract sea birds, which mistake it for food, ingest it, and feed it to their young. It's not good for the parents, and it kills the chicks—up to a third of them. Other sea life also ingests particularized plastic, with deadly results.

The plastic in the Pacific Gyre primarily comes from China and North America. Much of it is due to illegal dumping. The Pacific Gyre is only one of five such gyres around the world. Particularized plastic has accumulated in all of them. There are a few cleanup efforts underway. One of the most promising technologies was developed by a young Dutchman, Boyan Slat, founder of The Ocean Cleanup (www.theoceancleanup.com), but there are several others under development.

NOTES

1. Chant and translation from June Gutmanis, *Na Pule Kahiko: Ancient Hawaiian Prayers* (Honolulu, HI: Editions Limited, 1983).
2. Hawai'ian gods can take many different earthly forms. Kanaloa can appear as a man, an octopus, a squid, a banana tree, or various medicinal plants. Oddly, as lord of the ocean, Kanaloa is also the god associated with fresh water.
3. This is the author's invention. However, she was informed by a Moloka'ian woman of great learning and wisdom that the Ali'i, the elite nobility among the ancient Hawai'ians, came from the Americas—so in this version of history, the Menehune came with them. The more conventional theory is that the Ali'i came from Tahiti, and the Menehune were the original inhabitants of the islands, migrants from the Marquesas Islands, later subjugated and marginalized by the conquering Ali'i.
4. One of Kama Pua'a's bodily forms is the humu-humu-nuku-nuku-apua'a, the reef triggerfish and state fish of Hawai'i. The name means "triggerfish with a pig's snout." Kama routinely uses this form to escape trouble—usually of his own making.
5. "Do you have some chocolate?"
6. "Thank you, Auntie."
7. www.disappearednews.com/2008/12/life-of-land-files-motion-to-intervene.html.

REFERENCES

Beckwith, Martha Warren. *Hawaiian Mythology*. Honolulu, HI: University of Hawaii Press, 1970.

Carroll, Rick. "Incident at `Ili `ili `Opae Heiau." *Weird U.S.* Accessed October 22, 2017. http://weirdus.com/states/hawaii/stories/iliili_opae_heiau/index.php.

"E MauAna O Kanaloa, Ha'i Hou." *Kaho'olawe Island Conveyance Commission*. Accessed October 22, 2017. http://kahoolawe.hawaii.gov/KICC/12 E MAu Ana O Kanaloa Ho'i Hou.pdf.

Gutmanis, June. *Na Pule Kahiko: Ancient Hawaiian Prayers*. Honolulu, HI: Editions Limited, 1983.

"How to Speak Hawaiian like a Haole." *Instant Hawaii*. http://www.instanthawaii.com/cgi-bin/hawaii?Language.

Kamae'eleihiwa, L.K. *He Mo'olelo Ka'ao o Kamapua'a (A Legendary Tradition of Kamapua'a, the Hawaiian Pig-God)*. Honolulu, HI: Bishop Museum Press, 1996.

Kamakau, Samuel Manajakalani. "Ka Po'e Kahiko (The People of Old)." Translated by Mary Kawena Pukui. *Ke Au 'Oko'a* Honolulu, HI: Bishop Museum Press, 1964.

"Kanaloa." *Kumukahi*. Accessed on October 22, 2017. http://www.kumukahi.org/units/ke_ao_akua/akua/kanaloa.

"Kauhuhu, the Shark God of Molokai." *The Internet's Sacred Texts Archive*. Accessed on October 22, 2017. http://www.sacred-texts.com/pac/hlog/hlog12.htm.

"The Legend of the Night Marchers." *To-Hawaii*. Accessed October 22, 2017. http://www.to-hawaii.com/legends/night-marchers.php.

Malo, David. *Moolelo Hawaii (Hawaiian Antiquities)*. Translated by Nathaniel B. Emerson. Bernice P. Bishop Museum, 1898.

"Night Marchers." *Hawaiian Myths*. Accessed October 22, 2017. http://hawaiianmyths.weebly.com/history-of-sorts.html.

Westerveld, W.D. *Legends of Gods and Ghosts (Hawaiian Mythology)*. Boston: Press of Ellis Co., London, 1915.

Wianecki, Shannon. The Sacred Spine. *Maui No Ka 'Oi Magazine*. http://www.mauimagazine.net/Maui-Magazine/September-October-2012/The-Sacred-Spine/index.php?cparticle=2&siarticle=1 - artanc.

Wight, Kahikāhealani. *Illustrated Hawaiian Dictionary*. Honolulu, HI: Bess Press, 2005.

K.D. KEENAN worked in the high technology industries for thirty-plus years as a content creator and public relations expert. She founded her own PR agency, named one of Silicon Valley's Top 25 PR agencies for ten years running by the *Silicon Valley Business Journal*. Today, she focuses on her fiction writing, her grandchildren, and a long list of things she'd like to do if there were more hours in the day.

Keenan has always been a voracious reader. Having worked through her grandparents' extensive library of Victorian children's literature, she began reading fantasy and science fiction at the age of nine—a move that curbed her tendency to write with a mid-nineteenth-century flair that was never really appreciated by her English teachers.

The Obsidian Mirror, the first book in a trilogy, tells the tale of a Silicon Valley PR executive whose life takes a turn for the weird when a fast-talking coyote appears on her doorstep and plunges her into a whirlwind of hijacked technology, ancient evil, and environmental threat. *Fire in the Ocean* picks up Sierra's story as she embarks on a tropical vacation but instead encounters the ancient magic of the "isle of sorcerers" as she fights to protect the precious natural environment of Hawai'i.

Keenan and her husband of forty-five years have two grown children and two grandchildren.

Printed in the USA
CPSIA information can be obtained
at www.ICGtesting.com
JSHW031709140824
68134JS00038B/3604